‘Ella,’ she said quietly, ‘there is something I think you ought t’ know. You won’t get upset if I tell yer, will you?’

‘Try me,’ was all that Ella said.

‘Well, I don’t want yer mum to find out that you ’eard it from me, but Connie Baldwin reckons she’s ’aving a baby.’

‘What, young Connie Baldwin whose mum an’ dad live over the paper shop?’ Ella asked, frowning.

‘Yes, that’s the one.’

‘Do her parents know about it? She’s not sixteen yet, is she?’

‘Sorry, luv, but it’s no t’ both of those questions as far as I know, and what her mum an’ dad are gonna say when they find out, the Lord only knows. Won’t be long before they do, though, mark my words. Half the street knows already.’

Ella stared in disbelief, thinking to herself that Nellie was enjoying telling folk about a young girl’s misfortune. Aloud she said, ‘Wonder if the fella will be man enough t’ marry her?’

‘He won’t,’ Nellie said smugly.

Ella was watching her closely and she couldn’t fathom what the look on Nellie’s face was supposed to mean.

WHEELING AND DEALING

ELIZABETH WAITE

sphere

SPHERE

First published in Great Britain in 2006 by Time Warner Books
This paperback edition published in 2006 by Sphere

Copyright © Elizabeth Waite 2006

The moral right of the author has been asserted.

A CIP catalogue record for this book
is available from the British Library.

ISBN-13: 978-0-7515-3611-9
ISBN-10: 0-7515-3611-3

Typeset by Palimpsest Book Production Limited,
Grangemouth, Stirlingshire
Printed and bound in Great Britain by
Clays Ltd, St Ives plc

Sphere
An imprint of
Little, Brown Book Group
Brettenham House
Lancaster Place
London WC2E 7EN

A Member of the Hachette Livre Group of Companies

www.littlebrown.co.uk

PART ONE

1952
Going Upmarket

Chapter One

DENNIS DRYDEN DROVE HIS Jaguar along the tree-lined avenue and into the drive, which was bathed in brilliant sunshine. He turned the key in the ignition but it was a few minutes before he got out of the car. When he did, instead of walking straight up the flight of stone steps, he stood still and surveyed the front of this lovely old house. Who in hell's name would have thought that he, a lad from the East End of London, would ever have ended up owning a place such as this?

In Epsom in Surrey of all places.

The steps leading up to the house ran straight on to a veranda which stretched the whole length of the front part of the building. Four tall upright pillars supported the roof of the porch, and the massive oak front door had to be seen to be believed.

Still, he hadn't bought this property for the look of it from the outside, had he? It was the inside that had knocked him for six, and what was more, with a bit of ducking and diving and because he had the readies available, no mucking about with bank managers or mortgage companies, he'd got it for a knockdown price.

3

Mind you, he was well aware that he owed a great deal to his old man. A man who lived by the code of the East End and expected everyone he did a deal with to do the same. And woe betide anyone who didn't adhere to that code of honour.

When Ted, his father, had first asked if he wanted to come and have a butcher's at a country mansion, he thought the old man had gone bananas. A place that belonged to a real lady; her husband had died some years ago, she was eighty-six and lately had become very frail. Sheltered housing seemed to be the only answer.

How come his father was on such intimate terms with her ladyship?

Trust. Right from the beginning. Through the grapevine Ted Dryden had heard that what with death duties and debts of one sort and another the old lady was desperate. The truth was, he had known the old girl for years through meeting her at various racecourses.

A few years ago Ted had been running a book at Cheltenham. Her ladyship had backed a rank outsider, and as the leading horses galloped towards the line the crowd had erupted in cheers and shouts. As Ted was paying her out she had got so excited.

'God, I've won a whole lot of money, haven't I?'

With that remark she had swayed on her feet and would have fallen to the ground had Ted not caught her in his brawny arms. A couple of brandies in the clubhouse and he had driven her home.

You could say these two people were as different as chalk and cheese, but for all that they had become good friends. Each of them was lonely, she having lost her husband and never having had any children, while Ted's wife had been dead for twelve years. They had become good friends, with Ted visiting her at least once a month.

Money-wise, and health-wise, matters for her ladyship

had gone from bad to worse. With the exception of Dorothy Sheldon, her paid companion, who was herself in her late sixties, she had no one, having long since paid off the rest of her staff.

With his father doing the business, Derek had bought the place for a knockdown price. That was what happened when you dealt direct with folk. No agents slicing the cream off the top, and as Dennis had the ready cash to cover the whole house as it stood, lock, stock and barrel, except for the family heirlooms and a few of her ladyship's favourite items, it had all been plain sailing.

There had been another bit of luck, proving that it wasn't what you knew but who you knew in this life: his father had managed to secure a marvellous roomy apartment in leafy Chelsea for the old lady. The place was well run, with staff, including a warden, on duty twenty-four hours a day, a lift to all floors, a restaurant on the premises which would serve meals to residents' rooms should they not wish to come downstairs to eat, and several well-heated and nicely furnished public rooms if residents felt the need to socialise.

Dennis had no misgivings that Lady Margaret had been done down. If he hadn't bought the place someone else would have, and while he knew he had got a good deal, he also knew that his father had been fair, seeing, as far as he could, that her ladyship's move went as smoothly as possible. She had made it clear from the start that she wanted not only enough money to clear her debts and live comfortably for what remained of her life, but also, apparently, to get away from this big, lonely house as quickly as possible, taking with her only what would fit into her new home.

He placed the key into the lock of the heavily built front door, but it was all of half a minute before he managed to turn it and was able to open the door. The large, high-ceilinged hall smelt damp and dusty. After closing the door, he stood with his back to it for a few seconds before walking towards the middle of the hall, to stand on a large Persian rug and gaze up the high-panelled staircase.

Well, now he had some sorting out to do and no mistake.

Ella, his wife, was right about two things. One, this time he might have bitten off more than he could chew! And two, she and their two children were never going to agree to come and live in this gloomy, dark house. On the second count he knew his Elly would be unmovable. She was an East Ender born and bred, and wild horses wouldn't make her move from her beloved London.

Slowly he climbed the stairs and on reaching the first landing stared down at the grounds that surrounded the house. The state of the lawns, flowerbeds, trees and shrubs cried out that it was many a long day since a gardener had worked there. Poor old soul. Seemed like most of her ladyship's friends must have deserted her. Or even more likely, most of them were already dead.

The fact that she had turned to a man like his father for help spoke volumes.

Ted Dryden was a good man at heart, but a rough diamond at the best of times. Though born and bred in the East End of London, he could polish himself up when the need arose. He was the sort that had come from nothing without any privileges and had made it to the top by sheer undeniable guts and determination. He had the confident manner of a successful bookmaker without any airs or graces. A damn good friend who always made sure he repaid a favour.

But you wouldn't want him as an enemy!

And I'm his son, Dennis thought, allowing himself a wry smile.

Dennis was fifty but looked younger, in a rough-and-ready kind of way. A boyish face and a way with the ladies; intense bright blue eyes with lots of lines across his forehead. A thick mop of dark hair, his sideboards going a bit grey, though unlike his father he had never grown a moustache. He did match his dad in height, each of them standing six foot three in their stockinged feet.

He turned away from staring down at the overgrown grounds, walked a few yards down the corridor, pushed through a heavy door and stepped into a deep-carpeted small lounge. Dust-sheets covered three armchairs, probably thoughtfully placed there by Dorothy Sheldon. Apart from that there was no other furniture and basically the room looked awful. The decor hadn't been touched for years: the once expensive wallpaper had faded and the ceiling, which should have been white, was now a dirty brownish colour.

Going further into the room he stared at the large open fireplace. Great log fires must have burnt there at one time was his immediate thought. It was then that his gaze fell on a small footstool on which lay two old racing programmes, one for the Derby and one for the Oaks. Alongside was a pair of ladies' spectacles, still attached to a long silver chain.

He had always considered himself a hard man, but at that moment he felt utterly gutted, and the lump that had formed in his throat was threatening to choke him.

There must have been a time when racing was a great part of her ladyship's life. Especially with the glorious downs of Epsom and the great racecourse right on her doorstep. Maybe she and her husband had even owned their own horses.

How had Lady Margaret sunk to such a low level?

Folk still talked about her husband as being a thorough gentleman.

Some gent! He'd left his wife almost penniless, with a

huge house that she could not afford to keep in good repair. If tales told were true, in his lifetime the house had had a host of servants, and he had employed a coachman who drove his horse-drawn carriage even after he had acquired two motor-cars. And naturally he went to shooting parties and rode with the local hunt.

Dennis hadn't known him, and neither had Ted, but they'd had many a discussion about this gentleman in the last six months and they were both of the same mind. A gentleman looks after his family and makes provision for them when he's called to meet his Maker. No decent man lives so much beyond his means that when he dies his poor wife struggles on a pittance until it comes to the crunch and she is forced to sell not only her house, but almost every stick and stone inside it.

Dennis sighed heavily and walked slowly back across the room, closing the door softly behind him. As he descended the stairs he was shaking his head. His face was thoughtful and his eyes were sad. What a way to end one's life.

Poor Lady Margaret! Poor soul!

Chapter Two

ELLA DRYDEN WRIGGLED HER plump bottom more comfortably into her armchair.

By God, her old man had done a damn silly thing this time. He had actually signed the contracts and everything had been completed legally, and now he was the proud owner of that musty old house miles away from London.

What in the name of God was he going to do with it?

He had been full of it when he took her down to see that place. But Ella had made it quite clear it wasn't for her. There and then she'd sworn to him that that was the first and last time she'd set foot in the place!

Dennis didn't need any telling what his Ella was thinking, but just got on with eating his dinner. Damn good cook was Ella. Steak and kidney pie today, with masses of vegetables and a jug of gravy the likes of which nobody else he knew could make. As for her pastry! Light as a feather. And he'd take a bet that she'd been to at least two other houses today and delivered a good hot meal to an old soul that was living alone. Always cooking and feeding half the blinking street was his wife. Talk about being lady bountiful. Old Mr Parsons loved her cheese scones, Ma Bristow's delight was Ella's fruitcake, while poor Mary Marsh and her two fatherless kids always got a free dinner every Saturday, and they were only the ones he knew about. More than likely there was half a dozen more that he was helping to keep.

Ella just couldn't keep her thoughts to herself any longer.

'You've really done it this time, Dennis.' She spoke sharply. 'I never thought you'd go through with it.'

'You said you liked the 'ouse,' he said, munching on a well-salted roast potato.

'Yeah, well, some of the inside I did.'

'Well, if I could persuade you to move you'd be living in the inside, you daft woman, not on the outside.'

'You're the daft one, Den. No matter what yer do with the place yer can't pick it up and put it down 'ere in London, can yer?'

'I thought you'd be glad to be rid of all the dirt and squalor around 'ere. All the local council and the land-lords are intent on doing is knocking down these old streets of houses and building high-rise flats. See how you feel about moving when it comes to that.'

'When! It ain't 'appened yet. No need t' meet trouble 'alfway. Besides, Babs and Teddy don't think much of moving. Got their mates and their school and they like it fine. Come to that, you'd 'ave to drag them screaming to get them away from their gran, an' you know it.'

'You've just been sitting there thinking up excuses. You could persuade yer mother t' come with us if you went the right way about it.'

'Not a chance in hell, Denny boy. You've 'eard Mum say often enough that she was born in that 'ouse an' she'll go out of it in 'er box.'

'Well, if that's the case, you'd better start looking for an old folk's 'ome for her, 'cos it's a dead cert that sooner or later they'll demolish all the houses in these back streets.'

'Oh yeah?' Ella now twisted her body round and faced him. 'The day will never dawn when I stand by and see my mother go into a home. You ought t' know by now you don't get my mother to go anywhere she doesn't want to. You get away with bullying me most of the time, but nothing you say or do this time will coax me into moving from London to live in the back of beyond.'

She lowered her voice a little and, changing her tone, said, 'Why do you always 'ave t' play the big I am? If you wanted us to move, why not buy a place near here? Buying an 'ouse out in the country won't make you into a country gentleman. Or is it that you've got yerself another young bit of stuff that you want to show off to?'

'Oh, you're not going to start off on that track again, are you?' Dennis said, sighing heavily.

Ella shook her head sadly as she added, 'I know I'm not growing old gracefully, I'm nothing like the young, slim girl you married, but then you're no oil painting. But you flash money around and that's the only reason the young women flatter you.'

'You finished?'

'Yeah, we'll leave it for the present, but there's lots more I could say. Just don't ever play me for too big a fool, Den. I can smell cheap scent, and it's me what scrubs the lipstick off yer shirts. Perhaps you should stock up with some of that new kiss-proof lipstick they've got in Woolworth's.'

'Oh, we're going to 'ave all the old rigmarole today, are we?' Dennis said, reaching for the crusty end of the loaf of bread, which he used to wipe his plate clean.

Ella was about to tell him a few more home truths when the sound of another war of words cut her short. Babs and Teddy were at it again! It was bad enough when they were just bickering, but from the sound of the noise now coming from upstairs it had gone beyond that stage.

'I'd better go an' see what they're up to,' she exclaimed impatiently.

Dennis laughed. 'Leave 'em to it. You were about to tell me what a rotter you really think I am.'

'You don't need me t' tell you. Try looking into yer own conscience once in a while.'

And with that she pulled herself up from the depths of her armchair and marched out of the room, shouting, 'Teddy! And you, Babs!'

She was halfway up the stairs when her twelve-year-old son, Edward, named after his grandfather, stuck his head over the banisters and called down to her, 'Mum, can't you keep this blinking sister of mine out of my bedroom?'

Ella paused for a moment and looked up at him, saying, 'Whatever she's done, do you have to make such a racket? You'd better not have laid into her, or your father will tan your backside.'

Teddy drew back and she went quickly up the remaining stairs, calling, 'Babs, are you all right?'

On the narrow landing she pushed open the door to her son's bedroom to see her young daughter, just eight years old, deliberately tearing pages from a book and adding them to a pile of screwed-up ones that lay beside her. She couldn't believe her eyes, and yelled at the top of her voice, 'Good God, girl! What on earth do you think you are doing? If there is one thing I've taught you in your short life, it's to treat books with respect.'

Babs let go of the torn page she was holding and turned her face towards her mother, crying, 'I'm getting my own back. He's pulled all the lovely curls off my best doll's head, the big china one that Gran bought me. I'm going t' get Dad to kill him, I am.'

'Shut up! You are both as bad as one another.'

Ella now looked at her son. He was a big lad for his age, well built, with bright blue eyes and a thick mop of curly hair. Oh yes, he was the image of his father. She glared at him as she said, 'One of these days you're gonna go too far. I'm warning you, even yer father won't give in t' you for ever. Why did you do it?'

Teddy's lips tightened now as he said bitterly, 'She sneaked in here an' she's torn up at least six of my fag-cards. I only left them out of the box 'cos I was going to exchange them with Johnny Riley. You wanna tell her to keep her hands off my belongings. Besides, she thinks she knows everything. Teacher's pet 'cos she can do adding-up in her head. But she knows nothing about sport.'

'All right, all right, so you're both different, which is a good thing.'

'She's spiteful an' horrible,' Teddy screamed. 'Just what did she get out of destroying my cards?'

'That's enough!' Ella was shaking. 'Whatever the reason, boys should never hurt little girls. You've been told that often enough.'

'She's not a little girl. She's nearly as big as me and she kicks me often enough.'

Ella turned round now, took hold of her daughter by her shoulders and shook her, saying, 'That was a horrible thing to do. You know how much his collection means to him. Why did you do it?'

There was a sulky look on Babs's face now as she said bitterly, 'Because he's such a know-all and a big-head and he's Dad's favourite. Dad gets him all those cards and he knows the names of all the cricketers and footballers, but when it comes to school work he's almost bottom of the class.'

'Oh God above, give me strength,' Ella muttered. Then, pointing to the door, she said, 'Come on, Babs. Out! This

13

is his room and each of you should thank yer lucky stars that you've got a room of yer own. There's a great number of kids that have never known that luxury.'

Babs got off the bed and walked out. Her long dark curls swinging, she went across the landing, thrust open the door to her own bedroom and went in, shutting the door firmly behind her.

Little madam, her mother said to herself, a fact that she partly blamed her own mother for. Babs could do no wrong in the eyes of her grandmother.

She turned to her son and stared hard at him for a moment before she said, 'Don't look at me like that, Teddy. It's only right that yer father and grandfather take yer to football matches and help you to keep up with all forms of sport, but it won't 'elp yer to know all the famous names when it comes to earning your own living. Girls won't like you either if all you ever think and talk about is sport.'

'Who cares about girls, they're all dead soppy,' he answered defiantly.

Ella changed the tone of her voice. 'Why do you do it, son? Why must you always be fighting with yer sister? And I know for a fact that when you're at school, you want to boss everybody.'

'Because I want to be like me dad an' me grandad. They're their own bosses an' nobody gives them any stick.'

The words sounded so much like a challenge, they startled Ella. Teddy was only twelve, and he was speaking as a man. She hadn't imagined that her son was already thinking that he wanted his life to run as his father's did.

When it came to their physical needs, Dennis was a good father and a good husband. He saw to it that Ella always had enough money to feed the children well and put good clothes on their backs, and he made sure they went to school. No wagging off like a lot of the young lads round here did. For a moment she pondered. It was great that Teddy had been taught to be interested in sport and to stand up for himself, but had these two things become an obsession with both his father and his grandfather?

She didn't need any telling that Edward Dryden had had a hand in her Denny buying this big house out at Epsom. It was near a racecourse for one thing, and what with Ted being a bookie, horse-racing had become an obsession with both her father-in-law and his son. And now she had to face the fact that Teddy had the urge to be like them.

Oh, life was difficult.

Ella chewed on her lip as she went slowly back down the stairs.

When all was said and done, she hadn't married Dennis with her eyes blinkered. She had known from the beginning he was a Jack-the-lad. A good many girls had had their eyes on him, and she had been proud that he had looked her way.

She sighed and told herself she might have done better, but watching some of the goings-on round these parts, she wondered. There were young women living with men who had never married them, and others with husbands who knocked them about unmercifully or gave the bulk of their wages to the local pub owners. It was the plight of the children of these families that sparked pity in her and caused her to readily admit that she could have done worse than marry Dennis Dryden.

Oh yes, much worse. A whole lot worse.

Chapter Three

'YOU'VE GOT YOUR WAY over the Epsom house. I've put two applications in to the council, one for turning the whole place into flats and the second one for renovating the place and maybe using it as a hotel.' Dennis Dryden's voice was harsh as he told his wife what his options were. She was still dead set against moving. No matter how hard he had tried to persuade her, she was absolutely determined that she was not going to live anywhere but London.

Ella nodded, but did not reply. She sensed that Dennis had more to say. She stared out of the kitchen window at the small cobblestoned back yard and watched her two lines of washing blowing in the breeze. At last she said, 'It would be nice to live in the country, just for a while now and again, to be able to keep your house and your clothes so much cleaner, but by God I'd miss the shops, the markets and most of all me neighbours.'

'Oh yeah,' Dennis agreed, 'we'd all miss the bloody neighbours!'

His sarcasm ruffled her feathers and she went on, 'You probably wouldn't, but could yer live without yer local pubs and yer dad's betting shop? An' another thing, what about all the blokes you've got working for you on yer dodgy deals? Would they be willing to travel out into the sticks every day to get their orders from you?'

Stifling his anger, Dennis nodded dumbly. Ella's current life was pretty hard; she took such good care of their two kids and her mother. His father too, come to that, 'cos there weren't many Sunday dinnertimes that he wasn't round here with his feet under their table. Dennis made sure he didn't keep her short of money, yet her whole life seemed to be one long struggle against the dirt and grime of these back streets of London. He sighed as he did his best to smile at his wife.

'Trouble with you, Ella, is fear of the unknown. You've never known anything different and you don't particularly want to, do yer?' he said resentfully.

Ella lifted her hands in a helpless gesture. 'I was born here and we've all survived the war, so why should we up and leave it all behind now just to satisfy your ego?'

He stared at her for a moment before picking up his coat and thrusting his arms into the sleeves. He walked slowly across the room towards her, then stopped within an arm's length of her. In a low voice, now, he said, 'You're very fond of calling me a big-head, aren't you, Ella? In the past you've called me brash, and on one occasion you even said I'd stop at nothing to pull off a deal. That's right isn't it?'

'Suppose it is, if you say so.'

Dennis lowered his head and thrust his face closer to hers. 'You don't like the deals I do, but all the same you and the kids benefit every which way there is. I supply the wherewithal so that you can be the kind-hearted woman who is generous to the needy. Well, my dear wife, here's something for you to think about. Whichever plan the council gives their approval to, I shall be employing

17

a darn sight more men than I do now. Bricklayers, carpenters, plumbers, you name them, and I'll have no difficulty in finding them. Why? Because it will be steady work and they know that I will pay them well. So it won't be just me that makes money, will it?'

Ella's large bosom rose and she let out a long breath before she said, 'So according to you, everyone is 'appy to go along with whatever you decide except me.'

'That's the message I'm getting, far too often if you want me to be blunt. Tell me straight, Ella, just what is keeping you here?' He was dismayed by her dull tone of voice and her lack of enthusiasm.

Ella pursed her lips. That was the big question. She had always considered herself ordinary, contented with her lot, and she wanted her two children to be the same, but not Dennis.

Oh no, not him!

He'd been fighting his way all his life, ambition driving him, determined that he was going to move his family up the scale. She was no fool; she knew Dennis regarded her as a hindrance, thwarting him at every turn. She was well aware that although she was twelve years younger than him, she hadn't worn so well. She had borne two children and from then on had become plump, and that was putting it kindly. She was always clean and tidy and so was her house, yet he was forever telling her she had no style, whereas the type of women he took out could wear old sacks and still appear attractive, because he always chose younger women who were very slim. When Dennis had a few beers inside him and was admiring the ladies who happened to be in the pub, he would look at Ella and say unkindly, 'Can't stop me from looking.'

More often than not, she would cast her eye over the bunch of girls sitting near the bar and her reaction would be, 'Skinny lot, a damn good meal would do them good.'

Dennis would laugh loudly and say something along the lines of 'The nearer the bone, the sweeter the meat.'

Sadly, these days that didn't apply to her.

She looked down at herself, her baggy, shapeless dress covering her wide hips and fat legs. Could she move away from London? Live out in Epsom? She doubted it. She'd be like a fish out of water!

This house might be old-fashioned, with none of the mod cons the youngsters were always on about, but it was clean, comfortable and more to the point it was her home. Apart from cracks in one wall, a few slates off the roof and every window having been smashed, it had withstood all of Hitler's air raids. There were parts of London where whole streets had been destroyed, and if the German bombers hadn't driven her out of her home in those awful years, she saw no good reason why she should move away now.

What Dennis wanted was to get away from this colourful, noisy working-class area. He hated the back-to-back houses and long, narrow streets hemmed in by factories, and the street markets where men shouted their wares from early morning until as late as ten at night, when huge paraffin lamps would still light up their stalls. Of course all that had stopped during the war, what with the blackout and the food shortages, not to mention the fact that all fit and well men had been sent to foreign shores to fight for their country.

Things were getting better, though. The Government had set up a special committee to ensure that all houses which were still standing had the glass replaced in every window and all structural faults put right.

The men who had been lucky enough to come home had discarded their uniforms. They mostly wore overalls during the week, but on Sundays they wore trousers and jackets or their demob suits. And for the lads who were still single, a trilby hat worn jauntily to one side was an absolute must.

On the whole, life was getting back to normal. And now Dennis was asking her to pack up and move away to live an entirely different life. Mix with different people, be a bit more upper-class. Could she do it?

'No! No! Never!' She had shouted the words out loud.

From the look on Dennis's face, she thought he was going to blow a gasket.

Ella stood in the middle of the room, eyes cast down, looking at the floor.

'Yeah, take a good look. How many other houses in this street 'ave got carpet on the floor?' he raged at her. 'You, Ella, when it comes to me, are a bleeder! You bleed me dry. I provide and pay for every last damn thing that comes into this house, but what do I get in return? Sod all. Well, you've gone too far this time, but don't for a minute think you'll put the kibosh on my plans. Not this time you won't. Stay here with the kids, live yer dreary life. I'll see you don't starve but I don't 'ave t' let you drag me down with yer.' Dennis had hissed the last words at her.

Ella was frightened. He had never threatened her like this before. 'I didn't mean that you shouldn't have bought the house.'

'Didn't you?' with a scornful look. He was glad that he had raged at her; it had given her something to think about. He was fed up to the teeth with her never wanting to do anything worthwhile. Stuck in a rut, her and her bloody mother. There was simply no pleasing either of them.

Ella sank down on to a chair as Dennis stormed out of the room. She listened to his footsteps go along the passage, and when the front door slammed, tears trickled down her plump cheeks.

He was right. He was a damn good provider.

When the going was good, that is. At times Dennis had a convenient memory. How about the times when things weren't going the way he wanted them to? Then anything and everything he could lay his hands on was taken out of the house and sold. It was no joke. One week he'd had a radiogram delivered to the house, and then, to the sheer delight of both Babs and Teddy, their father had taken them out and allowed them to choose at least two dozen records. For days on end they played music and sang along with the records. Never before nor since had Ella seen her children so happy.

Then one morning the kids had come down for their breakfast and found the whole caboodle had gone. In fact the front room had been stripped bare. For a mere five and a half weeks the children had thoroughly enjoyed that radiogram. Oh, good old trustworthy Dennis had replaced it, but not until seven weeks later, and the presentation hadn't seemed the same the second time around.

That was only one incident.

Most worrying of all was that Dennis would disappear for days on end. Why did she worry herself at such times? Because how was she to know that he hadn't had an accident? But voice her concern and Dennis would laugh and just say that every businessman had to be away from home at times. Quite so, but without telling his family where he was?

The erratic behaviour of their father took away a feeling of security the kids should have. Not just for worldly goods, but for a steady, permanent way of life with a dad who could be relied on to always be there.

Ella busied herself clearing the breakfast table. Going through to the scullery, she stacked the dirty dishes on the wooden draining board, then filled the kettle from the cold tap, placed it over one of the gas rings, struck a match and lit a low flame beneath it.

Talking aloud to herself she said, 'While the kettle's boiling I may as well go up and make the beds.'

It was dead on the stroke of eleven when she came downstairs, arms full of more dirty washing. She smiled to herself as she heard the front door open and her mother calling out loudly, 'It's only me, luv.' Regular as clock-work, Winnie Paige arrived at her daughter's house at the same time Monday to Thursday. Fridays she came earlier because the two of them went to the market, while Saturdays and Sundays she kept herself to herself in case Dennis was around. They had never exactly seen eye to eye.

For as long as Ella could remember, her mother had been the local flower-seller. On weekdays she had sat outside the underground station with her basket of blooms. She had long since given up working during the week, but although she was in her late seventies, she still worked on a Sunday, getting one of her neighbours who was a totter to trundle her wheelbarrow up to the London Hospital, where she did a roaring trade.

Ella said, 'Hallo, Mum, you look smart this morning. You off out somewhere?'

It was true, Winnie did look good, and Ella sighed, wishing she could look more like her mother. Winnie Paige was only five foot four, and slim in build. She dressed smartly although her face was florid and weatherbeaten. Her motto was 'God helps those that help themselves', and so she did her best using a little make-up and a lot of face-powder. Her hair was marcel-waved and peeped out from her smart hat to cover her ears. She wore a brown costume that had seen better days but still showed signs of having been an expensive outfit when first made. She wouldn't thank you for telling anyone that she bought her clothes from a second-hand stall run by a middle-aged couple who often acquired garments from well-to-do ladies.

Ella had now reached the bottom of the stairs and she gave her mother a look that went from top to toe. You never look like that on Sundays, she grinned to herself. And that was true. Come Sunday, a black shawl and an old felt hat was Winnie's uniform; she wanted her customers to feel that she needed them to buy her flowers.

'I feel a bit fed up this morning,' Winnie said frankly as she walked into her daughter's kitchen. 'Sarah Brown from Brady Street died yesterday. She had been ill for a long time, but she was a good friend and I need cheering up a bit. I thought you and I might go out somewhere.'

'Nice idea, Mum, as long as we're back in time t' meet the kids from school.'

'Course we will be, an' we'll take them into Joey Lyons, buy them hot chocolate and a cupcake.'

'I'm nowhere near ready yet, though. I haven't washed up, and there's all this laundry,' Ella moaned.

'Oh Ella, for God's sake. I'll wash the pots while you get changed, and the laundry can wait till tomorrow. Go on, and wrap up warm. These last few days of March are very cold and damp. I'm glad Easter is late this year. Let's 'ope the weather improves before the kids break up.'

Ella knew she would get nowhere arguing with her mother, so she smiled at her affectionately and did as she was told.

Winnie looked serious as she watched her daughter shrug her arms into her long coat. How she wished she could do something about Ella's image. Some mornings when she arrived, Ella was sloshing about in her nightdress and dressing gown. Why didn't she wash and dress herself as soon as she got up; perhaps even walk the children to school? There was so much Winnie wanted to say, but she knew things weren't that good between Ella and Dennis so she had to tread carefully.

'Ella,' she began as they walked arm in arm to the tram stop, 'would you let me buy you a new outfit?'

'Oh 'ere we go, Mum. You always have to start. You're not saying that I need new clothes, you're telling me, as you always do, that I'm too fat.'

'Well, luv, it's only because I hate to see you slouching about. You don't make the best of yourself, now do you?'

'You've always said I'm like me dad was, and he was a great heavy brute, wasn't he? So I guess it was how I was born.'

'Yes, I suppose you do have a lot of your father in you,' sighed Winnie. 'But I still say you don't make the best of yourself. Will you let me sort a few things out for you today?'

Loath as she was, Ella gave in. 'All right, but can we have something to eat before we go to the shops or up the market?'

'Course we can, but then . . . Well, we'll wait and see, but by the time I've finished with you, that 'usband of yours will be seeing you in a different light.'

As the day wore on, Ella began to think her mother had gone over the top. They were weighed down with bags. Most of the items they had found on Winnie's favourite stall, but a couple had come from a select shop in the London Road. Looking at herself in a full-length mirror and listening to the complimentary remarks not only from the sales ladies but also from Winnie, Ella had to admit her mother knew what she was talking about when it came to clothes, and today she had given Ella a magnificent boost.

She began to feel grateful to her mother. She knew she

had let herself slide, and that fact alone had played a big part in spoiling things between her and Dennis. She would make an effort, she promised herself, perhaps even have her hair shampooed and set, wear one of her new outfits.

Would Dennis look at her in a different light?

Hopefully he would. She was willing to meet him halfway over lots of things, but there was still that problem about moving out of London. She just could not give way on that.

Then a bright thought came to mind. Whatever Dennis decided to do with that property, when everything was completed to his satisfaction, he'd be able to sell it at a huge profit.

She smiled to herself. There was nothing in this world that her husband loved more than making money.

When his pockets were full, life was great. Times when he was broke, it was a question of God help them all.

Chapter Four

ELLA HAD LAIN AWAKE half the night listening for Dennis to come in. Now she laid her arm across the bed to where he should be lying, yet she already knew he wasn't there. She wished she hadn't had so much to say: why oh why had she had to rub him up the wrong way? She could just as easily have gone back to Epsom with him and given the house another look over. Made suggestions, aired her views, even gone along with his plans. That wouldn't have meant she had to move there; she could have gone on stalling. But no, she'd jumped in with both feet, adamant she wasn't moving come what may, and Dennis wasn't going to forget it.

He hadn't come home last night, and God alone knew when he would make an appearance again.

She struggled to sit up, threw the thick patchwork quilt and the blankets to the end of the bed and swung her legs round until her feet touched the thick bedside rug. Feeling under the bed, she brought forth her slippers and slid them on: at this time in the morning the oilcloth that covered the floor of the bedroom always felt icy cold. She crossed to the window and drew the curtains back. It was already light, and she gazed over the back yards and the slate-covered rooftops. The tall chimneys of the factories were already smoking, and soon the shrill sirens would blast the air, signalling to the workers that the morning shift was about to start.

When she'd given the children their breakfast and seen them off to school, it would seem a long morning until her mother came in. Dennis hardly ever left the house before ten.

Oh well, she'd stated her case firmly enough; she wasn't moving from here and so she'd just have to grin and bear it.

Three weeks later and still Ella hadn't seen sight nor sound of her husband.

Her mother kept saying, 'Stop worrying, he's got it made. From what I hear down at the King's Head, your Dennis is doing all right for himself, got workmen swarming all over that place he bought out at Epsom.'

Ella was silently wondering where he was living. Surely he wasn't sleeping in that huge house while all that work was going on? She might not admit it, but she missed her Den, very much, especially now that Teddy had joined the Boys' Brigade and Babs went to the Brownies and she had some evenings on her own. She wasn't worried about money; she knew Den would turn up sooner or later, if only for his clothes. Besides, she had been going through his wardrobe, brushing the shoulders of his tailored suits and checking his pockets, and had found a leather wallet that held one hundred pounds in small notes, winnings from horse-racing as well as dogs, she had no doubt, and she felt no qualms about carefully using it for housekeeping money. She folded his pile of shirts more neatly and hung his flashy ties on the rail that was fixed to the inside of the wardrobe door.

Ted, her father-in-law, still came round, sometimes for

a meal, other times just long enough to have a cup of tea. He never left without leaving at least a couple of pound notes on the table.

Saturday morning, Babs and Teddy were playing out in the street with a lot of other children. Ella had warned them to stay out of trouble, Teddy especially, because he was in danger of becoming a real terror now his father wasn't around.

Ella and her mother were just about to set out to do their shopping when Ted Dryden pulled his car into the kerb, lowered the window and called out, 'How about you two joining me for a drink in the Globe tonight? I'll pick you up about 'alf seven.' Without waiting for a reply, he put the car in gear and drove away.

Mother and daughter looked at each other in amazement. The Globe was a posh pub, quite a way from this area, but it was also known as a meeting place where crafty crooks did dodgy deals.

'What d'yer reckon?' Winnie asked as the pair of them exchanged meaningful glances.

'You go,' Ella urged her mother. 'I can't leave the kids on their own.'

'Don't make excuses. You know darn well Janey Brown from next door t' you will willingly come into your place and stay with them. She's sixteen, so she knows what she's doing, and I'll give her 'alf a dollar.'

Ella shifted her shopping basket to the other hand and linked arms with her mum. Laughingly she said, '*You* want to go, don't you?'

'Well, it's not every Saturday night that we get asked out, is it?'

'No, you're right there. So we're going, are we?'

'Yes, we are, an' for once do me a favour, try dressing yerself up. I'll come round early and heat the tongs up and see what we can do with your hair.'

'I'll wash my hair when we get back and give it a jolly good brushing. Isn't that good enough?' Ella said.

'No it isn't.' Winnie patted her own permanent-waved hair theatrically. 'You won't know yourself by the time I've finished with you. You've let yerself go for far too long, but today I'm taking you in hand.'

Ella knew her mother was speaking the truth, so she just squeezed Winnie's arm and kept silent.

The weather during March had been really depressing, the gale force winds beating against the old houses, feeling almost as if they were penetrating the walls, and howling down the chimney pots, sending clouds of smoke into the kitchen and making it nigh on impossible to keep a good fire going. But today everything was much calmer: the wind had died down, the streets were dry, and a weak sun was doing its best to shine through the fluffy clouds. This change in the weather had brought the world and his wife out, and everywhere you looked there were crowds.

Ella and Winnie took the bus to Bishopsgate. As they stepped down on to the pavement they smiled at each other. The atmosphere was different, real East End; people smiled and had a bright word as they passed. Across the road, on the corner of Middlesex Street, stood one of London's most famous pubs, known far and wide as Dirty Dick's. Of course that wasn't the name that appeared on the justice's licence. The real name of the delightful old-fashioned pub was actually The Old Jerusalem.

Winnie suggested they should pop in and have a drink. The pub was full, noisy and bustling, as was to be expected on a Saturday, but today it was even busier than usual, and there wasn't an empty seat to be seen. Winnie pushed her way into the snug and ordered two glasses of the house speciality beer served straight from giant hogshead barrels. It was a strong but refreshing

29

drink. They had almost drained their glasses when someone's elbow caught Ella in the back and she said, 'Let's get out of here, Mum.'

They made their way out through the rear entrance, through the alley, and into Middlesex Street. Real cockneys called this street 'The Lane'. In reality, there were several streets, narrow and cluttered by stalls and impassable to all but pedestrians. On Saturdays this great street market sold mostly china, household goods and food. Fruit and vegetables, meat, fish, home-made bread and cakes. Ella loved the different smells, and listening to the totters shouting that the china tea services on their stalls were pure English bone china and at the prices they were asking they were practically giving them away.

They were not without competition. A father and son were flogging bed linen, and their ribald comments as to what would happen if you were to put their sexy sheets and eiderdowns on your bed were beyond belief.

As for the meat van! Two brothers owned it, and there was always a wide choice of meat for sale both for roasting and stewing, as well as bacon, sausages and chickens which, although dead, still had their feathers on and needed to be plucked when you got them home. The brothers would skin rabbits for you and hold on to the skins because a dealer in fur would pay a good price for them. These two young men were using a microphone and their saucy jokes were a bit near the mark.

It was jolly good free entertainment to visit these London markets.

'Are we going to have something to eat before we do our shopping?' asked Winnie.

'I 'ope so,' was Ella's reply, walking more quickly towards the café.

Winnie looked irritated when they found the café to be as busy as the pub had been, but a familiar voice shouted out, 'Come over 'ere, Win, there's a couple of empty seats at our table.'

Ella elbowed her way to the counter. The café was stuffy and the windows were steamed up, but it was a good meeting place. Customers mostly knew each other so there was plenty of gossip going on, and you always got damn good food and a decent hot drink.

Ella came back with a tray that held two large mugs of tea and a plate piled high with hot buttered toast. She plonked her backside down on the only empty chair, smiled and said hello to Pam and Bill Edwards, who were old friends of her mother. She also nodded to an elderly man with grey hair and a moustache who was sitting with them. Bill merely said, 'This is Boris Lindsey, a neighbour of ours; this is Win's daughter, Ella Dryden.'

Ella gratefully grasped her huge mug in both hands, sipped her tea and then began to munch at a slice of toast while her mum and Pam chatted away nineteen to the dozen, but she felt a little uneasy. This Boris hadn't taken his eyes off her.

Suddenly he reached out and touched her arm. 'You ain't Dennis Dryden's wife, are you?'

'Yes, I am,' she replied with surprise, looking into the man's bright eyes.

'I'm glad t' meet yer,' he exclaimed, 'I've 'eard a lot about you lately. Got two kiddies, ain't yer?'

'Yes, I have,' Ella said quietly.

The man shook his head. 'That makes it worse. I'm ever so sorry, luv. Wasn't much I could do about it, though.'

'Would you mind telling me what you're talking about?' Ella said, puckering her forehead.

'I suppose I 'ave t' come straight out with it now.' The man's face showed shock and he sucked his lips. Then, taking a deep breath, he blurted out, 'The minute Bill said yer name was Dryden I put two an' two together.

31

Your 'usband has been taking my granddaughter out. She brought him round t' my place the other night 'cos her mother wouldn't 'ave him in the 'ouse. I didn't let him in neither, told him to wait in that big flashy car of his. I couldn't 'elp but think he were dodgy. My Anne's barely half his age.'

Ella leant her elbows on the table and said quietly, 'Don't let it worry you, Boris. Your Anne's not the first an' it's a dead cert she won't be the last.'

She was doing her best to put a brave face on but she was finding it hard. It was no surprise, but it was hurtful if she admitted the truth. To be told something like this by a total stranger, and worst of all to know that he was sitting there feeling sorry for her. She felt awkward to say the least, and breathed a sigh of relief when her mum looked over at her and suggested that it was about time they started their shopping.

'Goodbye, luv, take care,' was shouted back and forth, and they were back outside in the cold fresh air.

An hour later, loaded down with bags of shopping, Ella would have been more than pleased to go straight home. Her mother had other plans.

Head held high, and a look of determination on her face, Winnie led the way through side streets that would bring them out into a different kind of market. Here all the stalls were covered in on three sides with sheets of canvas, giving customers a sense of privacy. The goods on offer for sale were also very different. Some sold rings, bracelets and necklaces. One stall had a wonderful display of timepieces: clocks of all shapes and sizes, pocket watches with chains for gentlemen, and for the ladies not only wristwatches but some very ornate fob watches which Ella glanced at with envy.

The owners of the last stall in the row were also the

proprietors of the glass-fronted shop which stood directly opposite on the pavement.

Winnie Paige had become acquainted with this family some years ago and had benefited greatly from the friendship inasmuch as she was able to wear really good clothes that had not cost her a fortune.

Mother and daughter were still walking when Isaac Cohan stepped in front of them and blocked their passage. Arms flung wide, he spoke loudly. "Allo, Winifred, where the 'ell 'ave yer been? Sight nor sound of you we 'ave not seen. Come 'ere.'

A flush of pleasure rose in Winnie's cheeks as she looked at this short man with the broad smile on his face. He was wearing a smart pinstriped suit with narrow lapels, a sparkling white shirt and a dark blue tie.

She dumped her shopping bags at her feet and willingly went into this portly old man's arms.

Even passers-by paused to look, and Ella watched with pleasure as these two old friends greeted each other. It was a show of warmth and affection. When they broke free, Ella was surprised to see that her mother's eyes were brimming with tears, and it came to her that although her dad had been dead for years, her mum must still miss him. It was then that she told herself that in future she mustn't take Winnie for granted so much, and must remember not only to tell her that she loved her, but to show her that she did.

'And how is our Elly?' Isaac asked. Without waiting for a reply, he herded both of them towards the shop, shouting through the open doorway, 'Wally, come and see to the stall.'

A tall young man appeared, and as soon as he spotted Winnie he said, 'Winifred Paige, how nice to see you. My mother will be pleased.'

'And this is her daughter Ella. I don't think you have

33

met each other before, but we have known her since she was a little toddler, though we haven't seen her for years, not since she married and got a family of her own.'

Isaac's son shook hands with Ella and told her he was pleased to meet her, then he crossed the road and went to stand behind their stall. Ella turned her head; she had to give this young man a second look.

Walter Cohan was a lot taller than his father, and in his early forties, Ella guessed. He had deep dark brown eyes, a handsome tanned face and a head of thick black wavy hair. Ella couldn't have said why, but despite the short acquaintance, she liked him and the friendly way in which he had treated her and her mother.

The inside of the shop was much larger than it had appeared from the outside. Ella looked about, her eyes darting from side to side with unconcealed curiosity. There were blouses, jumpers and cardigans expertly displayed in glass-fronted cabinets. Two waxwork dummies stood against a wall, one dressed in a businesslike navy-blue two-piece costume, the other one attired more modestly in a perfectly plain high-necked, long-sleeved black dress that fell to just about calf length. What made the garment look so glamorous was that the last six inches of the dress was covered with an adornment of heavy black silk fringe.

Ella's imagination was running riot. Imagine dancing, wearing a frock like that! Get real, she scolded herself, you'd have to starve for six months to even get into it.

Sadie Cohan put down the pen with which she had been writing and came round from behind the counter. She was not very tall, and her dark hair was fastened back and secured into a neat twirl at the nape of her neck. She was wearing a beautiful tailored suit in a worsted material of soft brown with a beige silk blouse beneath the jacket. She was an attractive woman, with fine black eyebrows, her face lightly powdered, her features outlined by lipstick and a hint of rouge.

She grasped both of Winnie's hands in her own, squeezing them tightly. 'At last, at last you come to see us. Please come through to the sitting room. So much shopping you have done. I must make you some refreshment. You will take a glass of lemon tea with Isaac and me?'

Then, realising that she had not greeted Ella, she smiled at her with genuine pleasure and spoke to her in a warm tone. 'Please, come, sit down. You must be Winifred's daughter of whom I have heard so much, though it is many a long year since I have seen you. It is nice that you visit us now.'

'It is nice to meet you too,' Ella said politely.

It was then that they heard voices coming from the shop. 'I will attend to the customers. You stay, my dear, and chat with our friends.' Isaac looked at Winnie. 'Please excuse me, duty calls.' He inclined his head with that grave courtesy of his and went through to the shop.

Sadie crossed to the stove and within a few minutes had returned with three glasses on a small tray. She handed one to Winnie and then, giving one to Ella, said, 'You have not had lemon tea before, I think, but you will like it. I hope you both enjoy it.'

Ella sipped the hot drink and to her amazement found she really liked it. Black tea, lemon-flavoured, with pieces of real lemon and herbs floating in it, and it was sweet and hot. She had never tasted anything like it before, though she didn't feel that she should mention this.

When Winnie had drunk half of her tea she set the glass down on a coffee table and took the bull by the horns. 'Sadie, I need you to do me a favour. It's for my Ella really.'

Poor Ella, she wished that the floor would open up and

35

swallow her as she listened to Winnie telling Sadie Cohan how her daughter had let herself go, only dressed in loose, flowing dresses, old cardigans and coats that had seen better days, and never bothered to use a bit of paint and powder. There was so much conversation going on between these two old friends and it was all about her, Ella was on the point of leaving. She stood up, feeling gutted that her mother should say such things about her, and more so to this total stranger.

'Where d'yer think you're going?' Winnie asked crossly.

'Well I'm not staying 'ere to listen to you describe me as a fat, blowzy old woman. I'm going home,' she said miserably.

Total silence descended and two pairs of eyes stared at Ella.

It was Sadie who broke the silence. 'I am so sorry. You are absolutely right. We talked as if you were not here and that is unforgivable.'

Ella was thunderstruck.

Winnie's cheeks had flushed a deep red, but she got up and came over and patted Ella's arm. 'I was only doing it for your good, Elly, please. You're far too young to dress the way you do, and it's only because Dennis doesn't pay you much attention these days and all your time and money is spent on the kids. What about your own life? You should be allowed to live a little as well, as other people do.'

Ella was so surprised that her mother hadn't yelled at her, she was speechless.

Sadie gave her a sweet, understanding smile and said, 'If you will let me, I can really help you. Has your mother told you we buy clothes that have been worn by high-class women? We also buy from theatrical wardrobes. Our stock is not new but we have home-workers who do repairs and every article is cleaned before we offer it for sale.'

Ella couldn't think of an answer; she just looked at her mother, who nodded her head and solemnly gave her a thumbs-up sign.

'Ella . . . do you prefer to be called Ella or Elly?' Sadie asked.

'I don't mind. It was Elly when I was at school, but since I've got older I seem to be more of an Ella.'

'Well,' Sadie laughed, 'sit down and I am going to give you your first lesson. You are not to be offended, because what I am going to tell you about is what you wear under your clothes. Have you ever heard of a corselet?'

'Well, yes, but I've never seen one,' Ella stammered.

'I am wearing one and I'd guess your mother is also. It is a modified corset combined with an uplifting brassiere. We sell them and they are brand new.'

The three women looked at each other and their combined laughter filled the air.

It was a moment or two before Sadie turned to Winnie and said, 'I think it better if you disappear for a little while, leave Ella and me to work a few things out.'

'All right,' Winnie said with a shrug. 'Maybe I'll go over to your stall, see what Wally is getting up to.'

Sadie closed the sitting room door behind Winnie and turned to Ella.

Ella felt a lot more comfortable with her mother out of the way. 'Why do you have a shop and a market stall?' she asked.

Sadie grinned. 'Because the men of my family are so well organized. Clothes on the stall are cheaper, within the reach of poorer folk, and the turnover is faster. In the latter years the shop has always been Wally's domain, though he doesn't let on: Isaac still regards everything as his territory. Wally is young, such ideas he has, this son of ours,' she murmured, shaking her head. 'But first I go to our stock room while you take off your clothes down

37

to your underwear. Nobody will come in; you will not be disturbed.'

Left alone, Ella was flustered. *Take her clothes off!* Finally she did as she had been told, then, catching a glimpse of herself in a tall cheval mirror which stood in the corner of the room, she gasped and hastily put her coat on to cover herself.

Sadie's arms were full when she re-entered the room. One look at Ella and her heart was filled with sympathy. Without appearing to even notice that Ella was wearing an outdoor coat, she put the pile of clothing down and held up a long brassiere-type article. Smiling broadly, she looked straight at Ella and said, 'Believe me, pet, this is a girl's best friend, so come on, no shyness with me. I fit women every day.'

Ella's top half was soon laid bare, and she slipped her arms through the shoulder straps while Sadie, standing behind her, did up the long line of hooks and eyes.

'Lift your bosoms into the cups and fiddle them around until you feel comfortable,' Sadie suggested. Then, coming round to stand in front of Ella, she gasped in admiration. She had guessed well at what size to bring.

'Come, look into the mirror and see for yourself the transformation,' Sadie said in a soft voice.

Ella could not believe it! She had been wearing a bra, but it hadn't done much for her. This corselet had at least five inches of material below what would be a normal brassiere, and its lining was finely boned, which held her ribs in. She found that if she stood up straight, shoulders back and tummy in, her figure certainly looked a darn sight better.

Sadie slipped a dress over her head and Ella was suddenly transformed.

It was a soft woollen dress with a full skirt, long sleeves, pearl buttons down the front and a large white linen collar, and although it had been darned a little way along the hemline, its simplicity and the rich colour, which could be likened to that of port wine, added to the impression of elegance. This young woman could be quite beautiful, Sadie thought, intrigued by the difference an undergarment and a second-hand dress had made. Her hair needed attention, yet the colour, dark copper, was real enough, and if washed and treated it could be shimmering. Her features were also good if only she weren't quite so plump, and she seemed such a nice, unassuming woman. Sadie badly wanted to help her.

She was not wrong in these assumptions. In her younger days, Ella Paige, as she was then, had been something special, only a slip of a girl but a real beauty.

'You're very quiet, Ella,' Sadie said. 'Do you not like the dress?'

'Like it!' Ella had been turning this way and that, seeing herself in the long mirror from every angle. 'Doesn't it make a difference to me?'

'Yes, it does, but remember, a lot of that is down to your corselet. Now, slip the dress off. I have a skirt for you to try, and two tunic blouses that will both tone in so that you will be able to alternate your outfits.'

'Sadie, how much are all these clothes going to cost?' Ella asked suspiciously, her heart thumping wildly.

'No more than you can afford,' Sadie said, then she whispered, 'Besides, your mother insisted to me that the cost was to be her treat.'

'Oh, I'm not going to let her do that,' Ella said rather sulkily. 'It's kind of me mum to offer, but I can pay me own way.'

'Let's get sorted what you are going to buy first,' Sadie insisted as she helped Ella to take off the dress. As Ella bent her head and leant forward, her hair, her thick, dark auburn hair, fell across her outstretched arms.

'Tell me why you have neglected yourself so much,' Sadie said.

'You wouldn't understand.'

Sadie shook her head. 'Try me. It might help just to talk.'

Ella sat down, now wearing only her stockings, big bloomers and this lovely silky-feeling corselet. Her vest with its wide shoulder straps lay on the floor with her coat, tweed skirt and thick woollen jumper.

'It didn't seem worth while getting dressed up,' she sighed. 'I only went out shopping or to meet the kids from school. I suppose I've got slovenly. Dennis is only interested in younger, slim girls. He tired of me a long time ago.'

'Men! They think they know so much and they yearn for their youth. Sadly, we all grow old, but you are nowhere near that stage in your life yet, Ella.'

Having said these wise words, Sadie picked up two skirts from the pile of clothing she had fetched from the stock room, asked Ella to stand up and held each one in turn up against her. She cocked her head to one side and screwed up her eyes, looking at the skirts carefully and critically. Both were well tailored and had originally been expensive.

'What do you think?' she asked Ella.

'The black one is a bit fussy, too many pleats, but I do like the dark green one, if yer don't mind me saying so.'

Sadie smiled faintly. 'You don't need much teaching. You are perfectly right. The green one is the ideal colour for you. It will show off the glints in your hair once you get it washed and tamed.'

Ella frowned. 'I have let it get matted. I'll buy some shampoo on the way home.'

'Buy some conditioner as well. It will make all the difference.'

'Mum said that later on she will curl it with the hot tongs for me.'

Sadie stared at her, stupefied with horror. 'Is that what she does?' She croaked the words.

'Sometimes. I think it makes it look nice,' Ella admitted sheepishly.

'Well, Ella, my dear, dear girl, Winifred is doing you no favours. Hot tongs will eventually ruin your gorgeous hair. Learn to wash it regularly, comb it well and leave it to dry naturally, and then practise putting it in different styles. Just a touch of oil rubbed between the palms of your hands and gently smoothed over your head will give your hair an even better gloss.'

Ella seemed doubtful, and was frowning and biting her lip as Sadie slid the green skirt over her head.

'It could have been made for you,' Sadie declared. 'A little tight around your waist, I think, but we can move the button nearer to the edge, and when you lose a little weight you can move it back or . . .' Sadie stopped talking for a moment and grinned. 'Leave the original button in place, sew a second one on, and when you can fasten the skirt on the first one comfortably you will know your figure is more trim.'

'Yeah, when!' Ella said crossly.

'Keep the skirt on, I've two overblouses for you to try,' Sadie said firmly, ignoring Ella's small burst of bad temper.

The first top Ella tried on was a creamy beige in colour, long-sleeved, soft to the touch and had a neat collar and lapels which were edged with a satin ribbon of the same colour and fastened with shiny crystal buttons down the front. It fitted very well across the shoulders, but as Ella made to tuck the blouse inside the waistband of the skirt, Sadie cried out in horror.

'No, no, that you never do, not unless you are very slim and can wear a wide belt. You leave the blouse hanging

41

outside your skirt, look, see, it has slits up the side which are very fashionable, and hanging loose it hides a multitude of sins.'

Once again Ella twisted and turned in front of the cheval mirror. Suddenly her emotions got the better of her and the backs of her eyes stung with unshed tears. She wouldn't have believed that she could look so different, neater and a good deal smarter. She turned to thank Sadie Cohan, but the words wouldn't come, and she stood still and just stared at this kind Jewish lady, wide-eyed. Eventually she said, 'How do you do it?'

Sadie smiled. 'It's easy when you know how.'

Ella swallowed hard. 'I thought I was a bit old to keep up with fashion.'

Sadie raised her eyebrows. 'If you are too old, what does that make me? Would you mind, Ella, if I ask how old you are?'

Ella hung her head. 'I'm thirty-eight, thirty-nine this year.'

Sadie was shocked. This poor overweight young woman looked at least forty-five. She did her best to hide her astonishment, but Ella said quietly, 'I know what you are thinking.' Then, very bravely, she said, 'My husband is twelve years older than me, and more often than not he looks younger than me.'

Sadie answered kindly with a smile, 'That's men for you.'

Ella felt she could confide in Sadie and she quickly said, 'We were married for six years before I had my first child, and during those early years our marriage was great. Dennis was proud to show me off because then I looked good.'

'And you will again,' Sadie was quick to reassure Ella. 'You do know how to dress, you just haven't bothered. It's time you showed that husband of yours that you aren't going to be left behind. Anyway, this second top is exactly the same as the cream one, so you have no need to try it on.'

She tossed a garment to Ella, who immediately held it up and gasped with pleasure.

The material was a much paler green than the skirt that Ella was still wearing, and was perfectly plain apart from a dark green motif embroidered on the breast pocket.

'A perfect match, I'd say,' Sadie remarked, looking at Ella's smiling face. 'So, one dress, one skirt, two blouses and your friendly uplift, will that do for today?'

'Oh, yes please, Sadie. I don't know how to thank you.'

'Then don't try.'

While Ella was putting her own clothes back on, Sadie was taking great care over the packing of Ella's new garments. Each article was wrapped in tissue paper and all were placed in an elegant carrier bag which was embossed with just one word raised in capital letters: *COHAN'S*.

Winnie had a short conversation with Isaac and Sadie, but she had her back to Ella and therefore Ella had no idea how much money her mother had spent on her this afternoon. It did help her to see the wide, beaming smile on her mother's face as she put her purse away in her handbag, picked up the carrier bag and said, 'I can't wait for us to get home. You can give me and the kids a fashion show.'

'Hmm, Babs might think it's great fun, but can you see Teddy sitting still long enough to watch?' Ella said with laughter in her voice.

Sadie hugged them both and kissed them each on both cheeks. Isaac, gentleman as always, wrapped his arms around Winnie, giving her a big bear-hug, then he actually kissed Ella's hand, a gesture which in most men she would have found rather queer, but somehow it was part of Isaac's old-world charm.

'Say goodbye to Wally as you go out,' he said, then, wagging a forefinger at Winifred, he said, 'Not so long you leave it before you visit again.'

Sadie had to have the last word. To Ella she said, 'You have the beginning of a new wardrobe, and you have a very smart mother. Listen to her and heed her. Meantime I know your size now and have a good idea of what you like, so I shall be putting aside any article that I think for you would be good. Be sure you come again soon.'

Ella thanked Sadie again for all her kindness and for the lemon tea.

Outside, Wally asked a customer to excuse him for a moment and came over to them. He gripped Winnie's hand firmly. 'Goodbye, Winifred. Thank you for coming to see my parents. Nothing gives them greater pleasure than to see old friends.'

Turning to Ella, he said, 'I think we shall become friends too.'

Ella's face was serious as she nodded and murmured, 'Goodbye, Wally.'

Loaded down with shopping bags, mother and daughter struggled to board the tram. Once seated, Winnie said, 'Are you pleased with yer new clothes?'

'Am I pleased? More than that, I can't wait to show you everything.'

'I knew I was doing the right thing, taking you to see Sadie. I trust her judgement, she has such good taste,' her mother said with a satisfied smile on her face.

'By the way, Mum, I want to stop at the corner shop and get some shampoo. I'm gonna wash my hair if we're going out tonight.'

'Not so much of the if. We *are* going out and you're going to be done up to the nines.'

Winnie wasn't about to listen to any excuses. The invitation from Ted Dryden to take them both to the Globe for a drink had been on her mind all day. There had to be more to it than he was saying, else why had he driven off without giving either of them a chance to ask any questions? It had taken a bit of thought on her part, but she felt sure she'd got it right. Nice as Ted was, and always good to Ella and the kids, he was still Dennis's father. Dennis was going to be in the pub, Winnie would lay a pound to a penny. Those two men had got some scheme going.

Well, when they set eyes on my Ella tonight, they're in for a real surprise, she thought, knowing that she was being vindictive but not caring one jot.

Chapter Five

AN ASTONISHING AMOUNT OF time had been spent on getting Ella ready to go out for the evening. 'Anyone would think we were going to a royal do,' Winnie muttered as Ella stooped down to pull on the pair of black court shoes that her mum had lent her.

'I'll never be able to walk in these blinking shoes,' she groaned. 'One's all right, but the right one is pinching my toes.'

'Well, thank yer lucky stars that you ain't got t' walk anywhere tonight. Ted is picking us up and as soon as we're in the pub you can kick my shoes off and keep yer feet tucked underneath the table.'

'All this fuss an' bother, I'll end up looking like a dog's dinner,' Ella said ungratefully.

Winnie had also given her daughter a pair of nylons, one of the best things to have come over with the Yanks during the war. Even the worst pair of legs looked better clad in silky, shimmering nylons than in the thick lisle stockings that were the only hose which had been available for years.

Eyeing Ella from top to toe, Winnie was well chuffed.

Her daughter really and truly did look totally different. Her hair especially.

Ella had washed it twice, put conditioner on and left it for five minutes to soak into the roots. When it was towel dry, she had alternately brushed and combed it until it gleamed. It had taken ages before she had got the style right. Eventually she had taken some of the long strands and slowly began to coil them on top of her head, pushing a great many hairpins into the coil to keep it in place and letting the rest of her hair hang free down on to her shoulders.

To tell the truth, she had got the idea from taking notice of Sadie Cohan's rich dark hair, and though she had not managed to achieve the exact same result, for a first attempt she was more than pleased with herself.

Teddy was staring at her, not quite able to work out what all the fuss was about. 'You look ever so different,' was all he said.

Babs was jumping up and down and running round Ella until Winnie was driven to shout, 'Babs, will you please sit down and stop running around like a blue-arsed fly.'

'Well, Mum looks like a real posh lady and I want to know why me and Teddy can't come out with you,' Babs moaned.

Janey from next door pacified Babs by showing her a huge jigsaw puzzle she had brought in with her, then whispered to Teddy, 'I've got quite a few sweets, and I've brought you in one of my brother's books of true adventure stories.'

'Oh good-o, thanks, Janey.' Teddy sounded as pleased as Punch.

The sound of a honking motor-horn told them that Ted was waiting outside. Winnie, dressed elegantly herself, reached for her fur-collared black coat, but as Ella put out a hand to take her own coat down from where it hung on a hook on the wall her mother cried, 'You don't imagine I'm going to let you ruin everything by wearing that old coat.'

Ella looked down at herself. She was wearing the soft woollen dress that Sadie had so kindly advised would suit her. The wide white collar lay high and flat around her neck and emphasized the make-up that her mother had insisted she put on her face. Winnie had told her she could keep the lipstick and Ella was thrilled. It was in a flashy gilt case and the colour was called Russet Rose.

Winnie had come by it when working in the cloakroom of a London hotel. A guest had handed her coat over the counter and the lipstick had fallen out of the pocket. Winnie had gone down on all fours to retrieve it and popped it into her own handbag. Later, when the lady came for her coat, she hadn't mentioned it and Winnie had told herself that by the look of her fur coat she could well afford to buy herself another lipstick.

'If I can't wear my coat I'm going to freeze,' Ella said, looking bewildered.

'You should learn to trust me more,' her mum said. 'I have thought of everything.'

From her old shopping bag Winnie produced a white shawl. It had been hand-crocheted in the finest of wool and edged with a heavy knotted silk fringe. Ella was struck dumb as she watched her mother fold the shawl into a triangle and then drape it around her shoulders, crossing it over her chest. Ella nestled her cheek into the softness. It felt so luxurious.

'Oh Mum, I don't deserve you,' she murmured with a sob in her voice.

'There's days when I would agree with you,' Winnie laughed. 'But right now we are going to have a night out, so goodbye, kids, and if tomorrow Janey tells me you have both been good, I will give you a tanner each.'

'Cor, thanks, Gran,' Babs cried, well pleased.

But Teddy grinned and said, 'Make it a shilling, Gran, an' I'll be a saint.'

Winnie did her best to hide her smile as she answered, 'You, my old son, will get more than you bargained for if Janey tells me you've so much as said a word out of place. Yer mother doesn't 'ardly ever go out. She deserves this treat and she don't want to be bothering her head about you all night. You got that?'

'Yes, ma'am.' Teddy struggled to keep a straight face while giving his gran a mock salute.

'Cheeky little sod, he gets more like his father every day,' Winnie muttered to Ella as they closed the kitchen door and made their way down the passage.

'Blimey! What's got into him?' Ella muttered, when they saw her father-in-law standing on the pavement and holding the rear door of his car open for them.

'Looking forward to a night out then, girls?' Ted chirped as Winnie got in the near-side door and Ella walked round the back of the car and settled herself comfortably beside her mother in the back passenger seat.

It was a clear night, no rain, no fog and no wind, a fact that Ella was grateful for. This shawl was beautiful around her shoulders but it wouldn't keep the cold out, and she hoped the pub, once they got there, would be nice and warm.

Luckily enough there was a vacant space only yards from the front door of the Globe, so Ted had no bother in parking his car.

The public bar was crowded as usual, but Ted ushered them both through into the saloon. A few couples were chatting noisily at tables on the far side of the room, and a young couple were gazing dreamily at each other over their glasses at a corner table.

'Ain't love grand,' Winnie murmured enviously as Ted

49

indicated a large round table that was not occupied. Once seated, Ted asked, 'What would you gals like to drink?'

'I'll have a gin an' it,' Winnie said with no hesitation.

Ella pondered for a moment before saying, 'I think I'll have a milk stout.'

'No you won't,' her mother contradicted her.

Ella felt her cheeks burn and for one awful moment she thought her mum was going to tell her that was what made her fat.

Ted felt the tension. 'How about a Southern Comfort, Ella? Nice drink that is.'

'OK, thanks, Ted,' Ella quietly agreed, cheeks still flaming.

Ted left them to go to the bar. Winnie took her coat off and laid it across an empty chair, and Ella undid her wrap and let it lie loosely around her shoulders.

Conversation was sparse between mother and daughter until Winnie let out a yelp.

'I knew it, I damn well knew Ted hadn't brought us for a drink out of the goodness of his heart.'

The look of outrage on her mother's face and the ferocious sound of her voice made Ella turn her head and look in the direction that Winnie was gazing in so savagely.

'Oh no, I should have known it was too good to be true,' Ella whispered sadly.

The colour had drained from her cheeks and her hands were trembling. Her first thought was to get out of this place and go back home. Her husband was standing by the bar talking to two men, and the three of them were surrounded by smartly dressed, good-looking young women.

Ted brought their drinks over, smiled at them, then turned on his heel and without saying one word returned to stand at the bar with his son.

Ella took a sip of her drink and sat there listening to

her mother rant and rave on about how crafty and sly Ted Dryden was. She finished her long, angry, aggressive speech by adding, 'What I want to know is why the pair of them have gone to such lengths to get us here tonight.'

Ella couldn't bring herself to answer. Her heart was heavy. Dressing in her new clothes and taking so much trouble over her hair had been a sheer waste of time. She sat there staring at the mat on which her glass was placed, not really seeing the advertisement that was printed on it. When her mother at last calmed down, Ella forced herself to raise her head and look towards the bar.

The girls that surrounded Dennis and his mates were not only much younger than herself, they were also a darn sight slimmer. Ella's eyes filled with tears as she watched her husband place his arms around the shoulders of a pretty blonde-haired girl and draw her close until her slim body was leaning against his huge frame. Then he lifted her up and seated her on a bar stool. Once settled, she pointed the toes of her high-heeled shoes downwards to the floor and began to swing her silk-clad legs in a very suggestive way.

He must know by now that I am here, Ella told herself angrily. More than likely it had all been prearranged between himself and his father. Like her mother had said, she would give a lot to know the reason why they had been set up.

She sighed heavily as she gazed at her husband's big frame, his broad shoulders and dark good looks. Why was it that men didn't go to seed as quickly as women did? Because they didn't have to bear children or grapple with the day-to-day troubles that came with bringing them up, she supposed.

Once folk had said that she and Den were the ideal couple. He hadn't altered much; he still reached for the sky and invariably got it. It was she who had become shabby and disappointed with his expectations of how life should be led.

As if he was aware of her watching him, Dennis turned and met her eyes, a slight smile playing at the corners of his mouth. She lowered her gaze first, and confused and hurt looked down, gripping her hands tightly together in her lap.

Little did she know that Dennis was asking himself if he was seeing straight.

He just could not believe the difference in his wife and was wondering how and when it had come about. And more to the point, why? Who the hell was she trying to impress? Not for one moment did the thought enter his head that it might be for his benefit.

He wasn't the only one to have noticed Ella and her mother.

One of Dennis's associates, Stan Wilson, grinned. 'The sooner you unwind yourself from that tart who is wheedling up to you, Den, and get over to talk t' your missus, the better, I'd say.'

'Yes,' Pete Jarvis, the third man in the group, agreed. 'Your missus is looking pretty sharp tonight.'

'Makes yer wonder what's going on there.' Stan put his oar in again.

'Good Lord Almighty!' Dennis roughly pulled the arms of the platinum-blonde from around his shoulders and moved a step nearer to Stan. His temper was boiling over. 'Anybody ever tell you you're a nosy git, Stan?' he hissed, his blue eyes glinting angrily.

'We were working out a good deal 'ere, but just you remember, Stan, business is one thing! My family life is down t' me and sod all t' do with you.' Then, turning his head, he said, 'You wanna remember that an' all, Pete.'

Stan Wilson nodded. He wanted to laugh at the absurdity of this daft situation but had a feeling that right now wasn't the time for joking. Indeed, it was Ella Dryden that he felt sorry for, but as Dennis was pointing his finger into his face, Stan Wilson knew when to back off. Dennis was not only far bigger than he was, he had a reputation for going utterly crazy when annoyed.

'I was paying a compliment to your Ella,' Pete said quickly, doing his best to play the peacemaker.

Dennis sniffed loudly and, ignoring the question of his wife, said, 'We gonna settle this deal tonight or not?'

The three men closed ranks. One look at their faces and the good-time girls knew when to take the hint. They picked up their glasses and moved to the far end of the bar.

Even Ted, who was standing to one side sipping Scotch, looked warily at the three men and decided they were best left alone for a while.

As he walked to the men's toilet he was thinking about his daughter-in-law. There certainly was a change in her tonight. And very much for the better was his decision. He had been bowled over at the sight of Ella; she really was done up to the nines. He had his own idea as to why his son had asked him to bring Ella and her mother here tonight, but he wasn't dead sure. In fact he was hoping that he was wrong. He needed no telling that his son played his cards very close to his chest, and just lately he was beginning to wonder whether Dennis had any conscience or real feelings. All married couples had their tiffs, and men the world over strayed after a fresh bit of skirt, but to walk off and leave yer wife and kids, no, that wasn't on. He was certainly baffled by the fact that both Ella and her mother had turned themselves out as if they were going to a dinner and dance. There was tension in the air, you didn't need to be able to read the tea-leaves to be aware of that much. What the bloody hell is going on? Ted wondered for the umpteenth time.

The answer he came up with was that a lot more than Dennis had admitted was being sorted here tonight, and Ella did not deserve to be brought into it.

Ted felt awful knowing he couldn't trust his own son, at least not a hundred per cent. He ran his hands through his hair, feeling his face burning with embarrassment. The truth as Dennis told it was that Ella was being awkward, refusing to move out of the East End, but there were two sides to every story. Not in a million years could he see Ella and her kids fitting into that big house in Surrey. In fact in his opinion it would take dynamite to shift Ella from the East End.

But that didn't give Dennis the right to treat her like dirt.

Dennis drained his drink in one gulp as his father rejoined them at the bar and looked straight into Ted's eyes. He felt sure he knew exactly what his father was thinking.

And he was right.

Taking big strides, he crossed the bar and sat down on the empty chair opposite his wife. He nodded his head at his mother-in-law, who drained her glass and gulped down the strong gin before saying, 'I know when I'm not wanted.'

Taking her empty glass with her, she went straight to where Ted stood and said loudly, 'Do you expect one drink to last me all night?'

Dennis and Ella stared at each other, each reluctant to make the first move. Then, taking a thick envelope from the inside pocket of his jacket, Dennis slid the packet across the table saying, 'That should keep you and the kids going for a while.'

If he expected a thank you from Ella, he was in for a long wait.

Quickly he said, 'You know I would never see you and the kids skint. How are Teddy and Babs?'

Ella stared at the floor. It was as if she was deaf.

'I have a right to know.' He looked at his wife, really looked at her, and sighed.

Ella shook her head. 'Suddenly you're concerned? All these weeks and what 'ave you cared? You've always said Babs was your golden girl, the apple of yer eye, your precious favourite. What is she supposed to do now?'

Dennis felt a moment's pang of guilt and it showed.

Ella was glad. It proved he had a streak of humanity in him after all. Once started, she felt she was fully entitled to rub salt into his wounds.

'They come 'ome from school telling me their friends' dads 'ave taken them to the zoo or to the pictures. What am I supposed to say? Daddy's too busy doing up a big posh 'ouse out in the country which in the end will make him a load of money?'

That is, she thought, if he doesn't end up getting caught buying building materials and tins of paint that have fallen off the backs of lorries.

'Teddy says he likes Grandad better than you 'cos at least he takes him to watch the football on Saturdays.'

Dennis laughed. 'He don't mean it, does he? He knows I 'ave to work. I didn't think he'd miss me living at home.'

'Course you didn't. That's your trouble, you never think about anything except making money.'

He looked at her and sneered.

'Well, luv, I don't see you refusing what's on the table, and I know for a fact you had what was in one of my suits. You an' the kids ain't been living on fresh air.'

Ella looked at her empty glass and said in a sad voice, 'Teddy and Babs need new shoes, and I've kept up the rent so far, but . . .'

'There's more than enough in there to keep you going for a while.' Using one finger, Dennis edged the package nearer to Ella, and this time she picked it up and put it into her handbag.

'I'll get us both another drink,' he said, reaching for Ella's empty glass.

'That's right, Den, money and booze will cheer us both up.'

He shook his head in despair as he walked slowly back to the bar.

His mind was in a whirl. Never had he seen Ella look so smart; nor had he heard her sound so cocksure of herself. He had asked his father to bring her here tonight to let her see that he was doing all right. Coping well on his own. Yet really hoping that she would plead with him to return home.

He didn't want to be the one to climb down. That would mean losing face and give Ella the upper hand, but he missed his family and he missed Ella's cooking. Sad but true, things hadn't turned out at all as he had planned.

In fact he was in two minds as to whether or not she had already turned the tables on him.

In the Globe that Saturday evening the landlord felt uneasy. Jack Riley had been in the business a long time and he had a nose for trouble. He had seen more than his fair share of bar brawls, and right now he could sense one brewing.

At first he paid no attention to Dennis Dryden and his mates, drinking hard and fast in the corner of the saloon bar. It was the scantily dressed young women who were playing up to them that bothered him. It wasn't unusual for women to go for well-dressed men, knowing that they would be bought a good many drinks. The situation did not often get out of hand, mostly being good-humoured banter with the men taking just a few liberties.

Tonight it was different. Dryden's wife and his mother-in-law were in the bar. Dennis had left the group and gone over to talk to his missus; whatever it was that had been said had left him with a thunderous look on his face. He had soon rejoined the others back at the bar.

He picked his glass up and took a gulp, then wiped his wet mouth with the back of his hand.

'You know what, Dad? I've lived in that poky little 'ouse ever since me an' Ella got spliced, an' both our kids were born in that upstairs bedroom. Yer could say I've managed to keep the wolf from the door one way or another, couldn't yer?'

His father nodded, wondering what Dennis was getting at.

'I don't treat Ella badly, the odd slap now an' again but only when she's out of order. Neither she nor our kids 'ave ever gone hungry. I might 'ave strayed a bit now an' again, but what man can put his 'and on his heart and swear he's never played away from 'ome? Besides, take one look at my Ella sitting over there. When did you last see her looking like she does tonight? A bloody long time ago if ever! You know darn well I'm only speaking the truth. She's run t' seed and that's a fact. Wearing tent-like dresses and flip-flop slippers is how I see her when I get home, an' in the bedroom, well, if she ain't got an 'eadache it's like mounting a camel, only even the humps are flabby.'

Ted was getting worried. Winnie was still standing at the bar and her face had turned white with temper. Suddenly she pushed aside Stan Wilson's restraining hands and made for Dennis. She pulled her arm back and then swung it, hitting him full in the face.

Dennis staggered back, blood streaming from his nose.

Winnie wasn't finished. She gave him a mighty shove and he fell in a heap on the floor, but still she wouldn't leave him alone, slapping him round his head with her handbag, kicking his legs, and all the while shouting abuse.

57

Ted came up behind her and lifted her away from his son as though she were a baby.

Stan and Pete hoisted Dennis to his feet as Winnie struggled to free herself from Ted's vice-like grip.

'Put me down, you rotten sod. You're as much t' blame as he is, letting him talk about my daughter as if she were dirt beneath his feet. Just let me get at 'im! I'll swing for 'im!'

'Stop it, Win, you're old enough to know better. You shouldn't go losing yer temper at your age, it's bloody stupid.' Ted looked over to where Ella was still sitting. 'Look at your gal, she's going potty. Go on, go over and sit with 'er and I'll bring a brandy over for each of yer.'

Winnie grinned sheepishly and dusted her skirt down. 'It's not fair the way Den goes on about her. Heart of gold that girl 'as and he don't give a damn for her.'

Dennis was on his feet now, gingerly leaning on the counter still holding a blood-stained handkerchief to his nose.

Ted looked at the empty glasses. 'What yer all 'aving? Same again, or d'you want a short?'

'I dunno as I wanna drink 'ere while that hell-cat an' my bloody missus is still 'ere,' Dennis said.

Ted grabbed his son's arm. 'Look, Den, you were out of order, went a bit over the top. I take it that yer talk with Ella didn't go down so well. Didn't she go down on her knees an' beg yer to come 'ome?' he asked sarcastically. 'Forget it, son. 'Ave anuvver drink and keep quiet fer Gawd's sake.'

Dennis was embarrassed that his father had hit the nail right on the head.

'I ain't gonna plead, no way. I'll get at her through the kids; she'll come round, you'll see.'

Ted laughed, and called to the landlord, 'Come on, Jack, fill 'em up.'

Digging in his back pocket for his wallet, he added, 'I'm gonna take a brandy over to Ella and her mum an' then I'll take them home.'

''Ope it chokes the pair of them,' Dennis muttered.

Ted did his best not to smile. He was only sorry that his son might soon come to realize what he had lost.

The way things were looking tonight, Ella might just stand her ground this time and refuse to dance to his tune.

Chapter Six

JUNE HAD BROUGHT THE promise of a good summer. So far there had been days of constant sunshine and clear blue skies. Ella kept telling herself that she would get out more, and that as soon as the children broke up from school for their six-week summer holiday she would make picnics and take them to various places; maybe Battersea Park, anywhere out in the fresh air.

Promises were one thing; keeping them was an entirely different matter.

She didn't have the inclination to do much these days, and if it weren't for her mother's perpetual nagging she more than likely wouldn't have kept herself looking as neat and tidy as she did. Winnie made sure that she watched her figure, kept her copper-coloured hair glossy and smooth and wore decent clothes.

Ella knew she meant well, because she'd overheard her mum say to a neighbour, 'Anything to avoid my poor Ella falling into a fit of depression.'

Three months had passed and Dennis had not returned home to live. He had cut her adrift and she had no one to blame but herself.

Surprisingly, he had remained friendly, often dropping in, mostly on the off chance. Some Sundays he'd turn up with his father for his midday roast dinner. Her mum always went on about how daft she was to feed him, but Ella looked at it from a different angle. It made the kids happy to sit round a table and enjoy a family meal with their dad and grandad rather than just her.

It also kept Dennis in touch with his children, and money-wise he had been fair, coughing up seven pounds a week; well, most weeks! She could never totally rely on him.

Ella was never completely relaxed when Dennis was around. She always felt that she had to be on her guard. If he should arrive and find his mother-in-law there he would turn tail and make a hasty retreat, but not before he had let them know exactly what he thought of the pair of them.

One wrong word from Ella or one complaint about the shortage of money and he would blow his top, grab her roughly, push her to the floor and storm out into the street.

Dennis hadn't changed; he still had a short fuse.

Teddy teased his sister something rotten because their father often took him out, mostly to watch a football match on a Saturday afternoon, but he never took Babs anywhere. Whether from a feeling of guilt it was hard to say, but after one of what he and Teddy called their 'men-only outings' he always brought back a decent present for Babs. Secretly Ella thought that the reason Dennis made sure his young son still favoured him was because she had told him, that night in the pub, that Teddy thought more of his grandfather than he did of his father.

Neighbours had stopped asking awkward questions and by and large they looked out for Ella and her two children. Always willing to give her a hand if and when she needed help.

Yet to Ella, each day was so monotonous. Every morning she was up bright and early. She laid out the children's clean clothes, did a bit of housework, and then put the porridge on to simmer while she got the children out of bed. All washed and dressed, the three of them sat round the table and ate breakfast, chatting like they always did.

'On Wednesday, Mum, can I have some flour, sugar, margarine and a few currants or sultanas, oh, and two eggs if you can spare them, please.' Proudly, Babs puffed out her chest. 'Teacher said we're going to start cooking lessons an' we can bring the cake home what we're gonna make.'

'Well I've been doing woodwork classes for a long time and I'm making something special for you, Mum.' Teddy wasn't about to be outshone.

'I think you're both getting on ever so well at school,' Ella said as she sprinkled spoonfuls of sugar over their porridge.

With time to spare, Ella cleared away the breakfast things while the children packed their books into their satchels and got ready for school. At half past eight they were ready for the off, both of them looking neat and tidy in their uniform. Several children came out of the line of terraced houses and they all joined up, chattering away nineteen to the dozen. Ella stood at her doorway and watched until they had turned the corner, then went back indoors mumbling to herself, 'Another long, miserable day. Still, I've got a great pile of ironing to do, that will pass the morning away.'

It was not to be.

Hardly had she got a blanket spread over the kitchen table and an old sheet that had a good few scorch marks on it laid over the top and the two flat irons set on to the top of the hob to heat up, than there was a rattle of her letter-box and a voice called out, 'It's only me, Ella.'

Ella didn't need any telling to know to whom that voice belonged, and in a way she was glad of the distraction.

Ah well, she sighed as she went up the passage to open

the front door, even Miss Turner had to be better than having no one to talk to.

Putting a smile on, she said, 'Good morning, Miss Turner, have you come for a chat or are you in a hurry?'

'Now, now, Ella, how many times have I asked you to call me Nellie? It ain't everyone gets that liberty but you are different,' Nellie Turner said, pushing her way past Ella and walking towards the living room.

Ella had to laugh to herself as she looked at this middle-aged woman. She certainly was a character. She was scarcely taller than five foot two, dressed in a blue frock that looked as if it had come out of the Ark, and her navy blue cardigan had seen better days. Her greying hair was pinned tightly in a bun and the glasses she wore were plain and steel-rimmed.

This woman let everyone know that she was *Miss* Turner because she had never been married. Very kindly she had devotedly looked after her elderly parents until they had died, which had been within three months of each other. She missed them terribly but would be the first to say that they had left her comfortably off. Now she was the proud owner of their very nice house, which they had bought and paid for years ago. Alone and often lonely, with time on her hands, Nellie Turner lived her life by poking her nose into other folk's business. There was still a lot of good in this sad lady. She'd do anything for someone in trouble but she spread gossip faster than a forest fire took hold.

Seeing that Nellie had settled herself comfortably in what had been Dennis's armchair and was undoing the buttons of her cardigan, Ella said, 'I'll make us a cup of tea as soon as I've folded all these bits an' pieces.'

Nellie was up on her feet in an instant. 'You put that iron back on the hob an' see t' the tea and I'll fold the ironing,' she insisted.

With the table cleared and a cup of tea and a plate of

biscuits set out, they sat drinking their tea in comfortable silence until Nellie sat her cup down on her saucer with a clatter and her face suddenly became serious.

'Ella,' she said quietly, 'there is something I think you ought t' know. You won't get upset if I tell yer, will you?'

'Try me,' was all that Ella said.

'Well, I don't want yer mum to find out that you 'eard it from me, but Connie Baldwin reckons she's 'aving a baby.'

'What, young Connie Baldwin whose mum an' dad live over the paper shop?' Ella asked, frowning.

'Yes, that's the one.'

'Do her parents know about it? She's not sixteen yet, is she?'

'Sorry, luv, but it's no t' both of those questions as far as I know, and what her mum an' dad are gonna say when they find out, the Lord only knows. Won't be long before they do, though, mark my words. Half the street knows already.'

Ella stared in disbelief, thinking to herself that Nellie was enjoying telling folk about a young girl's misfortune. Aloud she said, 'Wonder if the fella will be man enough t' marry her?'

'He won't,' Nellie said smugly.

Ella was watching her closely and she couldn't fathom what the look on Nellie's face was supposed to mean.

'How the 'ell can you be so sure?' Ella sat up straight and her body was rigid as she looked directly into Nellie's eyes. She didn't like what she was seeing, and she leant across the table and stabbed her forefinger into Nellie's chest.

'I'm not daft, yer know, Nellie! You've come 'ere this morning t' tell me something. Something I ain't gonna like. I've got it in one, 'aven't I?' Without waiting for an answer, Ella stood up, prodded Nellie again and said, 'Well, say yer piece. I'm warning you, I'm not the most patient person in the world.'

Nellie was shocked. She hadn't expected Ella to react in such a nasty manner. She met the younger woman's eyes and could see that she had pushed her further than she should have.

Ella grew tired of waiting. 'I'm warning you, Nellie, for the last time, whatever it is you think I should know, spit it out. Don't make me lose me temper.'

All the colour had drained from Nellie's face and it took a great effort for her to get the words out, but eventually she croaked, 'According to Connie's friends, your Dennis is the father,'

'Hmm, some friends! Poor little cow, she sure as hell don't need any enemies,' Ella murmured sadly.

She plonked herself down. All the wind had gone out of her sails.

Dennis, Dennis, Dennis, she was saying over and over inside her head, have you really sunk so low?

She sighed deeply. At times he could be so charming and the trouble was he knew it. He would look straight into a young girl's face, smile at her with those big blue eyes and know straight off that he could lead her on like a lamb to the slaughter.

He was well aware of his good looks. He had a decent, trim body with broad shoulders, and his height seemed to fascinate females both young and old. But to put such a young girl in the family way must be a new experience for him. Surely it couldn't be true.

Please God don't let it be true, she prayed silently. If it were, she would lay her last penny that the day would come when he'd live to really regret it. If that day hadn't already dawned.

Nellie drained her teacup to the dregs and hastily began to button up her cardigan. She hadn't got the reaction from Ella that she'd hoped for and it would be just her luck for that mother of hers to turn up, and then she would be for it. She knew Winnie Paige didn't like her much; she'd called her a nosy old gossip to her face on more than one occasion. All the same, I came here in good faith, she told herself, hoping against hope that she could get out quickly.

Too late! The sound of the front door opening and then being slammed shut had Nellie trembling in her shoes.

'Ella, you there, luv? Come an' give me an 'and with this load of shopping. Sorry I had to kick the door shut.' Winnie sounded as bright as a button.

Ella stared at Nellie as if she was something the cat had dragged in. 'Sit down again an' stay where you are,' she ordered as she went to meet her mother in the passage.

Nellie's expression froze. Stay there, Ella had said. Don't look as if I've got much choice now. She knew she'd dropped a clanger. Telling tales about Dennis Dryden to Ella was bad enough; now with her mother to face as well she'd have to do some hard thinking to wriggle out of this one.

Winnie poked her head round the door. ''Allo, Nellie,' she greeted her daughter's visitor. 'I only went in t' the greengrocer for a bag of spuds and two women told me you was 'ere visiting my Ella. Don't suppose you were the bearer of good news, were you?' Sarcasm was clear in her voice and she was smiling broadly.

That fact alone threw Nellie. 'I 'ave t' get back home. Your Ella can tell you all about it. I've told her all that I know.'

'I bet you 'ave,' Winnie said, looking at her with contempt.

'OK, Nellie, you get off now. By the look on my mum's face she's already been told all there is t' tell.' Ella's voice was hard now, as were her eyes. 'But just one thing: try keeping yer tongue between yer teeth, 'cos if my kids come 'ome crying that someone has taunted them about their dad, I'll come after you. I mean it, I will, Nellie.'

Winnie had taken all of the shopping through to the scullery. Now she stood dead in front of Nellie Turner and stared at her coldly.

'I will see you later, Nellie, and you can tell me the whole story and explain to *me* how you come to know so much. And believe me, it had better be bloody good.'

Nellie Turner held her breath as she slid past mother and daughter, thinking what a fool she'd been. She wished she hadn't got out of bed this morning, let alone come along here to tell Ella Dryden that her husband had been playing around with a very young girl.

When she was finally out in the street she felt faint with relief.

She decided there and then that she would steer clear of both those women from now on. At least she'd do her best to.

Not a word was said until they heard the front door close. Then, suddenly, Ella went to pieces. Choking on the words she said, 'Mum, I take it that you've 'eard about Den and Connie Baldwin.'

With an aching heart Winnie nodded her head.

'What about Babs and Teddy, Mum? I've done my best to keep them happy, their lives normal, that's why I've never minded when Den comes in for a meal. Folk will talk, their kids will listen to what their parents are saying, and before you know it they'll be jeering at my two that Den is going to be father to another child.'

Winnie couldn't find words to say that would do any good, so she murmured, 'I'll go and put the kettle on.'

Ella sat down, covered her face with her hands and began to cry softly. Her temper, for the time being, had run its course.

Her mother took her time, but finally she came in from the scullery carrying a tray which held two steaming cups of tea, two china side plates and a jam sponge sprinkled with icing sugar.

'Come on, Ella,' she urged. 'A nice cuppa and a piece of cake will do us both good.'

'Don't be so daft, Mum, how the 'ell will eating and drinking solve the ruddy mess we're in?'

Her mother rolled her eyes in exasperation. 'Ella, listen t' me. We 'aven't got much to go on yet, so let's wait and cross our bridges as we come t' them. I don't know why you let that silly spinster come in t' yer house, though I suppose it was better to hear the news while you were indoors.'

Winnie stopped talking suddenly, threw back her head and let out a great belly laugh. Ella was so startled that she took her hands from her face and stared at her mother.

'Oh, luv! If someone, anyone, 'ad come up t' you in the street and told you that your Dennis had put a slip of a girl in the family way, you wouldn't have stopped to think whether it were true or not. You'd 'ave punched them in the mouth so hard they'd 'ave been knocked into the middle of next week. And more than likely they would 'ave needed to see a dentist.'

Much as she didn't want to, Ella saw the funny side of what her mother was saying. Tears still brimming from her eyes, she got to her feet and hugged the slight figure of her mother close.

'Thanks, Mum. You're marvellous. Always there when I need you.'

Winnie used her handkerchief to wipe her daughter's face before saying, 'When I was told about it in the greengrocer's I thought even Den wouldn't go that far and I was hoping it wasn't true.'

'So was I,' Ella murmured sadly. 'So was I. But if it *is* true, Den has showed me up good an' proper this time, ain't he?'

Winnie decided it was better not to answer that one.

Chapter Seven

ELLA WAS FINDING EACH day a sad and worrying time. She was almost afraid to go out. Neighbours were so ready to stop her and sympathize, and that was exactly what she did not want. Some were just being inquisitive.

She was well aware that it had to be even worse for Mr and Mrs Baldwin and their poor young lass, not that she had had any contact with them. There was nothing she could do or say that would make matters any better, and more than likely any attempt on her part would end up making matters a damn sight worse.

Connie Baldwin was the youngest of her parents' four daughters. Why in God's name had Den had to pick on her? Probably to prove to himself that he was still man enough to pull young girls.

Ella gave a wry little smile as her mother came down the stairs, having been up to say goodnight to the children. She was shaking her head and talking to herself, but quite loud enough for Ella to hear every word.

'Those kids miss their dad, I know they do, and it's only natural that they should.'

Ella knew only too well the truth of what her mum

was saying, but she was at a loss to know which way to turn.

Winnie made straight for the dresser and picked up a bottle of sherry. 'I bought this while I was out shopping this morning, thought a glass or two might cheer us both up.' Taking down two glasses from a shelf, she filled each one almost to the brim with the rich dark cream sherry. Passing one to Ella, she pulled an armchair round and sat down facing her daughter.

'Den not been round?' Winnie started the conversation with a question.

'Mum, you know darn well he 'asn't. Don't suppose he's proud of himself; more likely he's afraid t' show his face, though I did think he would have kept in touch with the children.'

'Yeah, I thought that, especially Teddy. He so looks forward to Saturday with his dad, doesn't he?'

'Used to, you mean! I think he's given up now. Can't blame the boy. For the first few Saturdays he got himself ready and nearly wore the mats out walking from the front-room window to the gate, watching for his dad to come down the road. He don't bother now.'

'Selfish bastard Den is, always was and always will be if you ask me.'

Ella wasn't surprised at her mother's comments. She had never had a good word to say about Dennis from the day Ella had brought him home. For the first six months of their married life they had lived with her parents, and Dennis had got on really well with her father. Not so with her mother! Life had been anything but easy. They only had what had been Ella's bedroom, and the walls were paper thin. Ella had longed for a sister to talk to, but she only had two brothers. Since her dad had died, they came round about once a year to see their mum. Winnie's fault: she didn't like either of her daughters-in-law, so she was only running true to form by disliking her one and only son-in-law.

Ella sighed and told herself to be fair. The relationship between herself and her mother had always been good, and there wasn't anything that Winnie wouldn't do for Teddy and Babs. It was true she often had a go at her daughter, but Ella knew that it was always for her own good.

The trouble was, once her mum got started on airing her views as to what a bounder Den was, Ella knew there would be no stopping her, and for once she decided that Dennis was not *all* bad.

The early years of their marriage had been happy enough and she had always felt quite special because, of all the girls that were around at the time, he had chosen her. And she could say, hand on heart, that he had never overstepped the mark sexually before he put a wedding ring on her finger. Inwardly she laughed; not that they hadn't come pretty close on more than one occasion!

To begin with Dennis had worked for his father, going off to various racecourses and often being away two or three days at a time. Always great when he came home! It was after Teddy was born that he had become involved in dodgy deals. It was almost unbelievable that he had never got caught. Several of his so-called mates had been sent to prison, but Den, together with whoever else had got off scot-free, had made it his business to see that the families of the men who were locked up for long stretches were well taken care of.

Dennis never told Ella any details; she wasn't sure she wanted to know what he got up to anyway. Perhaps she was a coward. But the less she knew, the better, as far as she was concerned.

Still thinking back, Ella remembered how, when she had first found out that Dennis had been taking other women out, she had been so hurt she had just given up and let herself go. It was only recently, since her mother had taken her to visit the Cohans' shop, that she had made a great effort to keep her appearance up to scratch. Sadly, it would seem she had left it far too late.

As Winnie saw the hurt in her daughter's eyes, she felt the urge to really do some serious harm to Dennis Dryden.

'Let it go, Ella. He's not worth worrying over,' she urged.

Ella was baffled for a moment, felt her temper rising. She told herself to relax and to try and calm down, but instead she got to her feet and stood facing her mother. Big fat tears were rolling down her face as she shouted, 'You've never had one good word to say about Dennis, but you wanna think on. There hasn't been a Christmas since Dad died that you ain't spent under his roof. OK, right now he's broken my world in two, but remember, Mum, having a baby takes two. Does he face up to his responsibilities? No, I'll agree with you on that point. He disappears, where to, God only knows. All I do know is that he ain't gòt the guts to come an' tell me about it himself.'

Winnie's mouth gaped open at Ella's sudden outburst.

Once started, Ella decided it was time she stood her own ground for once.

'I've spent a long time scraping together pieces of information that others have been only too willing to tell me, and by now I think I've gathered most of the facts bit by bit. I've come to the conclusion that in more ways than one Dennis is a bounder, but when it comes to this business with Connie Baldwin, my 'usband is not entirely t' blame.'

It was a very long time since Winnie Paige had felt she was being chastised. This angry outburst had come out of the blue. She decided her best option was to keep her mouth closed tight.

Staring at the shocked look on her mother's face, Ella let out a great sigh and looked upwards. 'Dear God, give me strength.' For a moment she hesitated, in two minds as to what to do. But somehow, despite her regrets and doubts, her instincts remained strong. For too long she had turned a blind eye to whatever Dennis got up to, and now, simply because she had refused to move out of London and live deep in the country, he had left her and the children. At least that was what she had believed, until this matter of Connie Baldwin had been brought to the surface.

During the past few weeks she had dithered and been frightened to even think of a life without Dennis around. For too long she had done nothing but sit around feeling sorry for herself. Now that she had made her decision, she was going to face all her troubles head on.

It was in this fighting mood that she made up her mind that it was time her mother stopped thinking that Dennis was all bad.

Taking a deep breath, she began.

'Connie Baldwin's always been aware of her own good looks and slinky figure. She was apparently known as something of a flirt and at fifteen developed a crush on Dennis. It doesn't take a great deal of imagination to believe that she was flattered that a smart man like Den paid her attention. Then again, all things being equal, I suspect that the fact he had a big car and flashed his money about went a long way when she was boasting to her friends about where he was taking her and what he was buying for her. I don't think Dennis would have had to twist her arm, do you, Mum?'

'Hmm!' For what seemed an age, Winnie looked grumpily at her daughter. Eventually she said warily, 'It's a devil of a mess whichever way you look at it.'

Ella gave a small, bitter laugh. 'One minute we were

73

jogging along, coping with the ups and downs of everyday life as married couples do and then I find the bottom has dropped out of my world.'

'Yeah, well, you're not the first wife to find out that her 'usband has got a young girl into trouble, and it's a dead cert you'll not be the last. But you will have to deal with it.'

And though she made no further comment, Ella knew her mother spoke the truth.

There was no getting away from it. Trouble lay ahead, and she already had the feeling that it would be big trouble.

Chapter Eight

WHETHER IT WAS BECAUSE Teddy had played her up all evening, as good as saying outright that it was her fault that their dad didn't live with them any more, or because she had run out of money and was going to have to go cap in hand to her father-in-law because she hadn't set eyes on Dennis for weeks, Ella didn't know. Whatever the reason, she had slept badly, dreaming a lot and waking in a cold sweat. Now, having given the children their breakfast and seen them off to school, she stood in front of the mirror combing her hair and telling herself she looked like something the cat had dragged in.

Deciding she would make a fresh brew, she turned towards the scullery. As she held the kettle underneath the cold tap she heard the front door open and footsteps coming down the passage. Oh God, not me mother this early in the day, she moaned softly to herself.

She turned towards the living room and was shocked to see her husband standing there, still as a statue. She felt the colour drain from her face.

'What the 'ell . . .'

'Hallo, Ella, long time no see.'

His voice sounded different. She felt nervous of him. It was weird, unnerving, seeing him standing there.

'I see you were about to put the kettle on. Don't let me stop you, I could murder a cuppa.'

Ella laughed, she couldn't help herself. 'My, you've got some nerve, Den, walking in bold as bloody brass as if you've never been away.'

With all the confidence in the world he pulled out a chair and sat down. 'Watch what yer saying, Ella my love, this is still my 'ouse.'

'Is that so? Well, I 'ope yer wallet is bulging, 'cos I 'aven't been able to pay the rent for the last two weeks and me and the kids ain't been living it up like lords either.'

As Ella had been stating her case she had been studying him. She hated to admit it even to herself, but he did look good. He had always dressed well, but today he looked elegant. He also looked very sure of himself, a fact that made Ella aware that things were going well for him.

Dennis gave her a saucy grin. 'Go on, gal, make us that brew. You know full well I'm here to give you some dosh. Come what may, I'd never see my family starve.'

Ella was really rattled now. 'No, you'd shut yer blinking eyes and carry on buying drinks for all the scroungers in the pubs.'

She banged about out in the scullery as she made the tea, deliberately giving Dennis a big chipped mug, and was on her way back with it when she felt she couldn't keep her mouth shut. He was in the wrong, not her.

Setting his tea down in front of him, she sat herself down opposite, making sure that she could look him straight in the eye as she spoke.

'You weren't man enough to face me with the truth, were you? It were the neighbours and yer so-called friends that made sure I was kept well informed. The one good person in all of this rotten mess 'as been yer father. He filled all the blanks in for me, and when he says something at least I know it's the truth.'

Dennis leant across the table and would have taken hold of her hand. Ella wasn't having any of his soft soap. She drew her hands back like a scalded cat and sat with them tightly clenched in her lap.

'Oh, Ella!' he sighed as if he were the one being wronged. 'I would have preferred t' tell yer meself, but I 'eard that you'd been got at. Who was it that came t' you with a likely tale?'

'As if you didn't know! Who would it 'ave been other than the street gossip, Nellie Turner? I warned her that if our kids got t' know they were gonna have a brother or a sister, I'd swing for 'er.'

'My God! What a bitch that Nellie can be. Teddy and Babs don't know, do they?' Dennis sounded so concerned, and yet Ella knew it was an act he was putting on.

'Come off it, Den, you ain't even asked how the kids are. Remember what they look like, do you? Even you can't convince anyone that you live in cloud-cuckoo-land. I told Teddy and Babs straight that what people were only too willing to tell me might be the truth, but until you had the guts to face me and tell me outright that you'd been with a young girl and made her pregnant, we couldn't be sure.'

'What did you 'ave to tell the kids for?' He was getting more angry by the minute.

'Don't be so stupid, Den. Teddy 'eard everything from the kids at school, and Babs came 'ome in tears because some of the girls taunted her that her dad was going to 'ave a new baby that wouldn't be part of our family. How the hell do yer think that made me feel? What was I supposed to say to her?'

'I'm sorry, Ella. Honest to God, if I could turn the clock back . . .'

'Yeah, yeah, you're sorry now, but not 'alf as much as me and the kids are. As to that little word *if*, what was it you used to say to me? If yer aunt 'ad balls she'd be yer uncle.'

Dennis was fighting to defend himself but damned if he was going to crawl.

'I was drunk, you know how these young girls come on to us men, and they're half-naked when they walk into the pub. Connie Baldwin was asking for it.'

'You know what, Den? You're unbelievable. You sit there and tell me that you couldn't 'elp yerself. Next you'll be asking me to believe that you haven't been taking that girl out, showing her a good time and having an affair with her, that it was all just a one-off.'

Tears were stinging the backs of her eyes now and she was annoyed at herself for letting him upset her so much.

Dennis clenched his fists. 'Trust you t' believe the worst of everybody. Boiling it all down, you can't exactly blame me for looking elsewhere. You're always such a bloody miserable mare, and all the years we lived together you walked about looking like a rag-bag, and a fat old bag to boot.'

'Listen here, Dennis, I'll give way on some of what you say. I did get fat, a lot of women do when they've had two kids, and of course I didn't exactly dress meself in the latest fashion. How could I, even if I had wanted to? I never knew where I stood with you. Some weeks you were really generous, buying God knows what for the kids, but lose on the gee-gees or do a deal that went down the pan and you'd storm in and sell everything you could lay yer hands on. It was those weeks that always frightened me. You'd give me barely enough to buy food, let alone put shoes on the kids' feet and clothes on their backs.'

Dennis took an envelope from his pocket and laid it on the table between them. Ella lifted the flap and stared at the thick wad of notes in disbelief.

She sighed as she said, 'While you're about it, you'd better settle up with your father. It's only what he's been handing me that has kept us going.'

He didn't answer her.

She shook her head. 'All you really care about, Dennis, is number one. You've made that pretty obvious. Look at you. New suit, and the shoes on yer feet must 'ave cost a pretty penny. Suppose you've been staying in some posh 'otel. I ain't even had the money for Teddy to go on his school trip. Time an' time again your son has said, "I bet my dad will pay for me to go," but you've never bothered to come near nor by. The pity of it is for weeks on end he waited every Saturday for you to come and take him to football, 'cos he said over and over again, he didn't care what *anyone* said, you were *his* dad. That's why I get so cross when I 'ave to tell the kids that they can't have things 'cos you haven't sent us any money.'

Now Den was really angry and for a moment she thought he was going to hit her.

'You know where an' when t' hurt a man when he's down, don't you, Ella?'

'Hmm! You are neither down nor out, you're just bloody mad that the son you're supposed to think so much of is beginning to realize what you are really like.'

Dennis sighed and gritted his teeth. 'Ella, listen to me. I had to get away for a time. I had business that needed sorting, but as you so rightly say I am not down and out and I won't leave you without funds again. You shouldn't believe all the gossip nosy folk round here tell you. Young Connie Baldwin is a right little flirt. *If* she is carrying a baby, it could belong to anybody.'

'Oh, she's carrying a baby all right!' Ella's voice was

rising, though she was trying as hard as she could to control it and her temper. 'That girl passes my front window five mornings a week and I ain't blind. This affair has been going on for a lot longer than I've known about it. Though you'd 'ave me believe different.'

Dennis sniffed. His whole face was red as he stared at her hard.

'If what you're claiming is true, then it's like I've said before, you've only got yerself to blame,' he said, punching his clenched fist down heavily on to the table, making his now empty mug fall over on to its side.

'My fault! All the pain and aggro you've caused me and the kids, and now you've got the cheek to suggest it's all my fault . . .' Her voice trailed off as she had to stop and draw a deep breath.

'Yeah, a marriage is supposed to work both ways. You, Ella, are a taker, never willing even to meet me halfway. I had plans, big plans. My old man did me a favour when he asked me if I wanted to buy that house at a knockdown price. Most women would have been over the moon having a deal like that dropped in their lap. But oh no. Not you. You'd rather stay in this dingy little 'ouse that is damp an' 'asn't seen a lick of paint since before the war. Why? 'Cos you're dead lazy. Couldn't get off yer backside and come an' see if there was anything you could do t' help. You'd rather sit drinking tea all day, or chatting over fences to women like yerself what ain't got no ambition. Is it any wonder that I turned to another woman? I'll tell yer again, 'cos it doesn't seem to have sunk into that thick 'ead of yours, you make no effort. Dead scruffy, that's what you are most days when I come home.'

Ella gave a sarcastic laugh.

'Oh, it's easy to blame me, helps t' ease yer conscience, does it? I might be a lot of things, Den, but soft in the

80

'ead I ain't. You're making a big mistake if you think you can get away with coming out with these old woman's tales. First off, Connie Baldwin is not a woman, she is a young girl who is at least five or six months pregnant, I'd say, and I don't for one moment think that she conceived the very first time you ever took her out. No, you had to butter her up first, show 'er what a great man you was, big car, plenty of money, knew yer way around London. I reckon the first time you got in that young girl's knickers was way before you or your father knew that old lady was thinking of moving from her big 'ouse. Me refusing to uproot our two kids and live out in the back of beyond had nothing whatsoever to do with you 'aving your filthy way with Connie Baldwin. You 'ad the sweets, Den, and now you 'ave to put up with the sours. Just a pity that your own kids 'ave to suffer in the process.'

Dennis closed his eyes. He had never seen Ella in this kind of mood before. Her moaning he was used to, but today she was being a right pain. He leant towards her and whacked her full force in the face.

It felt as if her face was on fire as her head rocked backwards.

Pushing the table until it was resting hard against Ella's chest, Dennis stood up and pointed to the envelope that still lay on the table between them.

'Will that lot keep you going for a while?'

Ella nodded her head slowly.

'Never let it be said that I keep you or the kids short of money.'

She couldn't bring herself to answer.

'Did you hear what I just said?' Dennis bellowed menacingly.

'Yes,' Ella said reluctantly.

'Well, don't go telling folk that me not living 'ere is a hardship for you,' he shouted back over his shoulder as he made for the door. Then, grinning, he said, 'Tell Teddy and Babs that I'll be seeing them soon.'

After she'd heard the front door slam, Ella sat still for a good five minutes, just staring into space. She didn't know which hurt the most: her painful cheek, the thudding in her head, or the fact that she hadn't been able to throw his money back into his face. Sad but true, she needed the money to feed and clothe her children, never mind pay the rent.

That was the moment when she decided she was going to get herself a job.

Chapter Nine

ELLA HAD GIVEN A young lad a threepenny bit to take a note around to her mother. All she had written was that she had an errand to run and would call in on her way back. That had been an hour and a half ago, and Winnie was curious. For the umpteenth time she went into her front room and walked over to the window, and now she watched as her daughter walked down the street, her shoulders stooped as if they carried the weight of the world. 'Now what's happened?' Winnie murmured thoughtfully. 'Poor Ella, life can't throw much more at her.'

Shaking her head, she straightened her lace curtain and hurried to the kitchen to put the kettle on. 'It has t' be something more to do with Dennis,' she said to herself. 'That man is a right selfish sod.' From her shopping bag she took out a bag of six jam doughnuts and set them one by one on a plate, which she placed on a small table covered with a pretty tablecloth.

'You timed that well, Ella,' she called out as she heard the front door open and Ella walking down the passage. 'The kettle has boiled an' I'm just about to make the tea.'

First glance told her something wasn't right. Ella looked terrible. Her copper-coloured hair that she had been taking such good care of lately straggled across her face.

Winnie walked across the living room to her. Ella put her hands up to her face and tried to turn her face away from her mother.

'You all right, luv?' Winnie asked, knowing full well it was a daft question.

Ella nodded her head.

Very gently her mother took hold of her chin with one hand and used the other to uncover her face. Ella flinched.

The very look of her made her mother's blood boil, because despite the fact that Ella had powdered her face, it hadn't covered the ugly bruise that ran across her cheekbone.

'Bloody men! I don't need to be told who done that to you,' Winnie said, and Ella could tell she was bristling with anger. 'Come on, luv, sit yer down an' I promise yer one thing. I'll make damn sure that 'usband of yours will live to regret the day he laid a finger on you. It was Dennis, wasn't it?'

'Yes,' Ella admitted quietly.

'I guessed as much, but let's have our tea and a doughnut and then you can tell me what's 'appened to make him lose his rag.'

What she really wanted to do was ask a load of questions. But she knew better. Wait, and Ella would tell her all in her own good time.

'I'll fetch the tray. They're nice jam doughnuts. I got 'em from Bloomers, the posh bakers. Still warm they were when he 'anded me the bag.'

Returning with the tea tray and two fancy plates, Winnie would have gone on chatting, but something about the way Ella was sitting hunched up and quiet made her pause.

'Ella, luv, what's really up?' She came nearer. 'Don't

tell me that ol' man of yours whacked yer one 'cos you asked him for some money? What the 'ell does he think you and the kids are living on, bloody fresh air?'

When Ella raised her head, her mother saw tears rolling down her swollen cheeks and knew there was something very wrong. Quickly moving the tea tray out of harm's way, she knelt down beside her.

'You don't 'ave t' tell me your Den has put in an appearance. I can see that for meself, but what I want t' know is what he had t' say for himself, 'cos it couldn't 'ave been very nice seeing the state he's left you in.'

Not yet able to open her heart to her mother, Ella bowed her head again and looked away.

Carefully Winnie wrapped both arms about her. 'Something big 'as upset you, I can tell.' Laying her face on Ella's head, she murmured, 'I'm here, luv, I always will be. Just think about it, you can tell me. I might even be able to help.'

A moment passed. Feeling loved and safe in her mum's arms, Ella sobbed quietly.

Winnie released her hold, saying, 'I'll pour the tea out. Don't know why, but a cuppa always seems to help.'

They each sipped their tea, and the everyday sounds of the street coming through the open window made Ella realize that life had to go on. Winnie got up and pulled a coarse linen tea-towel from a drawer in the dresser. Handing it to Ella, she said, 'Wipe yer face and try an' eat a jam doughnut.'

Ella looked into her mum's face and managed to smile. 'And that will make me feel better, will it?'

'Course it will, but don't go getting sugar all over me best tablecloth.'

Winnie grinned as she watched her daughter pick up a sugary doughnut and take a big bite. If only I could sort out her problems as easily! she thought.

Some time later, Ella actually did start to feel better. She gave her face, and especially her lips, which were smeared with jam, another good rub with the towel, then took a deep breath, looked at Winnie and said, 'How am I supposed to cope with all this, Mum? Dennis didn't deny that he was the father of Connie Baldwin's baby, but according to him everyone else is responsible for the mess we're in; none of it is his fault. First off he went mad 'cos Nellie Turner had told me about the affair, called her every wicked name under the sun. Then he pleaded with me not to tell Teddy and Babs, and when I told him that I'd already had to tell them the truth because the kids at school were 'aving a field day, well, that was like adding fuel to the flames. I thought he was going to burst a blood vessel.

'Then, well, you wouldn't believe it. Accusations were coming from all corners. He was drunk at the time, couldn't help himself. Young girls come into the pubs half-naked just asking for it. When I told him there was no way I was going to believe it had been a one-off, and that I was well aware he had been taking Connie out and buying her things for months . . . that was when he stuck his face close to mine and—'

'He put his fist in yer face?' Winnie screamed the words.

'No, Mum. Not at that point. What he did do made me feel a darn sight worse.'

'Lord Almighty!' Winnie jumped up fast, nearly knocking the teapot flying. 'Sorry, luv, carry on, I'm listening, but the more I hear, the more I'm sure Dennis Dryden was born bad.'

He told me *I* drove him to it. Said I was a miserable mare, a fat, lazy old bag, and the clothes I wore weren't fit to put in the rag-bag. Without thinking, Mum, I needled him. Told him he was selfish. Always buying himself good clothes, real leather shoes, and riding around in a flash car, while his kids and I had to wear whatever we could get. That really rattled him. But still I hadn't the sense to leave it there. I had to push me luck.'

'No one could blame yer, gal,' Winnie cut in. 'About time somebody told that bloke a few home truths.'

'You ain't heard the worst of what I said yet.' Ella's voice was low.

'Well, go on, let's 'ave it all out in the open,' Winnie urged.

Ella put her hands to her head. It was aching like mad, and her cheek felt as if it was on fire.

'I told him I might be scruffy and miserable, but at least I did me best to bring the kids up well and I led a far more decent life than he ever did. He wanted to know how I worked that out. I told him outright it was him that was turning schoolgirls into whores and young Connie Baldwin into an unmarried mum.'

Ella's voice was rising in panic and Winnie's temper was almost out of control.

'That was when he grabbed my chin with his hand and pulled my face towards him and told me I needed to watch my mouth 'cos he could always take the kids away from me. I tried desperately to pull away from him, and that's when he pulled his right arm back and slapped me in the face.'

'Some slap!' Winnie murmured.

'That's not all, Mum. He punched me in the stomach just as I stood up, and I got the full force of his fist. I don't know what hurts the most, me stomach or me face or me head.'

Winnie stood up and started to pace the floor. 'Oh, you poor luv. I'll see Ted gets to know what his son is really like, but you've got to calm down and start thinking. There's more than one way to skin a rabbit. First question, did he leave you any money?'

'Yeah, he did, but t' be honest, Mum, I would have given anything to be able to tell him to stuff it. Teddy needs new shoes, though, an' I'm behind with the rent, so . . .'

'You could talk to me more. You know I can manage a little every week.'

'You shouldn't have to, Mum, and you buy far too much for me and the kids as it is. But there is something else I haven't told you yet.'

Winnie raised her eyebrows and sighed heavily.

'Go on then, we might as well get it all out in the open.'

Ella tried, unsuccessfully, to sound optimistic. 'I've made up my mind. I'm going to do my best to get a job. However, I still feel really shattered, so I thought I'd leave the job-hunting for a few days.'

'You're doing the right thing.' Her mother grinned, showing her good white teeth; she was very proud that at her age she still had no false teeth. 'But before you even start thinking about looking for work, you and I are going to pay a visit to Sadie and Isaac Cohan's shop. Sadie will sort you out a couple of smart outfits, my treat, and that Dennis of yours will regret the fact that he called you a rag-bag. You'll see. And I think getting a job is a jolly good idea, shows you've still got some go in yer. You'll find a decent job, I know you will. It'll give you a bit of independence, and get you out an' mixing with other people.

'But for now, you take yerself upstairs and have a lie-down while I wash these cups and plates and make myself presentable.'

'Well, if you're gonna do yer face and dress up to the nines, that will be the day gone.' Ella really smiled for the first time since she had come into the house.

'Why, you cheeky moo! I can see Dennis hasn't completely knocked the stuffing out of you. Anyway, I think we both deserve a break. How about we do a bit of shopping, then 'ave pie an' mash or fish an' chips if the fancy takes yer, then we'll go an' meet the kids from school and buy them a treat. How does that sound?'

'Mum, what would I do without you? You wanna know something? You're better than any tonic. Far, far better. You might get on me nerves sometimes with yer nagging, but I love yer t' bits.'

Ella laughed loudly and swiftly ducked as her mother picked up a cushion and threw it at her.

Chapter Ten

'WELL, ELLY, ARE YOU feeling any better?'

Sitting side by side on the low wall that fronted the school, Winnie had lapsed into using her daughter's pet name, that had suited her so well when she was a child.

'No lies, mind,' she warned. 'I'll know if you're not telling me the truth, though I still think I should have taken you up to the hospital.'

'Mum, Mr Greenway cleaned up my cheek and forehead all right, and the witch hazel he gave me will ease the burning and help the bruising, he said, so stop yer worrying.'

'Yes, old Mr Greenway is a marvellous chemist. Folk 'ave been going t' him for years. He's just as good as any doctor an' a damn sight cheaper too.'

'Also, Mum, I felt so sick all the while we were out until we had our pie an' mash, but since then I've felt much better.'

'It's like I'm always telling you, keep the inner man fed well an' you can cope with anything. Now, no brooding tonight, and bright an' early in the morning we're off to see what Sadie can do about some decent everyday clothes for you.'

Ella didn't bother to answer. School was out and she could see her two children surrounded by their mates running across the playground.

'I can't believe how fast Teddy is growing. It seems only last week that I bought those long trousers, and look at them now, they're up round his ankles.'

'Makes yer feel proud just looking at him,' Winnie declared, a grandmother's love shining in her eyes.

'He's so like his dad,' Ella remarked sadly.

'Only in looks,' his gran quickly commented.

Teddy was very tall for his age, with long, lean limbs and a thick, wild shock of unruly dark hair exactly the same as Dennis's; he also had his father's bright blue eyes.

As he drew nearer, Winnie said, 'The lad does seem to 'ave shot up all of a sudden. But then, so has Babs. A few more years and she's going to be a real beauty, an' no mistake. I tell yer, gal, with that long chestnut-coloured hair, and those big brown eyes, both of which she gets from you, she'll drive the fellers up the wall.'

She pointed to Teddy, who had stopped running and was waiting for his sister. As she drew near, he held out an arm and she put her hand into his.

'See that, he knows we're watching, but I'm sure one way an' another he'll always look out for her.'

Both mother and daughter chuckled and Ella added, 'I'll try and remember that next time they're going for each other like two tom cats.'

Both children came bounding up and were greeted with hugs and kisses from their mum and their gran. Teddy was busy telling his mother how he was going to be sent up to the senior school, and that he had put his name down for woodwork classes. Winnie was cuddling Babs, telling her how she thought she must be the prettiest little girl in the whole school. 'Did you do all right today?' she asked.

'Yes, why?' Babs's smile was as bright as ever.

'Just wondered, that's all.'

'Well, I did my best, at least I think I did, but . . .'

'But what?'

Babs shrugged. 'Nothing really. Just some nosy kid thinks she knows more about my dad than I do. Gran, I'll always love my dad.'

Winnie closed her eyes in distress. Her grandchildren meant the world to her.

'Of course you will, darlin'. Of course you will.'

As she put her arms around Babs again, inwardly she wanted to cry. Why should it be that when families ran into trouble, it was always the kids who suffered the most?

Although Ella's attention had been taken up with Teddy, who had asked what had happened to her face – 'My own fault,' she lied, 'I didn't look where I was going' – she had heard what Babs had said and it hurt her to the quick. She forced herself to keep her voice soft and calm as she said, 'Who wants to choose where we go for a treat?'

She was doing her best, acting like this was a special day.

Teddy pulled a face. 'That depends on whether we're going to get something to eat first. I'm starving, Mum.'

'Me too,' Babs declared.

Even Winnie grinned. You couldn't help laughing at Teddy. Food always came first with him.

Ella smiled as she said, 'Going for something more like an ice-cream was what I had in mind.'

Quickly Winnie cut in. 'You two kids choose where you would like t' go and what you fancy to eat, an' we'll say it's my treat this time. That's if yer mum says it's all right.'

Teddy and Babs both grinned and in agreement said, 'Hot dog and a milkshake, please, Gran.'

Ella smiled once more. 'OK. You two could charm the hind legs off a donkey.'

Babs and Teddy were sitting on high stools, noisily sucking through straws at their strawberry milkshakes and waiting for their hot dogs to be cooked. Ella and her mother were seated at a corner table in this cosy café with a toasted teacake and a pot of tea in front of them.

'Have you decided what you're going to do about Connie Baldwin?' Winnie asked cautiously.

Ella thought it was hardly surprising that her mother had once again brought this subject up.

'What do you suggest I do, Mum?'

'Time's getting on; that baby will be born before you know it.' Winnie sighed.

'I know what you're trying to say, Mum, and I think I know what you want me to do.'

'Oh yeah, and what's that?'

'You think I should see a solicitor and go for a divorce, don't you?'

'That's for you to decide, Ella luv. There's nobody on this earth who can make your mind up for you where that's concerned. But while you're deciding, think on this. That young girl is gonna be walking up and down your street wheeling a pram with your Dennis's baby in it, and she ain't going to make no secret of it. I reckon you should ask someone to tell you whether or not she is going to keep the baby.'

'Thanks for the advice, Mum. God knows I need it at the moment, but who the hell do you reckon that someone should be?'

Winnie looked at her daughter. 'By rights it should be your Dennis, but it don't seem like you're going to get much joy from him. So then, Ella, you tell me what you are thinking of doing.'

The tone of her mother's voice made Ella aware that she was fast losing patience with her.

'What I wish is that Dennis would take the flipping girl as far away as possible, live with her and her baby and leave me and my children alone.'

'Is that what you really want, Ella? For Den t' go miles away? What about Teddy and Babs? They're his children as well, you know.'

That was the nagging worry at the back of Ella's mind. Whichever way she turned, it seemed likely that she would be depriving her children of their father. Hadn't she heard her own little girl tell her gran that she would always love her dad?

Pushing these thoughts impatiently away, she nodded warily. 'I'm not sure what I want any more. I only know it would take a miracle for our lives to go back to being what they were before.'

She leant forward in her chair and covered her face with her hands. Gingerly, she felt the swollen side of her face. Earlier on the pain had been so bad she had thought Dennis had broken her cheekbone, but thankfully Mr Greenway had assured her it was just bruised.

Winnie scowled at her. 'It's a pity, but nothing will really get sorted until one of us has a talk with Connie's parents.'

'Well it's not going to be me.' Ella bristled slightly. 'I'm not going anywhere near them.'

'Did you ask Dennis if he had discussed the matter with the girl's father?'

Taken aback, Ella stared at her mother for a moment. 'You're 'aving a laugh, aren't you? Den face Mr Baldwin! That would be some meeting, that would. Probably end up with murder being done. More than likely, all he's done is tell the girl to get rid of it.'

For a while they sat silently eating their teacake and

sipping their tea. Finally Ella changed the subject and asked, 'Mum, do you think I drove Dennis away? Was I so lazy and scruffy all the time?'

Her mother took a long, deep sigh. Reaching out her hand, she held Ella's, and the look she gave her was soft and loving. 'I'd never lie to you and I would never willingly hurt you,' she said. 'Never in a million years. But you don't need me to remind you that Connie Baldwin is not the first girl that your Den has gone astray with.'

'You think I don't know that?'

'All right, Ella, but you have to face the facts, hard as the truth is to bear. Dennis is and always will be a ladies' man. The younger they are, the more attracted he is. Since you ask, yes, maybe you did let yerself go a bit, but he hasn't been the perfect husband by any means. A few weeks of the year he'd be rolling in money, treating you like a queen and buying the kids God knows what. The rest of the time you never knew where yer next shilling was coming from half the time. So do me a favour, stop taking his guilt on your shoulders.'

Seeing the look on her daughter's face, and sensing the uncertainty, the misery and the loneliness that Dennis had brought down on her, Winnie decided she would have to interfere.

Doing her best to smile, but feeling embarrassed, she said, 'I'll tell you what I'm going to do. I'm going to arrange to meet Ted Dryden and try and get some answers. Just him and me, we'll meet somewhere quiet and I'll tell him straight that if his son can't or won't sort things out, then he had better get to the truth of the matter himself. I'll also remind him that his son already has a wife and two children, and that those two children are his grandchildren.'

'But, Mum, Ted has been like you, good t' me and the kids. I don't want to start quarrelling with him. At the moment, without his grandad there would be no men in our Teddy's life, an' that wouldn't be good for him. But I am grateful and I do agree that if anyone can sort this mess out it will be Den's father.'

Having said that, Ella gave a soft sigh of relief. For too long they had done nothing but listen to gossip. Now perhaps her father-in-law would face Connie and her parents dead on and some kind of solution might be found.

Seeing that Ella had faith in her and had agreed to accept her offer, Winnie half wished she hadn't been so brave.

I only hope I'm doing the right thing, she said to herself.

Chapter Eleven

ELLA AWOKE TO SEE the sun was streaming in at the window of her bedroom. She lay for a while staring at the thin flowered curtains. How many times had she washed and ironed them? They were getting so thread-bare, it was about time she had some new ones.

Then she remembered, and she was so thrilled that she swung her legs around to the side of the bed, got up, flung the curtains back as far as they would go and opened the top of the window.

It was going to be a glorious summer's day. It had to be. She had a job; or rather, she was going in Thursday morning for a couple of hours just to be shown the ropes, then a trial run starting this coming Friday at six thirty. It was only Tuesday, plenty of time to get her hair done and do something about her clothes.

Talk about coincidence, or was it fate?

She and her mother had been coming down the street yesterday, both loaded with shopping, when they almost crashed into Mike Murray.

'You wanna watch where you're going, Mickey, dashing about like a madman. Skiving off for a few hours, are yer?'

97

Mike was brought up sharp by the sound of Winnie's voice.

'Oh, hallo, Win, Ella, sorry, me mind was miles away. In me head I'm trying to piece together an advert to put into the *Borough News* and if I don't get it in today it won't be in Friday's edition.'

'What's so important? What's the ad for?' Winnie couldn't help being nosy. After all, Mike Murray was the manager of the British Legion working men's club and they'd all spent many a great night in that place, especially when her Alf was alive. Different when your husband dies and you're left on your own, she thought. Don't get out and about so much. A woman on her own was always regarded suspiciously by married women.

'I don't know, Win, gal, don't seem t' be able t' keep staff five minutes these days. Half the young men have their fingers in the till and the bits of girls yer get t' work behind the bar would turn the place into a knocking shop if they 'ad their way. Pull a pint, they can't pull their own knickers up, 'alf of them.'

'Sounds rough, Mickey. Perhaps you ain't treating your staff all that good.'

Mickey looked amazed. 'Thought you knew me better than that, gal.' He was watching Winnie's face and suddenly he said, 'You wouldn't wanna job, would yer?'

Winnie groaned. 'What, me, stand on me feet all them ruddy hours? Not on yer Nellie.'

'I've never worked behind a bar, but I could wash glasses.' Ella's voice was quiet but she sounded desperate.

'Well, well,' was all her mother said.

Mike turned to face Ella and looked at her with respect. 'If you mean it, Ella, I'll start you on whenever you say. You'd be quick to learn, I know yer would, and I'd make sure the other staff gave you a bit of help.'

Ella was astounded. She felt herself blushing furiously. What on earth had made her jump in like that?

'I couldn't do all day, Mike, especially now when me kids are soon gonna break up from school. Summer holidays are about six weeks, yer know.'

'That's all right, luv, we'll sort something out. Evenings and weekends is when I'd need yer most. Thirty bob a session to start with, but five quid if yer do two sessions on a Saturday.'

'I'll come to your place and look after the kids.' Winnie had sounded really enthusiastic.

Now, in her excitement, Ella couldn't believe all that had really happened. She ran down the stairs, not bothering to put her dressing gown on, but as she waited for the kettle to boil, doubts began to creep into her mind. Would she be able to hold down a job? Busy place was the Legion.

The back door opened and her mother came in, smiling bright as a button and really smartly dressed.

'Morning, my luv, thought I'd get round here before the kids go off to school, then I can clear up while you're seeing t' yerself.'

'What's the hurry, Mum?'

'I wanna get you over to Sadie's nice an' early so you an' she can take yer time sorting through whatever gear she has in stock. Got t' 'ave you well turned out when you start yer first day down at the Legion, ain't we?'

'Mum . . .'

'You don't need t' tell me, luv, you're 'aving a fit of the collie-wobbles.'

'Well, yes, I did kind of jump in with both feet, an' now I'm not so sure I'm up to being a barmaid.'

Her mother stared hard at her. 'Don't put yerself down, Ella. Being with Den all these years has sucked away a lot of your confidence, but you just listen t' me, gal. You're good enough to work anywhere. Yer brain might be a bit rusty, but you're certainly not dim, not by a long chalk you're not. A few days and you'll take to serving behind that bar like a duck takes t' water.'

She moved closer and laid her hands reassuringly on Ella's shoulders.

'It's only natural for yer t' be a bit scared at the thought of facing all them customers. But you'll be fine. Think of all the people you'll meet. I bet there'll be a good many you know already, and you'll make new friends 'cos there's always a good social life down at the Legion.'

Ella stared at her mother thoughtfully. Winnie was right. This job could be a turning point in her life. It would certainly make Dennis sit up and take notice. And she liked the sound of a social life.

Winnie could imagine what was going through her daughter's mind and she quickly said, 'You never know, luv, this might lead to a whole new way of life for you.'

That did set Ella thinking, and suddenly a feeling of excitement stirred within her and for the first time in God knows how long she began to take a lively interest in the future.

'You're right, Mum,' she said, grinning. 'When I woke up this morning I wasn't sure that I hadn't dreamt that Mike had offered me a job. Now talking to you I'm OK. Mike said two weeks' trial, so if I get through that all right I shall stay on, do me best and see where it leads.'

'That's the spirit, gal, an' you'll feel even better after our visit t' Sadie. Now you get yerself upstairs an' get yerself dressed. I'll see t' the kids. I'll even walk them t' school.'

'Mum, d'yer mind holding yer horses for a bit? I'd just put the kettle on when you arrived and I ain't even got round to making a pot of tea yet. Sorry, but I can't pull meself together until I've had at least two cups of tea of a morning.'

'You waste 'alf the day, you do,' her mother muttered.

Ella heard what she'd said and laughed.

'Just 'cos you get up at the crack of dawn 'cos you're too wicked t' sleep.'

'Get on with yer, you saucy hussy, and pour that blinking tea out if you're going to.'

It was a quarter to ten when they got off the bus opposite Dirty Dick's pub and began to walk down the side streets that would lead them to Cohans' shop. There were no stalls set out today.

Ella pushed the glass door, holding it open for her mother to step into the shop first. She was right behind her, and for a moment she felt envious. The shop and the clothes on display were even better than she had remembered. But envious was the wrong way to feel. From what her mum had told her, she knew the Cohan family had worked extremely hard to get their business up and running.

Having heard the ping of the bell as the shop door had opened, Sadie came through from their living room. Seeing Winnie, she ran towards her, wrapped her arms around her and kissed her on each cheek. Releasing her hold she said, 'It's so good to see you. And you too, Ella,' she added before kissing her as well. 'You listened to what I said.' Sadie was nodding her head and smiling.

Ella looked a bit bewildered.

'Your hair, it looks gorgeous. In fact you look different altogether. If I didn't know your mother so well, I'd say there was a new man in your life.'

Winnie laughed, but Ella didn't.

'You couldn't be more wrong,' Winnie said. 'The man in my daughter's life ain't worth the air he breathes and he puts my Ella down at every turn. If he had his way he'd live the life of old Riley while she'd spend her whole time scrubbing, cleaning, doing the weekly wash and

101

making sure a damn good dinner was put in front of him every night. Well, between us we've decided it's pay-back time. Ella is going to have a life of her own. That's why we're here: she's got a job, starts on Friday, and she needs some everyday good clothes.'

'You come to the right place, I'm pleased to say.' Isaac was standing in the doorway that led from their private quarters. His voice was so full of pleasure that it made Winnie feel glad they were here.

He was wearing Prince of Wales check trousers, and a fawn shirt open at the neck with the sleeves rolled up to his elbows. As he embraced Winnie he apologized. 'If I had known you two ladies were coming, I would have worn a suit.'

A flush of pleasure rose to Winnie's cheeks, as it always did when she came face to face with this dear old friend.

He held out his arms to Ella and she gladly went into them for a warm and welcoming hug. 'So our little Elly is going out into the big world to earn her own living. I heard right, did I not?'

'Well, I'm going to try.' Ella looked briefly at her mother, who nodded her encouragement.

Isaac rubbed his hands together. 'Now then, best that your mother and I disappear and leave you in the capable hands of my beloved Sadie, but we shall be kind to both of you.' He paused and winked at Winnie. 'We shall make each of you a glass of lemon tea and bring it through to here.'

'Good,' Sadie said happily. 'Ella and I can manage quite well without help from either of you, but the tea will be much appreciated.'

Sadie was a good-looking woman and she knew it. Why? Because she worked at it. She had lovely dark eyes, long dark hair that had a sheen to it, and her styling was different from time to time. In fact there was nothing about Sadie Cohan that one could take for granted. As on the first occasion they had met, she was wearing an immaculate worsted suit, which should by rights make her look businesslike. Ella decided it must be the way that she did her make-up and her hair, because Sadie looked sexy. Then again, maybe it was the way that she held herself and the way that she walked, full of confidence. Ella sighed. She was sure she herself would never be able to acquire such self-assurance.

They sipped their hot lemon tea and talked about everyday life. Yes, both of Ella's children were doing well at school, though they both missed their dad.

'I gathered from what your mother said that you were having marital problems,' Sadie said with feeling.

'That's putting it mildly,' Ella exclaimed.

'Well, in that case, let's get on to happier things, find out if I have any clothes that take your fancy, shall we?'

'You are joking.' Ella looked around the shop and raised her eyebrows. 'Anyone would 'ave t' be really picky if they couldn't find several things they would die for in this shop.'

'If only that were true,' Sadie murmured. 'Some days I get more than one customer there is no pleasing, no matter how hard I try.'

'I promise I won't be like that,' Ella said quickly.

Sadie patted her shoulder. 'First things first, strip off to your underwear.'

Ella couldn't help it: she still felt embarrassed, even though this time she had come prepared.

As she removed her cardigan and undid the buttons of her blouse, Sadie clapped her hands. 'Oh good,' she cried. 'You are wearing your long bust bodice.'

Ella kept quiet. She wasn't going to tell Sadie that she only ever wore it when she was going out. Around the house it felt restricting, but she knew she would buy another one today, because if she really did get the job at the Legion, she would wear this type of brassiere every day to work. So it would have to be one on and one in the wash.

It was as if Sadie read Ella's mind.

'Do you find it very uncomfortable?' she asked.

'Not now I've got used to it, and since my mum has encouraged me to lose a bit of weight, it does seem to minimize my bosoms.'

Sadie eyed Ella's still large but quite shapely breasts as she slipped a simple black linen dress over her head. Ella did up the line of buttons that fronted the dress while Sadie moved backwards and eyed her from top to toe.

Winnie had helped her daughter a lot. Ella did look a good deal thinner, much smarter, younger even.

Ella was smiling at her image in the three-cornered looking glass. 'I've never had a black dress before.'

With a businesslike air Sadie examined her. 'Well, it suits you to a tee. Black always looks smart.'

It was true: the design was simple, seeming to reduce her tummy and skimming over her hips.

'Maybe with your first week's wages you might buy yourself a nice pair of black shoes that would go with any outfit,' Sadie suggested.

'Wouldn't I need a touch of colour with a dress like this? I don't have any what you'd call good jewellery.'

Sadie turned her back on Ella, walked to a glass-fronted cabinet and from a drawer withdrew two silk scarves, one emerald green and one red, each with a delicate, intricate pattern woven down both sides. First she draped the green scarf around the neck of the dress, tossing one long end over Ella's left shoulder.

Ella gasped in surprise. The difference the scarf made was dramatic.

Laughing at the expression on Ella's face, Sadie

removed the green scarf, replacing it with the red one, only this time she allowed both ends of the silk to dangle to the front of the dress, tying a loose knot to keep it in place.

'See, two different outfits. And there are many more ways one may wear a scarf. You just need to practise.'

Ella considered this. Would she ever be able to adapt clothes to make herself look as elegant as Sadie did? She doubted it, but by God she was going to have a damn good try. She half turned to gaze at herself in the mirror again. She was more than pleased with her reflection.

'What you need now is a basic good skirt with which you can wear blouses or jumpers. I suggest navy blue. What do you think, Ella?'

Ella considered for a moment. She would much rather leave the choice to Sadie but she didn't want to appear to be too dim. 'Yes please, Sadie, I think navy blue would suit me fine.'

Sadie produced three skirts. The first one Ella did not like; the material was good but it was a pinstripe. Hesitantly she looked at Sadie. 'If you don't mind, I think that one is too mannish.'

Sadie roared with laughter. 'Oh, Ella my dear, I am thrilled to hear that you have an opinion of your own.'

'Then you are not going to put me down as an awkward customer who has ruined your day?'

'Certainly not. How about this one?' Sadie took a skirt by its waistband and flung it neatly so that the all-round pleats spread over the carpet.

'Beautiful,' Ella said quietly, 'but not for me. Sadie, can you see those pleats fitting over my hips?'

'You are not only getting bolder, you are acquiring more dress sense by the minute! However, my stock of skirts is pretty low at the moment, so it is this third one or wait until your next visit.'

Having taken off the black dress, which Sadie carefully folded, placing both scarves on the top, Ella sat down on the gilt chair and pulled the tailored skirt up over her hips. The waistband was fine, and she was able to do the top button up without any difficulty. She stood up and ran her hands down her sides. The skirt felt slinky, and as she looked into the mirror and noticed there was a slit to the side which reached nearly up to her knee, she turned to Sadie and they both laughed.

'Go on, say what you're thinking,' Sadie urged.

'Sexy,' Ella said, drawing herself up to her full height.

'Exactly. Now all I have to do is find you two or three decent tops and you'll be fit and ready to become part of the business world.'

One long-sleeved white blouse was added to the pile; also a very pale blue twinset, and when Ella protested that she wouldn't be able to afford so much, Sadie told her to be quiet. Fully dressed now, Ella asked if she might buy another long-line brassiere and Sadie said she had to go upstairs to fetch that.

Ella sat shaking her head in disbelief. She was so lucky, and if her mother would pay half of the amount she had spent today, hopefully she would be able to pay her back in weekly instalments out of her wages. With that thought in mind she started to silently pray. Dear Lord, let me be good at this job, please don't let me end up a complete failure, the kind of useless slag that Dennis has come to believe I am.

Sadie came back holding not only the bra she had gone for, but also a pink blouse.

'This is my present to you, a good-luck omen for you to wear at your new job.' She was holding the blouse up high for Ella to see, and only one word came to her mind: exquisite. 'It will tone perfectly with the navy skirt,' Sadie assured her.

'But redheads can't wear pink,' Ella protested.

'Whoever called you a redhead? Deep copper-coloured hair such as you have is a rarity, and don't let anyone tell you any different. Take a good look at that blouse and tell me you don't want it.'

Ella took the blouse and looked at the workmanship on the collar and cuffs. It was the most delicate and intricate that she had ever seen.

'Hold it up against you and look in the mirror.'

Ella did. 'Brilliant,' she said softly. 'Sadie, how can I ever thank you?'

'By enjoying your job and making a new happy life for yourself.'

Ella couldn't answer. Tears were choking her, her eyes glittering.

After a friendly argument as to who was going to pay for what, mother and daughter said their goodbyes, promising to come back soon and let Isaac and Sadie know how Ella was doing.

'Happy?' Winnie asked as they walked to the bus stop.

'Absolutely, Mum.'

'Well, it's still early. What say we get the bus and go up West for a change?'

'All right with me,' Ella agreed happily.

It wasn't long before they were standing at a coffee stall on the corner of Hyde Park, eating what could only be described as wonderful bacon rolls, and sipping strong tea served in thick white china mugs.

The sun had brought out the smell of the grass and the flowers, which looked a picture. Their lunch finished, they decided they would sit by the Serpentine for a while.

Late afternoon found two very tired but happy women trudging their way home.

Chapter Twelve

'SO HOW'S THAT THEN, Mike?'

Placing a brimming pint of old ale on the bar next to a pint of Guinness, which had a creamy head about half an inch deep from the rim of the glass, Ella grinned.

Mike seated himself on one of the bar stools and eyed her with satisfaction. 'Told yer, practice makes perfect.'

'You're just being kind. Took me four goes before I got that Guinness right.'

'Ella, slow but sure. That is one of the most difficult pints to pull. In one afternoon and with not much waste in the slop trays, you've learnt how to change an optic, and attaching that device to an upside-down bottle of spirits is no easy task. You know you have to keep the ashtrays emptied and cleaned whenever you have any spare time. You've also been down the cellar with me and watched me change a barrel, not that there will ever be the need for you to have to do that, I hope. We've a couple of good potmen who also know their way around a pub cellar. Yes, looking at those two pints, all in all I'd say you've proved yer worth this afternoon. How do you feel about taking the job on?'

'Well, Mike, I'll admit I was scared t' bits when I walked in here, but yeah, if you're willing to give me a chance, I'd like to try an' do the job.'

'You'll be fine, Ella. I knew you would be. Of course it will be different in here at the weekend, what with the entertainers an' what have you. It can get pretty noisy. Just don't ever let yerself get flustered. Myself or one of the bouncers will always be within earshot. Anyway, there's a whistle beneath the bar; one blast from that and the whole place will go silent.' He grinned broadly. 'You only blow that on very rare occasions. Most arguments can be dealt with easy enough. Blokes know that once chucked out they stay out, and as the prices in here are far cheaper than the pubs, none of them want that.'

Mike turned from looking at Ella to watch Sam Richardson sliding on to the stool next to him.

'Hallo, Sam, you're early. What's brought you here at this time of the day? Oh, by the way, this is Ella Dryden. She's going to start working here tomorrow night.'

Ella smiled knowingly at Sam, and he smiled back and said, 'Long time no see, Ella. You all right?'

'Yes thanks, Sam, I'm fine.'

'I take it you two know each other then,' Mike said, nodding from one to the other.

'You could say that,' Sam smiled sadly. 'Ella and my Lottie went to the same school, were in the same class for years, great friends, weren't you?'

'The best,' Ella answered quietly.

Mike Murray was well aware that Sam had been on his own for years. Only twelve months after he had married Charlotte Fuller, she had suffered a miscarriage, and lost so much blood she herself had died. As far as Mike knew, Sam had never looked at another woman.

'So, Ella, you're going to be a working woman?' Sam remarked.

'Hopefully. Mike has been kind enough to offer me a two-week trial. How about you, Sam, you don't work 'ere, do you?'

'No, I'm a partner in a firm of accountants, Hirst and Richardson. I'm here because we do the books for the Legion.'

'Always knew you would do well, Sam, but you moved away after Charlotte . . . Oh God, what 'ave I said?' Ella flushed with embarrassment.

'Please.' Sam reached out and touched her hand. 'Don't upset yourself. It was a long time ago and it's nice to meet someone who was so friendly with Lottie. Another time perhaps we'll have a chat about old times. All right if I go through to the office, Mike?'

'Yeah, course, mate. I'll bring yer a drink through when I've finished talking to Ella.'

'Probably be seeing something of you then,' Sam said, smiling at Ella as he bent down, picked up his briefcase and walked away.

Mike came round the bar to stand beside Ella. 'You can get off home now if you like. I hope you feel confident enough to come back tomorrow to really start work.'

'Yes, I do, and thanks, Mike, I promise I'll do me best.'

'That'll be good enough for me then, Ella.' He leant his back against the edge of the bar and folded his arms. 'Strange that, ain't it? You and Sam Richardson meeting up again like that.'

Taking a deep, calming breath, Ella said, 'I hope I didn't upset him talking about his wife. Has he never married again?'

'No, not t' my knowledge. I don't think he's the type to be pushed into anything.'

'I wasn't pushing nor prying,' Ella retorted sharply. 'There was a time when him, Charlotte, my Den and me used to go around as a foursome, but like a good many

110

more, Sam found out that a little of my Dennis went a long way. Den would keep bragging about whatever it was he was up to.'

'I know what yer mean.' Mike's voice was all concern. 'Oh, by the way, while we're on the subject, Ella, you do know that your Dennis is a member here, don't you?'

'Yes, I've been here with him an' me family many a time, though it was a while ago.'

Mike smiled warmly. 'Yer right, it's ages since he has drunk in here, but you never know. When word gets around that you're working 'ere he may just saunter in for the hell of it. But don't let it bother you. Just remember, any trouble, I'll deal with it.'

Ella laughed. 'Oh, he won't upset me. I'm rather hoping Den does come in for a drink. I'd dearly love to serve him just t' prove that I can do something worthwhile when I put me mind to it,' she said defensively. Then added quickly, 'Mike, I am grateful t' you for this chance.'

'You don't have to be, Ella, it works both ways.'

As Mike Murray let Ella out of the side door, he was thinking how she had smartened herself up and a smirk twitched at the corners of his mouth. He wouldn't mind seeing Dennis Dryden walk in while Ella was around.

He'd lay odds she'd be able to hold her own.

Chapter Thirteen

ELLA DRYDEN WAS AS happy as a lark as she pushed open the side door of the Legion. It was not yet six o'clock in the evening and her shift didn't start until six thirty. Her mother had taken Teddy and Babs to the pictures, so she had thought she might just as well come to work as stay at home on her own. She had been working here for a month now and she loved the job. To begin with there had been endless gossip, and some queer reactions from members.

She smiled as she recalled the first weekend that she had been behind the bar, when Mrs Baldwin had fronted her, stating loudly that she was not going to be served by the likes of Ella Dryden.

Mike had been fantastic.

'Give me one good reason as to why you do not wish to be served by Mrs Dryden, and I will sack her immediately.' His voice had been quiet but menacing. The whole bar had suddenly gone silent.

Alf Baldwin had stuttered and stammered, doing his best to calm his wife and persuade her to keep her voice down. She paid no heed to him, yelling loud enough for everyone to hear. 'You know damn well what 'er old man has done to our Connie.'

Mike had remained quite calm and in a firm voice had said to Kate Baldwin, 'Would you care to explain to this crowd exactly what Mr Dryden and your daughter's affairs have to do with Mrs Dryden? Apart from the fact that I would say it is her and her children who have been sadly wronged.'

'Aye, that's right.' Many heads were nodding and the mumblings seemed to reverberate around the hall.

Kate Baldwin had been stunned. She had anticipated an entirely different reaction from her neighbours. She looked up into Mike's face first and then turned her gaze on Ella, and what she saw there made her flinch.

She lost her temper again, this time having a go at her husband.

'You silly old sod, I told yer we shouldn't come in 'ere tonight. Everyone has been only too willing to tell me that Ella Dryden was working at the Legion.'

Alf Baldwin was dying for a pint and he decided it was time he got one.

'You, Kate, can do what yer like an' go where yer like, but my throat is parched and I'm staying right where I am. As Mike has just pointed out, what's going on in our family had nought to do with Ella. I for one admire her. She ain't sat on her backside and moaned, she ain't come to our 'ouse spoiling for a fight with our Connie; she's picked 'erself up an' got 'erself a job, and if Mickey's satisfied with her that's good enough for me. If you don't like it, then sod off 'ome an' I'll follow you when I'm good and ready.'

For a short moment Ella had felt quite sorry for Mrs Baldwin, who had sheepishly made her way to the nearest empty table and sat herself down without saying a word. Alf had looked at Ella but stopped short of saying he was sorry. Instead he said, 'Gis a pint of best bitter, a gin an' tonic and take one for yourself, Ella.'

With a straight face she had served him and then said, 'Thanks, Mr Baldwin, I'll 'ave half of shandy.'

From that day onwards everyone had not only shown Ella a bit of respect but had let her know that they were on her side.

She had got herself into a routine and in fact looked forward to coming to work. There was many an evening when she thought it was better than going to the Hippodrome. Fridays and Saturdays were a laugh a minute. Several of the male comedians told jokes that were near the mark and some were downright blue, but the customers, all adults, loved them, and as long as the money kept coming into the tills, Mike was happy.

There were two well-built men, Tom and Derrick, both in their early forties, serving behind the bar besides herself and Molly Riley. By the time Mike called last orders both Molly and Ella were ready to drop, feet hot and sweaty, legs aching like billy-o, and there was still all the clearing-up to do.

Cleaners came in every morning, even Sunday, to hoover the carpets and give the toilets a jolly good clean, but all four bar staff pitched in and left the tables cleared and wiped down and the dirty glasses stacked behind the bar.

The weekly pay packet that Mike handed each of them meant so much to Ella. It went a long way to making her feel independent but also gave her a feeling of self-respect.

The strangest thing that had happened so far was only three days ago, yet it was still vivid in her mind. She grinned. Until she had come to work at the Legion, she had never realized how the other half lived.

It was Saturday evening and Janey, her neighbour, had offered to stay with Babs and Teddy so that Winnie could come to the Legion for a drink. Probably because it was a hot night and there was nowhere at the club for folk to sit outside, trade had not been so brisk.

When Mike had called time, he'd whispered to Winnie that she was welcome to stay behind and have a quiet drink with the staff, and he would put her and Ella into a taxi so that they got home safely.

The usual crowd had left the pub, and Mike closed and bolted the double front doors before settling down to a drink with all the staff, including the two potmen. They had chattered amongst themselves until Molly's Irish blood came to the fore and she had started singing. Such a sweet voice she had and one would have had to have a heart of stone not to have been moved almost to tears as she sang, one after the other, the old, dearly loved Irish ballads.

It was turned one o'clock when Ella and her mother got out of the taxi, and Winnie made no objection when her daughter insisted she stay the night at her house.

Janey was in bed with Babs, one arm around her daughter, the other flung outside the bedclothes. Both were fast asleep. Next Ella looked in on Teddy. He too was well away, and she bent and, smoothing his thick hair off his forehead, gently kissed him.

Next morning she crept quietly downstairs, filled the kettle, placed it on the stove to boil, and then, having made a pot of tea, drank her usual two cups before washing and dressing herself.

There was no sound of movement coming from upstairs and Ella decided it wouldn't hurt to leave them all to have a good lie-in. It was a gorgeous morning and she felt so much better. Today she was wearing her smart navy blue skirt teamed with a crisp cotton blouse with a high neck, long sleeves and cuffs with six buttons. Her chestnut hair was piled up into a bun on the top of her

115

head, but she had allowed a few tendrils to fall round her face and she had used a light covering of make-up, shaping her lips with a very pale lipstick. She was proud of the fact that despite her life having been turned upside down, she had got on with it and wasn't doing too badly. Daytime mostly she could cope, especially now she had a job that kind of brought a social life with it.

Nights were still awful.

She'd be a liar if she said she didn't miss Den. She still turned over in her big double bed and reached out an arm to cuddle up to him, and all she ever found now was empty space. Also, she would never be able to forgive Den for what he had done to their two children. She knew she was partly to blame for him having a roving eye and a yearning for much younger women. She had let herself go and now she was paying the price. Babs and Teddy were a different matter altogether. Each, in their own way, adored their father and he had disdainfully rejected them.

And for what? Although she knew she had no say in the matter as to what would happen to Connie Baldwin and her baby, it didn't stop her feeling sad. Whichever way you looked at it, that young girl's life would never be the same.

If she had the baby adopted, for many years to come she would constantly be thinking of that child. Ella hoped with all her heart that if she kept it her parents would always be there to help with the problems, because God knows problems there would be!

Would Dennis stand by Connie Baldwin?

Well, I wouldn't put my money on it, was the answer Ella gave herself. He'd practically deserted his older two kids. She smiled to herself. Dennis changing napkins and helping with a newborn baby. Well, that would certainly be a first!

As she had neared the pub later that morning, she saw that Mike was standing outside on the pavement eyeing a top-barrow that was upended in the gutter loaded with old iron and various bundles of what looked like clothes.

'Was this here when you went home?' he asked Ella.

'I dunno, it was dark and I'd 'ad a few drinks,' she laughed.

'Oh well, somebody will claim it later on, I suppose,' Mike said, turning and leading the way in.

Only Tom and Ella were going to man the bar this lunchtime, and as they set to laying out the beer mats and making sure that all the optics were in working order, Peggy Briggs, one of the cleaners, called out, 'Anyone do with a cuppa tea?'

'Not 'alf,' Tom said quickly. 'Yer must 'ave been reading my mind.'

'How about you, Ella?'

'You're a life-saver if ever there was one,' Ella told her. 'I'll just take meself into the ladies' and tidy meself up and then I'll sit down and enjoy a cup, please.'

'We ain't got round ter doing the ladies' yet; we've done the gents, though,' was Peggy's answer.

'I'll take me chance in the ladies' if you don't mind,' Ella told her as she picked up her handbag and went into the ladies' cloakroom. Two steps and she couldn't for the life of her have said what was wrong, but her every instinct told her that something was.

She looked up at the window. The curtains had gone! And the vase of flowers which sat on the windowsill was also missing. She had always greatly admired those heavy brocade curtains, and although the flowers were artificial, they had been tastefully arranged in a truly lovely heavy vase.

Suddenly there was an unearthly sound, like a grunting pig, which made Ella turn very quickly, and it was then

117

she let out a scream that had Mike running, thinking that poor Ella was being murdered.

'Where the bloody 'ell did he come from?' Mike said angrily, his hands on his hips as he stared down at the spectacle of the scruffy old man stretched out on the floor in the far corner of the cloakroom.

'I don't know,' was all Ella could manage to say as she too stared at the white-haired old man, who was struggling to sit up. His tatty overcoat and boots were caked in mud. Across his legs were draped the missing curtains and the vase of flowers stood by his feet.

Mike stepped nearer. The man's face and hands were filthy and the pong coming from him was disgusting.

'I got locked in,' he mumbled, saliva dribbling from between his thin lips. 'I'm sorry, mate.'

'Don't you "mate" me, yer bloody filthy tramp. Just tell me how yer got in here an' why you had the damn cheek to pull our bloody curtains down.'

'I didn't mean no 'arm.' He sighed heavily and leant his head back against the wall. 'I'm Sid Thomas, the totter man.'

'I know who you are right enough, but how the 'ell you got in 'ere is what's puzzling me.'

'I'd 'ad a good day an' I thought I'd treat meself to a pint 'fore I went back t' me yard, but the pub was empty when I pushed the door open, not a soul about, never did get me drink. I needed to 'ave a slash, so I came in 'ere, an' when I finished suddenly the 'ole place was plunged into darkness. I sat in 'ere an' I must 'ave fell asleep, an' . . .'

'You didn't get a drink in this pub because it must have been well after time, but any fool can see you'd had far too many pints before you landed up here.'

'Well, it was late an' I was tired out an' cold.'

'And you decided our curtains would keep yer warm?

Yer must 'ave yanked 'ard at them. You not only brought the curtain pole down, you've brought 'alf the bleeding wall with it.'

Ella had the urge to ask about the flowers but thought it better to keep her mouth shut.

'I checked on both sets of toilets, I know full well I did.' Mike was angry.

Ella thought it was a good job that this bloke was still down on the floor, because if he'd been standing up Mike would have knocked him down for sure.

'Then I went down t' the cellar to turn the pumps off, and that must 'ave been when he wandered in, 'cos I came straight back up, locked the side door and turned all the lights out.'

'I've 'urt me back an' I can't get up,' the totter moaned. 'A drop of brandy might do me good.'

Ella giggled.

'You got as much chance as a snowball in hell,' Mike yelled at him. 'And another thing, we ain't picking yer up, not in the state you're in. I suppose that barrowload of old junk outside in the street is yours as well.'

'Oh, fank the Lord it's still there. An 'ole day's work that was.'

Mike had had enough.

'Ella, go phone the police. I don't want him charged, I just want him out of here. It will soon be opening time and we've this place to get cleaned up. One thing I do know, the smell of him will take some getting rid of.'

Holding her handkerchief to her nose as she went to make the call, Ella was in total agreement with Mike's last remark.

In less than fifteen minutes a uniformed policeman had arrived. He stared at Sid Thomas with a murderous look in his eye. 'I'm gonna nick yer for breaking, entering and trespassing on British Legion property,' he growled. 'But

I ain't soiling my uniform by helping yer t' yer feet. I'll phone for the Black Maria and it wouldn't surprise me one little bit if the boys don't take yer out in the yard and put the hose on yer.'

'What about me barrow? That's me living, that is,' Sid implored.

'We'll get some lads t' push it to yer yard. I'm sure your missus will be only too pleased to give them a couple of bob.'

'A couple of bob! Cor blimey, you've got t' be 'aving me on. An' anyway, who said anyfing about bringing me missus in on this?'

'Oh don't worry, Sid lad, we'll be more than happy t' let yer missus know where you are, and if she won't come and stand bail for you, I'm sure our sergeant will find a nice cell for you.' He took a large white handkerchief from his trouser pocket and blew his nose hard before adding, 'Of course, that is, after our boys have thought of a way to really clean you up.'

During the last twenty minutes or so there had been moments when Ella had wanted to laugh. However, as two young constables led a sorry, tired and totally dejected totter man out to the black police van, she felt an enormous amount of pity for him.

It had been nearing closing time when the policeman had returned and walked into the saloon bar, where Ella was serving. She was looking forward to going home to the good Sunday roast dinner which she knew her mother would have prepared.

'Just thought you'd like t' know, our boys really cleaned your old totter up and his missus came to the station t' take him home.'

All the staff had laughed.

'Bet he wasn't very pleased to see her,' Ella remarked.

'You've hit the nail on the head there all right, miss.

First thing Mrs Thomas wanted to know was where he'd been all night. He could 'ardly admit he'd been in the ladies' toilet, could he?'

'Thanks for letting us know he's all right,' Ella said, smiling at him. 'Are yer gonna have a drink while you're here?'

'I shouldn't 'cos I've still an 'alf-hour t' go before I'm off duty, but . . . well go on, then, I'll 'ave a pint.'

Ella took a clean glass from the shelf, and as she held it under the tap and pulled on the beer pump she could feel Mike's eyes on her. She placed the filled pint glass on a towelling mat and went to pick up the half-crown that the policeman had put down.

Mike beat her to it.

He picked up the coin and returned it, saying, 'Have that one on the house. Never know when we'll need you boys in blue, and we're more than grateful that you dealt with our intruder so quickly.'

Later, as Ella had walked home in the sunshine, she had been smiling. Talk about you meet all sorts in a pub. Her day-to-day living had certainly altered, but there was one thing she'd have to admit to: life was never dull now.

Chapter Fourteen

CONNIE BALDWIN WAS TALL, blonde and very pretty, but her flirtatious manner towards any man who gave her a second look had not endeared her to other women. A few of the neighbours felt pity for her because she was only sixteen years old and heavily pregnant by Dennis Dryden, a fifty-year-old man who should have known better. By and large, though, the general opinion was that she had only got what she had asked for. Dennis had flattered and spoilt her, given her presents galore and taken her out and about to places she had never before seen the inside of.

What she was too young to have realized was that in this life everything comes with a price-tag.

Today she was dressed up to the nines. As pretty as she was, she was empty-headed when it came to common sense. One attribute she did have was dress sense, and she knew it. She was wearing a black suit, the jacket left unbuttoned, the maternity skirt of the new-look length, the white blouse she wore hanging loose to cover her bump. She wore sheer black silk stockings with fancy heels and a slender seam, and black stiletto high-heeled shoes, and was carrying a leather handbag which must have cost more than most young women earned in three months.

Her father placed her suitcase down by her feet and stood beside her. Her mother was in the front porch, leaning against the wall, her arms crossed over her skinny chest.

'Try and behave yerself, luv,' Kate called, 'and tell yer Auntie Harriet that we'll come up to bring yer home whenever she's 'ad enough of yer.'

'Don't keep on, Mum, I'll be all right,' Connie said quickly. In fact I'll be glad to get away from here for a while, she added under her breath.

'All right, Con? You're dressed up. Going somewhere nice?' Len Evans, their next-door neighbour, was leaning over the low wall.

'Only to Croydon to stay with me mum's sister,' she said as a taxi came into view and drew up outside the house.

Kate Baldwin sighed heavily as she watched her husband hand the suitcase to the driver, help Connie into the back of the cab and then climb in beside her.

'The break will do her good,' Len Evans remarked as the cab drew away from the kerb.

Kate laughed cruelly. 'A break would do me an' her father some good, but that ain't likely to 'appen.'

She looked agitated, and Len was embarrassed. He looked into his neighbour's tired eyes and felt a moment's sadness. She wasn't a bad woman nor a bad mother, and as for Alf Baldwin, he worked every hour that God Almighty sent and all he asked in return was a quiet life with a few pints of beer over the weekend.

This business of their Connie having a baby at sixteen was a hard blow, as it would be for any working-class family. Gossip from all sides, Connie getting most of the blame, and it wasn't even born yet.

Trying to help, Len Evans said, 'I know me and my wife have said it before, but we do mean it. If there is any way in which we can 'elp you only 'ave t' ask. Has Connie decided if she is going to keep the baby?'

'Neither me nor her dad 'ave got a clue, and t' be honest, I don't think our Connie has either. She day-dreams. That I do know. Always on about how that sod Dennis Dryden will marry her and take her somewhere bloody posh t' live. We all know it ain't gonna 'appen. Thanks anyway for yer offer, but you've enough on yer own plate with four youngsters to feed an' clothe, so you go indoors and do yer best to sort out your own problems and let us try and sort out ours, eh?'

Kate Baldwin gave a sharp nod in her neighbour's direction, then, head high, she turned and walked into her house, shutting the front door firmly.

The train was already in the station when they arrived, and Connie's father was grateful. At least they wouldn't have long to stand about on the platform.

Surprising himself, he suddenly said, 'You know, luv, I don't agree with yer mother sending yer away, even if it is only t' your aunt. I don't care what she says, when there's trouble, families should stick together. Yer sisters, they ain't turned against yer, and if anyone talks about you in their hearing they give them a sharp answer, that I do know.'

Connie was thinking her father was an absolute darling. He saw good in everyone, and as she stood looking into his tired eyes, tears of distress began to trickle down her face. Alf gently took hold of her hands and squeezed them.

'Oh, Dad,' she whimpered, 'what am I gonna do?'

He had no answer to give her. Putting his arms around her in a comforting hug, he longed to be able to turn the clock back. Could he have made things turn out differently? Who knows?

A guard was walking along the platform, slamming carriage doors. 'Come on, my luv, up you get.' Her dad put his hand under her elbow to assist her, then handed in her suitcase. 'Don't forget, it's only a couple of stops, so be on the lookout. East Croydon is a very busy station, so stand still until yer Uncle Jack spots you. He promised me faithfully he'd be there to meet you.'

'All right, Dad, don't worry about me so much,' Connie said tearfully.

'Do me one favour, try and get along with yer Aunt Harriet. Her bark's worse than her bite,' he grinned.

Connie sighed, a long, deep sigh. 'I'll do me best, Dad.'

'I know yer will, lass, an' don't forget you've got the telephone number of the corner shop. Mrs Taylor said she will always take a message.'

It was too late for any more talking. A shrill whistle rent the air and the train began to move.

Connie stepped back from the window and sank down in a corner seat. Early afternoon and the train wasn't full. She gave another great sigh and raised her eyes to heaven.

'Dear God, please help me to make the right decision.' Her mind was in a turmoil. When she was with Dennis, she had no trouble in believing everything he told her. Away from him, doubts crept in. Would he really divorce his wife and marry her? He said he would for the sake of the child she was carrying. Yet he already had two children, and what message did that send out to her? He said they would move away from London, that she would want for nothing and that he would always love her and the baby. What about her leaving all her own family and friends? What about his wife and their family?

Was he going to be true to her or were his promises going to turn out to be like pie-crust? For too long she

125

had dilly-dallied. Soon, very soon, she was going to have to decide just what was the right thing for her to do.

Left alone, her father didn't move straight away, but stood staring after the train long after it was out of sight. Up until now he had kept his thoughts to himself. However, he had known Dennis Dryden for a good number of years and his opinion of him had never altered. He was a horrible, sly, devious git who had always fancied his chances with the ladies.

The trouble was, Dennis had never known what it was to need anything. His father had seen to that. Spoilt him rotten, more so since his mother had died. Some would say that Ted Dryden bought his son's company, because when it came down to brass tacks, he might be a rich man – most bookies were – but all the same he was a lonely one. A decent one too by all accounts. Pity he hadn't taught his son to live by his set of rules.

As Connie walked up the steep slope from the platform at East Croydon, she felt disgusted. Her Uncle Jack looked like a tramp. His trousers and jacket were crumpled, his shirt none too clean, and he hadn't even bothered to have a shave. He had no manners either. Twice he had stopped to relight his rolled fag, and although she had placed her case at her feet and breathed a heavy sigh, he still had not made any attempt to take the case and carry it for her.

'You've been 'ere before, so yer know it's not far t' walk, but Longfellow Road ain't got any shorter.' He laughed. 'It's still a long bleeding road.'

Jack Briggs was right. It was a very long, steep road and sod's law being what it was, his house was right at the top end of it. By the time he opened the front door, Connie was sweating buckets and her breathing was slow and heavy.

'So you've arrived, young Connie.'

'Oh.' Connie stared at her aunt, thinking she must have been standing behind the door. Harriet Briggs was a big sharp-faced woman with dry frizzy brown hair, and at this moment she didn't look at all pleased to have had her niece forced upon her. It was true, she had only agreed to have Connie to stay because she felt sorry for her sister, Kate. She had never been over-fond of this girl; even as a toddler she had been nothing but trouble, right bossy, forever throwing tantrums if she didn't get her own way. Always had been pretty, though, pretty as a picture, and everyone used to say she would break many a man's heart when she got older. That prophecy had now become a reality.

'Come on through,' Harriet said more kindly than she felt. 'I've got the kettle boiling, and we can 'ave a chat over a cuppa an' you can bring me up to date as to what's been 'appening.'

Although the thought of having to spend weeks in the company of her aunt and uncle did not make Connie feel very happy, she knew the best thing she could do right now was play along and do her best to keep the pair of them sweet.

'I could murder a cup of tea, please, Aunt Harriet,' she said as she took off her jacket, hung it over the back of a chair and then sat herself down in a big squashy armchair. Glancing about her, she came to the conclusion that this front room was very nicely furnished, light and airy and very clean.

Sighing with relief, she remembered what her mother had told her. Harriet had been a nurse before she had married Jack Briggs, and during the early years of their marriage she had trained as a midwife. Apparently many of the local families had good reason to be grateful to Harriet Briggs. She had delivered many of their babies, slapping the breath of life into some of them.

127

'Tea won't be long.' Harriet half-smiled at her niece, but turning to her husband she looked him up and down. 'You dared to go an' meet our Connie looking like that?' she sneered. 'You ain't got an ounce of respect left in yer. When you called out that you were going to the station I thought you had washed and changed. I would 'ave had you back by the scruff of the neck if I'd seen yer.'

'Oh, I'm sorry,' he said mockingly. 'I thought the girl was 'ere with us 'cos she's in the pudden club and the neighbours were giving your sister a hard time 'cos she'd let 'er daughter run wild with a married man. I didn't know yer wanted me to treat 'er like royalty.'

Harriet curled her lip in contempt. 'You're such an honourable man, never put a foot wrong in yer life, is that what you'd 'ave us believe?'

Jack mimicked her voice. 'No, my dear, you're the saintly one in this family, but now I know where I stand I shall do me best to mind me p's and q's.'

'I don't want any special treatment,' Connie said, trying to lighten the situation.

Her uncle grinned nastily. 'You won't get any, at least not from me.'

Harriet felt guilty that Connie hadn't been in the house two minutes and already she had had to witness how things stood between herself and her husband.

'Jack,' she pleaded, 'go wash your hands and come an' have some tea. I've made sultana scones.'

'I don't want any tea,' he said irritably. 'I'm going for an evening paper.'

'Well, take the dog across to the park. He could do with a good run.'

'Trying to get rid of me now so you an' she,' he nodded towards Connie, 'can 'ave a good old natter about how terrible life 'as treated both of you?'

Harriet rolled her eyes to the ceiling.

Jack moved nearer to Connie and, resting a hand on each side of the armchair in which she was sitting, leant his head down until his face was only inches from hers.

'You, young lady, had better keep yerself t' yerself while you're under my roof. I don't want fellows coming knocking on my door 'cos they think my niece is an easy touch.'

She flinched away, but she wasn't going to let him think that she was frightened of him.

'You don't need to threaten me, Uncle Jack. I don't want any men, not even for company, thank you very much. Christ knows I've come unstuck with the one I've got, haven't I?'

He took hold of her chin and waggled it.

'Just remember what I've said.'

Without another word he shrugged himself into his jacket and walked out. His wife did not say goodbye to him, and neither did Connie.

Harriet brought a loaded tea tray in from the kitchen, placed it in the middle of the table and sat down, telling Connie to come and sit beside her.

'I really am sorry you had t' listen to all that,' she said. Then she grinned. 'He likes to think he's such a big man, does my Jack. Coming to meet you all scruffy-like is his only means of protest. He won't work himself, never been able to hold a job down longer than a month, and of course he doesn't like it that I do still work. He's a dog in the manger, is Jack. He doesn't want me to earn money but he doesn't mind me paying all the bills.'

Connie nibbled on a scone. It was very good, better than those her mother made. All the same, she wasn't sure that leaving home and coming here to Croydon was the right thing to have done. The way things had started off, it certainly didn't seem that they were going to settle down to play happy families!

Her whole life was an utter mess. What she felt she needed right now was a damn good weep.

However, she still had some pride left and she wasn't going to let her aunt see her cry. Why, she asked herself, did she always have to play it the hard way? Never let folk know what she was really feeling?

She reached for her cup of tea and took a long, steady drink, telling herself that God had made everyone different. Wondering once more if she had she jumped out of the frying pan into the fire by coming here.

She couldn't answer her own question, she was too uncertain. But sensing that neither her aunt nor her uncle really wanted her here had given her yet another problem to think about.

Chapter Fifteen

CONNIE WATCHED HER UNCLE closely. She detested him. His very nearness gave her the creeps. She had formed the opinion that given half a chance she wouldn't be able to trust him any further than she could throw him.

During the fortnight that she had been living in Croydon, she had come to really like her aunt, though in a funny kind of way. She felt sorry for her, despite the fact that on most occasions Harriet had proved that she could hold her own. Not only with the nasty piece of work that was her husband, but also with their weird son, who had turned up out of the blue.

Connie vaguely remembered her cousin being known as Reggie when they were all young children, but when he had arrived unexpectedly the day after Connie, he had insisted that he now went by the name of 'Duke'.

Her uncle had taken Duke's homecoming in his stride, but Connie had been shocked when all the colour had drained from her aunt's face as she stared at her son, muttering, 'Christ, where the hell 'ave you turned up from?'

'All you need to know, Mother, is that I'm home now,

at least for a while.' And that was all he had been prepared to say on the subject.

Much later, when they had been alone, Harriet had told Connie the little she knew about her own son. He was sixteen when she had last set eyes on him, and that had been three years ago. Where he had been and what he had been up to she hadn't got a clue. On the whole, these were unhappy times for Connie.

Most days her aunt was out of the house for two to three hours at least. Connie forced herself to go for a walk rather than stay in the house with her uncle. The way he looked at her, and his nasty tongue when and if he spoke to her, was more than she could take.

It was a relief to have Duke in the house, although he never got out of his bed until eleven o'clock in the morning. By midday he was all spruced up, his natty clothes cleaned and pressed, his hair shiny with Brylcreem. If her aunt was at work, Connie would prepare a light lunch, or a late breakfast as Duke called it, and they would sit in the garden to eat it. He would talk to Connie about any number of subjects which she found very interesting, but if she asked questions as to what he intended to do that day, or indeed for the rest of his life, he would close up like a clam. Regularly each evening he left the house at seven, never returning before midnight.

'May I come out with you?' Connie had been bold enough to ask him one evening.

'What! And 'ave me mates thinking I might be the father to that baby you're carrying? You have got t' be joking.' That and a great shrug of his shoulders was the only answer he'd given.

'Where *are* all yer mates?' his mother had asked one evening as he stood combing his thick jet-black hair and admiring himself in the mirror that hung on the wall over the fireplace. 'There used to be hordes of them coming

132

round here for you and mostly I thought they were a good bunch of lads. Always polite t' me, they were.'

'Most of them are in the nick,' said Duke despondently.

His mother made no reply.

Duke looked from Connie to Harriet, and the looks on their faces had him shrieking with laughter.

Was he joking? Connie wondered.

Suddenly she felt very lonely shut away from her family. She missed her mum and dad, her sisters, and the jokes and friendly patter of her East End mates.

Harriet's mind was also working overtime. Her son had come home with some really decent clothes and he certainly didn't seem to be short of money. He hadn't been in the house five minutes when he had called her aside and given her sixty quid.

'It's a small fortune,' she had protested.

In a rare show of affection he had put his arms around her and held her close for a moment, patting her back and kissing the top of her head. 'Make sure you spend it on yourself, Mum, no handing it over to me father. You promise?'

Harriet couldn't have answered; she had been softly crying. She couldn't bring herself to question where or how he had come by the money, but she was thinking he wasn't all bad; there had to be a lot of good somewhere in this only son of hers.

Connie felt tired and irritable as she looked at the calendar. It was already the last week in August and the hot weather was getting her down. Every day seemed to be longer than the previous one, and being pregnant was no joke. She could barely walk to the park let alone down into Croydon with this heavy weight dragging her down morning, noon and night. These days her affair with Dennis Dryden did not seem so glamorous.

Where was he?

Probably miles away upcountry, doing some dodgy deal or at least finding work from councils or big offices and sub-letting the contracts to middle men for a whacking backhander. He had laughed himself silly one night when he had had more than enough to drink and opened up and told her a few details of what he actually did for a living.

'Never do for yourself what someone else is willing to do for you,' he had said was his motto, but had hastily added, 'so long as you've made sure you've creamed off your share of the profit first.'

Ducking and diving would be her term for what Dennis had openly bragged about. She shouldn't be grumbling about him really, she chided herself. She'd known what she was getting into, and although first off she had given a few thoughts to the fact that Dennis had a wife and two children, you only had to take one look at him to know that if he wasn't showing Connie a good time, it would be some other young girl. He was that sort of a man.

Besides, when he had first paid attention to her she had thought the sun shone out of his backside, as did an awful lot of people. There was no two ways about it. Dennis was a natural charmer.

When she had told him she was pregnant, he had surprised her. To be honest, he'd made no bones about it. Promised her everything, even marriage. But how long was it since she had set eyes on him?

Too long.

Facing up to the truth, Connie felt tearful, thinking of the good job she had had to give up, the dances she went to with her mates every Saturday night, the lovely smart clothes that used to fit her. All that she had lost.

Now she was fat and ugly and nobody really wanted her. With both hands she clutched the rim of the kitchen sink and began to cry.

An arm went around her shoulders and she turned quickly, shuddering as she looked into the face of her Uncle Jack.

'What's the matter, girl? What are you doing out here on your own?'

His voice sounded full of kindness, but Connie wasn't fooled; indeed, she was frightened.

He saw she had been crying.

'Has that son of mine been upsetting you?' His voice had changed and was harsh. ''Cos if he has, I'll kill the little rotter.'

'No, Uncle Jack, Duke has always been all right with me. It's just . . .' A great sob strangled her words.

'I know it can't be easy for you, but you can tell me what's troubling you an' I'll help if I can. Here, wipe your eyes,' he said, handing her a big handkerchief.

Connie found it hard to believe how nice he was being to her. Using the handkerchief, she rubbed her face and then shrugged her shoulders. 'It's just everything suddenly seemed to get on top of me.' She did her best to smile to counteract the sadness in her voice.

'Come here and give yer old uncle a hug.'

As he cuddled her, Connie was thinking of her dad. She was so glad Jack was being nice to her. She badly needed to feel someone liked her, that not everyone was against her.

'Go and sit in the front room and I'll make us a cup of tea. It shouldn't be too long before your aunt gets back, and she always knows how to cheer you up, doesn't she?'

Connie wondered briefly about this sudden change in her uncle's attitude. She leant back in the armchair, tiredness sweeping over her. It didn't ring true; her uncle was up to something, she knew he was. Eventually it would come to light. Then again, perhaps she was misjudging him.

At least she hoped she was.

It was about time somebody gave her a break.

Chapter Sixteen

'WHO WOULD HAVE BELIEVED it?' Mike Murray was almost dancing for joy as he and Sam Richardson surveyed the completed extension of the British Legion club. 'Finished well on time and it looks wonderful, well worth while.' Mike's voice held a note of admiration for both the builders and the architects, who had, each in their own way, convinced the board of directors that this venture was sorely needed.

'Brought in well within budget.' Sam, ever the accountant, smiled. 'I am more than a little impressed.'

The club's main building had always been solid and substantial but as the club membership had grown, a wooden barn of a place had been erected within the grounds. For a good many years it had certainly served its purpose. Fund-raising dances, whist drives and coffee mornings had all been held there. However, the fact had remained that although there had been a basic kitchen within the building giving provision for coffee and tea, no licence to sell alcoholic drinks had ever been granted for that part of the club, so a bar had never been installed. Therefore it had hardly been popular with the men. If they were there at a dance with their wives they had to cross the yard to the main building in order to get an alcoholic drink from the bar. This went against the grain, especially during the winter months when the snow underfoot could be treacherously icy, and certainly did not do much to encourage the men to leave the comfort and warmth of the main clubhouse and their beloved darts board and snooker tables.

Mike Murray's biggest problem had always been that this hall being separate from the bar kept the takings down.

Few had been surprised when a year ago the wooden barn had finally given up the ghost and the roof had collapsed. Even fewer had mourned its passing when the news had been announced that an extension was to be built directly on to the main building and that the extra premises were to be licensed. The suggestion had been put forward and accepted by the committee that a restaurant should also be incorporated in the plans.

A few seconds passed before Sam exclaimed, 'It's all gone much smother than I imagined. We didn't come up against too many hiccups, did we?'

Smiling, Mike nodded his agreement. 'No, we didn't, but don't let's start counting our chickens before they are all hatched. There is still quite a bit of interior decorating to do, and most important of all, we still have to obtain a licence to sell alcoholic drink within these new premises,' he said matter-of-factly.

'Oh, don't go all sober-sides on me, not now we've come this far. I can't believe even now that at every stage the Legion committee came up with the cash.'

Mike reached out and touched Sam's shoulder lightly. 'You, my old son, can take a huge chunk of the credit for that. Once you'd seen the professional plans, you worked out the cost practically to the penny.'

'Oh, come off it,' Sam exclaimed loudly. 'I like what you're saying but it's not true. There was a whole team working on this project from start to finish. Anyway, shall we leave the congratulations until the official opening night finally comes around?'

Mike grinned broadly. 'That'll be a night to remember!'

'I'm sure it will be,' Sam laughed, then quickly added, 'Have you forgotten you've a darts match on here tonight, and it's a qualifying round, isn't it?'

'Jesus wept an' well he might!' Mike shouted, showing his irritation. 'I 'ad forgotten all about it.'

'Blowing yer top won't help. Besides, I know the staff have it all in hand. I spoke to Ella and Molly this morning and they said they were snowed under with enough food to feed an army. The draymen are down in the cellars now, so I presume Tom and Derrick have everything under control.'

Molly and Ella didn't need any reminding that it was darts night.

This was the busiest night Ella had seen since she had started working at the Legion. The visiting team from the Crown and Anchor had brought quite a few supporters. Tom, Molly and Ella were serving drinks in the public bar, leaving only Derrick and Mike's wife Beryl to do a spell in the saloon. During the matches the three of them behind the public bar were kept very busy. There was little time for conversation, let alone to keep the bar wiped down. As the evening wore on and the two darts teams became more excited, both Ella and Molly thought their heads would burst with all the noise, and the air being thick with smoke didn't help. Every time a winning dart was thrown, the cheers that rang out were enough to deafen everyone. The only time there was complete hush was when the caller announced that a double top would secure the match for the home team.

No problem for Wally Stebington. He toed the line, spat on his hands and rubbed them together. A single arrow was all that he needed.

Straight and true it flew from between Wally's fingers to bed itself in the narrow space between the two wires at the top of the board.

'*YES!*' The unanimous cry rose to the roof as the regulars celebrated their victory.

The visiting team weren't quite so happy. Having stuffed their faces with quite a lot of the good food that the Legion had provided, most of them and their supporters left to get a last late drink back at the Crown and Anchor.

Both Molly and Ella sighed a huge sigh of relief as Mike called, 'Last orders, please, ladies and gentlemen.'

Glancing round the bar, Molly muttered, 'Looks as if a ruddy bomb hit this place tonight.'

'Yeah, and I feel as if I've gone ten rounds with a heavyweight boxer,' Ella answered. She wasn't feeling very good-tempered. There had been a few customers who had gone out of their way to let her know that they had seen Dennis from time to time. Mostly the gossipmongers were nosy old biddies whose biggest aim in life was to make mischief. As she poured the slops into the troughs and stacked the dirty glasses that Molly was collecting, Ella reflected on the different versions she had had to listen to over the past few weeks.

Her Dennis looked so well, was living off the fat of the land. One day he was supposedly living in a big house in Hampstead wearing well-tailored suits and expensive shoes. The next story would have him living in Windsor.

'In a royal apartment of the castle?' she was tempted to ask. Instead she had learnt to keep a straight face and her feelings well under control.

'Whenever I see your old man he's never short of female company.' One spiteful old biddy threw her twopennyworth into the conversation, not caring whether it was true or not.

But on that occasion it had been one remark too many, and Ella had thrown caution to the wind.

Leaning across the counter, she cupped the woman's chin in her hand. 'Would you like me to give you a face-lift?' Ella's voice was low, heavy with menace. As she saw the fear in the woman's eyes she felt an urge to punch her in the face.

The woman dropped her eyes and tried to back away, then she felt Ella's fingers make contact with her hair. One mighty tug and Ella was holding a few strands. She let go, shoved the woman in the chest and threw the hair into her face.

'I hear another word from you about my affairs and so 'elp me God I'll strangle yer. You got that?'

'Yes, yes,' the woman stammered, trying not to show her fear as she shifted her weight from one foot to the other. One thing was certain, she had learnt that it wasn't safe to wind Ella Dryden up.

With the darts match over, Ella and Molly set about the clearing-up like a couple of zombies. Dead tired, and longing to put her feet up, Ella suddenly noticed that Alf and Kate Baldwin were standing by the door, looking at her with some concern in their eyes. The expressions on their faces bewildered Ella, and suddenly she felt so sorry for them both. It was a shame, she thought, the disgrace their daughter had brought on them, and it wasn't over yet. Not by a long chalk it wasn't.

Suddenly she realized they had been staring at her in silence for quite a while.

'Is there something you wanted to ask me?' she found herself saying.

Alf Baldwin straightened his shoulders. 'I know we've no right to question you, Ella, you've more than enough on yer own plate, but our Connie's time is drawing nigh and we wondered if you had any idea what your Den was going to do.'

Ella leant her weight on the nearest table and sighed heavily. What in God's name could she say to these parents? When first it had become known that Connie was pregnant and that Dennis was the father of the baby, Kate Baldwin had gone more than halfway to blaming Ella. Still, it didn't do to bear grudges.

'I haven't seen my Den for some time,' she managed to say. 'As to his intentions regarding your daughter, your guess is as good as mine. I did 'ear that you'd sent her to stay with your sister. How's she been doing?'

'I don't think she's all that happy in Croydon,' Kate Baldwin said quickly. 'It's hard t' know what t' do for the best. We don't want her to end up bringing the baby up all on her own. The council will only allocate her some dirty, poky flat in a grim, tumbledown back street. We're overcrowded as it is with only three rooms over the shop.'

Ella looked at her in silence for a moment. 'I don't know what I can do.' She felt she was becoming a little too involved, but she wanted to help if only she knew how. 'Tell yer what, Dennis's dad, Ted, is coming t' dinner with me termorrow. I'll 'ave a word with him. Maybe he's been in touch with Den. Anyway, we'll see. No 'arm in asking him, though whether we'll get a straight answer is another matter altogether.'

'We've no right t' ask fer your help, Ella, but we can't think straight at the moment. Thanks anyway,' Alf Baldwin said gruffly.

Ella felt tearful then, thinking of all the trouble Dennis had caused. Not only to Connie Baldwin and her parents, but also to her own two children. It was going to take a long time before young Teddy and Babs gave up hoping that their dad would come back home and their lives

141

would return to what they were before this storm broke over their heads.

No matter which way you looked at it, her Dennis was a devil, a selfish devil who gave no thought to anyone but his bloody self!

She shuddered and glanced back in the direction of the bar, which was by now packed high with dirty glasses. 'I'd better get back ter work or Mike will think I'm slacking.'

She turned away quickly; the look on Kate and Alf Baldwin's faces was making her stomach turn.

'I'll let you know if Ted tells me where Dennis is.'

She spoke the words softly, and the Baldwins both nodded their heads.

'Thanks for talking t' us, Ella,' Kate said as she buttoned up her coat and took hold of her husband's arm.

Ella went back behind the bar, her mind in a whirl as she found herself dwelling on the conversation she had just had with Connie Baldwin's parents. She had seen such despair in the eyes of that father and mother. None of this trouble was of her making, she knew, yet her face was flushed and her hands were shaking as she bent over the sink.

Den had had the sweets and buggered off and left everyone else to pick up the pieces. She wondered if he was sorry for all the trouble he had caused.

Of course he wasn't, she answered herself angrily, otherwise he would at least have kept in touch with his children. Babs hadn't been the same since her dad had left home. Young as she was, she knew she had been rejected. Gone from being Daddy's little sweetheart, spoilt rotten, given hugs and kisses every day of her life, to almost having no dad at all. Kids at school taunted her that her dad was going to be someone else's father. The nastiness and cruel words hurt more than blows would have done.

Teddy was only four years older, but he seemed better able to cope with the fact that his father didn't live with them any more. Maybe it was because his grandad was around and took him out and about. Teddy was tall and lean, cheeky, noisy and sometimes a bit rough, but always lovable.

Babs was totally different, which was only to be expected, a dainty little girl with long chestnut-coloured hair and big brown eyes. She took after her grandmother's side of the family and was the apple of Winnie's eye. But no one, least of all her mother, could fathom what she was thinking. It grieved Ella more than anything else that Den could have walked out of his daughter's life almost without a backward glance when previously he had been so protective of her.

Oh well, nobody had ever said that life was going to be fair, Ella told herself as she gave the long bar a final wipe-down with a towelling beer-mat.

At least she had pulled herself together and got this job, for which she was eternally grateful. This was her life from now on, and the sooner she accepted the fact that Dennis was no longer part of it, the better off she would be.

When Ella woke the next morning she could barely lift her head from the pillow. She still felt dead tired and utterly weary. Then the bedroom door opened and her mother was there holding out a steaming cup of tea.

'Oh, Mum! Whatever would I do without you? If I live to be a hundred I'll never be able to pay you back for all you've done for me over the years. Never. But one day I'll make it up to you in one way or another.'

'Of course yer will, darlin'. You do anyway just by letting me share yer life.'

Suddenly Ella sniffed and then in great haste placed

her now almost empty cup down on the bedside table and swung her legs over the side of the bed.

'Jesus! That's roast beef I can smell cooking, isn't it? I forgot all about Ted coming to dinner today. What time is it? How long before he turns up 'ere?'

Winnie laughed. 'Stop asking so many questions. Everything is under control; all you've got t' do is get washed and dressed. It's almost one o'clock an' Ted's been 'ere since ten. He brought loads of fresh veg with him, and took both the kids out and bought them a present. Babs has been 'elping me make pastry for the apple pie and Ted, daft as a brush, is out with all the kids from the nearby streets playing cricket in the alley. He sent Teddy to buy sticks of chalk so that he could draw stumps on the end wall. Never grow up, Ted won't.'

The dinner was a great success, with Ted declaring that Win's roast beef melted in the mouth.

'That's 'cos it's cooked on the bone; none of this boned and rolled rubbish,' Winnie declared firmly.

Ted leant across the table and said to Ella, 'I bet the butcher wants t' run and hide when he sees your mum coming!'

'I 'eard that, Ted Dryden, an' I notice you wasn't so damn cheeky until after I fed yer.'

'We 'aven't finished dinner yet, 'ave we, Gran? What about our apple pie and custard? I rolled the pastry out, didn't I?' Babs's whole attitude was full of indignation. They didn't get pudding every day of the week, so how could her gran possibly forget that they were supposed to have pie and custard?

Ella felt good as she watched everyone laugh, and at that moment she could have taken her young daughter in her arms and almost crushed her to death, such was the love she was feeling for her.

All in all she was feeling good today.

That was until Ted, having scraped his pudding bowl clean, began to talk about his son.

'I've got a message for you, Ella, from Den,' he began.

'Hang on a minute,' Winnie cried as she got to her feet and reached for her purse, which lay on the dresser. 'We grown-ups are going to 'ave a decent cup of tea, but I forgot to fetch any drinks for you two. Teddy, take Babs to the corner shop and let her choose a bottle of whatever she wants.'

'Cor, can I 'ave cream soda, Gran?'

'Course yer can, me darlin'.'

'An' can I have a bottle of Tizer?' Teddy wasn't going to be outdone.

'Yes, luv, but don't leave go of yer sister's 'and as yer cross the road. That can be a busy corner sometimes.'

'Oh, all right,' Teddy agreed, but none too happily. Boys didn't hold their sisters' hands.

'Now,' Winnie said with a sense of achievement as she watched the two little 'uns scarper, 'I'm gonna take meself off out into the scullery and you two can say what yer got t' say, but you should both know better than to discuss what is happening to their father in front of Teddy and Babs.'

Winnie expected Ted's reply and she got it.

He apologized immediately.

Alone, Ted took a good look at his daughter-in-law. He was amazed at how well she was coping with the two children. She was a good mum, and she'd put herself out and about and found herself a full-time job. Another point was she looked and acted so differently than she had when his son had been around. She certainly wore different clothes.

He was embarrassed. He didn't like being the messenger. Nothing would give him greater pleasure than to see his Den and Ella back together again, but no matter

145

how hard he tried, he wasn't able to achieve much headway. When it came to being obstinate, there wasn't much to choose between the pair of them.

Den was no saint, Ted was well aware of that, but he was a red-blooded man, and most men played away from home at some time.

Noticing Ted's hesitation, Ella spoke up sharply.

'Come on then, spit it out, this message that Dennis couldn't deliver himself.'

'Den's turned over a new leaf, you know, Ella.'

'Huh,' was all she said.

Ted wasn't pleased at her reaction and it showed.

'Try an' 'ave a little faith, gal, give way a little bit, 'cos honestly Den's doing his damnedest to lead a different life. You wanna see what he's managed to do with that property he bought at Epsom. I'll take yer t' see it if yer like, you've only got t' say the word. It's being beautifully restored, especially those great big rooms. When Den's finished with it it will be absolutely fabulous and he'll make a mint if he sells all those apartments.'

'You'll be telling me next that Den has done most of the work himself.'

'Well, he tells me he's done a fair bit of it. Why don't you let me set up a meeting for the two of yer?'

Ella was trying her best to picture Dennis in overalls with his sleeves rolled up and actually working. Doing what? He always said himself he was a Jack of all trades and master of none. Yet as she lifted her eyes to look at Ted's face, he didn't appear to be joking.

'Are you serious?' she asked, her voice cracking.

'Never more so,' he said, reaching out to take her hand in his. 'I wish for nothing more than to see you two back together and the kids bright and happy, a real family like you used to be.'

Whose fault was it that they were a broken family? And

if she and their children were still of such great importance to Dennis, why wasn't he sitting opposite her now instead of his father?

Her thoughts were suddenly of Connie Baldwin and her sad parents, and she felt her temper rising, but before she could decide what to say to her father-in-law, he spoke again.

'Maybe Den *is* different now. Couldn't you have him back, Ella? Give him another chance? Maybe he has changed.'

The truth was, she argued with herself, that she wanted to believe what Ted was telling her. But how many times had she had promises of changing for the better from Dennis himself?

Suddenly this was more than Ella could stand.

'Yeah!' she said loudly. 'And maybe he's still a lying, cheating bastard.'

Chapter Seventeen

'SOD IT!' JACK BRIGGS swore loudly, feeling something sharp pierce into the ball of his right foot. He leant against the wall of the kitchen and shoved his foot up on to the seat of a chair.

'It's a bloody drawing pin,' he sniffed as he wiggled the round top of the pin loose before he was able to withdraw it from his flesh. He hobbled to the one armchair which stood beside the fireplace, and once he was sitting down lifted his right leg to rest across his knees and did his best to examine the bottom of his bare foot, which stuck out below the leg of his cotton pyjama trousers.

His wife leant forward and slapped his leg, causing him to bring his sore foot down hard on to the floor. He winced. 'What did yer do that for? You can see I'm in pain,' he complained loudly.

'Serve yer right,' Harriet retaliated. 'You shouldn't be walking around the house with nothing on yer feet and half-undressed this time in the morning. Just look at yer! Yer 'aven't had a wash let alone cleaned yer teeth or combed yer hair. You're a disgrace at the best of times, but I thought you'd 'ave made an effort with our Connie staying in the house. Instead I reckon you've got steadily worse. I'm beginning to wonder whether you're doing it deliberately just to annoy me.'

Connie was sitting at the breakfast table nibbling a piece of toast.

Oh Christ! she murmured to herself. Don't let them start on at each other, not so early in the day. Mind you, the very sight of her Uncle Jack was enough to start her heaving. His pyjama jacket was unbuttoned, showing his hairy chest, he hadn't shaved for at least two days, there was enough grime beneath his fingernails to plant a pot, and his bare feet were none too clean. He just sat there oblivious of what his wife or his niece thought of him, merely watching as Harriet lifted the heavy steaming black kettle off the hob and carried it through to the scullery.

Connie heard the rattle of the big enamel bowl being lifted down from the shelf above the stone sink. As Harriet came back into the living room she threw a piece of Lifebuoy soap into her husband's lap, took an old tea-cloth from the dresser drawer, quickly ripped it in half and tossed one of the pieces at her husband saying, 'Yer can use that for a flannel. So move yerself, get out there and give yerself a good wash from top t' toe, 'cos Connie and I are going upstairs to make the beds, and when we come down I want to see you looking reasonably clean and dressed properly.'

Aunt and niece watched Jack stumble to his feet and leave the room clutching the piece of clean rag and the bar of red soap. They heard the echo of the bowl rattling in the sink and then the scalding water being poured into it. They both smiled as they heard Jack muttering.

'Bloody bossy bitch. Just 'cos she's got a job, messy one at that, delivering babies, how could anyone enjoy doing that with all the blood an' guts coming out all over the bed.'

Harriet caught hold of Connie's arm and steered her towards the stairs. 'Come on, luv, let's leave him to it. We'll do the beds then I must be away. I've two women I have to check on today, but I'll do a bit of shopping down in Croydon, see if I can find something nice to eat that will tempt you, and when I get back we'll go for a walk over the park and eat our lunch sitting on one of the benches. How's that sound?'

'Oh, Aunt Harriet, that sounds real good. I'll change into that loose cotton dress you made for me and I'll be ready and waiting. Shall I bring a bottle of cold tea?'

'No, luv, we'll 'ave a treat today. I've still got a couple of bottles of my homemade elderberry wine hidden away. We'll sneak one of those out with us.'

When they came downstairs, Harriet was dressed in what she called her everyday uniform, ready for work. Connie was wearing a loose cotton dress and carrying a book, intending to go and sit in the garden and have a quiet read.

Jack Briggs responded to the surprised look on their faces by giving them a mock salute and bending from his waist to make a regal bow.

'You don't 'ave t' bow an' scrape,' Harriet grinned, 'but I will say you don't polish up bad when you make the effort.' To herself she was thinking what a pity it was that he didn't try a bit harder every day.

'Thank you, my dear wife, for those kind words,' he mocked. 'And how about our Connie? Does she approve of her uncle today?'

'Yes, I do now,' Connie quickly answered.

Jack was wearing black shoes and socks, plain grey trousers, a blue checked shirt and even a tie. The same thought immediately came to both of the women. The tie was one of Duke's. They managed to suppress their smiles as Harriet said, 'Well, I must be off. I'll be back about one o'clock.'

Connie went to the front door with her aunt and stood watching her walk down the street until she was out of sight. As she turned to go back inside the house she had a premonition that everything was not as it should be. She suddenly felt fearful. Of what, she couldn't have said.

'Got the whole place to ourselves,' her uncle leered at her. 'Shall I make us a fresh brew?' he asked, holding the big teapot in his large hands.

'Not for me, thank you, Uncle Jack, I've had enough to drink. I'm going to find a shady spot and sit out in the garden.' There was more than a little fear in Connie's voice. She didn't like the idea of being on her own with him and she wished she could slip upstairs and wake Duke up. She glanced at the big clock that stood on the mantelshelf over the fireplace. It was only just turned nine. Duke wouldn't thank her for waking him at what he would call an unearthly hour.

'Come for a walk with me, Connie. I'll buy yer a drink later when the pubs open,' he suggested, moving closer to her and stroking her bare arm.

Connie knew trouble was brewing, and she wanted to back away, yet she made herself stand still. 'Drink is the last thing I need, Uncle Jack, the very smell of it makes me feel sick, but you go, you're all spruced up and it's a lovely day. Won't get many more days like this, two more and we'll be in September.'

She knew she was talking for the sake of it. Her uncle was standing far too close; she could feel his hot breath on her face. She had to get away from him. Her every instinct told her that he was plotting something. If only she could go home. If only she hadn't been daft enough to be flattered by Den Dryden's attention. If only . . .

Connie looked out of the kitchen window, staring into

the peaceful garden. She could go on for ever saying to herself 'if only', but all the talking in the world wouldn't let her have her life back as it used to be.

Her uncle stepped as near to her as he could get and, with his face only inches from hers, said, 'I don't know why you're trembling. I've never laid a finger on yer, 'ave I?'

Connie clutched her hands together tightly, pressing them against her swollen belly.

'I have to sit down or I shall fall down,' she pleaded.

'So! No one's stopping yer,' he said, cupping a hand beneath her elbow and steering her towards the armchair.

'I'd rather go and sit outside in the fresh air. You come out there too, it's so hot in here.' Right now her instinct told her to get out of the house. If he tried anything on with her out in the open she could at least shout and scream and the neighbours might hear her. Here indoors he could place a hand over her mouth before she could shout loud enough for Duke to come down. Anyway, Duke would still be dead to the world. If only he would get up now and come down those stairs! Another 'if only'.

Her uncle practically pushed her down into the armchair then stood swaying above her, looking down at her with a broad smile on his face. It was then he started to talk, his words little more than a whisper, almost as if he were talking to himself.

'You come into my home, queening it over everyone. Not an ounce of shame in yer that yer carrying a baby. Don't suppose yer really know who the father is. Don't look like Dennis Dryden is gonna let you lumber him with it, does it? Ain't seen sight nor sound of him, 'ave yer? It's yer poor mum an' dad that I feel sorry for. Neighbours do love to gossip and cast stones. Life must 'ave been bad for them to turn yer out of house an' home an' dump yer on me and 'Arriet. What 'ave we ever done that we should be made to house yer an' feed yer?'

Heart thumping like mad, Connie pushed her head sideways. If she spoke quietly and stayed calm he might back off.

'Uncle Jack, listen to me. Please. You and Auntie Harriet have been so good to me, but if my being here has upset you so much, I will go home today. Maybe it's best that I should. I can't have much longer to go an' I wanna be with my mum when the baby comes.' Her voice trembled and she wasn't far from tears.

That made no different to Jack Briggs. He had set his course and he was going to have his way while he'd got the chance.

His arm shot out, his hand grasping her hair, and at the same time he was pulling her forward. She opened her mouth to scream but he had anticipated this; he fished from his pocket the rag that Harriet had given him to use as a flannel and suddenly her scream was muffled as he shoved the ball of cloth tightly into her mouth.

'I tried being the nice kindly uncle but you didn't want to know, did you? Oh no, you've been playing Lady Muck, and I was dirt beneath yer feet. Well, I'm fed up with the way you've taken over my home and the bloody way you've looked down yer nose at me. I've put up with all of that, and right now I think I'm within my rights to 'elp meself to a bit of pleasure. You've put it about a bit before you came 'ere, that's obvious, and yer know what folk say, "A slice off a cut loaf is never missed."'

Connie wriggled from side to side, trying to get her hands free so that she might take the cloth out of her mouth, but that only brought her a hefty slap across the side of her face and she felt warm, sticky blood trickle from her nose.

She saw stars and at the same time felt him grasp the front of her dress. With one violent swoop he ripped the material from the neck to the waistline.

From that moment on there was no fight left in Connie.

Time passed as her uncle bent over her swollen breasts, stroking them gently in turn. Then abruptly he pulled her bra straps from her shoulders, letting her big breasts fall free. Now he became a wild animal, sucking at her nipples, biting down hard on the first one and then doing the same to the other. Squeezing, pinching, digging his fingers into her tender flesh, and the more she winced with pain, the more excited he became.

Her nipples had been sore for weeks now, and biting them was the worst thing he could have done. The burning pain he was inflicting on her was more than she could bear. She wanted to be sick. She wanted to die.

Yet he wasn't finished yet.

Straightening himself up, he bent low, grabbed both of her ankles and pulled hard until her body slid forward and she was lying flat on the floor. It only took seconds to roll up the bottom half of her dress and petticoat, and rip the crotch of her knickers apart.

He freed himself of his clothes until he was totally naked and then he was on top of her, pinning her to the floor. Connie was past caring. She prayed to die. She did her best to close her mind to what was happening to her body. She did feel anxious about the baby, but what good would it do to cry out now?

Eyes screwed up tight as they would go, hands balled into fists, she lay there, hurting, burning, suffering pain like she had never imagined.

Still her uncle repeatedly, roughly rammed himself into her as hard as he could go. He was having what he regarded as his revenge on her.

At last! It was over.

Grunting happily, her uncle rolled away from her. He lay on his side, panting for a minute or two, before he stood up and pulled his pants and trousers back on. It wasn't enough that he had raped her. Now he lifted his foot and kicked the side of her body.

'Get up and get some clothes on, you filthy little whore! At least now you know what I think of you.'

Connie hadn't died, no matter how much she wished she had.

There was only one thought in her mind. Get up off this floor. She needed to wash and scrub herself and leave the house before her aunt got home or her cousin came downstairs.

The side of her face was sore, and as she gently touched it she could tell her cheek was swollen and that there was dried blood around her nose and on her top lip. Her aunt would know something was wrong, but how could she tell Harriet that her husband had raped her, or tell her cousin that his father had used her as he would a whore off the streets.

She staggered to her feet.

Her uncle grinned as he finished dressing himself. 'You look like a tired-out whore. Go and change yer dress an' we'll tell yer aunt yer went for a walk and bumped into a lamppost. You've only got a bit of bruising, don't look like you've been in a car crash or anything like that.'

Connie didn't answer; she was crying softly. She felt so sore, it was as if her whole body was screaming, even her insides.

'You tell yer aunt any different and by God I'll make you sorry.' He hissed the words at her.

Connie lifted her head and stared hard, and he could feel the hate beaming towards him.

'Look, it's like I said, it's not as if you were a virgin. Tell yer what, I'll make us a cuppa and something nice to eat while you're tidying yerself up.'

She nodded, resigned now that it would be pointless to argue with him.

The sooner she got out of this house, down to the railway station and home to her mum and dad the better. She just knew she wouldn't feel safe or even clean until her dad put his arms around her.

Chapter Eighteen

THE LONG WALK SEEMED never-ending. Her back was aching and getting worse with every step. Her swollen stomach had made her tend to throw her weight backwards, which didn't help.

Finally she arrived at East Croydon station.

With a heartfelt sigh of relief, Connie sat down on a platform bench and placed her brown paper carrier bag between her feet. There wasn't much in the bag, and she hadn't bothered to pack her case. Her one thought had been to get out of that house and on her way home. What she had just suffered at the hands of her Uncle Jack had been a nightmare she wouldn't inflict on her worst enemy. Why did her Aunt Harriet put up with him? He was downright selfish and lazy, and after what he had done to her this morning she considered he was no good to man or beast.

She had had a great deal to think about as she trudged along the roads.

Nothing in her world made sense any more; nothing could be classed in black or white. Everything she did or touched went wrong. Was it just her? She didn't think so.

No one was wholly bad, and no one person was perfect either, least of all herself. They say as you sow so shall you reap. Well, if sowing wild oats was what she was supposed to have done, then the harvest had been a sour one. Was she so bad? All she had longed for was a bit of fun, a few nice clothes and someone to take notice of her, make a fuss of her.

God knows, she'd grown up like most of the youngsters of her age. Hating the war, hating the fact that two oranges had to be shared between all of the family – that was the few times they ever saw a piece of fruit. As for sweets, a penny bar of chocolate, a few fruit drops and maybe one gobstopper and that was the ration for a month. When it came to clothes, all they ever wore were hand-me-downs. For three winters running she had worn a coat that her mother had made from an old grey army blanket. Her eldest sister had very bad feet because she had been made to wear shoes that were too small for her, because there were not enough clothing coupons to enable their mum to buy her a new pair.

Then suddenly the war had been over.

London could once more have bright lights everywhere, though not all signs of the bombing had yet disappeared: wreckage, ruined buildings and masses of debris still scarred many parts of the city. Dance halls had reopened, so had theatres and cinemas. Young women could take their pick of the new-look clothes that every shop suddenly had a good stock of. To go up to Marble Arch and Oxford Street, look around C&A and Selfridges was such a joy. The only problem now was not a shortage of clothing coupons but money. As a family they didn't do badly, but it was always sufficient, just enough, rather than extravagance.

Then Den Dryden had come into her life. Snappy dresser, loads of money and not afraid to spend it. But most of all he owned a car! Leather upholstery, walnut dashboard, oh, the very smell of the interior of Den's car had always sent shivers of delight up her spine whenever he opened the door and handed her into the front passenger seat.

Of course she had showed off, bragging to her mates about the places he had taken her to. Naturally each and every one of them had been envious, and if the truth be told there wasn't one amongst them that wouldn't have gone out with Den if they had been given the chance.

But it wasn't one of those girls that Den had chosen. It was me, Connie told herself as she placed her hands over her big belly and smiled wryly.

Was she feeling bitter now? Of course she was.

Den had promised her so much. Even when she had told him she was pregnant, he'd assured her he would cherish both her and the baby. They would want for nothing.

That was a laugh if ever there was one!

How long was it since she had set eyes on him? Even his own father didn't know where he was, or if he did he wasn't telling.

It was Connie who had been left to face the gossips and the sneers from all sides, including those coming from her so-called friends. As for money, she had less than four shillings left out of what her father had given her. For all Dennis knew, or cared it would seem, she could have starved to death.

What had happened to her today had been the last straw. Her Uncle Jack might not be a blood relative. Still, would it have hurt him to show her just a little respect? To be honest, respect was probably asking too much.

A lot of what he had said was true. She had let an older man make love to her, make her pregnant, and she *had* known from the beginning that Dennis was a married man and that he already had two children.

That still didn't give Jack Briggs the right to rape her. Especially as he had done it in such a crude, spiteful way. Even animals didn't treat each other with such brutality.

Ah well, sitting here won't get me home, Connie thought. She felt in her pocket: yes, she had her ticket safe; she had bought it at the ticket office before she had ventured down the steep slope to the platform.

What would she do when she arrived at Victoria? She hadn't got enough money for a taxi. She could telephone Mrs Taylor at the corner shop, and she'd send someone round to tell her mum and dad that she was at Victoria station. She had kept the slip of paper her dad had given her, with Mrs Taylor's number written on it, safely in her purse.

What I need, Connie told herself, is to make sure that I've got my story exactly right in my head. The first thing her parents would ask would be why she had returned home so unexpectedly. Not in a million years could she bring herself to tell them the truth.

There would be ructions! Jack Briggs would be damned lucky if her father stopped short of killing him, and that would be like adding fuel to the flames where the gossips were concerned. Her father would be arrested, and even if he only gave her uncle a good battering, he might still have to go to prison. No, she couldn't talk about it. Far better to keep her mouth shut and her thoughts to herself. She would just have to swear to her parents that she was homesick.

What was done was done and couldn't be undone, so why cause her family more heartache? Bad as she was, she didn't want to heap more trouble on her parents.

The train shuddered to a stop in front of her, and with a thankful sigh she waited whilst a well-dressed lady opened the door and stood back, allowing Connie to precede her into the carriage. With difficulty she climbed the high step and eased herself on to the nearest corner seat.

The carriage was empty apart from a working-class man who was seated in the opposite corner. He appeared to be engrossed in his copy of the *Daily Mirror*. In actual fact, he had taken his eyes away from his newspaper to cast an appreciative glance at the smartly dressed lady.

As his eyes automatically turned to Connie, he raised them heavenwards, his disapproval plainly showing.

She wasn't wearing gloves and her finger showed no wedding ring. Connie knew instinctively what he was thinking. Like a good many others, he was condemning her for being immoral. She was going home and she would have to face the gossips once more, and most of them would probably judge her to be just as evil as the look this stranger had given her. Still, it wouldn't be too long before she had her baby in her arms, and she would love it and care for it against all odds. After all, the wee mite hadn't asked to be born and things might turn out for the better once it was here.

Wasn't her mother always saying that inside every cloud there was a silver lining? She would do her best to keep that thought uppermost in her mind, though the way her life had turned out, God alone knew what a hard job it was at times to look on the bright side.

Within a few minutes a whistle blew and the train began moving along the tracks. Connie wriggled in her seat, thinking she would never feel the same again. Her whole body was sore and her thighs hurt so much she felt they must surely be black and blue with bruises. The moment she got home all she longed for was to be able to have a good long soak in a hot bath. She smiled wryly. Even that would be an impossibility. In the flat above the shop where her family lived, no one could have a bath on demand. There was a bathroom but no running hot water. A gas copper had to be filled with cold water and lit, and one had to be patient and wait for it to be heated. Even then it was a right carry-on transferring the hot water from the copper into the bath.

To arrive home unexpectedly and ask to have a bath! She would need a very good explanation.

Watching idly as the London buildings and the blocks of ugly, dirty-looking flats flicked past the window, she felt sorry for the tenants who had to live in these buildings. Rows and rows of washing were strung out on iron balconies. The thought crossed her mind that most of the washing would be dirty again by the time it was dry. What with the fumes from vans and lorries plus the sooty smoke coming from the railway lines, surely anything white would turn grey on the line.

The train was gathering speed and it sounded as if the wheels were squealing. Now, suddenly, the lady sitting opposite leant forward and held out a hand to Connie.

'Would you like a barley-sugar, my dear, they do help if you're feeling a bit queasy.'

'Thank you,' Connie smiled as she took the sweet. Unwrapping the paper, she popped the barley-sugar into her mouth, and as she sucked it she immediately felt better. Mostly because of the kind action a complete stranger had shown towards her, and also because it tasted good and had begun to make the inside of her mouth feel so much cleaner. She shuddered. For one awful moment she could actually feel the tongue of her beastly uncle being thrust into her mouth.

Good God! What was happening?

The noise was suddenly terrific, and the train seemed to be swaying from side to side. Connie wanted to steady herself and put out her hands for something to grip. She touched netting and a kind of pole and knew that it was the luggage rack, that had fallen down from overhead.

Without warning the carriage was full of thick dust and there was a smell of burning.

She was so frightened she could hardly breathe.

She tried to stand up, but before she could find her balance, there was an almighty crash and, in a moment of total horror, another line of carriages loomed in towards them. There was a crash, far worse than any clap of thunder, as tons of metal clashed together at great speed. Then, with a thunderous roar, the carriage Connie was in tipped and rolled over on its side, throwing her backwards. She was hurting everywhere as she was buffeted about amongst broken seats, shards of glass and twisted metal.

It seemed ages before the banging and clattering stopped and they were left lying in a confused state. Where was the kind lady who had befriended her? Connie reached out and they managed to just about touch each other's fingers across the twisted metal that seemed to be everywhere. Their attempt to make contact must have moved something because more shattered glass showered down on them and they heard the male occupant of their carriage scream out in agony.

The noise of grinding and crashing metal continued. It was horrific. Then the carriage gave a great shudder as it settled.

Connie felt a hard blow to the side of her head and something heavy hit her across her chest. She struggled to protect her baby. She wanted to put her hands across her swollen belly or at least lift off whatever was pinning her down. She couldn't move either arm. She felt a terrible pressure, a great weight holding her down.

Her body had felt battered and bruised when she had got on the train, but now she knew her unborn baby had been hurt because in her belly there was such awful pain, burning and throbbing.

She heard male voices urging folk to stay as still as possible. She wanted to laugh. Stay still on this filthy floor with what felt like a ton weight on top of her? Did she have any choice?

Mercifully, it wasn't long before she was drifting in and out of rational awareness. Time had lost all meaning. Then voices were calling, 'There has been a terrible train crash but help is at hand. We'll get you out, you will be all right.'

Would she? Connie didn't believe she would ever be free of this heavy weight which was pinning her down. But she didn't have the energy to voice her thoughts; she was finding it difficult to breathe, it hurt so much.

Someone had once told her that God paid his debts without money.

Lord Jesus, please, I know I have sinned over and over again, but do I deserve what is happening to me today? I just want this awful, terrible pain to go away. Please, please, make it go away. And please, I want to see me mum and me dad.

Part of her prayer was answered. She no longer felt any pain. She had lost consciousness.

Chapter Nineteen

BAD NEWS TRAVELS FAST!

Winnie Paige came into her daughter's living room so quietly that Ella immediately knew she was the bearer of bad news.

For a moment her mother remained still. The news she had just been told had been such a shock and the events of the previous weeks were crowding into her mind. Then she roused herself, and taking the large pin out of her hat, she placed the hat and her gloves on the table and then took off her coat. Moving to the range, she lifted the kettle, which was already full of water, and pushed it nearer the hot plate to boil. The kettle had been black-leaded and like everything else in Ella's kitchen was sparkling clean. Unlike most folk's ranges, Ella's had two ovens, one large and one small. The smell that was filling the room told her that Ella was roasting a joint but also had made a bread pudding, which was in the smaller oven. The smell of fruit and cinnamon was mouth-watering.

'Well, lass, you've been busy this morning. I'll make us a brew an' hope that bread pudding will be ready to eat. What time does your shift start today?'

Winnie's voice was over-bright and she certainly was acting uneasily, her movements all quick and jerky.

'Mum,' Ella set two cups and saucers down on the table and turned to face her mother, 'I'm not daft, yer know. You've got something to say, and as you're taking for ever to spit it out, I can only imagine that it's bad news. Why don't you tell me what has happened? Get it over an' done with.'

The knuckles of Winnie's hands were showing white as she gripped the edge of the kitchen table. She took a deep breath and said, 'You heard about that train crash that happened midday yesterday, didn't you?'

'Yes, bad do, wasn't it? Not far out of Croydon apparently. Everyone was talking about it in the bar last night; it made the evening papers.'

Winnie's voice was thick with emotion as she said, 'Young Connie Baldwin was on that train.'

Ella's hands flew to cover her face. After a while she shook her head from side to side murmuring, 'Oh no, oh no.' Then, 'Was she badly hurt?'

'Plenty of tales flying around but nobody seems to know the full story. Her aunt and uncle and their son Reg are over here, stayed the night with Kate and Alf Baldwin from what I hear.'

Ella shuddered. 'I feel I should go and visit Connie's parents, ask if she's been badly hurt, but I'm probably the last person they would want to see. I'll more than likely hear more news when I get to work. There's not much goes on that doesn't get discussed in the Legion.'

Winnie looked anxious as she asked, 'You know Pete Jarvis, don't you?'

'Only that he's always been pretty friendly with my Den. I don't like him much, never have. Why are you asking?'

'Most folk believe that he's a right bent old lag, sell

fridges to Eskimos he could. It figures, 'cos a man is known by the company he keeps,' Winnie stated sharply. 'None the more for that, it seems he was in the district and apparently went straight to the scene of the crash and did all he could to help.'

'Did he see Connie? Or find out if she was badly hurt?'

'Not that I've heard, but Mr Taylor said he came into the corner shop for some cigarettes just as he was closing up and he looked so awful that he took him into their back room and Mrs Taylor gave him a mug of strong tea with a drop of the hard stuff in it. Apparently he poured his heart out to them. Best thing he could 'ave done, 'cos they reckon he was in a right old state of shock.'

Ella was getting exasperated. Why did her mother have to be so long-winded in getting to the point?

'Thought you were going to make the tea. I'm going to put me washing in the copper to soak and then we'll sit down and you can tell me what you know all in one piece, because dribbling a bit of news here an' there is driving me mad.'

'All I know is hearsay,' Winnie grumbled, but she did as Ella had bid, spooning three heaped teaspoons of tea into the big brown teapot then covering them with boiling water from the black kettle, all the time wishing that there was a drop of whisky knocking about here, but Ella didn't keep spirits in the house since Dennis had left. She had listened to Mrs Taylor's version of what Pete Jarvis had had to say, and the very thought of a pregnant young girl being involved in such a disaster had made her feel sick to her stomach. I hope to God they got her out safely, poor kid, she prayed.

Now, seated round the table, tea in front of them and a plate each which held a piece of steaming hot bread pudding, they were both silent, their heads buzzing with thoughts.

Ella's main thought was, Shouldn't Den be contacted?
Suddenly she voiced that question aloud.

'Not for us to interfere, is it, luv? I do think you're right, but whether or not the Baldwins will feel the same way is another thing entirely.'

'So you still don't know whether young Connie was hurt or not?'

'No, but according to Pete Jarvis, there couldn't have been many that escaped unharmed. He said the crash site was like nothing he had ever seen before. Coaches of one train were lying on their sides and another train had crossed into the oncoming track and been hit by a third. Wreckage was piled on either side of the second engine and two carriages had been forced on top of one another. Pete said the smells were awful, burning, oily grease everywhere, not to mention the blood. According to him it was a major alert: there were workers everywhere, firemen cutting into the smashed carriages, doctors and nurses crawling about in the wreckage helping the injured that they could manage to get to. Loads of ambulances. Policemen were guiding some of the casualties on to the sloping banks and sitting them down. Even those, Pete said, were all injured, bloodstained and covered with filth. Neighbours in the houses near by were very kind and helpful. Pete went with two other men to collect blankets that were offered. The ambulancemen did have their bright red blankets, but of course there wasn't nearly enough to cover all the folk that needed them.'

'Oh, Mother! All the things we've said about Connie, and to think she had to be caught up in an accident like this. I feel awful. Not knowing what to do is driving me mad.'

'Oh for God's sake, there's nothing you or I can do at the moment,' Winnie told her angrily. 'We just have to wait and see. If the girl has been injured she will be in hospital, and if not, please God, she'll be home with her family and then perhaps they will want to get in touch with Dennis. He has a right to know, especially if the baby has been hurt. There's one thing that Mrs Taylor told me this morning that's got me wondering. Connie's parents hadn't been expecting her home; they didn't seem to know how or why she was on that train. When Len Evans – you know, their next-door neighbour – came in the shop this morning, he didn't know what had happened to Connie, but he said Kate's sister and her husband arrived quite late, and it was nearly midnight when their son turned up, and Len said there was a hell of a ding-dong going on in there. Shouting and swearing by all accounts.'

'Ah well,' Ella sighed, 'I can't sit here all day nattering. I've got to get ready for work. Are you going to meet Babs from school this afternoon?'

'Yeah, course I am. Teddy won't come near nor by me, though. His mates call him a sissy if he walks home with his gran.'

Winnie stood up and fastened her hat securely with her hatpin, then shrugged her arms into her coat. 'I think it's more likely that you'll hear first if young Connie has been hurt; anyway, I might pop in the Legion myself at dinner time. Be great when they have the new part up and running. I'll be able to have meals in there on a regular basis then.'

Ella stood up too. 'Thanks, Mum, for coming in so early and telling me that Connie was on that train. I'd rather have heard it from you. I'll come to the door with you.'

'That's all right. Just don't get yerself worked up, no matter what you hear.'

'I won't, but I do hope somebody can contact Dennis.'

'Stop worrying over him. A bad penny always comes

back. I'll lay yer ten to one that his old man knows where he is.'

Ella closed the front door and leant against it, her heart beating nineteen to the dozen. She felt dreadful.

The information her mother had given her was a bit garbled and Ella was unsure of what to believe. Why had Connie Baldwin not told her folks that she was on her way home? She tried to comfort herself with the thought that no news was good news. In any case, she was bound to find out more once she was behind the bar of the Legion.

Fully dressed now, Ella glanced in the mirror. No one could describe her as plump and dowdy now. Since having been lucky enough to get herself a job that brought her into contact with people from all walks of life, she knew she was a different person. She worked hard and that had helped her to lose some weight, but the difference in her appearance was mainly down to the influence of Sadie Cohan. They had kept in touch, and Ella regarded Sadie as a true and valuable friend.

Today she was wearing a beige-coloured, plain, slim-fitting dress with a tailored coat made from matching material that hung neatly from the padded shoulders down to her calves. Her plain court shoes and her handbag were almost the same colour as her thick copper-coloured hair. She missed Dennis, of course she did, but in some ways his leaving had done her a power of good. It wasn't ambition that drove her, or the desire to have expensive things. It was the freedom to be herself, never having to be at the beck and call of Dennis when he came home in the early hours of the morning. Never having to lie awake wondering where he was and who he was with when she and the children hadn't seen him for days. Another great feeling was that having proved she could hold down a responsible job, she did not have to depend on others.

However, her insistent thoughts gave her little peace and she was relieved when it was time to leave for work.

As Ella pushed open the swing doors of the saloon bar, Mike Murray spotted her immediately and strode quickly to be by her side.

'Hallo, Ella,' he said, his voice full of sympathy. 'I take it you've heard the news?'

'Yes, pretty dreadful, isn't it? Have you heard if Connie Baldwin was hurt?'

'Yes,' he answered, and she knew he had been expecting the question. 'I'm afraid she's in hospital. Apparently they had to cut the poor lass out of the wreckage. We've just had the news on the radio. Nineteen dead and over fifty injured at the last count.'

Ella's face drained of colour. 'That's awful.'

'Yes,' Mike agreed. 'Folk 'ave been coming in telling us some ghastly stories. It must 'ave been a hell of a crash.'

'So who told you about young Connie?'

Mike sighed heavily, which told her more than any words could have done that Connie was in a bad way.

'Come on,' he said, taking hold of her elbow, 'take your coat off and I'll get you a brandy. In fact, I'll 'ave one with you.'

There were more customers than usual in the bar for this time of the day. They picked their way through to get behind the bar and soon they were leaning against the counter each with a glass between their hands.

Ella needed no telling that Mike knew something hideous had happened to Connie, but she didn't prompt him to talk about the details. He'd tell her in his own good time.

The silence between them was broken when Alf Baldwin came to the bar. The haggard look on his face had Ella expecting the worst, even though the poor man hadn't said a word.

171

'Just come from the hospital, 'ave yer, Alf?' Mike asked quietly.

'Yes, I've left her mum and her aunt up there sitting with Connie. We've come home to see to a few things but we'll be going back shortly. I'll 'ave a pint, please, Mike, and what will you 'ave?' he asked, turning to the tall, broad-shouldered young man standing at his side. 'This is me nephew, Reg. It's his mum an' dad that our Connie has been staying with.'

Reg was a tall, well-built young man with a head of slicked-back dark brown hair. He wore navy blue trousers and a white striped shirt with a dark tie that had been jerked loose and hung like a noose around the collar of his smart dark leather jacket.

His face seemed to tighten and he clenched his fists as he nodded at Mike before saying, 'I'll 'ave a pint and a whisky chaser.'

Ella stood where she was for a few minutes, her eyes on the young man. Something was eating away at him. Mike handed both men their drinks before asking for the latest news on Connie, and Ella felt that the question had been like putting a naked flame to a pool of petrol.

It was Reg who quickly spoke. 'If it weren't for my old man, my cousin would never 'ave been on that bloody train.' His voice was a sheer blast and every person in the bar turned to stare at him.

'Now, now, son, you had yer say t' yer father last night when you arrived. Let's leave it like that fer now. We don't want our dirty linen being washed in public, do we?'

'You can say what you damn well like, Uncle Alf, but I'm for letting the whole world know what a toerag my dad is.'

Ella drained her glass and moved further along the bar to start work.

It didn't take much working out, she thought.

Her mother had said that Reg had arrived at the

172

Baldwins' house very late last night, a while after his parents. Len Evans had said that no sooner had the son arrived than there had been a helluva bust-up. Connie apparently was on that train running away from something or someone, since neither of her parents had had any notice that she was on her way home.

Reg had downed his whisky and drunk more than half of his pint of beer, but the drink had not calmed him down. Quite the reverse.

Molly Riley stood close to Ella and quickly made the sign of the cross. 'Jesus holy Mary, will yer listen t' that young man's language?'

'Mike's letting him get away with it because you only have to look at him to see how upset he is,' Ella said.

'Our Connie was trapped in that bloody disaster for hours before the doctors and the paramedics could cut her free, and God alone knows if she's gonna make it.' Reg's voice was so full of anger that he was almost choking on his words. 'I'll tell yer what, though, Uncle Alf, if our Connie does die, then so will that lying, cheating, filthy shyster that passes for my father. I don't know for sure what it was he said or done t' Connie, but she didn't leave our house and get on a train without saying goodbye to me or me mum without some very good reason. If you hadn't pulled me off him last night I would have got the truth out of him, but the very fact that he shot out of the house the minute I accused him said it all for me.'

'Reg, will you leave it, please, people are listening to every word you're saying,' his uncle pleaded.

'OK, but sooner or later I will get the truth out of him an' then I'll 'ave the bastard, and make no mistake, I'll flatten him.'

'Sorry, Mike. I'll make sure he keeps his voice down.' Alf jerked a thumb at his nephew.

Mike leant towards Ella and whispered in her ear, 'He's

a holy terror, that young lad, but I bet he's got his facts right. Young Connie wouldn't have upped and left that house without so much as a word to anyone if something hadn't driven her away.'

'You're probably right, Mike, and I wouldn't be in 'is father's shoes when he does find out, 'cos I know him of old. That boy's got a temper. Always did 'ave, even as a child, an' I wouldn't guess it's got any better as he's got older.'

Just then the bar doors opened and two policemen came inside.

Mike came quickly from behind the bar and hurried towards them.

A quiet conversation was carried on, then Mike turned his head towards Mr Baldwin, nodded and beckoned him to come forward. The taller of the two policemen approached and he and Alf Baldwin each covered half the distance that lay between them. The quietness and patience of the constable's speech was enough to tell folk that he was the bearer of bad news. Whatever had been said had certainly sapped what little energy the poor man had left.

Dragging his feet, he returned to the bar, caught hold of his nephew's arm and very quietly said, 'Come on, Reg, we have to get back to the hospital.'

Ella shook her head in despair as she watched Alf Baldwin and his nephew follow the policemen.

Mike picked up the two dirty glasses and stared at Ella, and she raised her eyebrows at him. It was one of those rare moments that occur in everyone's life.

One of those times when there really isn't anything to say.

Chapter Twenty

ALF AND REG ARRIVED back at the hospital at two o'clock to find Connie's three sisters sitting in the corridor, empty coffee cups on a table beside them and looks of sheer misery on their faces.

'I take it there has been no change?' their father asked, not really expecting to receive a reply.

Amy, the eldest daughter, started to rise, but Reg laid a hand on her shoulder and said kindly, 'Sit where you are. I'll get us all a fresh coffee.'

The hot liquid brought a little colour to the girls' cheeks, and both Alf and Reg drank theirs gratefully.

'Who's sitting with yer sister now?' their father asked.

'Just Mum and Aunt Harriet.'

'Have yer seen anything of yer Uncle Jack?'

The three girls glanced at each other, but it was Sheila, the youngest, who answered. 'Oh yes, he turned up here all right,' she said sarcastically. 'Practically threw himself across the bed and kept muttering over and over again about how sorry he was. Two male nurses dealt with him very efficiently, told him not to come back at all today, and not even tomorrow unless he cleaned himself up and was sober.'

'See, I knew all along I was right. Something he said or did frightened the life out of Connie and made her start for home.' For a change Reg's voice was low, but that gave more emphasis to his words than if he had shouted them.

Suddenly Alf Baldwin was struggling to his feet. His chest was heaving, and he seemed unable to speak. He clutched at his chest, shaking his head slowly as tears filled his eyes. Swaying, he would have fallen if Reg hadn't wrapped his arms around his taut body and held him close.

'Sheila, go quietly, but fetch your aunt, and a doctor if you can find one. If not, bring a nurse. Be as quick as you can.'

It was Amy who took charge of the situation now. 'Reg, if I help you, shall we see if we can get my dad into the waiting room. It's only just over there.'

Within minutes Kate Baldwin had rushed into the room and dropped to her knees in front of her husband. He was sitting back in an armchair with his eyes closed, his face drained of colour.

'What's wrong, dear?' she asked, her voice trembling with concern.

Alf opened his eyes. 'It's just this sharp pain, it feels so tight right across here.' He rubbed a hand over his chest. 'I'll be all right in a minute.'

Kate was telling herself not to panic. She didn't like the look of her husband at all. His face was a terrible colour and he was having a lot of trouble breathing. She took hold of one of his hands and held it between both of hers, and using soft circular movements she massaged his fingers, which felt bitterly cold.

Suddenly there were people in white coats, and two trolleys were being pushed into the centre of the room. A male voice issued a command.

176

'We need to get him on to the floor, lying flat. And clear this room.'

No sooner were the words heard than all the Baldwin family and Reg Briggs were being herded out into the corridor.

Kate just succeeded in patting her husband's knee before scrambling to her feet. 'The doctors are here now, Alf, an' they'll help you.' All the while she was telling herself to stay calm, not to let her husband see how worried she really was.

Once on her feet she managed to gently kiss his forehead, but she couldn't put a smile on her face as she assured him, 'I'll be back in a minute.'

Next thing she knew, she was being led out of the room by a young nurse, and it sounded so dreadfully final as the door closed behind her.

A few whispered words and the ward sister quickly got the message.

'Come along, Mrs Baldwin, I've sent your family along to the canteen, and Mrs Briggs – your sister, isn't it? – is still sitting with your daughter, so we'll wait in my office.'

'He will be all right, won't he, Sister?'

It was such a sad question, and one that the sister could barely bring herself to answer. However, she did her best.

'Mr Baldwin couldn't be in better hands. We'll know more when the doctors have had a chance to examine him.'

'Whatever it is that's wrong with him must have caught him unawares. He didn't complain of feeling ill this morning.'

'Well, neither of you have had much sleep. All the stress and strain you've been through since the train crash has probably caught up with Mr Baldwin.' The sister put her hand on Kate's arm. 'Shall we both silently say a little prayer?'

Kate Baldwin covered her face with her handkerchief and between sobs prayed like she'd never prayed before. 'Dear God, my Alf doesn't deserve this. Please don't let him die. Not now. Our Connie needs him. I need him. Please help him.'

Brian Holmes had been a doctor at St Thomas's for almost fifteen years. He was a kindly man, tall and well built, with a shock of dark hair. Despite the fact that he had had to break bad news many times, he had never got used to doing it. Wasn't it bad enough that the Baldwins' young daughter lay lingering between life and death? Her parents had barely left the hospital since she had been brought in.

Obviously she had lost the baby she had been carrying. Her injuries were so severe he found it hard to believe that she hadn't given up the ghost herself by now. Three times she had almost died, and yet something or someone had kept her holding on.

Now, with no warning whatsoever, her father had suffered a massive heart attack and died immediately.

Some time had passed before Dr Holmes gave a light knock on the door and entered Sister's office. The doctor exchanged glances with her.

Oh dear God above! How were they supposed to break the news to Mrs Baldwin?

'Well, Doctor,' Kate spoke abruptly, 'how bad is my husband? He's never been ill in his life. You won't have to keep him here in the hospital, will you?'

Brian Holmes raised a hand to silence her.

'I am so sorry, Mrs Baldwin, there is no easy way of telling you that your husband suffered a massive heart attack and died almost instantly. There was nothing I or anyone else could have done for him. If it is any consolation to you, he didn't suffer.'

'No!' Kate screamed. 'You can't be telling me that my Alf is dead.'

The sister broke all the rules. She took the terrified woman into her arms and held her close, rubbing her back and speaking softly.

'You must try and be brave, Mrs Baldwin, you can't afford to break down. Connie still needs you. No one knows what's going to happen. She might regain consciousness at any time, and if you go to pieces that wouldn't help anyone.'

'First thing she'll ask for is her dad,' Kate sobbed into the sister's shoulder.

Less than one hour later a sad group were gathered around Connie's bed. Her mother, her three sisters, her Aunt Harriet and her cousin Reg.

It was as if Connie gave a gentle sigh, then passed away.

Harriet Briggs also sighed as she squeezed her sister's hand. But her sigh was one of relief. If Connie had lived she would have been crippled for life, and the fact that the baby had been crushed to death in her womb would have haunted her for ever. Keeping those thoughts to herself, Harriet whispered, 'God works in a mysterious way. Think about it, Kate. Connie is not on her own, her dad has gone with her, they'll make the journey together.'

At that point in time none of what Harriet was saying made any sense at all to Kate. She was grateful that her three other daughters were there, and they each held on to her as she bent over the bed and kissed her youngest daughter goodbye.

It was early evening by the time they all got out of the hospital.

'A drink is what we need,' Reg said loudly as he looked

179

at his watch. 'Yes, it's turned opening time. Let's make for the nearest pub.'

His mother was in two minds about her son. This last couple of days he had come through with flying colours. No one could have asked more of him. But she could read his thoughts as he sipped the dark whisky. She needed no telling he was not finished with his father yet.

'Come on, Auntie, drink up that Scotch,' Reg urged, 'then I'll get us a taxi. The quicker I get all of you home, the better. There's nothing we can do tonight except see you get some rest. Time enough in the morning to start to sort things out.'

Luck was still not on their side. To get a taxi to stop at that time of the day was an impossibility. Every passing cab already had a fare.

'Duke, Duke!' A large black saloon car had pulled in to the kerb a few yards up the road and a young man was calling and beckoning.

Reg took to his heels and ran. Opening the passenger-side door, he poked his head into the interior of the car and a hurried conversation took place. Running back to his family, he gasped, 'Christ, that's a bit of luck. That's Charlie Seymour, he's doing a favour for a car hire firm, picking that car up from being valeted and taking it back to the showrooms. He'll take us all home; he's got his own big van back on the site.'

'He'll never get us all in, will he?' Harriet asked.

'Come on, he can't hang about for long. There's a bench seat in the front; you, Mum, and Auntie Kate can sit there and I'll squeeze in the back with the three girls. Even if I squat down on the floor it's got to be better than getting on an' off of buses.'

Reggie's mate had kept the engine running. They piled in, and within minutes were on their way.

'The car showrooms are just off the King's Road, so

180

'I'll let you lot out by the Albert Bridge. Wait for me there. I'll only be five or ten minutes, then I'll get you all home.'

Reg nodded. 'You're a bloody good mate, Charlie. You'll never know how glad I was t' hear yer calling me.'

'Been a bad day, 'as it?'

'You can say that again, pal, but you've turned up trumps.'

Charlie drove across London by way of Hammersmith and soon they were heading down the King's Road, then turning into Oakley Street, with the wonderful Albert Bridge at the end of it.

'Shan't be long,' Charlie shouted as they piled out.

With the five women safely on the pavement, Reg jumped into the front passenger seat and the car sped off.

'What a day,' Harriet Briggs murmured.

No one answered her.

The three girls were walking up and down, each lost in her own thoughts. To have lost a sister and their father all in the space of one afternoon was a pretty heavy blow. How the hell was their mother going to cope?

Amy suddenly realized that being the eldest, all the problems of arranging the funeral would fall on her shoulders. She felt sick to the bottom of her stomach. Would there have to be two separate funerals? God above, she wouldn't know where to begin.

Harriet had her arm around her sister's shoulders as together they leant against the brickwork and stared out at the wide, quick-flowing River Thames. All around them life was still going on in London: people were hurrying home from work, tugs were hooting, gulls were scavenging for food, and the smell was like no other.

Kate gave a deep, heavy sigh as she placed her hand on top of her sister's.

'I knew in my heart it would be better if my Connie

died, her injuries were so bad, but now . . .' Her voice trailed off.

'I know, luv, for Alf to be taken like that is a mighty shock. The only consolation is that Connie has him with her. She's not on her own.'

Kate leant forward, put her elbow on the ledge of the bridge and rested her forehead in the palm of her hand. With her other hand she clutched her sister's arm.

After a bit, 'What do you think, Harriet?' she asked.

'About what?'

'Was my Connie a real bad lot? Her carrying on with Dennis Dryden has ruined the lives of two families, and there's still so many questions to which we don't know the answers. Why do you think she upped and left your house without so much as a word to you?'

Harriet bit her lip, took a deep breath, and then spoke, her voice coming out clear and full of concern. 'We both know Connie was not a bad lot, as you put it. That Dennis Dryden could charm the birds out of the trees and Connie is not the only young girl who has been caught by the likes of him. You don't need much imagination to know what he promised her.' Her voice was tight with temper as she added, 'I bet he promised her the moon and the stars to go with it.'

Kate lifted her head high and managed a slight smile as she looked at her sister.

'How did she act while she was staying with you? Did she behave herself?'

'She was fine,' Harriet answered sadly, 'she really was.' She shook her head as tears flooded her eyes and blurred her vision. 'I'm blaming meself. I should never have left her in the house alone with Jack.'

'What are you talking about?' The implications of what her sister had just said had Kate's mind working over-time.

Harriet wished she hadn't said anything. She stared at Kate, guilt filling her mind, and tried to turn her head away, but Kate caught her chin with one hand and tilted it up so she had no choice but to look at her.

'Wasn't your Reg in the house when Connie left?'

'Yes,' Harriet whispered, trembling inside, 'but when I questioned him about it, he admitted he was still in bed. He hadn't seen Connie at all that morning.'

'Harriet! For Christ's sake. Am I hearing right?'

'Wait, luv, just hold yer horses. I don't really *know* anything. Honestly, Connie was a real gem while she was with me, but I saw the way Jack had been watching her.' She looked into her sister's face, pleading for understanding.

'So what your Reg has been hinting at may well be the bloody truth. Christ Almighty, I don't know what t' believe. Over these last few weeks, one minute I've been blaming my own girl for all the trouble she'd caused, an' the next minute I've been persuading meself she'd been wronged and left stranded to deal with it all on her own. My Alf didn't blame her, she was the apple of his eye, the last-born, the baby of the family.'

The honking of Charlie's horn stopped any more speculation.

The two older women linked arms as they walked towards the roadway where Charlie had parked his white van. Never had Kate felt so heavy-hearted. What had started out as a terrible day was getting worse as the hours went by.

Reg sat up front with Charlie while the women travelled in the back of the van. No one bothered to speak, though there were plenty of questions that needed asking, and answers would have to be found at some stage.

Kate watched the different expressions flicker over her sister's face and heaved a great sigh. Harriet looked awful.

Her straggly grey hair, usually so neat, had escaped from beneath her hat, and her dear kind face was the colour of grey slate. What was she blaming herself for? If Jack Briggs had assaulted Connie, the blame couldn't be laid at Harriet's door. She was the one who went out to work, brought home the money that put food on the table and paid the rent. Kate couldn't remember when Jack Briggs had ever held down a decent, steady job.

But surely not. The very idea was unthinkable! Connie was his niece. Yet there had to be a good reason for her to leave the house and get on a train to come home without saying a word to anyone. Not even getting in touch with her father to meet her at Victoria station.

Had she had a row with her uncle and stormed off?

If half the accusations Reg had thrown at his father last night were any way near the truth, then by God the man deserved to be hung, drawn and quartered.

Why oh why did I ever send her away from her own home?

Pride! Downright stupid pride. Because neighbours talked. My Connie wasn't the first girl that got herself pregnant by a married man, and it's damn sure she won't be the last. I should have stood up for her. Kept her home where she belonged, shown her that no matter what she had done, her family loved her.

Too late now to tell her anything.

Charlie brought the van to a halt in the middle of the long row of old terraced houses. Blackshaw Road, where everyone knew their neighbours' business.

Charlie opened the back doors of his van, and he and Reg were helping the women down when suddenly Reg turned and ran towards the house. The look on Harriet's face frightened Kate half to death.

Jack Briggs was sitting on the pavement, his back

184

propped up against the wall. The very look of the man was appalling!

Reg was the first to reach him. He shook him roughly, shouting at him to get up. Then he quickly stepped back; the sour smell of Jack's breath was revolting. That was not enough to deter his son, though. Reg stared down at his father's face. Jack had not shaved or washed, and by the look of his jacket he had vomited.

'You filthy swine.' Reg's face was dark with fury. 'You couldn't even keep your rotten hands off a young girl who was a member of yer own family. I should have known why Connie was afraid of you. Because she was pregnant, you tried t' 'ave her over right under me mum's nose.' The words were emphasized by sharp kicks.

'Keep your voice down! Do you want the whole street t' know what's been going on? You wanna remember, Reggie, we've got t' go on living here.'

Reg shook his head as if to shake off his temper. 'I'm sorry, Aunt Kate. I'll get Charlie to give me a hand with him. We'll put in the back of the van and then we'll sling the bastard in the river, and don't tell me my dad can't swim, 'cos I don't give a monkey's if he dives deep down to the bloody mud.'

Kate looked at Harriet. Under different circumstances they would have had a good laugh, but right at this moment they both doubted they would ever laugh again.

'Come on, girls, it's about time we took charge,' Amy declared loudly. 'Let's leave the men to it and get ourselves inside the house. Sheila, you put the kettle on. What our mum and Aunt Harriet need is a good strong cup of tea.'

If they were ever going to get any sleep tonight, she needed to see that their tea was well laced with a good strong dose of whisky.

And she had already decided that she would make sure they got it!

Chapter Twenty-one

ELLA WAS WASHED AND dressed when the children came downstairs, the table was set for breakfast and the bread board was piled high with thick slices of bread ready for toasting. Even though it was still August, there was a bright fire burning in the grate. It paid to keep the fire going most days because the back boiler made sure there was hot water for washing, the two ovens were constantly used for cooking and the big black kettle was always simmering away on the top of the hot range.

Babs and Teddy were scrambling to sit up to the table when they heard Gran's voice calling out, 'It's only me,' as she let herself in and came down the passage.

'Morning, Mum,' Ella muttered.

'Morning, Gran,' the kids said in unison.

'You're up and about early,' Ella commented.

'Well, there wasn't any more news about Connie Baldwin, only that she was holding her own, but I did hear about Alf Baldwin from the milkman. What a shock, eh?' Winnie said, sounding really upset. 'I guess all of you at the Legion were told last night.'

'Yes, Mike had given the Legion's number to the family

and told them if they needed any help not to hesitate to ring. But nobody expected Mr Baldwin to pop off like that, did they?'

'Poor man, too many worries piled on his shoulders one after the other. Didn't expect him to have a heart attack and go as quick as that, though. Nice ordinary bloke he was; if he couldn't do you a good turn he certainly wouldn't do yer a bad one. Not a fair world, is it?'

'No one ever promised it would be, my luv,' Ella said, giving her mother a hug.

'But Mum, I feel so guilty for all the nasty things I said about young Connie.' A single tear trickled from Ella's eye, down her cheek, and she quickly brushed it away.

Winnie lifted a hand to stroke her daughter's face. 'Try not to worry, Ella, none of this is your fault.'

Ella leant over the sink and put a handful of soda crystals into the washing-up bowl. If what her mother was saying was true, then why did she feel so bad about everything?

There was a commotion at the table as the children argued over the use of the sugar-pot for their porridge, and Ella tutted with anger.

'Stop quarrelling. Get on and eat it while it's still hot,' she ordered. 'You staying for a while, Mum? If so, start making the toast for me, will yer.'

Just then Babs tugged at the milk bottle that Teddy was doing his best to hold on to, and as was bound to happen, it went flying, spraying milk all across the table.

'Behave yerselves, I've enough to cope with today without you two playing up,' their mother yelled.

'It was her fault,' Teddy grumbled.

'No it wasn't. He always wants to grab everything first.'

Ella thumped her fist on the table. 'Enough! Get on an' eat yer breakfast, else I'll whack the pair of you and then I'll know I've got the right one.'

Brother and sister glared at each other, then Teddy took advantage of the brief lull in hostilities to grab the first piece of toast his gran put on the table.

Babs tried to take it from him but he slapped her hand away. 'You're a pain in the neck, you are,' he muttered.

'Oh yeah?' Ella stood with her hands on her hips. 'You, my son, will 'ave a pain in yer arse if I whack yer backside with my shoe.'

Winnie was worried. It wasn't very often that Ella lost her temper, and certainly not with her own children. By and large she had the patience of Job.

'Come on, you two, eat up and then get yerselves ready and I'll walk to school with you. Maybe I'll even treat you both to a packet of sweets to eat in your lunchtime.'

That put a smile on the kids' faces, but Winnie was being crafty. She knew Teddy wouldn't want to be seen walking with his gran, so a bribe was necessary. Besides, the sooner she got Babs and Teddy out of the house, the sooner she might find out exactly what was niggling away at her daughter this morning, 'cos a hundred to one something very bad had upset her.

By the time Winnie returned to the house, clutching a bag of freshly baked bread rolls, she was pleased to notice that her daughter's temper, which had flared so quickly, had receded somewhat.

With a fresh pot of tea, a jar of marmalade and a full round of butter laid beside the rolls all set out on the table, mother and daughter sat themselves down facing each other.

'So, are you going to tell me what's eating you, luv, or did you just get out of bed the wrong side this morning?'

'Mum.' Ella's voice was low, and the very sound of it rang warning bells in Winnie's head.

'Mum.' She tried again. 'It's obvious you've heard that

188

poor Mr Baldwin died very suddenly, but what you don't seem to know is that his daughter died soon after he did.'

Winnie's hands flew to cover her mouth and the colour drained from her face. Some minutes ticked by before she was able to speak. Then, shaking her head slowly from side to side, she muttered, 'Dear Jesus, that poor woman, what she must be going through.'

One phrase was going through Ella's mind. Over and over again she was asking herself, Where the hell is Dennis? Surely he should be here shouldering some of the responsibility.

Last night, when the news of Alf Baldwin's sudden death had reached the club, Ted Dryden had been in the bar. Connie Baldwin was still alive when Ella had decided that she was unable to stay neutral. She had approached her father-in-law with the suggestion that at least his son should be made aware of Mr Baldwin's death and the fact that poor Mrs Baldwin was having to cope with the likelihood that Connie might also die.

Her father-in-law's voice and manner had been abrupt but not unkind. He had said he couldn't say where his son was to be found, but on the other hand he hadn't said he didn't know. Played his cards very close to his chest, did Dennis's father.

Winnie pulled herself together, poured milk into each cup and then, lifting the teapot, filled the cups to the brim. Talking as if to herself, she was saying, 'You don't expect your children to die before you do, but to lose your husband and your youngest girl both within the space of a few hours must be more than a body can take. Oh, that poor, poor woman.'

'Yeah, I know, Mum, my heart aches for Mrs Baldwin. Her Connie and my Den didn't know what they were starting, did they?'

'They didn't stop to think, Ella, none of us do. So often we let our hearts rule our heads.'

Ella sighed at hearing her mother's true words.

They ate their breakfast in silence, though neither of them managed more than one bread roll.

'It's a queer how-d'-yer-do,' Winnie remarked as she helped her daughter to clear the breakfast table. 'According to what his father has told you, Dennis has disappeared off the face of the earth. When yer think about it, that young Connie Baldwin got the rough end of the stick, didn't she?'

'How do you work that one out?' Ella asked.

'Well, to be shoved off to live with an aunt and uncle just 'cos her mother was feeling the shame of having a sixteen-year-old-daughter pregnant by a married man wasn't right, and by all accounts all the time Connie was away, Dennis never once made contact. Says a lot for your ol' man, don't it? Full of big talk, supposed to think the world of his children, but first sign of trouble and he scarpers, leaving everyone to fend for themselves. Still, that's always been your Den's motto. "I'm all right Jack!" Sod everyone else. He's always been a nasty piece of work. A big man with his fists when it came to keeping you in line.'

In spite of feeling as if she was drowning in sadness, Ella almost wanted to smile. There was something immensely comforting about her mother. No two ways about it, she always called a spade a spade!

'Mum, can I leave you to tidy up here and make the beds? I'd better get in to work a bit early today. You can bet your life the place will be packed this morning; half the East End will want to know all the gory details of what has been going on.'

'Yes, luv, I'll see to everything, you get yerself off.'

'Thanks, Mum,' Ella said as she slipped her jacket on. Somehow she wasn't looking forward to this coming shift.

★　　★　　★

190

She had only walked a few yards when Reggie Briggs came out of the corner shop.

'Off t' work, Ella?' he asked cautiously.

'Yeah, needs must,' then, feeling that she ought to say more, she added, 'I am so sorry, Reg, so . . .' but she couldn't find words to describe the way she was feeling, because although none of these terrible happenings were of her making, and certainly not her fault, she had never felt like she did now. Never in her whole life.

'I know, I know, Ella, none of us know what to say or what to think.' Then, taking hold of her arm, he said, 'I'll walk to the Legion with you. I could use a drink.'

As they walked, it was Reg who started the conversation.

'It's my Aunt Kate I feel the most sorry for, she's blaming herself for so much.'

Ella knew what he meant. 'D'you know, Reg, your aunt and uncle had the happiest marriage I've ever known. They lived for each other.'

'I know, only makes it a bloody sight worse, don't it? Me aunt won't know how to live without him.' He stood still for a moment and took a deep breath before saying, 'We can all be so damn clever after an event. It was a mistake to send me cousin to go and stay with me mum and dad. Don't get me wrong, my Aunt Kate thought she was doing it for the best. She says herself now she should have been bolder and not given a damn for the gossips, let them get on with it and say what they liked.

'My mum is a gem, though, and she really did her best to care for Connie. Up until now she's never willingly opened her eyes to what a slimy toad my dad is. By God, there are some evil so-an'-so's in this world, but he takes the biscuit. I may as well tell you now, 'cos sooner or later the whole town will get to know. He forced himself on our Connie.'

Seeing the look of shock on Ella's face, Reg quickly added, 'Oh yes he did, and when you think about it, pestering his own niece in the state she was in was really acting dirty.'

Ella stopped walking and stared at the strapping young man beside her. His eyes looked haunted and he looked far older than he was. She let him go on talking. That was all he needed at the moment, a good listener. It was the only way he would get some of this horror out of his system.

'When I was a kid, I used to have to watch my dad treating Mum so badly 'cos I knew I wasn't a match for him. I could never understand why she stayed with him. Many's the time he's knocked her black and blue. As soon as I could, I left home.' Reg's voice was very tense as he continued. 'But things are different now, and if he so much as shows his face near me again, he's gonna realize that. If he wants to bully anyone, he can 'ave a go at me, and I'll soon put him straight.'

Ella felt such pity for this lad. He might act tough and let everyone think he was streetwise and well able to take care of himself, yet what had happened had knocked him for six. He had been forced to grow up and face reality almost overnight. She didn't know what to say, and was relieved when they reached the club and Reg held the door open for her.

One foot inside the place and Ella pulled a face. There were three times the normal number of customers in the bar and the club was buzzing with a variety of different stories about what had happened to Mr Baldwin.

Ella left Reg to join his mates while she went behind the bar.

'Are we glad to see you, Ella.' Tom spoke for himself and Derrick. 'Haven't had a minute to go down and do any cellar work, an' the way things are going, both the mild and the lager barrels will need changing.'

'If nothing else, gossip about a tragedy is always good for trade.' Derrick grinned at Ella as he hung a towel over an empty pump. 'Will you be OK by yerself till Molly turns up?'

'She's just coming through the double doors now,' Ella told him. 'You two get away, we'll manage all right.'

''Allo, Molly, you're well needed here this morning, the news is all so sad.'

Molly only just managed to sound civil as she said, 'Good morning, Mrs Turner, don't need to ask you what's brought you out for a drink so early in the day.' With that she pushed by and went to join Ella behind the bar.

The two women hugged each other, both on the verge of tears.

'So hard to take it all in, isn't it?' Molly commented. 'And it's so wrong that folk don't all turn out for the best of reasons. There always has to be the street gossip like Nellie Turner.'

'You weren't on yesterday, Molly, so how did you get to hear the news?'

'I went out to do a bit of shopping in the afternoon and the whole street was shocked that Mr Baldwin had died so suddenly, but you know I live opposite the Baldwins', and earlier on I had seen Jack Briggs slumped down half on the pavement and half in what you could call their front way. Wasn't nothing t' do with me, I don't deal with drunks. Then later in the evening a big van draws up, and oh dear, it doesn't bear thinking about.

'Kate and her girls and the aunt got out of the back of the van, and then you never heard such a commotion in all your life. The noise drew me to the window, and hellish it was to see a lovely young man laying into his own father, and him on the ground as it so happened.'

'You mean you actually witnessed Reg giving his father a good hiding?'

The conversation had to be put on hold there. Customers were clamouring to be served and the two barmaids were run off their feet.

'Are there going to be any meals today?' more than one customer wanted to know.

'Do you know if there is?' Molly asked Ella.

'When I came in, Mike told me that Beryl was going to rustle up a few dishes, but so far I haven't even seen so much as a sandwich.'

Ella was concentrating on pulling a pint of Guinness when the creamy flow ceased and all she could get was a hiss and spitting. She could see the top of Mike's head where he stood at the end of the bar, and she shouted, 'Mike, will you call down and tell Tom that the draught Guinness has gone.'

With a few minutes' lull, Molly answered Ella's question.

'Yes, more's the pity, and there was me thinking he was such a nice, kind and considerate lad.'

'I think you got it right first time around, Molly. Anything that was dished out to Jack Briggs would seem to me well and truly deserved.'

'And how would you be knowing that?' Molly asked with a toss of her head.

'Well, from piecing bits of information together, it turns out that he had been making Connie's life a misery every time she was left alone in the house with him. That's why she was on that train coming home. He violently attacked her.' Ella was choked as she wiped tears from her eyes. 'If it hadn't been for that dirty old man, that young girl would never have been on that train and she would still be alive today.'

Molly made the sign of the cross and murmured, 'Holy Mary Mother of God, are you saying that her own uncle raped her?'

'It would seem so. I suppose he thought that since she was under his roof and pregnant, he was entitled to take liberties.'

'Good gracious me!' Molly was appalled. 'This goes from bad to worse.'

'You can say that again,' Ella said as she pulled hard on the pump. At least some things were going right. The Guinness was back to normal, rich and dark with a thick creamy head.

It was a long, tense morning shift and every member of the staff was more than relieved when Mike called, 'Time, gentlemen, please.'

Ella was moving amongst the tables emptying ashtrays, collecting glasses and wiping tabletops when suddenly she had a queer feeling that somebody was watching her.

She raised her head and immediately it was as if she was turned to stone. Her eyes were wide open and staring as if she was seeing a ghost.

For there, leaning against the wall, was her husband.

Chapter Twenty-two

REG BRIGGS HAD NO choice but to get down to the business of making the arrangements for the burying of his cousin and his uncle. His aunt was in no state to make any decisions.

'First off I'm going to get in touch with an undertaker,' he said whilst they were all sitting finishing breakfast.

'I'll come with you,' Amy offered.

'Thanks.' Reg accepted her offer eagerly. 'Wasn't looking forward one bit to going on me own. Before we set out, I think we should make a list, and for that we shall need your help, Aunt Kate.'

'Yes,' said Amy. 'It would be much easier, Mum, if you could let us know what you would like.'

Writing pad and pencil at the ready, the three of them sat around the table.

'Aunt Kate, which undertaker do you think? I don't know this area very well.' Reg lowered his voice every time he spoke to his aunt.

'Well, there's the Ashley brothers, they've always been known to do a decent, respectful funeral.'

'If that's what you want, Mum, though lots of people

prefer cremation these days.' Amy met her mother's angry look without flinching.

'Your father and your sister are getting a Christian burial, so we'll have no talk of cremation if you don't mind,' wailed Kate. 'It makes me feel terrified just thinking about burning people.'

'That's all right, Mum, that's why Reg is making a list, just to be sure we've got everything as you want it to be.'

A short silence followed that outburst until Reg asked, 'Next person to get hold of is a vicar, isn't it? You do want a church service for them both, I presume, and a vicar will be able to advise us on a plot in the cemetery.'

Discussing all the details and being relieved of most of the responsibility made Kate Briggs feel a little better. At least she wasn't on her own. 'Well, there is the Reverend Clifford James. He lives in the vicarage next to the big church behind the market. Can't say as how I've been a regular church-goer, except Monday afternoons for the mothers' meeting – I never miss that – and you were all christened in that church.'

'So the Reverend James knows the family?'

'Yes, slightly, but me mostly 'cos he always looks in of a Monday afternoon and has a cup of tea with us. You can talk to him about hymns, and maybe he will want to know a bit about Connie and your father.'

'That all sounds straightforward enough, Aunt Kate, but seeing as how my Uncle Alf has lived here all his life, don't you think we should put a notice in the local paper?'

'Well, we'll see. But first you've got to get a date for the funeral . . .' Kate Baldwin hesitated. 'Do you think it's necessary to have people come back to our house for a drink and a bite to eat? Some of yer dad's relations we ain't seen for ages, but people do usually travel quite a long way to attend family funerals. Besides, I think perhaps it helps, seeing old friends and relations; you can have a bit of a talk and remember old times, especially when our Connie was a baby. Somehow I think that will take the edge off all the sadness.'

The old-fashioned custom of having a wake had not occurred to Amy, but she thought it made sense. 'Yes, Mum, you're right. We'll organize something. I'm sure a couple of our neighbours will be only too pleased to help out with seeing to the food.'

'Well, that seems to be everything for now, so Amy and I will get going.' Reg got to his feet, folded his written list in half and placed it in his top pocket. 'You'll be all right, Auntie, won't you? Sheila's just put the kettle on; she's gonna make you a nice fresh cup of tea.'

Kate sat sipping her tea. She was still finding it hard to realize that she had lost two of her loved ones.

Suppose I ought to be thinking about flowers. Connie is easy, the prettiest posy that the florist can make. No wreath for her, at least not from her mum. Alf was a different matter altogether. As far as Kate could remember, he had never bought flowers for anyone in his life. Even for close family deaths the buying of the wreaths had been left to her. Alf had always been an honest, hard-working man, a good provider for the essential things in life, but buying flowers would never have entered his head.

Bless him. He shall have some beauties now. I'll go on my own to choose them, she vowed.

The final day had dawned. And that was the trouble.

They had bought two adjoining plots so that father and daughter could lie side by side. When the earth covered the coffins, what could be more final than that?

The narrow London street had never before seen anything like it.

In every house the blinds and curtains had been drawn before the hearse came slowly into view with a second one following closely behind. Each was drawn by grey horses, a black cloth draped across their backs.

All the women mourners were dressed from head to toe in black; each wore a hat stripped of any adornment and replaced by a wide black ribbon. The men had turned out in strength to pay their last respects. They walked tall and upright, smart in their dark suits, white shirts and black ties.

On the pavement men removed their hats and bowed their heads.

No one had set eyes on Jack Briggs since his son had laid into him, and the mourners were more than grateful that he had stayed away. Every member of the family knew they would need all the strength they could muster to get through today.

Kate Baldwin stepped out of her house looking very poised and dignified. As she neared the front gate she raised her head, and her eyes had to gaze on not one but two coffins.

The sad sight was too much.

Her body shook and she released great gulping sobs of pain and would have fallen to the ground had not the strong arms of two male mourners grasped her one each side and helped her into the motor-car.

There would be no harsh words of judgement against young Connie Baldwin. Not today.

Her sins had been well and truly paid for.

Dennis Dryden had suggested that both he and Ella should go to the funeral.

Ella had flatly refused. She was convinced that they would be the last people the Baldwin family would wish to see in the church.

She had sent a card of condolence, really aching inside for poor Kate Baldwin's sorrow, yet unable to find words that would truly express her sympathy.

At last it was all over. Friends had left the house first, and now all the talking between relatives was coming to an end. Reg and Amy, seeing them off, watched the last car disappear and then, with a great feeling of relief, turned and went back into the house.

For once Ella couldn't face serving behind the bar of the working men's club. Not tonight, she told herself over and over again. If some of Mr Baldwin's mates came into the club, all chewing over the facts of what had happened, airing their views out loud, never mind whether they were right or wrong, it would be more than she could stand.

'Please, Mum, go up to the corner telephone box and call Mike for me, will you?'

'And what am I supposed to say to him?'

'Tell him I'm not well, that'll do.'

'No, luv, I'm not gonna do any such thing. Go yourself, tell him the truth. You know darn well Mike will understand. He knows there's been a lot of pressure on you lately.'

Ella reluctantly made the call herself, and as usual her mother was right.

'Ella, you take a couple of days off if you like,' Mike said quickly. 'I should have thought on, it's been pretty rough on you one way and another. We'll see you when you've given yourself time to calm down.'

'Thanks, Mike, you're a good bloke.'

'You're not so bad yerself, Ella,' he said laughing as he replaced the receiver.

Heaving a sigh of relief, Ella came out of the telephone box, and was lost in thought when she saw Dennis. He was standing in the middle of the pavement, blocking her way. When he had turned up in the club they had spoken only a few words to each other and she had made it perfectly clear that that was how she wanted things to remain.

'Ella, please, we need to talk,' he begged. 'Go home, see to the children and then meet me somewhere. That's not too much to ask, is it?' Then he smiled. Nothing had changed. His smile had always been amazing, and it lit up his whole face, causing his brilliant blue eyes to sparkle.

Ella wouldn't admit it even to herself, but her heart was thumping like mad as he took hold of her arm and began to walk beside her.

She felt ill at ease, agitated by this unexpected meeting. She also felt her appearance was not up to scratch. Today having been so sad, she had not bothered to really do her hair nor to put any make-up on her face. There was, however, nothing she could do about it until she got home. Her feelings were made worse because he looked every inch a very successful man. Tall, broad-shouldered, wearing a dark suit that had obviously been handmade by an excellent tailor. He hadn't altered in that respect. Nothing but the best for Den.

He said, 'Is there anywhere you'd prefer to go this evening?'

'Do you really want to talk civilly and seriously to me?' she asked him doubtfully.

'I wouldn't be here if I didn't.'

'Haven't you anything better to do?'

'Like what?'

'Some dodgy deal to fix or someone's palm to grease so that you make sure you get a contract you're after.'

'Oh, please, Ella, you're not going to start all that again, are you?'

Ella smiled at him icily. 'Why not? You're not going to

201

try and convince me that you've changed that much, surely?'

'You're determined not to give me a chance, aren't you?'

'Can you blame me?'

'No.' He shook his head, accepting this.

She said, 'I must go home. Mum will be wondering what to give the kids for their tea.'

'Will you come out for the evening if I pick you up about half seven?'

She did not reply at once, and for a long moment Dennis thought she was going to refuse.

Then she smiled. 'All right.'

'Good. I'll take you somewhere nice, we'll 'ave a slap-up meal and then we can talk. Get down to brass tacks.'

Ella laughed bitterly as she said, 'A posh invitation from my own old man; I'd better spend some time putting on the powder and the paint. We can't have folk saying you've lost yer touch, Den, taking an old bird like me out on the town.'

They looked at each other and suddenly they dissolved into laughter, and Ella felt her heart grow lighter, because it was the first time they had laughed together for a very long time.

Had she done the right thing, agreeing to go out for a meal with Dennis tonight? So much water had passed under the bridge.

While her mother cooked tea, Ella sat looking through the children's homework with them, but her heart wasn't it. When young Connie Baldwin had died she had vowed that she never wanted to see Dennis ever again, mainly because of the upheaval he had caused in the lives of their children.

Seeing him today had reminded her of just how much she had missed him.

When she got into bed at night she would read a book for quite some time. On other occasions she would lie awake and remind herself that Dennis had buggered off and left her with two young children and more often than not without a regular income. First off, life without him had been so empty, but with the help of her mother and Sadie Cohan, she had found the strength and the determination to turn her life around. She was much more independent, dressed differently, looked different, and indeed she was a wholly different person. She was proud of the fact that she had pulled herself together, got a job and become independent.

With the light out and the house quiet, the big double bed seemed so empty, and she would be lying to herself if she didn't admit that she missed Dennis. There had been some wonderful times in the early years of their marriage. Then Den had changed, become Jack-the-lad, and family life didn't matter any more.

It was a big world out there, deals were there for the taking, and Dennis had made sure he got his share of what was on offer, whether by fair means or foul.

Ella spent a great deal of time getting ready. First she rubbed her hair with a scented oil that Sadie had told her to buy, then she brushed it hard until her arm ached. By the time she had put the bulk of it up into a French pleat and left tendrils to dangle across her forehead and down over her ears, she was well pleased with the result. It was glossy and the chestnut glints shone through. She had decided to wear a plain black dress that ran straight from the shoulders down to her calves. It had a square neckline and long chiffon sleeves. To the left-hand shoulder of the dress she fixed a sparkling emerald-green brooch. Sheer silk stockings and high-heeled court shoes gave the finishing touches.

Since Ella had worked at the British Legion, she had become a dab hand at putting on her make-up, and the result this evening was almost professional.

'Mum, how do I look?' Ella gave a little twirl and Babs exclaimed, 'Smashing,' while even Teddy said, 'Wow.'

Winnie was more cautious. 'You're living dangerously, if you ask me. I just don't want to see you hurt again, but your mind is your own. You make yer own decisions.'

Ella didn't answer her mother, because if she had done, she would have said, 'That's exactly what I intend to do.'

As she stepped out of the front door, she was struck at how wintry the weather had turned. It had been a dingy, cloudy day, but at least it had stayed dry for the funeral. Now it was a cold evening, with a strong wind blowing in from the river, and she was thankful that her mother had loaned her a white cashmere stole which she was aware looked very elegant draped around her shoulders. She smiled softly to herself. This stole must have come into her mother's possession via Sadie; they both had a lot to thank the Cohan family for.

Dennis had knocked at the door and then gone back to sit in his car. The minute Ella appeared, he was out like a shot and holding the front passenger door open for her. The first thing that struck her was that he had a different car, and when thoughts began to run through her head as to why he might have decided to change cars, she immediately told herself it was none of her business. Tonight of all nights she was not going to allow herself, or Dennis for that matter, to start raking over old coals.

'You look great, Ella, so different,' said Dennis.

All the effort had been worth while. At least he had noticed.

As soon as she was seated in the car, Dennis offered a travelling rug to lay across her knees.

'Thank you, Dennis,' she said, surprised.

'On our way then,' he said, turning the key in the ignition.

Ella watched the narrow streets and soot-stained buildings disappear, and soon the car had crossed the Thames and they were driving through Fulham. Once they had passed the great power station the whole outlook changed. There were terraces of tall houses, and trees growing along the pavements.

'Where are we going?' Ella felt compelled to ask.

Dennis grinned. 'To Crystal Palace.' Then he turned his head and, seeing Ella's look of astonishment, added, 'To Norwood actually.'

The only thing that Ella knew about Norwood was that it wasn't far from Croydon.

Den looked at her, and laughed at her expression of bewilderment.

'Up an' coming place this side of the river is going to be in the near future,' Dennis said with conviction. 'Bomb damage, decaying buildings and dilapidation in general have not been dealt with quick enough. Now things are on the move, redevelopment is going ahead fast.'

Ella caught on quickly. 'And you've submitted plans, bargained with a few men in the know and grabbed some very nice contracts for yourself.'

'I wouldn't put it exactly like that,' Den said anxiously, 'but in the main you're right. I have got work permits and contracts, which means I can offer jobs to a good many blokes.'

Ella felt herself go tense. 'Good Samaritan as always,' she said sarcastically, 'but you won't be breaking yer own back, will you, Den?'

'Come now, Ella,' Den wheedled, 'the piper calls the tune, and the conductor of an orchestra is in charge of the baton. Anyway, you should feel proud. In a few minutes we shall be passing some very high hoardings enclosing

205

a site where I have thirty men working, an' you can take it from me, they are all good craftsmen.'

'Good for you,' Ella muttered, but inside she was seething.

Not one question about Babs or Teddy. For twelve years he had been around for young Teddy, and for eight years for Babs. How could he suddenly stop loving them? Almost shutting them completely out of his life. With all that had happened, didn't he ever have feelings of guilt? Ella spent as much time with them as she could. She did feel that she was a good mother, the three of them bound tightly in a mother–child relationship, yet nothing she could say or do could compensate for them having no father around. She had to work; flush as Dennis made out he was, they hadn't set eyes on him for ages, and she could not rely on him giving her a regular income. She worried that there was less time for her to devote to her children, and every day she thanked God that her mother was around. Without her, she didn't know how she would cope.

She remembered that it wasn't so long ago that she had been fat and miserable, knowing that life was passing her by and that she was obsessive about her children. Now she had a good paid job she worried that she was neglecting them. Why did life have to be so full of problems?

In the car the silence was heavy now. Neither of them seemed to want to talk and Ella was pleased when Dennis drove into a small car park. It was well dark by now and there weren't many people about. He came quickly around to the passenger door, opened it and helped her out of the car.

Ella looked around with interest. This was a very nice-looking place, but exactly what it was was hard for her to tell. It could be a classy pub, or a smart restaurant, or even a club of sorts. The gardens surrounding the building were well tended and the building itself was lit with fancy lanterns.

206

Dennis held out his arm to Ella and she hooked her hand through his elbow as they walked up the steep flight of steps that led to the front entrance. Reaching the top, they had to part and enter in single file because there were revolving doors.

They went inside to a luxurious entrance hall and Ella was at once conscious of the smell of mouth-watering food. She hardly had time to loosen her stole before a giant of a man appeared from nowhere and with something of a flourish wrapped his arms around Dennis.

Ella looked on in astonishment. Next moment the two of them were slapping each other on the back. It was minutes before Dennis introduced the man as Jeff Anderson, quickly adding, 'He owns the place.' Then he winked, and both men threw back their heads and laughed. 'Even if he did only pull off the deal by the skin of his teeth.' This remark was for Ella's benefit.

Suddenly Dennis playfully punched Jeff's arm and said, 'God, you were a lucky bastard.'

'Don't I know it.' Jeff grinned. 'But you don't do so bad yerself, Den boy. Case of the devil looks after his own, eh?'

When he finally turned to Ella he said, 'Good evening, Mrs Dryden, I am so pleased that Dennis has persuaded you to accompany him tonight.' This big man had a soft, almost gentle voice, but Ella couldn't stop herself from thinking that he must be the most ugly man she had ever encountered. His bruiser's face was like that of a pug dog. At some time he had certainly broken his nose. Apart from his face, though, he looked great. He was immaculately turned out, and his huge frame suited the evening suit he was wearing down to a tee.

'Bar first or straight into the dining room?' Jeff asked.

'We'll eat first.' Dennis answered for the pair of them. 'Got some serious talking to do.'

'Fine, your table is ready,' Jeff said as he led the way.

Sliding glass doors led into the large dining room, with beamed ceiling and red flock wallpaper. The tables were set with starched white cloths and folded white serviettes. There were red candles in glass bowls and vases of fresh flowers on each table, and in a huge fireplace big logs burnt slowly, giving the room a warm glow. Most of the tables were occupied.

As Ella hesitated, Jeff snapped his fingers and a waiter appeared and led them to the one set in the bay window, which stood empty.

'Enjoy your meal, I'll see you later,' Jeff said, but Ella felt that he was only talking to Dennis, not to her.

'Thanks, mate,' Den said as Jeff slapped him heartily on the back.

When they were seated and studying the long menus, Dennis leant across the table and said to Ella, 'Don't let Jeff's looks put you off. He's a great bloke. Provided you don't upset him, of course.'

The waiter appeared again with an ice bucket from which he took a bottle. He wiped the outside and presented it so that Dennis could read the label. 'Fine,' was all that Dennis said, but Ella heard what the waiter had whispered to her husband as he took away their menus. Apparently their meal was not to be of their choice. Jeff Anderson had laid everything on for them in advance.

Ella hadn't realized just how hungry she was, and never in her whole life had she eaten such delicious food. They had got through four courses and two bottles of wine before the table was set with coffee and a cheeseboard that offered a great variety.

Ella was pouring cream into her coffee when Dennis said, 'I have a great deal of explaining to do, don't I?'

She stopped dead and stared at him coldly. 'I'd say that's putting it mildly.'

He had the guts to look guilty. 'I have a proposition to put to you. You don't have to answer me tonight, but Ella, please don't take for ever making up your mind.'

She stared at him in disbelief. Finally she said wearily, 'OK, let's hear it.'

'I want us to put the past behind us and start again, even if it is only for the sake of the kids.'

'Hmm, that's rich coming from you. You haven't given a damn about Teddy or Babs, not when things were going your way. Now when yer past has caught up with you and folk don't think of you as the great I am any more, you want to come crawling back to me.'

Dennis put his coffee cup down with a clatter.

'Hold yer bloody horses, Ella, and let me outline what I think would work a treat for all of us as a family. You've got to take up a bit of the slack as well as me, though. You've got to agree to move out of that decrepit old house where the streets are so narrow and all you women do is wage an endless struggle against the dirt and grime. I can offer you the choice of several houses, all this side of the river, where life is so much better and cleaner and there are good schools for the kids. We could make a fresh start.'

'How come you're suddenly concerned with the welfare of your own children?' she asked him coolly.

Dennis glared at her. 'Ella, I'll take you home now. We don't want a slanging match here. All I ask is that you give some thought to what I am asking of you. You can pick the house and the district, I can't say fairer than that.'

Ella rose and was about to drape her stole around her shoulders, but Den had different ideas. He settled her down in a beautifully furnished lounge and told her he would send a drink in to her. He had a bit of business to settle with Jeff and wouldn't be long.

Another drink was the last thing that Ella wanted. She left it untouched.

Sunk in the depths of a squashy, comfortable armchair, she let her thoughts run wild. Yes, she had had a wonderful evening, but it just wasn't real life. But then that was her Den. He was larger than life. He had amazing energy and ambition. She was well aware he hadn't altered.

Probably never would.

He would still be impossible to live with, still totally selfish, and when he couldn't get his own way, would he still be ruthless? She didn't have to think for long before deciding that she was not willing to take that chance. What he was suggesting was a total upheaval of her and the children's lives, and once set into motion there would be no going back. With Den's track record she would be mad to take such a chance.

It was midnight before they finally set out for home. When he drew the car to a halt outside her house he made no attempt to invite himself in, a fact for which Ella was grateful. Instead, he took her arm as they walked across the pavement and said, 'I'm going to be fairly tied up during the next two weeks, but promise me you'll think about what I've said.'

'All right, I'll think about it,' she said. Mainly because she was feeling so tired she wasn't able to think straight.

'Good, let's hope we've made a bit of headway tonight.' He put his hands on her shoulders and stooped to kiss her cheek. 'Good night, Ella, you're so much more like the girl I married now,' he whispered.

Pity I can't say the same about you, was what she was thinking as she went indoors and straight up the stairs to her bedroom. As she undressed and got into bed, she sighed. She had so much to think about.

She didn't get much sleep that night.

Chapter Twenty-three

FESTIVITIES PLANNED FOR THE opening night of the new extension of the British Legion premises had been put on hold. The death of Mr Baldwin and his daughter had affected so many people that Mike had felt it wouldn't be right. He had made his decision out of respect, and members of the club were in complete agreement.

However, life had to go on.

The first Saturday evening in November had been decided upon, and now, finally, the day had arrived.

Although the club did not open until six, every member of staff was assembled in the foyer by four o'clock in the afternoon. Mike did the honours and swung open the double doors. Looking around, he saw that there wasn't an employee who did not have a smile of satisfaction on their face.

And no wonder, the hall was really a sight to behold. Everything that they had been led to expect had been done, and more. A gleaming chandelier hung from the centre of the ceiling. There were discreet wall lights, a marvellous sprung wooden floor, rich, heavy curtains at the windows, a huge wide stage which could be enclosed by fringed velvet curtains. Many small tables each with four chairs were positioned around the walls, but for tonight only there was a head table which was set up for a party of twelve. All the bigwigs from the committee, who had had hardly anything at all to do with this venture, except perhaps sign the cheques, would be here in force.

The food would be exceptional, as would the dresses their lady wives would be wearing. Their jewellery would certainly glitter, because it was a dead cert it would be the real thing.

But all that was to come later.

Mike and Sam Richardson each opened a bottle of champagne and passed a filled glass to everyone. Then Mike broke their stunned silence by saying, 'Before we raise our glasses and toast the new future, I would like to say a few words. Thanks to everyone for their help and support during the whole time that this work has been going on. The architect did a marvellous job with the planning, but the man who has had to battle with the committee, coax and sometimes even twist their arms in order to secure enough funds for the work to be completed is Sam.'

Ella was standing next to Sam, and on hearing him praised like this, she took hold of his hand and squeezed it hard.

He rewarded her with a dazzling smile.

Mike hadn't quite finished his speech. 'I think the end has proved to justify the means. However, tonight is just the beginning. We'll let the committee have their moment of pomp and glory . . .' he paused, 'but remember, it is only a few weeks away from Christmas, and then they can say what they like. This is a working men's club, and over the holiday, we and our members will show them that good times can be had here. Right?'

'Right,' everyone chorused.

'OK.' He raised his glass. 'Here's to us who work here, our members who support us, and an enjoyable evening.'

Ella had never tasted champagne before and was unprepared for the bubbles that tickled her nose. But she soon found that she quite liked the taste and it wasn't long before she was holding out her glass to Sam for a refill.

The Legion had been granted an extension until midnight.

The place was packed, but both Molly and Ella were enjoying themselves just as much as the customers were.

Mike had booked a wonderful band, and early on in the evening they had watched the posh visitors dancing in a way they had never seen before in their lives and probably never would again. Working-class folk didn't do the tango!

The whole place was jam-packed. A lot of alcohol was being drunk and a lot of money was being spent.

'Now you've seen how the other half live,' Mike joked as he removed piles of notes and put more change into the tills which stood behind the bar.

Even with all that was going on, every now and again Ella found herself looking amongst the crowds to see if Dennis had turned up. He had said that he was going to be tied up for two weeks, but that after that he would be in touch, and that he hoped she would have given a lot of thought to the plans he had suggested. That had been more than a month ago, and no one had seen hide nor hair of him. Even his father denied knowing where he was.

Ah well, she sighed, at least he had taken her out and been charming to her for one evening. The ideas he had laid out for her to consider had been going round and round in her head. As he had talked, she had wondered, was a second chance possible? Could a family life be recaptured? According to Dennis it could be! She was doubtful. It would take some effort for her to be able to feel that she could really trust Dennis again. Part of her wanted to. Yet there were so many ifs and buts.

He had talked about setting up a new home, and how much better it would be for the children if they were together again as a family, yet not once had he asked to see Babs or Teddy. How could a father act like that?

She couldn't answer her own question.

When the band went off for their refreshment, the entertainment began. This was for adults only; the humour was a bit near the bone, but the stunts the comics pulled were side-splitting.

Members of the committee thought now was a good time for them to leave. Which was just as well. With them gone, folk could let their hair down and really start to enjoy themselves.

The top table was cleared of china and glasses, the tablecloths were folded, and the three trestle tables which had been joined together were dismantled, leaving much more space for dancing in the hall. The band came back on stage and the music altered, because the musicians caught the mood of the crowd and began to play a Latin American tune known locally as the conga.

Within minutes, women were pulling their men to their feet, insisting that they put their arms around the waist of the person in front, thus linking everybody together. A long single file was formed which moved forward in time to the music, the dancers making a series of steps and side-kicks. Up and down and round the hall they danced, like a human snake. Hardly a soul was left sitting down.

Then came the sing-song. 'My ol' man said follow the van', 'There's my gal, up in the gallery', 'She is my lily and my rose'. And of course no evening would be complete without 'Knees up Mother Brown'.

Ella couldn't stop herself from laughing as she watched her mother and most of their neighbours out there in the centre of the floor. Using both hands, they were holding their skirts up high and their legs were being nimbly worked up and down. Such high jinks had never before been seen in this club.

Come tomorrow half of them would be complaining about the aches and pains they'd all got.

Neither Molly nor Ella was entirely sorry when the lights were dimmed and the band played, 'Who's taking you home tonight?'. It was a joy to watch young and old couples alike, dancing the waltz and softly singing, 'Please let it be me.'

Then Mike called time.

Every member of staff had been worked to death, but the unanimous decision was that it had been a great night.

The place looked as if a bomb had hit it. However, everyone mucked in with the clearing-up, including Mike and Sam. Derrick said he'd run Molly home and Sam offered Ella a lift in his car, for which she was more than grateful. She couldn't wait to kick her shoes off.

When Sam stopped his car outside her house, it was almost two o'clock in the morning. He slid from the driver's seat and hurried round to open the passenger door.

'Thanks, Sam, I don't think me legs would have carried me home,' Ella said as she held out her hand to him. 'Thanks again.'

He took her hand between his own. 'It's certainly been a night to remember. It's been a long time since I've enjoyed myself so much.'

'You wanna ask Mike t' give you a job behind the bar,' Ella joked.

'I might just do that.' He laughed. 'Go in now, it's far

too cold to be hanging about. Got your key? I'll wait here until I see you safely inside.'

Oh, he's a nice man, Ella said to herself as she heard his car drive away. What a pity Charlotte had died so young.

I wonder why he never remarried.

Chapter Twenty-four

THE WORKING MEN'S CLUB was even more popular since the new hall had been added, especially at weekends, though weekdays it was used for darts matches, quizzes and board games.

Early one evening Sam Richardson came behind the bar to remove the till rolls and replace them with fresh ones. He noticed that Ella was looking despondent, most unusual for her.

'You all right, Ella? Or are things getting on top of you?' he asked.

'No, I'm managing,' she said patiently, then smiled and added, 'Well, just about.'

'Nonsense,' he replied. 'Here at the Legion everyone agrees you do the job so well you might have been born to it. Is it your children, are you coping with them all right?'

'Yes, my kids are smashing, it's their ruddy father, he must think they live on fresh air, and as for clothing and footwear, Teddy would have the arse out of his trousers and be running around bare-footed if it were left to Dennis.'

Sam felt embarrassed but he forced himself to say, 'Feeling the pinch, eh? Den should be giving you a regular allowance.'

'Dennis should be doing a lot more than he does,' she said resentfully.

'Have you given any thought to consulting a solicitor? You shouldn't have to work all the hours that you do. The courts would assess your husband's income and then stipulate how much he should be paying you each week. Naturally they would take into account that you are bringing up two children on your own.'

If Sam wasn't being so serious, Ella would have laughed out loud.

Sam Richardson lived in a different world to the rest of the folk around here. He might not realize it, but he had just made the biggest joke of the year! Whoever tried to work out what Dennis's yearly income was would have their work cut out. He never let his right hand know what his left hand was doing!

Den's whole working life had never been anything but bent. Schemes and scams, that was his life. Even if she were brave enough to get that far and a court order was made against Den, the chances of him paying regularly were nil, she thought furiously.

She had to get off this subject. Her pride wouldn't allow her to tell Sam the true state of affairs. It was bad enough that some weeks she had to accept money from her own mother, and she knew full well that when the coalman came Winnie ordered him to put an extra two hundredweight into her coal shed and paid him the difference.

Her father-in-law still came round, and he was always generous to the children regarding pocket money, but she supposed that he thought that because she was employed full time at the working men's club she had sufficient

218

means to get by on. When he came for the odd Sunday roast dinner, that her mother cooked so well, he would always leave a couple of pound notes on the table. God knows how far he thought a couple of quid went.

Sam was looking at her, showing concern, and she hoped he wasn't able to read her thoughts.

'I'd like more time to spend with Babs and Teddy, of course I would.' She forced herself to smile. 'Without my mum to take them out and keep an eye on them, they wouldn't fare half so well. I feel guilty and I'm always telling myself it isn't possible to go out to work and still be a good mother.'

Sam felt he wanted to take her in his arms, but instantaneous actions like that weren't in his nature. Instead he said, 'Now, Ella, you know that's not true. It is defeatist talk and that is not like you.'

Ella gritted her teeth. 'It is the truth. And as for going to court to get regular money out of Dennis, I'd be banging my head up against a brick wall,' she answered with a touch of sarcasm.

Sam looked thoughtful. 'Well, any time you need to talk, you know I'm here two or three times a week and Mike has my firm's telephone number. Meanwhile you take care, Ella.'

'Careful has become my middle name,' Ella said, and Sam could hear the bitterness in her voice.

He bagged up the till rolls. 'See you soon, then,' he said.

Although Ella was not aware of it, Sam had a great respect for her and the way she was handling this different kind of life that she had been forced into through no fault of her own. There was a lot he would like to do for her, but she was another man's wife and there was always the fact that her two children needed both a father and a mother.

*   *   *

The first few days of December came in with high winds and a raw coldness that ate into a body's bones.

The first snowflakes started to fall as Ella and the children stepped out of the front door, and Babs laughed with delight. Clapping her hands, she yelled, 'Lovely, smashing, will it lie and get thick on the ground, Mum?'

'We won't know until you wake up tomorrow morning, pet.'

'I hope it does.' Babs spread out her hands, trying to catch the falling flakes. 'They look so pretty, like someone is spreading loads of duck feathers.'

'Hang on, Ella, I'm coming shopping with you.'

Ella turned her head and was not the least bit surprised to see her mother coming along the road, walking sprightly and dressed as smartly as ever. On her head she was wearing a fur hat which exactly matched the collar of her coat. Ella hadn't seen this outfit before and immediately she smiled as the thought sprang into her mind. My mother's paid another sly visit to Sadie and Isaac.

As soon as the four of them reached the market, Ella said, 'Mum, don't go buying a load of gifts. We've already got quite a lot stacked away and the children will be over the moon when they see their presents, no matter what they get.'

Ella had spoken quite sharply to her mother as they trudged between the stalls.

'All right, all right.' Winnie stopped to take a deep breath. 'You worry about yerself and leave me to do my bit. It would be nice if you told me who was going to be with us for Christmas Day.'

'Well, I've already told Ted that he's more than welcome, and he has accepted, though I did think he might have said he was going to spend the holiday with Dennis. I've also asked Mr Parsons and old Mrs Bristow just for dinner, seeing as they both live alone and don't seem to have any relatives. Then there's Mary Marsh and her two kids, Lenny and Vicky. I've had them every Christmas since Bill Marsh was killed when he crashed his lorry; can't leave them out now, can I? Besides, Vicky and Babs get on well and Lenny often plays football with our Teddy, so they'll be good company for each other.'

Winnie heaved a sigh. 'You know what, Ella, you're a glutton for punishment. I make that about ten that'll be sitting round your table again this Christmas.'

'Better than being sad and lonely, ain't it, Mum?'

'Course it is, luv, and don't for a moment think that I'm knocking you, 'cos I'm not. If you really want to know what I think, you're a saint, and I know everyone you invite will appreciate it.' To herself she was saying, Pity that bloody husband of hers doesn't wake himself up a bit and realize what a good woman my Ella is.

'So you approve of our guest list then?' Ella was smiling broadly.

'Yes, just glad that you've told me. I must get a little gift for everyone, wouldn't want to leave anyone out when handing out the presents, especially Mary Marsh's two little 'uns.'

They shopped for the week's food but also added quite a few items that would end up being gaily wrapped and given as gifts.

'How about we go into the café by the bus garage an' 'ave a cuppa now. Babs and Teddy might like a bowl of soup and we could have a hot meat pie,' Winnie suggested. 'Being Saturday, don't suppose you'll get much of a break later on, will you?'

'I don't think I can spare the time. I've all this shopping to put away when we get home and I mustn't be late for work,' Ella moaned.

'Oh shut up and think of yourself for once in yer life. Half an hour isn't going to make that much difference.'

221

Ella found herself laughing as her mother used her backside to push open the door to the café.

Once they were seated, Cliff, the part-owner of the place, came through carrying two great mugs of steaming tea.

'What, run out of cups and saucers, 'ave yer?' Winnie asked cheekily.

Cliff put his hands on his hips and acted as though he were offended. 'Ladies, if you hadn't noticed, the market is extra busy today with the run-up to Christmas, and me and Eddie have been run off our feet. The food is still good and the drinks are hot, but there's no time for niceties.'

Mother and daughter looked at each other but found it hard to conceal their amusement.

Winnie said, 'It's all right, Cliff, you know I was only kidding.'

Clifford tossed his head and brushed a strand of hair from his forehead. 'You don't really mind a mug, do you?'

'Not so long as you ain't charging us extra 'cos it's bigger than a cup,' Winnie couldn't resist teasing him.

To tell the truth, she thought the world of Clifford and his partner, Edward. They ran a good clean café, and as he said, the food was always very good. Their private lives were their own business.

Clifford turned to face Ella and raised his eyebrows. 'As if we haven't got enough on our plate today, why did you have to bring your mother in?'

''Cos we've all got a cross to bear and she sticks t' me like glue,' Ella said, giving Clifford a sly wink.

'Oh don't mind me, I'll order me food, keep me mouth shut and pretend that I didn't hear the two of you slagging me off,' Winnie said huffily.

Cliff put his arm across Winnie's shoulders and pulled her close, saying, 'You know you're one of my favourite

222

customers. Didn't I bring you a hot drink the minute you walked through the door? Now decide what you all want to eat and I'll be back in a minute. Hot chocolate for you two, is it?'

'Yes please,' Teddy and Babs chorused. For a moment there they had been afraid their gran was going to have a go at Clifford, and had breathed out when they realized that no one was in a bad temper, it was all just a bit of a daft game. Adults seemed to like to goad one another now and again.

Minutes later, when Cliff returned to take their order, Ella was quick to say, 'Make it steak and kidney pie for all four of us, please, Cliff.'

Quietness reigned as they tucked into their meals. Winnie was the first to clear her plate and for a few minutes she was quiet as she drank the remainder of her tea. Then, looking across at her daughter, she asked, 'So is ten the final number that's going to be sitting round your table for Christmas dinner?'

Ella looked puzzled. 'Do you think that I've left somebody off my list?'

'It's up to you, but I didn't think you'd be inviting Ted round this year, not taking into account the way his son's treated you.'

'Oh Mum, you can hardly blame Ted for what Dennis has done.'

Ella's face was blank for a moment. It was a hard job trying to please everyone. Having gathered her thoughts together, she decided to be straight with her mother.

'I might just as well tell you now; you'll get it out of me one way or another, you always do. The truth of the matter is, Ted has offered to pay for the turkey and to bring a good supply of drinks. I could 'ardly not invite him. Besides, the kids think the world of him, and no matter what happens between Dennis and me, Ted will always be their grandfather. There's also another point to consider: you can bet your life he's spent pounds on presents for them. Much more than I can afford.'

'All right, no need to get shirty with me, but I still have to ask, what about Dennis?'

Ella was thankful that the children had gone off to the toilets. She had enough to contend with without them listening to this conversation.

The silence that followed was intense until Winnie tut-tutted. 'You're on about Ted being their grandfather; Dennis is the children's father,' she stated loudly.

'It's a pity no one has thought to remind him of that fact during the months he's chosen to stay away.'

'Well, you went out with him for the evening recently, an' at this time of the year you can't ask his father and leave Dennis out in the cold.'

'Can't I? When he dropped me off he said he'd be back in two weeks. Obviously he's lost track of time.'

'Give him a little credit, Ella. I know him an' me 'ave never got on, but I think he's trying to put the past right. According to what I heard, he paid for the funeral arrangements for both Connie and Alf Baldwin.'

'Oh, and that makes everything all right, does it?' Sarcasm was well to the fore in Ella's voice. 'Put money on the table and it will solve everything. All can be forgiven and forgotten. Is that what you're saying, Mum? 'Cos I hardly think Mrs Baldwin will agree with you.'

'You know darn well that's not what I'm saying,' Winnie retorted angrily.

'I should hope not. He hasn't exactly come back cap in hand. Besides, explain to me how a man can walk out on his wife and two kiddies he swears he adores, never see them for weeks on end, and send only a few quid now and again when the thought occurs to him that they might need money to live on. Every man has his faults, but Dennis has enough for a regiment of soldiers. Have you forgotten Connie Baldwin and the reason he left us in the first place, Mum?'

'No, I haven't forgotten Connie, bless her heart, she was a fool to herself. I'm sorry to say, though, Ella, the beginning of all this trouble was partly yer own fault. You wouldn't move out of the East End.'

'Rubbing salt in the wounds now, are you, Mum? Anyhow, since you know so much, tell me where Dennis is living now and who he's living with, 'cos his father swears on oath that Dennis is not staying at his place,'

Winnie shook her head. 'Nobody seems to know. One of you 'as got to make the first move, but God help us I don't think it will be you, Ella, you're too stubborn.'

'You're dead right there, Mother. Dennis made the decision to leave. I was too old and too fat for his liking. He went off with what was little more than a schoolgirl, and you wanna start thinking about the heartaches that followed.'

Winnie sat there silent and gloomy until Ella decided enough was enough. Not for the world would she upset her mother, but she was not going to take the blame for her family being split up.

'Maybe Dennis did me a good turn leaving me on me own like that. Because now I'm independent, I'm slimmer, I earn my own living and I've proved I can exist without him.'

'You're pretty good at singing yer own praises, I'll give you that,' her mother said stubbornly.

'Yeah, well, since we're talking home truths, the way Den treated young Connie didn't do much for his reputation, did it? I am truly sorry that she died. She was so young. But perhaps it's just as well that the baby wasn't born. Do you think Dennis would have been a good father to it? 'Cos judging by the way he's treated his son and daughter, I wouldn't have put my money on it.'

It was just as well that at that moment the conversation was cut short by the return of Babs and Teddy. Both children were smiling as they licked away at orange ice lollies.

'Where did you get them from?' their mother asked.

Teddy lowered his lolly and cheekily said, 'Clifford gave them to us, 'cos he said we had been on our best behaviour.'

Their mother and grandmother looked at each other and laughed loudly. As they gathered up their bags of shopping and got ready to leave the café, Winnie patted Teddy on the head and said, 'You should have told him, Teddy, handsome is as handsome does.'

Chapter Twenty-five

ALTHOUGH THE WEATHER REMAINED bitterly cold, the snow did not settle, much to Babs's disappointment.

'Never mind,' her mother said, 'there's still time for us to have a white Christmas.'

Pulling on her long tweed coat and wrapping a long scarf twice around her neck, Ella was ready to set off for work.

'I'll probably see you later on tonight, won't I, Mum?' she said to Winnie. 'Janey is coming in as usual, and her mother has said she can sleep here tonight as I'll be late getting home. There's still room for you, though, if you come to the Legion for a drink and want t' come home with me. You know how the kids love to wake up and find you here.'

'All right, I probably will do that,' her mother said gratefully. She hated Saturday evenings if she stayed indoors on her own.

So, Ella thought now as she walked to work, my mother thinks I should try harder to find out where Dennis is and invite him for Christmas, but I don't see it that way.

Good job she didn't come out with that daft suggestion in front of the kids; they'd have been all for it and I'd never have heard the last of it. On the evening that Dennis had taken her out to dinner, she had wavered half-heartedly in her attitude towards him. For a while during their meal she had felt safe and peaceful. It had been good to have him for company, more so because he was making a great effort to be charming.

Somehow he had made himself irresistible, coaxing her into believing that there was at least half a chance they could get back together again. For all his assurances, from that day to this she hadn't heard a word from him.

He leads a good life and outwardly has all the trappings of a successful businessman, and he doesn't give a toss for me and the kids. He makes promises that he has no intention of keeping; well, I've got used to it now, and if that's what he wants, it's fine by me. Just fine. At least I know where I stand.

So intent was she on her thoughts that she didn't notice Sam standing across the other side of the road until he called her name. Then she turned and he was there in front of her. Mostly she only ever saw him in the club; outside in the street on this winter's day he looked different. He was a strikingly handsome man, and for the first time she noticed his vivid clear green eyes. He was tall, though not as tall as Dennis, and neither did he carry the weight that Dennis did. A sudden thought struck her. Why was she comparing him with Dennis? Why not? God alone knew where Dennis was, but Sam was here and now.

His dark overcoat was of good quality and his shoes were highly polished black leather, but what made her smile to herself was the fact that he was wearing a bowler hat. Den wouldn't be seen dead in a bowler!

'Morning, Ella, let's get you inside the club. You'll freeze to death standing here.' Then he paused. 'That is, unless you've got time for a coffee before you start work.'

'Isn't Mike expecting you?' she queried.

'No, I rarely come to the club on Saturdays unless there is something special on, but I will make an exception today if you don't want to go to a tearoom.'

Ella was tempted and very surprised. Why not? she asked herself. Besides, he did look forlorn, even lonely.

She had to swallow hard before she could answer. In as natural a voice as she could manage she said quickly, 'I'd love a hot drink, but could I have tea? I don't like coffee much.'

Sam chuckled as he took her hand and looped it through the crook of his arm. Suddenly he looked younger and a great deal happier.

It was a cosy little café to which he took her. Well known to Ella and her mother because from time to time they treated themselves to a toasted teacake and a pot of tea. That was exactly what Ella ordered for herself now, while Sam decided on a coffee and two rounds of toast.

Ella didn't feel exactly at ease. Talk to him, she urged herself. About anything. Don't just sit here like some dummy, for goodness' sake.

That was what her brain was telling her to do, but she was utterly tongue-tied. They had finished eating and Sam ordered another coffee for himself, but Ella insisted that there was enough tea left in her pot.

It was with some effort but not much thought that she finally said, 'Won't be long until Christmas.'

It was a stupid remark seeing that the tearoom had Christmas decorations everywhere, and outside several strings of decorative lights had been hung from one side of the road to the other.

Quickly, to cover up her embarrassment, she tried to sound interested as she asked, 'What are you doing for the holiday?'

His forehead wrinkled. 'Nothing much.' Then he added, 'I mostly remember the first and only Christmas that Lottie and I had together; that's one thing to be grateful for, no one can take your memories away from you, but I still feel guilty.'

'Why on earth should you feel guilty?'

'Because Lottie died and I'm still alive.'

Ella felt even more uncomfortable. Trust her to have put her foot in it! She and Dennis had been at Sam and Charlotte's wedding, and then Charlotte had died within the year. It all seemed so unfair, because the pair of them had been so much in love and they would have made such wonderful parents.

'Oh, Sam.' She didn't know what to say or do. Had he been blaming himself all these years? Suddenly an idea hit her and she blurted it out. 'Sam, come to me for Christmas.' The enormity of what she had just said caused her to add, 'That's if you can put up with me kids, they can be pretty noisy at the best of times. But you wouldn't be my only visitor, there will be my mum, you know her pretty well, and two other men, one is a neighbour and Ted, my father-in-law, you know, so you wouldn't be amongst strangers.' After that long declaration Ella had to stop to draw breath.

He stared at her, too taken aback to try to hide his feelings. Since they had met up again he had tried to pluck up the courage to ask Ella to go out for a meal with him. Mike had known of his intentions and had contrived to bring the pair of them together. There were several reasons why he had hung back, the main one being he had got the impression that Ella still had feelings for Den. After all, no matter what had happened, he was still her husband and the father of her two children.

Nevertheless, there weren't many days when Ella had not been in his thoughts. She was a kind and thoughtful lady. One who hadn't sat about and moaned at the bad luck that fate had thrown at her. Instead she had buckled down, got herself a steady job and taken care of her children to the best of her ability.

Sam stifled a sigh. In his book, Dennis hadn't behaved at all well. Ella was a good woman going to waste!

He was sitting perfectly still and he was grateful for the fact that Ella couldn't have the slightest idea of what he was thinking.

A couple of minutes went by before he leant forward and touched her face gently. His voice was low as he spoke.

'Ella, nothing would give me greater pleasure than to come to your house on Christmas Day, but only if you agree to let me take you out for a meal one evening this week.'

'But . . .' She stared at him, too surprised to hide her pleasure.

'No buts,' he said. 'I'm old enough to know that life is too short for regrets. Just say yes, and we shall both be gaining something that hopefully will turn out really well.'

'Thank you, Sam, I would like to go out for a meal with you.'

He answered with a smile on his face. 'And I am suddenly very much looking forward to Christmas.'

It was a long, busy shift behind the bar that evening. But time and time again Ella asked herself, was she now going to be able to put the past behind her? Was she being offered a new beginning?

She also decided there was going to be no secret whispering or gossip being passed around when it became known that she was going out for a meal with Sam Richardson and that she had invited him to spend Christmas with her and her family. Come closing time, she managed to get Mike on his own for a few minutes.

'Mike, Sam has offered to take me out for a meal on Wednesday. Would it be OK by you if I take the evening off?'

Mike grinned slyly. 'At last he's plucked up courage to ask you then. Of course you can. Silly bloody question. I've been urging him to ask you for ages.'

'I've also asked him to come to us for Christmas, me and my mum, I mean.'

Mike really was chuckling now. 'Ella, why do you feel the need to tell me all this in advance?'

Ella found she was laughing with Mike and blushing like some silly schoolgirl. ''Cos I don't want folk making more out of it than there really is. If Nellie Turner gets wind of this you know what she's like, she'll spread the news like nobody's business.'

'Nellie is one person that you don't want to worry about. She thrives on gossip, and if there's a way to make trouble then she'll find it. That woman could cause bother in an empty house. No, you go and have a nice evening together.'

'You don't think badly of me then?'

'What the hell are you talking about? Why would I ever think badly of you, Ella?'

'I'm married.'

'Yes, you're still tied to Dryden, worse luck.'

'You don't like Dennis, do you?'

'No, I don't. Never said as much because he's a member of this club and used to be a damn good customer. But a straight question deserves a straight answer. I think he's been a right bastard, a rotten husband and a rotten father. He scarcely ever shows his face around here since he behaved so disgracefully with young Connie Baldwin. How a lovely person like you came to be tied up with the likes of him is a mystery to me.'

Ella said hopelessly, 'He wasn't always like he is now.'

'Well, all I can say is you deserve better. You have a nice time on Wednesday, Sam Richardson is a real gentleman.'

'Thanks, Mike.' Ella leant forward and planted a kiss on his cheek.

'Oh for God's sake don't go all sentimental on me. Let's get these glasses out of the way and the tables wiped down, else you'll never get home tonight.'

Wednesday came round very quickly. Rather to her surprise, Ella felt really at ease sitting in the front seat of Sam's car as he drove, but she was even more surprised when he asked, 'Did you know that I live in Hampstead?'

'No, I didn't,' Ella answered quickly, 'but I hadn't really given much thought as to where you do live, Sam. Must be nice to live outside of London.'

No sooner were the words out of her mouth than she was reasoning with herself, you had your chance. Even your own mother has told you that if you'd gone along with what Dennis wanted and moved down to Epsom when he first asked you to, it would have saved a whole lot of people a helluva lot of heartache.

Sam half turned his head. 'I couldn't stay in the flat that Charlotte and I had worked so hard on, not on my own, it just didn't seem the right thing to do. After giving the matter a whole lot of thought, I decided to get right away.' He paused and smiled. 'Didn't go far, though. Hampstead is only four miles from the centre of London.'

Ella asked, 'Is that where we're going now?'

'Yes, I thought it might make a nice change for you. The actual place we are going to is South End Green.'

Ella laughed. 'Southend is a real Londoner's seaside place; d'you know, Orange Coaches run evening trips down there in the autumn just to see the lights. It only costs three shillings and sixpence. Men go to have a good old booze-up but I think the women like the food. You know what Southend specializes in?'

Sam grinned. 'Can't say that I do.'

Ella soon told him. 'Real cockney food, sausages an' mash, jellied eels, cockles, winkles and whelks, that sort of thing.'

Sam looked about as thrilled as a turnip. 'Ella,' he said, 'I don't think you'll find much comparison between the place I'm taking you tonight and the Southend you have just described to me.'

Ella felt as if she had been rebuked and thought it best if she kept her mouth shut for the time being.

The journey did not take long, yet suddenly the whole scenery changed dramatically and she was wishing it wasn't so dark. There seemed to be so many open spaces with lovely views. The places that were lit up only made her want to see more.

Sam broke the ice by telling her that the huge pond they were now driving past was in an area known as the Vale of Health. When Ella made no comment he went on, 'Many, many years ago the Hampstead Water Company drained a swampy hollow and made this beautiful pond. I must bring you back another day and let you see the real beauty of it in the daylight.' Having said that, he took one hand from the steering wheel and patted her knee.

Friends again, she thought thankfully. Obviously his South End of Hampstead had nothing in common with her Southend by the sea!

When the car came to a halt and Sam came round to the passenger side of the car to open the door for her, Ella looked around and was gob-smacked. Facing her was a unique building; if asked to give a description, the only word for it that came to mind was a mansion. 'Is this a pub?' she asked hesitantly, knowing full well she was sounding ignorant.

'No,' he said firmly. 'Well, maybe one could use that description, but its main purpose these days is a restaurant, a continental restaurant.'

Sam was troubled. He had brought Ella to Hampstead tonight to impress her, but she was already out of her depth and the evening had hardly started. He had to do something quickly to put her more at ease.

'There are still quite a few ordinary taverns and inns in Hampstead,' he said frankly, 'like the Old Bull and Bush, the Spaniards' Inn and Jack Straw's Castle, but like everything else since the end of the war they have had to somewhat change their image and move with the times. This place where we are eating tonight has kept its original name, the Prompt Corner.'

Ella tried her best to smile but it was an effort. Odd name, she was thinking. Then she noticed there was a tall red postbox to the left-hand side of the entrance; that seemed unusual so maybe it had something to do with it. She was hoping against hope that the inside of this place wouldn't be too grand.

Sam held the door open and they went inside to a flagged passageway. As they walked along they passed open archways that led into small rooms with beamed ceilings and fireplaces where burning logs sparked and flickered. Ella sighed with relief. This building had an air of welcome about it. It might be hundreds of years old, but time hadn't altered it that much. Suddenly she was comparing this restaurant to the place where Dennis had taken her for a meal a few weeks ago.

There was no comparison!

One was modern, even a bit flashy. These thick walls, if only they could talk, would tell of bygone times. Even though it had most modern comforts, including electric light, Ella felt sure that she could smell paraffin lamps and newly baked bread.

As Sam slowed down, they saw an elderly man emerging from the darkness at the end of the corridor, walking into the light to join them. Ella noticed that he was dressed as a countryman, in corded trousers and a tweed jacket with leather patches at the elbows. He had a good head of hair that had probably been dark when he had been young but was now thickly white. He was tall, not far short of six foot, but thin as a rake.

'Evening, Sam,' he called jovially. 'I see you're dining with us tonight, booked a table for two, so I take it you won't be playing chess.'

Sam replied quite seriously, 'Evening, William, no, tonight I have company.' Then, turning to Ella, he made the introductions. 'Ella, this is my good friend Major William Lemington. William, this is also a good friend of mine, Mrs Ella Dryden.' They shook hands, he saying how pleased he was to meet her and she being surprised at the grip the elderly gentleman had.

Two waitresses appeared, one to take Sam's order for drinks and the other to show them to a table in a warm, cosy, old-fashioned dining room. Their drinks arrived and they were each studying a menu when footsteps sounded across the uncarpeted wooden floor.

Looking up, Ella saw a large lady, tall and well built, dressed in a cream woollen suit, an embroidered silk scarf tied loosely around her neck. 'Hello, Sam.' She held out her hand. 'William told me you were here.' Turning her head towards Ella, she added, 'My husband told me you are Sam's companion. I'm Margaret, it's nice to have you here.'

'Ella Dryden,' Sam answered for her.

'Well, Ella, enjoy your meal. I know Sam will, he's always had a good appetite.'

As Margaret Lemington left them, Ella was wishing

236

she was at home. She was out of her depth here. Almost before she could banish this awful thought from her mind, Sam was pointing to the menu again and asking her what she would like to order.

Sam decided on smoked salmon, Ella decided she was safer with the soup. For the main course he ordered for both of them, crown of lamb. Ella wasn't sure what crown meant, but lamb was one of her favourite dinners and she hoped they would serve mint sauce with it.

The meal was lovely, though she didn't like the wine that Sam had chosen. It was too sharp, almost sour to her mind. Then the sweet trolley was wheeled in. Oh my God. Ella just stared and wondered what her mother and her two kids would make of this lavish sight. There was such a wide choice and half of what was in the various glass bowls and china dishes she didn't recognize, so she played it safe and settled for sherry trifle, but her eyes nearly popped out of her head when the waitress set another bowl beside her sweet which was filled to the brim with thick cream.

Ella refused cheese and biscuits but was amazed to see Sam still tucking in to what he called a creamy, blue-veined Stilton, which he washed down with a large glass of port.

Behind Ella, quietly, three men, all bordering on old age, had come into the room. Sam, facing the archway, saw them approaching and immediately stood up.

'Oh, there you are, old boy. No chess tonight?'

'Unfortunately, no,' Sam said grimly.

That got Ella's hackles up. If he had wanted to play chess with these old fogies tonight, why the hell had he brought her along? The quicker he took her home, the better!

'Would you like a brandy to round the evening off?' Sam asked quietly.

'No thank you, Sam, I've had more than enough of everything. The meal was delicious and I do thank you for bringing me here.' She thought the least she could do was sound gracious.

'Well, I have ordered coffee.' He glanced up. 'Ah, here it comes. Let's go and sit nearer to the fire,' he suggested.

Settled in an easy chair, Ella lifted her cup of coffee from the small table and cradled it in her hands. Sam knew she much preferred tea, but she wouldn't dream of asking for that here. Coffee was obviously the after-dinner beverage. She watched Sam's face. All evening she had felt inadequate, and she was more than half regretting having invited him to spend Christmas with her. She had not been aware that his way of life was so entirely different from her own.

'Do you miss London?' she asked with a rush, already wishing she hadn't asked such a personal question.

Sam laughed. 'Hampstead is hardly a million miles away.'

Silence lay between them, until he said, 'You think I have only elderly people as companions?'

Ella made no answer, so he went on. 'When my Charlotte died I fled London because it had so many memories. For a long time I thought I had made a ghastly mistake. I missed the theatres, the cinemas, and the British Legion club. I was only renting a flat near here when I had a stroke of good luck, or maybe it would be more truthful to say, as everyone knows, that it is not what you know but *who* you know, and as it turned out, that is what happened to me. I was made an offer that was too good to refuse. To this day I do appreciate how privileged I am.'

'Now you have got me interested,' Ella told him. 'Tell me more about this wonderful offer.'

'Very well, if you're sure you want to hear this.'

Ella drained her coffee cup and set the cup and saucer back down on the table. 'I'm all ears,' she smiled.

Sam sat up straight in his armchair. 'Ten minutes' walk from here and down Fleet Road, you turn left into Quadrant Grove and you will come upon an unusual sight. There is a terrace of small cottages. Unusual type of housing, not to be found in this day and age, but then they were built a very long time ago. I was offered the freehold of the last cottage at the far end of the row.'

Ella was deep in thought. Were all men the same? It was the kind of thing that her Dennis would say. It is not what you know but *who* you know that gets you on in this world.

Sam broke into her thoughts. 'When Charlotte and I got married we had hoped to have children and we followed the advice of the firm I still work for and took out life insurance policies. When Charlotte died so tragically it seemed almost indecent to accept the company's payout. Our managing director lives in Hampstead and it was he and his wife who suggested a move might be the right thing for me. They informed me when this cottage became available and I used Charlotte's insurance money to buy my own home.'

Later, as Sam drove her home, she felt tonight had been an eye-opener in more ways than one. Several times she glanced at Sam's face and thought with grudging admiration that he had certainly made a new life for himself. Was he pleased with his day-to-day routine? One could hardly call it exciting. Work all the week, and from what she had heard, a game of chess with elderly gentlemen was the highlight of his world.

She hoped that both Babs and Teddy would still be awake when she crept in to their rooms to check on them. Even if they were fast asleep she would cuddle and kiss

239

them each in turn and thank God, as she did every day, that she had two such great kids.

Babs and Teddy, she repeated their names inside her head.

They made her life well worth living.

As Sam brought the car to a halt he smiled at Ella and asked, 'Are you glad you came out with me tonight?'

'Of course. I've had a great time.'

'I'm so glad.'

For a moment, she thought he was going to kiss her, but instead he leant towards her and put his arms round her and hugged her. 'Goodnight, Ella. See you at the weekend.'

And that was how they parted.

Chapter Twenty-six

THREE MORE DAYS TO go and it really would be Christmas, Ella consoled herself as she clambered out of bed. She shivered, reached for her thick dressing gown, pushed her feet into her slippers and went downstairs quietly so as not to disturb the children. It was only seven o'clock and school had broken up a week ago, so there was no need for them to get up yet. In the kitchen she reached out a hand and felt the side of the kettle. The water inside was hot because the fire had been well banked up the night before. Pushing the kettle to the centre of the hob, she murmured, 'That won't take long to boil.' She had, as always, set the breakfast table the night before.

Crossing the room, she pulled the curtains open and saw that it was snowing again, not heavily, but sleety flakes driven to swirling by the bitterly cold wind. Oh, she hoped for Babs's sake that the wind might drop and the snow would settle. Bare trees and muddy playgrounds would all be transformed should that happen. The effect of thick white snow on everyday dirty, untidy buildings would make for a grand sight. The kids would be overjoyed if it were to become thick enough for them to go out and play in it.

Steam was coming from the spout of the kettle and she made a pot of tea. She always had two cups before she was ready to face a new day.

Mike had been kind enough to say she need not do the morning shift, so the whole day until six thirty tonight was hers. Shopping for food was not one of Ella's favourite occupations. It wasn't so bad when her mother went with her, because she was always so enthusiastic about getting bargains, but today Winnie was coming round to stay with the children and help them to finish putting up the decorations in the front room. Ella couldn't bear the thought of trailing around the shops on her own. The crowds would drive her mad. You'd think the shops were going to be closed for a month or more, the amount of food people were buying.

Having eaten a slice of toast, she washed in the scullery and came back into the kitchen to dress herself. She had laid her clothes out along the brass fender to get warm and it felt so good to pull on her underwear. Fully dressed now, she went back upstairs to wake Teddy.

Her son was still asleep, looking so peaceful; his hand tucked under one cheek, his wild shock of unruly dark hair tumbled on the pillow.

'Teddy.'

He stirred, turned on to his back, yawned and opened his eyes.

'Teddy, I'm going out shopping. I want you to listen for Babs to wake up. Your gran will be here soon.'

'Umm, all right.'

'Are you properly awake?'

'I am now.' Sleepily Teddy sat up, rubbing his eyes. 'Are you going to buy Christmas presents?'

'Maybe, but you are not to go round the house searching for what you think I may already have hidden.'

He grinned. 'So there are some hidden?'

'Never you mind. Stay a while longer in bed if you want to, but it is nice and warm downstairs. I will be quite a while. I've a lot to do.'

She laughed as Teddy snuggled down under the bedclothes again, then she tip-toed into Babs's bedroom. Babs was still fast asleep, curled up and looking so small, her long chestnut-coloured hair in a heap around her pretty face. Ella didn't touch her – it would be a shame to disturb her – but instead crept out of the room and back downstairs.

Wrapped up warmly, Ella boarded the bus. Fifteen minutes later the driver parked in the bus terminal as the market clock struck nine. Ella was amazed. Already the morning was well under way. Shops were open and all the stalls were set up and doing a roaring trade. From a parked van two men were unloading crates of fruit and vegetables, bunches of holly and Christmas trees both large and small. Thank God she hadn't got to carry anything like that home on the bus. Ted had got their local greengrocer to deliver them a small tree, holly and even two sprigs of mistletoe. The kids were going to start to decorate the tree while she was out, but she wasn't supposed to know that: yesterday she'd heard Babs whisper to her brother that they should do it while their mother was at work. Teddy had agreed. 'Be a smashing surprise for Mum, that will be,' he had grinned.

Ella went from stall to stall like a dose of salts, making snap decisions over some things, pondering over others. A present for her father-in-law was the most difficult decision; finally she settled on a beige waistcoat. It was very smart and the label said it was pure lamb's wool. Woolly gloves for Mrs Bristow and Mary Marsh, a long warm scarf for Mr Parsons. Two more Dinky motor-cars, one for Lenny Marsh and one for Teddy; she already had a box of small presents for him. Two skipping ropes with brightly coloured wooden handles, one for Babs and one for Vicky Marsh, and a miniature china tea service as an extra present for Babs.

Next came the sweet stall, today looking entirely different from the usual display of boiled sweets and home-made bars of fudge. There would be four children in her house on Christmas Day, so she bought four nets of gold-wrapped chocolate coins, four coloured sugar mice, two white and two pink, all with long string tails which would be useful when it came to tying them on to the tree, and two chocolate Father Christmases, one each to be put in the stockings that Babs and Teddy would be hanging at the foot of their beds.

She stopped for a moment and breathed out. The only two she had to buy for now were her mum and Sam Richardson. Nothing was too good for her mother. She would go into Boots the chemist and buy her some decent perfume and a really posh lipstick. What about Sam? Well, he was writing and doing accounts all the time, wasn't he? She'd look for a fountain pen, one that was in a nice presentation box.

She had brought two large shopping bags with her and already they were bulging when she spied a really Christmassy stall. 'Don't forget yer wrapping paper,' the stall-holder was shouting, 'and yer labels, ribbons an' cards. If a job's worth doing, it's worth doing well.'

Ella just had to buy a little of everything, but the icing on the cake, so to speak, were the fairy dolls. Displayed on a large board to the rear of the stall, they looked dazzling. Tiny little dolls, all with blonde hair, wearing a white full-skirted dress of thin fine chiffon, adorned with sparkling tinsel. The tiny right hand of the doll was holding a silver wand topped by a glittering star. They were priced at half a crown.

Oh t' hell with the expense, Ella told herself, picturing in her mind's eye the way her daughter's eyes would light up when she gave it to her, and also how great it would look when fixed on the top of their small Christmas tree.

She couldn't miss the baker's stall. The smell of warm freshly baked bread and cakes defied anybody to walk by.

''Allo, Flo,' Ella greeted the rosy-faced plump woman in her spotless white apron. 'Busy today all right, eh?'

'Yer can say that again, Ella luv, but I ain't grumbling. Gotta make it while yer can. Only comes once a year.'

Ella had been to school with Flo, and her husband Pete had always been Den's mate. At least those two were still together. She couldn't help but feel a little envious; they had four children and she could imagine what a great family Christmas they would be having.

'I'll have a large bloomer, a large Hovis, 'alf a dozen jam doughnuts and a dozen mince pies.'

Flo said, 'Sorry, Ella luv, sold out of mince pies.'

'Oh Christ, an' I just ain't got the time ter make them now I'm working,' Ella said regretfully.

'I'll tell yer what, mate, my Pete an' my eldest boy will be baking all night. I'll get him to drop you in a dozen tomorrow. I'll put them in a tin for you.'

'Flo, you're a lifesaver, thanks, luv.'

Flo handed Ella a carrier bag containing the brown loaf and the white one plus the doughnuts, and then as an afterthought she popped a paper bag on top. 'There's just four mince pies there, can't sell 'em, they got a bit squashed, but you and the kids might like 'em when yer get 'ome. Give yer mum the odd one. 'Ow is she these days?'

'Fine, she'll outlive the lot of us. She's in my place minding the kids this morning.'

'Always was a goer, your mum. Tell 'er I sent me love.'

Ella paid Flo. Then she said, 'Flo, what about the mince pies Pete is going to bring me?'

245

Flo laughed. "Ave 'em as a Christmas box.'

Ella protested, but Flo cut her short. 'Over the holiday I'll make sure Pete brings me into the Legion. I know you're closed Christmas Day, but you're open Boxing Day, ain't yer?'

'Yeah, we are.'

'Well, you can buy me a drink then.'

'You're on,' Ella said, 'I'll tell you what, ask your Pete to make it two dozen mince pies and I'll buy yer three drinks on Boxing Day,' and they parted, both of them laughing as they called, 'Merry Christmas.'

Her visit to Boots the chemist was successful. She couldn't get over the fact that the girl behind the Elizabeth Arden counter had offered to gift-wrap the bottle of perfume she had bought, and a beautiful job she had made of it. Wrapped in silver paper, the small parcel was topped by an elaborate red ribbon bow. The cheapest Parker fountain pen was in a very nice box and the male assistant told her a diary for the new year came free with it. Good, Ella thought, she would wrap them separately. The diary could be a present for the children to give to Sam, because both she and her mum had made sure that there were at least two presents for Ted that would bear labels saying they were from the children.

Who's left now? she wondered. She reminded herself that most of today's shopping would not have been possible if it weren't for the fact that the Legion had given every member of staff an early Christmas bonus. Should she buy a present for Mike? If she did, she would have to do the same for his wife, and what about Tom and Derrick, she and Molly worked with them day in, day out. Oh dear, she sighed, there had to be an end to it somewhere. And she was pretty sure that Mike would make sure that all the staff got together for a drink sometime over the holiday.

She set off back down the street to the bus depot. She had spent enough money for today and she hoped that everybody would like what she had bought for them. She was pretty sure they would. God Almighty! The one person who by rights should have been top of her list she had forgotten. MOLLY!

Turning quickly she ran back into Boots. Quickly she made for the No 7 counter, Boots' own make. Having sought the advice of a very helpful assistant she was soon once again making her way to the bus depot. A glowing feeling of satisfaction made her smile. A gift of bath oil, talcum powder, scented soap and a very pretty nailbrush which were all neatly boxed had been the assistant's advice and once again the offer to have her purchase gift-wrapped was gratefully accepted. Molly would be really pleased with her present.

The children must have been watching for her. They came tearing down the street overexcited, yelling and tugging at her arms, urging her to hurry, there was so much they wanted her to see.

The front door was closed and Ella smiled: it was so she would notice that a wreath of holly had been nailed to the woodwork.

Once through the door, she had no option but to drop her bags of shopping in the passageway and allow herself to be pushed into the front room. Her eyes lit up as the Christmas tree was revealed in all its glory. The children, with a lot of help from their gran, Ella supposed, had done very well, and already the base of it was surrounded with brightly wrapped packages.

High up, near to the ceiling, the paper-chains that the children had made at school and so proudly brought home were looped the whole way around the room entangled here and there with balloons. All this must have taken a great effort.

Ella looked over the top of her children's heads and her gaze met that of her mother. Their eyes were glistening with unshed tears, but they were tears of sheer happiness.

'I'll make a pot of tea,' Winnie said softly. 'Kettle is boiling.'

Chapter Twenty-seven

'CHRISTMAS EVE, AND MIKE'S got an extension till midnight,' Ella remarked grimly to her mother. 'You can bet yer life it will be hectic in the club tonight. Are you coming back here to sleep or are you going home? Think on before you decide, 'cos the kids will probably be up and about wanting to know what Father Christmas has left them by about six o'clock in the morning.'

Her mother laughed. 'You were the same once upon a time. Anyway, I'll see you later. By the way, before you go, have you left a bit extra for Janey?'

'Yes, I've taken care of her. I gave her five pounds when I got my bonus. She said she'd rather have the money than a present 'cos she wanted to buy something nice for her mum.'

Thank God the customers were all in a festive mood. Almost every time they ordered a drink they said to the staff, 'Take one for yourself.' Molly remarked, 'Bejesus, if we drank half of what's on offer we'd never live to see Christmas Day.'

Mike had arranged that four cabs would be at the club

by twelve thirty, making sure that all members of staff had safe transport. God knows what the time was when Ella got home. She didn't know and she didn't care. Once upstairs in her bedroom she took off her clothes, let them lie where they dropped on the floor and climbed thankfully into her bed. She was asleep almost before her head touched the pillow.

The sudden noise was terrible. Ella heaved a hefty sigh and did her best to shove her head under her top pillow.

God! It only seemed like she had been in bed for a short while!

'He's been, he's been, come on, Teddy, wake up, Father Christmas has been, please Teddy, wake up, let's see what's in our stockings.'

Teddy wake up? The way Babs was going on, the whole bloody street would soon be wide awake.

Ella lay back, stretching her arms and legs, smiling as she remembered how good she and her mum had felt when filling those stockings for her children. They had both spent more on small toys and sweets than they could really afford, but the sounds of delight coming now from Teddy's room, where the two of them were comparing what Father Christmas had brought, made all the effort well worth while.

She found herself thinking back over the previous evening. It had been one hundred per cent better than anyone had anticipated. After all, Connie and Alf Baldwin's funeral hadn't been so long ago. Even Mike had said that might still have an effect amongst some of the members and that the festivities might not be so jolly this year.

Well, he'd been wrong.

Maybe the new premises and the bright decorations had all had something to do with it. Whatever, the evening had been great. Not one cross word. Drinks had flowed freely but everyone had remained friendly and jolly.

Mrs Baldwin and her daughters had not put in an appearance, but Ella supposed one couldn't expect that family to want to celebrate Christmas.

She reached an arm out of bed and yanked open the curtains. It was still dark, the streetlights were still on and she held the alarm clock near to the window. Jesus, it was only twenty minutes to six.

'All right, I give in,' she said aloud as she listened to the yells and screams and even a trumpet being blown. She couldn't tell the children to be quiet. Not today. She slipped her feet into her slippers and tied her dressing gown tightly about herself and half stumbled down the stairs.

Pushing open the kitchen door, she stared in astonishment.

'God, Mother, where do you get your energy from?'

The fire was burning merrily halfway up the chimney, almost every bit of floor space was taken up by presents and small toys which Father Christmas had supposedly filled their stockings with and the smell of roasting turkey and pork had Ella sniffing with delight.

Wiping a stray hair from her sweaty forehead, her mother smiled and said, 'Go and look in the front room, see if you approve.'

Ella did as she was told, and as she opened the door her breath caught in her throat. She cast her eyes around the room, and as she did so she muttered out loud, 'God above, this takes some believing.'

The extension leaves had been pulled out of their old dining room table, making it almost the full length of the room. A bed sheet had been used to cover the table and a sheet of red crêpe paper was set on top of that. Where on earth had her mother got it all from?

There were twelve places set. Winnie hadn't been too pleased when she was told that Sam Richardson had been invited, and had said sharply, 'Let's pray that your husband turns up as well.' Hence the twelfth setting, Ella supposed. Half-heartedly she was hoping the same thing, but there was no way she was going to admit it to her mother.

Slowly she walked the length of the long table. It was set beautifully, with lace place-mats and red candles in brass holders. There was a bowl of holly entwined with a couple of white Christmas roses in the middle of the table, and to top it all a fire had been lit in the black wrought-iron fireplace. Three strings of Christmas cards were strung across the wall above the mantelpiece.

Going back into the kitchen, Ella was at a loss to find words, so she just hugged her mum and planted a kiss on her cheek. She hoped she had conveyed just how grateful she was.

Babs and Teddy came tearing down the stairs and into the kitchen, where they plonked themselves down side by side on the hearth rug, still delving into the long stockings that Father Christmas had filled.

'Look, Mum, a London bus, and when you push it hard on the lino sparks come out of it. I've never seen one like this before, it's the bee's knees,' Teddy declared excitedly.

Not to be outdone, Babs was holding up pretty clothes that would fit a fair-size doll. She didn't know that her gran had knitted them all, and that the new doll would come later when everyone opened their presents.

Ella glanced at her mother as the children took out the various small gifts they had collected and secreted away over many weeks, all of which had been stuffed into the large stockings the children had hung at the foot of their beds. Each of them was choked. The joy on the children's faces and the way their eyes lit up was enough to make any grown-up want to cry.

Cry, yes, but not tears of sadness.

An hour later, when all the noise and laughter had died down, Ella, her mother and the two children were seated around the breakfast table.

Even breakfast was an extraordinary meal on Christmas morning. Home-cooked gammon, scrambled eggs and red pickled cabbage which Ella had salted away in screw-topped jars weeks ago. Plenty of toast with jam or marmalade to follow, because their Christmas dinner was not going to be eaten until four o'clock.

Well satisfied, Ella leant back in her chair, looked at her children and said, 'Well, are you both pleased with your presents so far?'

'Oh yes.' Babs was the first to answer. 'May I wear my new pink dress when Grandad gets here? And the silver shoes that Gran bought me?' She wanted assurance.

Gran had taken Babs with her to purchase these items. It would have been a disaster if on Christmas Day they had not fitted the child.

Teddy knew there were bigger presents to come and he was impatient.

'Why have we got to wait until everybody arrives before we open the big presents that are in the front room?'

Ella sighed. She had been expecting this. 'Because you know full well we are going to leave yer gran to get on with the cooking, and like we promised Babs's teacher, Miss Whitehead, we are going to a special church service this morning.'

'She's not my teacher, so why do I have to come?' Teddy crossly demanded to know.

'Because I said so,' his mother answered quickly in a voice that would brook no argument. 'You won't be the only boy there, I should think the whole school will attend seeing as how your headmaster wrote a letter to every parent which explained that it would be a simple thanksgiving service mainly for you youngsters. Besides, a little bird told me that you helped to make and set up the crib in the church. Don't you want me and your sister to see it?'

'Wasn't only me,' he said sulkily. 'All the boys helped, we did it in our woodwork class.'

'All the more reason for you to be there, and do you think, young man, that just this one day of the year you could do as you're told and we could have less of your backchat, please.'

Teddy's face broke into a broad grin. 'All right, Mum, but when we get back from church can we open our big presents?'

Ella playfully swiped her son around the head. 'Whenever you agree to do anything there has always got to be something in it for you. Now get yerself ready before I forget that it is Christmas Day and really swipe you one.'

While the children were putting their coats on, Ella had a few moments alone with her mother.

She said, 'Happy Christmas, Mum, and thanks for all you're doing.'

'Happy Christmas to you, my luv, now get going an' don't forget to say one for me.'

Ella felt happy and proud as she walked down the street, Babs holding one of her hands and Teddy the other one. They stopped several times to wave at their school friends and for Ella to greet her neighbours. Voices called out; other people gave one another a hug, everyone falling into step as they made their way through the huge churchyard.

'I already know what carols we are going to sing,' Babs said, tossing the end of her new long red scarf around her neck.

Teddy was horrified. 'You mean we've got to join in with the singing?'

'The choir will lead the congregation and we will all be handed hymn books.' Their mother was pouring oil on troubled waters.

As they went through the wide gates and down the path beyond which led to the wide flight of stone steps and the huge door of the church, for a moment Ella felt sadness overwhelm her. Dennis had carried each of their children into this church, wrapped in a beautiful shawl and cradled safely in his big brawny arms, and with her hand linked through the crook of his elbow they had gathered with a host of family and friends to have them christened. Where was their father today? Her mum was right: he should be sitting around the same dinner table as they were, but the last thing she could do was tell Dennis what she thought was best for him. He had a mind of his own, that had always been a well-known fact.

The children hesitated inside the church, and she gave them a gentle push. A kind lady wearing a very smart hat handed them each a hymn book. Ella thanked her and she wished them all a very happy Christmas.

'Come on, kids, see if we find somewhere to sit together.'

A great surge of sound from the organ and waves of music filled the church.

'O little town of Bethlehem, how still we see thee lie.' Ella mouthed the words

The church was already nearly filled, and they had begun to move down the centre aisle when a hand touched Ella's arm. A stout gentleman said, 'If all of us shuffle up a bit, there will be more than enough room for you and your two children.'

Ella said, 'Thank you,' and guided Babs and Teddy into the pew before seating herself on the end of it.

To the right of the altar steps there was a huge Christmas tree, lavishly decorated and twinkling with candles. To the left the nativity scene had been set: the three Wise Men, Mary, our Blessed Lady, and Joseph surrounded the crib which held the baby Jesus. As every year, the children who had at school helped to make the setting were being taught to commemorate the birth of Christ.

Ella squeezed Teddy's hand, letting him know that she was proud of the fact that he had been involved in setting up this festival tableau.

So far, so good. The children must all have been practising well-known carols at school, and they sang with passion, their voices filling the church. The choir sang just one hymn, and during their performance the congregation was still. The music was the only thing that mattered. If only Dennis had been there! But what was the use of if only? That was the one thought that spoilt the morning for Ella.

Walking home, Teddy asked, 'Mum, do you think Dad will turn up today?'

Oh my God! How am I supposed to answer that one?

Ella's expression was unreadable as she sought to find a suitable answer for her son.

'Maybe. But if I were you, Teddy, I wouldn't count on it.'

Chapter Twenty-eight

CHRISTMAS DINNER HAD BEEN a great success. Ella's biggest thrill was watching her own two children and Lenny and Vicky Marsh stare in wonderment as Winnie carried in the great dish that held an enormous Christmas pudding and Grandad Ted soaked the top of the pudding with brandy then set it alight. Blue flames danced merrily and the four children screamed with delight. A slice of pudding, a hot mince pie with a dollop of brandy butter, and there wasn't one amongst the eleven sitting around the table that could eat another morsel after that.

The ladies drained their one and only glass of wine while Ted poured another glass of brandy for Mr Parsons, Sam Richardson and himself. The table was strewn with the crumpled paper napkins, the remains of crackers that had been pulled and paper hats that had by now fallen off their heads.

Babs had for some time been looking longingly at the pile of fancy-wrapped parcels that still lay on the floor around the tree.

'Please may we get down from the table, and when are we going to open our big presents?' she whined.

'Right now, pet,' her mother answered lovingly. 'We'll leave all this mess until later and then your gran and I will clear it up after the parcels have all been given out.'

'Never seen such a rush in all me life,' Mrs Bristow laughed. The four children were on their knees and were reading aloud the words each label had written on it.

'This one's for you, Lenny. This one is for you, Mum, and this great big one is for me.' A delighted Teddy was already tearing at the wrapping paper. And so it went on. Even the adults were pleased to receive gifts, and the joy of watching the children was beyond description. Grandad Ted had been so generous: an exact model of a royal perambulator for Babs to wheel her dolls in, and the huge box labelled for Teddy had turned out to be the latest Meccano set.

Eventually things quietened down. Mary Marsh and Mrs Bristow had insisted on helping Ella and her mother to clear everything out from the front room and into the kitchen, and now all four were busy washing up. Ted had taken the leaves out of the table, folded it up and stood it against the wall, thereby giving the children a lot more floor space in which to play.

Teddy was looking through his Beano annual. Babs was engrossed in seeing what kind of underwear her new blonde-haired doll was wearing. Vicky too was cradling a doll in her arms and Lenny was busy assembling a wooden fort, which had twelve soldiers to go with it.

Suddenly there was a gentle tap on the front door. The women looked at each other and raised their eyebrows. A caller on Christmas afternoon? It didn't seem likely.

'I'll go,' Winnie offered, stepping over the bags of rubbish which lay in the middle of the kitchen floor.

Two minutes later she was calling loudly, 'Ella, will you come here a minute please.'

The front door was wide open, and Ella gasped sharply

258

as she stood and stared at the sight of two very expensive bicycles standing side by side on her doorstep. One was bigger than the other and bright blue in colour. It had brakes, a shiny bell on the handlebars, a crossbar and a large black leather bag strapped on the back. The other was obviously meant for a small girl. Mainly coloured silver, it had a pink basket attached to the front of the handlebars, and fixed to the back of the frame were two extra wheels which Ella knew were known as stabilizers. They could easily be removed once a child had got the experience and confidence to ride a two-wheeled bike.

Her eyes were brimming with tears as she stared at her mother.

'Yes,' Winnie said, 'there are labels on them. You don't need telling, but just look at them.'

Each tag read, 'Have a great Christmas, I love you, Dad xx'.

'No sign of him, I suppose?'

'No, I ran to the gate but he must have moved fast.'

'Bastard!' Ella couldn't help herself. 'He still thinks money buys everything.'

'I know, luv, I know. But just watch the kids' faces when they see these bikes, they'll be over the moon.'

'I'll have a damned hard job to hide them both until Christmas is over.'

'Why in hell's name would you do a daft thing like that?'

''Cos it makes what you and I have struggled week by week to buy for them look small and paltry. He either does nothing at all for them or else he goes over the top.'

'Come on, luv, at least he has tried.'

'And you don't think if he'd come into the house bearing no presents but just lifted them up in his arms and given them a great big bear hug that wouldn't have pleased them even more?' Ella's voice was very harsh.

'Don't let's go into the whys and wherefores, Ella, let's enjoy the rest of the day. Call the kids now, come on, at least their father has made an effort. Is that not good enough for you?'

'No, it's not good enough for me.' Ella pushed past her mother. 'If he really loved them he'd have wanted to see them and be with them, today of all days.'

Winnie followed her daughter down the passage without answering. She didn't blame Ella. Not after the way Dennis had treated her.

'Oh, all right.' Ella sounded cheesed off. She knew she had no choice, she would have to give in. She couldn't deprive her kids of such wonderful presents just because her temper had risen so high it was almost choking her.

Bloody Dennis, I was having a really great day from the moment I woke up until he rapped on the front door. Big-headed sod. Those two bikes must have cost him a fortune. She couldn't bear to go out front with the kids and watch them find what their father had left them. She asked Winnie to do it for her.

The squeals and screams of delight said it all, but the adults, who had by now all crowded around the front door, couldn't help feeling sorry for Lenny and Vicky Marsh. Those two children had lost their father a long time ago, and one would have to be blind not to notice the envy in their eyes as Teddy proudly exclaimed, 'Our dad bought them for us.'

Yet it was young Babs who echoed her mother's thoughts. 'Mummy, why did my daddy leave our bicycles on the doorstep?'

Then the words that her small daughter added felt like a knife being driven into Ella's heart.

'Wouldn't you let him come in?'

How was she supposed to answer that?

After a lot of persuasion, the children agreed that their

bicycles could be stored under the stairs, but only on the absolute promise that first thing in the morning they could ride them up and down the street.

With all the excitement damped down, and the fact that it was getting dark, Ella walked into the front room to pull the curtains. At the same time she slid the top of the window open a little because Ted had been smoking a cigar. She then threw two more logs on to the fire.

She was about to suggest that it was time they all had some tea: there was the Christmas cake still uncut, and plenty more mince pies that could be popped into the oven to get warm. Looking round, she had second thoughts. Sam and Ted were seated comfortably in armchairs one each side of the fireplace. Mr Parsons and Mrs Bristow were side by side on the sofa, their heads laid back on cushions, their eyes closed. Ella left the room, closing the door quietly behind her, deciding that teatime could be delayed a little longer. Then she climbed the stairs. The two boys were in Teddy's room and the two girls in Babs's. Harmony reigned; after all, they had plenty of new presents to keep them occupied today.

She came back downstairs and into the kitchen, where she reported that the kids were fine and the adults were resting. Winnie suggested that Mary, Ella and herself should stay in the kitchen and make a nice pot of tea just for themselves. This was unanimously agreed to be a good idea.

Back in the front room, Sam was fuming. Why had Dennis Dryden had to make such an expensive gesture? It wasn't at all fair on his wife, who had worked so hard to give several people a very happy Christmas, only to have all her good work undermined by him. How could Ella possibly have answered young Babs when she had challenged her mother as to why her father had not come into the house?

Sam held his temper and tried his best to sound casual

261

as he remarked to their grandfather, 'Children are thrilled with their bicycles, aren't they?'

Ted didn't answer him, and Sam quickly added, 'Pity their father didn't show his face.'

Ted had already heard the underlying anger in Sam's voice and decided it was time he spoke up.

'Don't go poking your nose in what is not your business.' He sounded friendly, but it was obvious he was sending out a warning.

'I don't think the man has any conscience, walking away and leaving Ella to cope with two young children on her own.'

'The man you're on about is my son, and Ella is not on her own. She knows I'm around if and when she or the kids need me.'

'I just think Dennis should play it a bit more straightforward, let Ella know where she stands. As it is, he comes and goes as and when he likes. It's no life for Ella or for the children. What about you, Ted? Do you agree with the way he is acting? You say you're there to help Ella, yet you deny that you know where your own son is living. Suppose one of the children were taken ill, are you saying you couldn't contact their father?'

Ted was out of his seat in a second, shouting, 'I honestly have no idea where my son is, but in the East End the jungle drums are quite effective. If I put the word out he'd be here within the hour. I hear from him daily, we have several mutual business interest, but his personal life is nothing to do with me and even less to do with you, so watch what you're saying and keep a tight rein on what you're thinking of doing, that's my advice.'

Ella, having heard Ted's raised voice, came quickly into the room, still drying her hands on a tea towel. Ted was still standing in the middle of the floor, his hands clenched into tight fists.

Ella gestured for him to sit down and then she glared at Sam.

'Whatever has been said between you two, just remember that you are in my house and it is still Christmas Day. I can't believe it. The kids are all being as good as gold and yet you grown men have to start a noisy slanging match.'

'Sorry, luv,' her father-in-law said, pulling a glass ashtray across the table and taking a cigar from the box which stood beside it. 'Sam here seems to think he has the right to interfere in your life. We all know that he'd like to—'

Ella held her hand up to interrupt him. She pointed a finger at each man in turn and then, with her voice full of irritation, said sharply, 'Strictly speaking I should be the only one dealing with Dennis, and I will in my own good time. Now, Mum is just bringing in a pot of tea and Mary and I have laid out lots more to eat. Unless the both of you want to clear off out and carry on your argument somewhere else, I suggest you make yerselves useful and put the table back up. You needn't put the leaves in, we can have our food on our laps.'

Mr Parsons looked relieved and Mrs Bristow smiled and said, 'Oh Ella, you're a saint, a cup of tea is just what the doctor ordered.'

Sam had never felt so ashamed in all his life. He knew he had overstepped the mark.

He had drunk far more than he was used to, yet he was aware that was no excuse.

Ella was staring at him, her big eyes never wavering even when she said, 'Well?'

She had no need to say more.

Sam got to his feet and held out his hand to Ted, saying, 'I apologize, really I mean it. You're right. It is none of my business.'

Ted Dryden shook his head sadly but he still put his

hand out and took Sam's. Then to Ella he said, 'For once, my gal, I think a cuppa tea will go down well.'

Peace was restored.

Despite the fact that it was less than three hours since everyone had declared they could not eat another morsel, they were now tucking into a typical Christmas tea.

Besides the cake, mince pies and a huge trifle, the table was covered with bowls of fruit, nuts, dates and chocolates.

Everyone had laughed heartily as Teddy had entered the room. He was wearing a football shirt which had been one of the presents he had received from his grandad.

'All right, is it?' Ted asked, tugging at one of the sleeves.

'Course it is, Grandad. West Ham colours, claret and blue, can't wait to show the boys at school, and the boots are smashing too. Maybe I'll get picked to play for the school team.'

Ted leant over and ruffled his grandson's hair, then said, 'I've got a surprise for you, my boy.'

'What, another one?' Teddy was bursting with excitement.

'It's not as good as I would have liked it to be, but all the same it's not bad.'

'Oh Grandad, stop teasing and tell me what it is.'

'Well, I was hoping to take you to see West Ham play tomorrow, but they haven't got a game on Boxing Day this year. They have got a match this Saturday away against Notts County, but I don't feel like travelling all the way to Nottingham. God knows what the weather will be like.'

Teddy was impatient. 'So how is that a surprise for me?'

Ted Dryden smiled. He adored his grandchildren.

'Hold yer horses, Teddy. My luck was in, I have managed to get tickets for the first Saturday in the New Year.'

'Great, Grandad.' A delighted Teddy was grinning from ear to ear. 'But where is the match, and who are West Ham playing?'

Ted couldn't hold back any longer. 'It's a home match, son. West Ham are playing Bury at the Boleyn Ground.'

Teddy shouted, 'Yippee! I'll wear this shirt and Grandad, will yer see if you can get me a big wooden rattle?'

'Course I will, lad, but you know what? If I got you the top brick off the chimney you'd want the stars out of the sky to go with it!'

Teddy was rolling about on the floor laughing, and every now and then he could be heard murmuring, 'Smashing, good old Grandad.'

Never had Ella loved her father-in-law more than she did at that moment.

Teddy used to look forward to regular visits to football matches with his father. Not that he had complained, but she knew the fact that his dad wasn't around had hurt him much more than he would openly admit.

Ella's eyes met those of her father-in-law and she mouthed silently, 'Thanks, Ted.' For a ridiculous moment she felt a bit weepy, but instead she crossed to where Ted was sitting, put her arms around him and hugged him tightly.

It hadn't been a bad day.

PART TWO

1953
A New Year

Chapter Twenty-nine

NEW YEAR'S EVE HAD been a great event in the British Legion. Mike had applied for and been granted an extension to stay open until half an hour after midnight. As Big Ben had struck twelve, the Thames had been lit up by the setting off of hundreds of fireworks, and every tug and ship on the river had answered with a forcible blast from their hooters. People had danced in the streets and sung their hearts out. The blackout and the shortages of the war years were forgotten. This was a different new world, everyone was optimistic.

Try telling that to the wounded soldiers, many of whom were still in Roehampton Hospital and other such places up and down the country. Still, one could not begrudge the public going mad on a night like this.

Tomorrow would be the start of a new year, and most folk were hoping for a new start. Everyday life would be a different matter. Ella was feeling a little despondent. Since the war, they had been told often enough how in future it would be a world fit for heroes. Oh yeah? How many men were unemployed? How many soldiers, sailors and airmen had lost their lives?

Customers were streaming back into the club, having seen the firework display. They all wanted a last drink, and as Ella pulled pints and held glasses under the optics, she reminded herself that 1952 hadn't been a great year for her.

She crossed her fingers. This year she would have a lot of decisions to make, but one thing was for certain: she had to make them herself, act as a capable adult and not be persuaded when other people thought they knew what was best for her.

Ted Dryden wore his Crombie overcoat, which made him look very successful – which he certainly was. Young Teddy was wearing long trousers, a shirt and two jumpers. Over the top of that lot he had pulled on his claret and blue football shirt, and to make his supporter's gear complete, his gran had bought him a hat and a long scarf in the West Ham colours.

Ella stood at the gate to wave them off.

Teddy turned, grinned at his mother and held his rattle high. Then he began to swing it round and round as he walked.

'That bloody awful racket,' Ella muttered. Thank God they were on their way. The sound of that football rattle being constantly swung this morning had her nerves in shreds. Still, going to a football match with his grandad was a wonderful way for Teddy to spend the first Saturday in the new year. Her young son was the happiest she had seen him for a long time, and for that reason alone she felt so grateful to her father-in-law.

Ella watched until Ted and young Teddy had turned the corner then she went back inside the house suddenly feeling very lonely. Her mother had taken Babs to the cinema; they were going to see Gene Kelly in *Singin' in the Rain* to compensate for Teddy going to see West Ham play.

It was her own fault that she was on her own. Sam had asked her if she would like to go up West with him, have a meal and maybe go to the theatre in the evening. She had made an excuse and refused.

Ever since Christmas afternoon when Ted and Sam had had a go at each other, she had felt she had to tread warily where Sam was concerned. Not that it was any of her father-in-law's business whether or not she went out with Sam, but she did feel, albeit half-heartedly, that Ted was right. Sam was acting a little bit overprotective. After all, she had only been out with him the once and she wouldn't have put that evening down in her book as a one hundred per cent success.

'I'll make meself a cup of tea and get on with the ironing,' she murmured, looking dolefully at the pile of crumpled clothes on the chair.

She had barely drunk her tea and was setting the ironing blanket to cover the kitchen table when there was a loud knock on the front door. She took her time walking down the passage, and as she opened the door her eyes widened with shock and she frowned deeply. There was a policeman standing on her doorstep.

'I wonder, is Mr Dennis Dryden here?' a gruff voice enquired. 'I'm Constable Didby.'

'No, no, I'm afraid he's not,' Ella stammered.

The constable nodded his head thoughtfully before saying, 'Is Mr Dryden any relation to you, ma'am?'

Ella was tempted to tell him to mind his own business, but looking at his uniform she decided she had better answer his question.

'Yes, yes, he's my husband.'

'Ahh,' he said, sounding as if he were clearing his throat. 'In that case, would you kindly ask him to contact me or any officer at the local station as soon as possible, please.'

'May I ask what this is about?' Ella had decided a bit more politeness might be in order.

'Of course, though I'm afraid it is sad news. Miss Dorothy Sheldon died two days ago and the hospital have been unable to trace any relatives. However, a firm of solicitors who were acting for Miss Sheldon had been given your husband's name as next-of-kin.'

Ella's mind was racing nineteen to the dozen. Dorothy Sheldon? As far as she could remember, she had never heard the name before. She found herself struggling to think of something to say.

All she could come up with was, 'I see.'

The policeman turned to go, then paused. 'Apparently her death was peaceful. A quiet end but the lady was all on her own.'

Ella felt guilty, but as to why she should, she had no idea.

She managed to speak calmly. 'Thank you for letting us know. I will ask my husband to get in touch with you as soon as possible.'

'Thank you, Mrs Dryden. Goodbye.'

'Goodbye, Constable Didby.'

Ella closed the door. All at once she needed to sit down. She perched herself on the bottom stair. Who the hell was Dorothy Sheldon? What had her death to do with Dennis? And another thing, how come Dennis had been named as her next-of-kin? There were certainly a whole lot of questions that needed answers.

She couldn't wait for Ted to get back from the match. Now maybe he could *prove* that he could get in touch with his son at any time.

He'd boasted about it often enough.

Ella had finished the ironing and still a lot of time stretched in front of her before her family would arrive home. She decided egg and chips would please both of her children for their tea. Meanwhile she opened the door to her big cupboard, took the flour jar down from the shelf and placed it on the table. To that she added margarine, lard, dried fruit and a two-pound jar of blackberry and apple jam. Having tied a bibbed white apron around her waist, she set to. A session of baking – a jam sponge and a few jam tarts – would keep her mind occupied.

Three hours later the front door almost came off its hinges as Teddy burst in yelling at the top of his voice, 'We won, we won! Great result, Mum, West Ham 3, Bury 2.' As he was reliving the excitement of the last goal that had decided the game for his team, he had taken a jam tart from the plate on top of the hob.

'Golly, that's blooming hot, it's burnt me mouth,' he moaned.

'Serve you right for helping yerself and not asking if you could have one,' his mother laughed. Then, making sure that Teddy was not watching, Ella gestured to her father-in-law that she wanted him to follow her into the front room.

With the door firmly closed, Ella told Ted of the visit from the policeman and did her best to explain why it was necessary for him to get in touch with Dennis.

Ted's face paled. He wasn't about to inform Ella that Dennis was at present in a police cell following a blazing row with builders who were working for him and were not only well behind schedule but were fiddling the cost of materials. He had been told the full story late last night but as usual had kept the matter to himself.

Stan Wilson, a long-term mate of Dennis, was in charge of the Wandsworth building project, and it went without saying that he was no fool. Duplicates of receipts for very large amounts of supplies had been slipped into the office.

Stan had had a word with Tom Cooke, the foreman. 'You must have been barmy, man, if you thought you could get away with it.'

'It wasn't only for my benefit. The whole gang thought a bit extra on top of their wages wouldn't be missed.'

'Well, me old mate, we live and learn, don't we? Now you're about to learn that you'd have t' get up early in the morning to put one over on Dennis.'

Dennis Dryden came leisurely out of the big shed that served as an office and walked across the site towards them. From his briefcase he took a pouch that held the wage packets of each of the workmen. Instead of handing it to Tom Cooke, as he normally would, he gave it to Stan.

'Hand these out, mate, and tell the men to be on site seven thirty sharp on Monday morning, when I'll 'ave something to say to them.'

Tom Cooke stood beside Dennis and watched silently as each man accepted his wage packet and cleared off faster than you could say Jack Robinson.

'And where's mine?' he said, trying to sound jocular.

Dennis gave him a blinding look. 'You've paid yerself twice over for the last two weeks. That wasn't very nice, Tom, I thought I was treating you well, paying you well over the odds.' Dennis's voice dripped with sarcasm. 'And another thing, duplicating invoices, that didn't impress me, that's kid's play. Thought you would have realized by now that I wasn't born yesterday.'

Then, without warning, Tom was knocked off his feet as Dennis lunged at him. Stan was trying to drag Dennis back by holding on to his overcoat, talking to him sensibly, willing him to calm down. Dennis pushed him out of the way. Using his feet to press home his point, he kicked Tom in the ribs, and as he lifted his head his face came into contact with Dennis's fist.

'Nobody robs me and gets away with it. Do you hear me?'

The workmen had needed no telling that their foreman was in for a beating, and one of them had phoned the police.

A police car roared on to the site. Slamming on the brakes, it skidded to a halt. Two uniformed policemen got out and stood in front of Dennis. Tom Cooke had staggered to his feet by now. Dennis pushed one policeman out of the way and smashed his fist once more into the side of Tom's head, saying, 'And that's yer bonus!'

The policemen took in the situation at a glance. One of them spoke to Stan.

'Do that bloke on the ground a favour and get him to a hospital. He looks like he could do with a bit of TLC.'

As the other officer pushed Dennis towards the police car, he said, 'You're nicked.'

Dennis's face was dark with temper as he lowered his head to get into the back of the police car.

He hadn't been given much choice. Still, he'd made his point.

Ted shook his head. Ella was still waiting for an explanation.

'I remember Dorothy Sheldon, of course I do, a really nice lady. So she's died, shame. She was younger than Lady Margaret, never thought Margaret would outlive her. Just goes to show, we never know.'

'How come I've never heard of her, and what's all this about Dennis being her next-of-kin?' Ella was confused, and couldn't wait to get to the bottom of the matter.

'Can't say that I know what all this solicitor business is about myself,' Ted answered warily. 'But I do remember the first time we all met; it was at Cheltenham racecourse. Officially Dorothy Sheldon was Lady Margaret's paid companion, but in all truth they were dear faithful friends.

'I need to get on the blower to contact my Den – what a pity you're not on the phone here, we'll have t' get that sorted – and I'll go with him to see this copper. Constable Didby you said, yes?'

'That's right,' Ella agreed, wondering as usual why Ted always denied that he knew where Dennis lived, yet he always knew how to get hold of him when he was needed.

Within twenty minutes Ted was walking through the front betting hall and on into the office of his main bookmaker. He owned three such businesses where bets were accepted and winnings were paid out, and nothing that went on in any of them got past his notice.

Being Saturday, business was brisk. Horse-racing might be finished for the day, but men were still placing bets. At three stadiums there would be dog-racing tonight.

Ted looked up the number for the local cop-shop, and as he waited he hoped for the best but prepared himself for the worst. Nobody seemed to know where his son was banged up.

'Elephant an' Castle police,' a quick, sharp voice answered.

'Oh, my name is Edward Dryden. I wonder, could I speak to Constable Didby?'

'Hold on, I know he's been out, I'll see if he's back in the station yet.'

Ted's heart sank. Hold on, that could mean a bloody long wait. But his fears were unfounded as a gruff voice came on the line almost at once.

'Constable Didby speaking, what can I do for you?'

'I'm Mr Dryden Senior, you visited my daughter-in-law this afternoon looking for my son, Dennis Dryden.'

'Yes, I had to deliver sad news, I'm sorry.'

'You said my son has been named as next-of-kin to Miss Sheldon. He wasn't related to her at all.'

The constable didn't speak for a moment, and when he did he sounded thoughtful.

'Probably the lady didn't have any family. Were she and your son friends? If so, perhaps he agreed to take on the duty of seeing to her affairs. He should contact her solicitor straight away.'

'Bit difficult,' Ted muttered down the line.

'How come?' Constable Didby was interested.

'Your lot has him banged up. I don't know where, but I'm told he was arrested in Wandsworth. Can I stand bail for him?'

'Depends.'

'On what?'

'Whether the magistrate agrees. When was he picked up and what for?'

'Yesterday evening . . . for brawling.'

'Pity it was the weekend. He won't be brought before a magistrate before Monday morning. You can attend the court and offer to stand bail but there is no guarantee that the judge will grant it. Then again, he might get off scot free or with just a fine, if he's lucky.'

'Oh, like that, is it? Anyway, thanks for your help.'

Ted replaced the telephone on its hook, put his elbows on the edge of his desk and cupped his face in his hands.

So there wasn't anything he could do over the weekend. He made a quick decision. He wasn't going to go anywhere near Ella, she'd be asking too many questions. Instead he would pay a long-overdue visit to Lady Margaret. It wouldn't take him long to get to Chelsea.

It had been a wise choice, Ted was saying to himself as he drove up the tree-lined avenue to the rest home.

Once inside, he introduced himself to a tall, smartly dressed lady with threads of grey in her brown hair.

Smiling, she said, 'Anne Riley, I'm the matron here.

Lady Margaret speaks of you so often, Mr Dryden, all the staff feel they know you. I'm so sorry I haven't been available on your previous visits. Lady Margaret still reads the sports pages of the newspapers and she greatly appreciates the fact that you always send her your race-card from the major meetings. It seems you keep her well informed where horse-racing is concerned.'

Ted smiled at the compliment. More than likely, Lady Margaret was still interested in horse-racing even if it was only from her armchair, and she would always associate him with the sport of kings.

Matron rode up in the lift with Ted and ushered him into a large bed-sitting room. His first impression was that it was old-fashioned but elegant. It was a much larger room and had a better view than the one that Lady Margaret had occupied on his previous visits.

His long-term friend was sitting in a deep armchair which was positioned so that she could see the beautiful gardens beyond the bay window. She turned her head as Ted stepped forward and blinked twice before saying, 'Edward, what a wonderful surprise, how well you look.'

Ted took her slender, bony hand between both of his. 'How well *you* look,' he replied. 'You haven't aged a day and you sound so happy.'

'That is because I am happy. The staff here have helped me make this my home.' Then, slowly, it was as if a cloud passed over her face. 'Dorothy's death has brought you here today, hasn't it?'

Ted nodded, for the moment too bewildered to speak.

'Sit down, Mr Dryden,' Matron said, indicating an armchair near to her ladyship. 'Would you like some tea or coffee, both of you?'

Lady Margaret answered. 'Your lovely milky coffee would be fine, please, Matron. I'm sure Edward will enjoy a cup.'

278

When Matron left the room the questions began and Ted started the ball rolling.

'Why has my son been named as Dorothy's next-of-kin?'

Such a deep sigh before Ted got an answer. 'Dorothy had no family, but I never thought I would outlive her. Because she was that much younger I even took out an endowment policy for her because I knew the small allowance I made her would cease with my death. When I had to move, your son was so kind and considerate to Dorothy. Having turned my big old house into four splendid apartments, he made it possible for her to purchase one. She was forever grateful to him for that. She loved living there. She used to visit me a lot until her health started to fail. However, we wrote to each other regularly.'

Lady Margaret stopped talking and a worried look crossed her face.

Quickly Ted asked, 'Is there something wrong?'

'Well, I suppose not, not now, since poor Dorothy is no longer with us, but . . .'

'But what?' Ted was quick to ask.

Lady Margaret sighed gently. 'Edward, within the last four months I have had the feeling that a gentleman, a resident in the same apartments, had been causing Dorothy some distress. She had a pet, a lovely old cat called Misty – actually it was my pet to begin with. She had to have it put down because it was so badly injured when it became entangled in some barbed wire. Dorothy couldn't prove anything, but Misty always used to make for the same patch of undergrowth whenever she let her out. She thinks the man, Mr Packard, hid that wire there deliberately.'

Ted felt he had to ask. 'Why would any man be so evil?'

279

'That was only one thing in a long list of nasty occurrences. Dorothy said he approached her soon after she moved in and asked her to sell her apartment to him. Naturally she refused. He pestered her time and time again to sell. Never giving her time to settle in. The Lord only knows why.'

Ted was seething with rage, and he vowed that he and Dennis would find out what had been going on.

He quickly changed the subject. 'Do you know who is going to make the arrangements for Dorothy's funeral?'

'All that will be left to our solicitor, Mr Trent, Mr James Trent. Dorothy and I made our wills a long time ago.'

A long pause while Lady Margaret gathered her thoughts. Then sadly she said, 'I don't suppose she will be buried until sometime next week. Shouldn't think many people will attend. Mr Trent will also arrange for light refreshments afterwards, perhaps in the lounge of a hotel in Epsom. I shall do my best to be there, though I rarely go out.'

Ted quickly offered, 'I will arrange for a car to take you and bring you back if you feel that you would like to attend.'

'Oh, Edward, that is so kind of you. I'll decide later on.'

'Are there any other details that my son should deal with?'

'No, I don't think so. Mr Trent will see to probate, the bank and whatever your son decides about her apartment. Everything including her personal possessions goes to him.'

Lady Margaret stared at Ted's blank face. 'Don't look so shocked. When Dorothy made her last journey up here to visit me, she told me that she had changed her will. Previously I think most of her belongings were to go to charity, but I truly believe that your son has been a good friend to her in her last months. I also have reason to believe that she knew she was very ill – not that she said a word to me.'

At that point Matron entered the room together with a maid pushing a small tea trolley.

'Oh,' Lady Margaret exclaimed delightedly, 'we are honoured, lovely savouries and a fruit cake to go with our coffee. Thank you, Matron.'

'You are both more than welcome,' Matron answered as she and the maid left the two old friends to help themselves.

Chapter Thirty

DENNIS HAD NEVER FELT such a fool in his life. He had
been placed high up in the enclosure used for the accused.
The magistrate was glancing through a folder which had
been set in front of him, and as Dennis watched he thanked
God he didn't have a record. He had listened to the
policeman's version of what had happened and then to
the testimony of Stanley Wilson as to his good character
and how well he treated his workmen.

The magistrate was now conferring with his colleagues
who sat on either side of him. They were murmuring and
nodding their heads in agreement.

Dennis turned his head and looked across at his father,
but Ted wouldn't or couldn't meet his eyes.

At that point Dennis would have freely admitted that
he was scared. He had never been to prison. He had been
in trouble enough times when he was younger, but
somehow his dad had always managed to smooth things
over. Now he felt he was entirely on his own. A film of
perspiration was covering his good-looking face and his
thick mop of hair was also damp.

Somebody was prodding him in the back, telling him

to stand up. Now he could hear the magistrate's voice loud and clear.

'Mr Dryden, this matter appears to have stemmed from a misuse of your business funds, and while the court does not take lightly the fact that you took matters into your own hands, the bench is of the opinion that you were severely provoked. Your site manager, Mr Cooke, has refused to press charges. However, you did cause an affray which led to a breach of the peace. You are therefore fined the sum of fifty pounds, but I add a warning that, should you appear before this court in the future, we shall not be of the same mind. Do you understand?'

Dennis quietly answered, 'Yes,' and then added, 'Thank you, sir.'

It was as if a burden had been lifted from his shoulders.

The experience of spending the weekend in a police cell had left him with an instinctive wish to avoid the police in future.

Two big men, both well over six foot tall, walked out of the court and into the nearest pub, where Edward Dryden ordered two large brandies. As they each tossed them back, it would have been hard to say which one of the men felt the more relieved.

'You'd better come home with me, have a wash and tidy-up before you go and see your wife, and don't forget that sometime today you have to contact that Mr Trent.' Ted's voice was low but firm.

'Thanks, Dad.' Dennis had no intention of paying Ella a visit. The less she knew about him having spent the weekend in a police cell, the better for everyone concerned. Instead he suggested, 'How about we go to Covent Garden first, get ourselves a slap-up breakfast? I'm starving; they didn't exactly feed me in the lock-up.'

His father grinned. 'Then you can thank yer lucky stars that they didn't bang yer up properly, 'cos I'll take bets you'd have lost a whole lot of weight before you came out.'

With a huge fry-up and two large mugs of tea beneath his belt, Dennis felt a whole lot better as he sat behind his father's desk in order to use his telephone.

'Gurney and Trent.' A young lady's voice answered his call.

'Oh good morning, I understand Mr Trent has been trying to get in touch with me.'

'Who shall I say is calling?'

'Oh, I'm sorry, Dennis Dryden, in connection with the death of Miss Sheldon.'

'Hold on a minute, please.'

Almost at once Mr Trent came on the line. 'Mr Dryden, so glad we have been able to contact you. Sorry about the sad news, but not totally unexpected.'

A good voice, strong and businesslike. Dennis felt better already.

'I've been told that I have been listed as Miss Sheldon's next-of-kin. Do I have to do anything in particular?'

'Oh no, Mr Dryden, you inherit, but Miss Sheldon asked that this firm be her executor. No other person is involved.'

'My father has been in touch with Lady Margaret; she told him you would be seeing to all the funeral arrangements and—'

Mr Trent intervened. 'All finalized. The first thing is that Miss Sheldon left instructions with my office that she wished to be buried with her parents. The family own a plot so that makes everything much easier. It is in Lambeth Cemetery in Tooting. Unfortunately quite a journey from Epsom. As for an undertaker, that has been dealt with, and as it stands, all documents being ready, the burial should take place next Tuesday, that's a week tomorrow. Not sure how many cars will be needed. Lady Margaret has promised to telephone or write to their few friends, and perhaps you could let me know if you will be attending and if anyone else will be accompanying you. Naturally myself and one colleague will attend and a booking has been made for the function room in the Spread Eagle Hotel in Epsom for a small get-together afterwards.

'By the way, have we got your telephone number?'

Dennis hesitated. 'I'm travelling a lot at the moment; best I give you my father's number, would that be all right?'

'No problem, we can always leave a message for you.'

Dennis gave him the number. 'Thank you again, goodbye for—'

'Mr Dryden?'

'Yes?'

'Don't ring off. Miss Sheldon was not a lady of great wealth, but you are the sole beneficiary. She had some savings, and her endowment policy will more than cover any outstanding bills and the funeral expenses. Her main asset is of course her apartment. I have to tell you we have already received an offer on this property, should you wish to sell.'

Warning bells went off in Dennis's head. His father had rattled on about another tenant, a Mr Claude Packard, who had been pestering Miss Sheldon to sell. Probably the same bloke; he sounded like a nasty piece of work.

'No way,' Dennis answered without stopping to think. 'We'll let the dust settle before we think about disposing of anything that belonged to Miss Sheldon.'

'A very wise decision, Mr Dryden. It is not a substantial legacy, but Miss Sheldon was anxious that you should

285

know how much she appreciated your kindness to her, especially because you negotiated terms that enabled her to live in what had been her home for a good many years.'

Dennis was embarrassed. 'I wasn't kind. I was just able to cut the price a bit on that remaining flat.'

Mr Trent chose to ignore that admission. Instead he said knowingly, 'I did the conveyancing when Miss Sheldon bought it from you.'

In other words he knows I knocked quite a bit off the price for her! 'I never thought . . . I didn't expect . . .' Dennis was embarrassed. The last thing he wanted was to be thought of as a do-gooder, or a gold-digger.

Oh, what the hell, it has nothing to do with anyone but me.

'Thank you,' Dennis couldn't think of anything more to say.

'A pleasure to be of help, though sorry it has to be under such sad circumstances. Goodbye for now, Mr Dryden, we'll probably meet at the funeral.'

Mr Trent rang off and Dennis slowly replaced the receiver.

Now he had to go and face his wife.

Bonus, though, he'd get to see his kids today.

Winnie Paige was alone in her daughter's house when a tap on the door followed by footsteps coming down the passage broke into her thoughts, and she called, 'Who is it?' and Dennis Dryden marched into the kitchen.

'Oh God above, it's enough to freeze the brass balls off a pawn shop out there! Probably gonna get some real snow this time, didn't have much before Christmas.' Dennis walked towards the hearth and, taking his gloves off and shoving them into his coat pocket, held out his hands to the blazing fire.

'It hasn't started to snow again, surely?' his mother-in-law asked.

'Not yet, Win, but it won't be long. Where's Ella and the kids?'

Winnie moaned to herself: why is it left t' me to tell this bloke where his wife is?

'Sit down and get yerself warm. I'll make a brew and I've made some pies if you fancy a bite to eat.'

'Win, I'd love a cuppa, I'm chilled to the bone, but first of all, remember, I asked you a question!'

Winnie pulled a face. 'They've all gone to a party 'cos Sam Richardson's firm didn't give one at Christmas, for what reason I don't know.'

'Where the hell does Sam Richardson come into this?'

'Sam is a kind of partner, I think, in a firm called Hirst and Richardson.'

'I know all that, don't I? Known Sam from years back, but that still doesn't answer my question.'

'All right, all right. At first Sam said he'd take Babs and Teddy, then he asked if Ella would like to go with them. He said it's always a good do and the kids get given lovely presents.'

'I can buy my kids all the presents they need,' Dennis said, sounding really churlish.

Winnie decided to give as much to Dennis as he was throwing at her.

'Yeah, and leave 'em on the doorstep and run away. Hadn't even got the guts to come into the house and see yer kids on Christmas Day, never mind the other three hundred an' odd days in the year.'

One look at Dennis's face and Winnie was having second thoughts. Perhaps she should have kept her mouth shut.

'Is Sam Richardson trying it on with my wife?' Dennis asked, letting his anger get the better of him.

'I don't know, an' if I did I wouldn't tell yer. You're such a big man, why don't you ask him yerself?'

This situation had suddenly become awkward and

neither of them spoke for a while. Then a surge of relief came over Winnie as Dennis got to his feet, went to the stove and lifted the big black kettle to the centre of the range. 'Thought you said we were gonna have a bite to eat and a cuppa,' he muttered.

Jesus, it was unbelievable!

This great big bloke was sitting here in his own kitchen, and she'd lay a penny to a pound that he was wishing it was him and not Sam Richardson that had taken his wife and kids out for the afternoon.

Oh, the madness of it all!

It was Dennis who made the pot of tea while Winnie took the cups, saucers and plates down from the dresser and set them out on the table.

'Only got cold pie, veal, ham an' egg, but I did make it meself, none of that shop rubbish. Got a big stew on the go back of the hob but it's nowhere near ready yet.'

'Thanks, Winnie.' He spoke softly now as she passed him a plate on which she had laid two thick slices of the pie. 'This will do me fine.'

She also put in front of him a plate of crusty new bread and a dish of butter. 'I've got plenty of salad or some pickles if you fancy some.' She was pouring the tea out as she spoke.

'Still pushing the rabbit food, Win? Sunday tea always included salad when we all used to come t' your place. No thanks to the salad but I will have some of that Branston pickle if you'd pass the jar, please.'

He had drunk his tea and Winnie was refilling his cup before he ventured to ask, 'Are the children all right?'

Without looking at him she said, 'Young Ted is the image of you, as you are the image of your father. Three peas from the same pod and no mistake. As for Babs, she's growing fast. A really nice little girl but she gets that beautiful copper-coloured hair and soft skin from our side of the family. I don't think she's in a hurry to grow up, though. She's . . . well, she's just Babs. Everybody loves her.'

Now Winnie did look at her son-in-law and she smiled, a small understanding smile. He smiled back at her, and they continued eating in silence.

Soon he was putting his coat, scarf and gloves on. Taking hold of her hand gently, he said, 'Perhaps it might be better if you didn't tell Ella or the kids that I've been here.' When she didn't answer, he shook his head slowly and said, 'I'm an ignorant fool, and I'm ashamed of so many things that I let happen.'

'Oh, Dennis, you don't need—'

He stopped her. 'Yes, I do need. And Winnie, nobody knows that better than you do.'

His remorse brought tears to her eyes, and she murmured something indistinct.

'What?'

'Well, do something about it,' she repeated.

'Such as?'

'Tell Ella, not me.'

The funeral was over. A quiet, dignified affair attended by just six women and five men.

Lady Margaret had decided against attending, and Matron had assured Edward on the telephone that it was a wise decision, with the weather being as bad as it was.

When each mourner had thrown a handful of the cold earth down on to the coffin and the priest had shaken hands with each of them, they all moved away and left the grave-diggers to get on with their work. Dennis shook hands with both Mr Trent and his partner. However, when Ted said that they would not be making the journey to Epsom, Mr Trent indicated that he needed a moment of Dennis's time.

'I have to go down to Epsom – these ladies and gentlemen who so kindly came to Miss Sheldon's funeral deserve the little get-together that I have arranged – but you and I do need to talk. There are a few matters that require your attention.'

Dennis looked thoughtful for a moment, then said, 'I can't make it tomorrow, but how would Thursday fit in with your plans?'

'You state the time and I'll make sure that I am free.'

'Ten o'clock, your office,' Dennis said without hesitation.

Mr Trent said, 'Good,' and, as though he were sealing their agreement, he covered Dennis's hand with his own.

Ted and his son stood silently watching the cars move down towards the cemetery gates. Then, heads sunk into the collars of their expensive overcoats, they walked away towards where Ted had parked his car.

Dennis was totally unaware that the death of Dorothy Sheldon and the events which were yet to unfold would have such a shattering effect on his future life.

Thursday morning, and Dennis was listening intently to what Mr Trent had to say. So far it was pretty much as his father had suspected, having listened to Lady Margaret air her fears as to the way her friend Dorothy had been treated. Now Dennis was beginning to form his own opinion as to why this Mr Packard was so anxious to purchase her apartment.

All legalities regarding the estate of Miss Sheldon had been dealt with and Dennis now knew exactly where he stood.

'Now, Mr Dryden, shall we move on to your actual property?'

Having got a nod from Dennis, Mr Trent leant across

his desk and said, 'I take it that when you had that beautiful old house turned into four apartments, which you then sold individually, you retained the freehold of the property?'

Dennis smiled. 'How did I know you were going to ask me that?'

It was Mr Trent who now smiled. 'How do I know that your answer to my question is yes?'

'To be honest, it was my father who steered me that way.'

'A real man of the world is your father. So, we can move on. We have established that you sold one apartment to a Mr Claude Packard, another to a young man . . .' Mr Trent paused and consulted his notes. 'Ah yes, Mr Alfred Marshall. He took out a mortgage in order to purchase, but after only two months his firm moved its business to Leicester. Having been offered an all-expenses-paid move, Mr Marshall wanted to sell in a hurry. Mr Packard applied for a mortgage and bought Mr Marshall's apartment. With that move Mr Packard became the owner of two of the apartments. From then on it would seem that a series of unpleasant happenings started to occur which made life very difficult for Miss Sheldon, and to a lesser degree the fourth owner also experienced unexplained accidents.' He paused again, turned over some pages and then carried on speaking. 'A widow lady, Mrs Hines, you met her at Miss Sheldon's funeral. Apparently she also has been approached by Mr Packard as to the prospect of her selling her apartment.'

'Thinks he's clever, this Mr Packard,' Dennis said with what was almost a sneer. 'We all know the property market is rising fast, but what he doesn't know is that anything and everything that goes on or around the area of a racecourse has always been a matter of great interest to my father. Packard has been putting feelers out to members of the local council as to what the chances are of obtaining planning permission.'

'I'm with you, Mr Dryden,' the solicitor murmured. 'There are a good many acres of prime land that go with your property. By the way, are you still using the original name?'

'Yes, Lady Margaret wanted it still to be known as Maple House.'

'Should Mr Packard be successful in securing both the flat that Miss Sheldon owned, which now belongs to you, and also Mrs Hines's apartment, it would mean that he owned the whole building.'

But not the freehold, Dennis was thinking, not by a long chalk.

'So,' he asked Dennis, 'if I were to agree to sell him what was Miss Sheldon's place, has this Mr Packard got the readies?'

Mr Trent had to think for a moment; readies was not a word with which he was familiar.

Finally he said, 'I wouldn't have thought so. Scraping the barrel more like! I've been given to understand that if and when he can say he has persuaded the owners of the two remaining apartments to sell, he would be seeking to take out a legal charge using the property as security for one huge loan.'

Dennis smiled, a truly wicked smile. 'Would he now! I would really like some concrete evidence as to why this Mr Packard can't wait to be the sole owner of all four apartments. Any chance you can put some feelers out?'

Mr Trent could not quite suppress a smile. 'Given your instructions, Mr Dryden, I can make discreet enquiries.'

'Please do that, Mr Trent.'

Chapter Thirty-one

EDWARD DRYDEN WAS TRYING to catch up on a backlog of ledger work and he was fast losing his patience.

'Why on earth do you want us both to go down to Epsom?' he asked Dennis, who was leaning up against the counter.

'Hard to know where to begin really, Dad, but before the funeral you were saying that you suspected that Mr Packard was giving Miss Sheldon a load of trouble; well, now I've got a problem with this geezer and the funny thing is I just can't put my finger on the cause. Dorothy was barely cold before he had telephoned her solicitor saying he wanted to put an offer in to buy her flat. Naturally, Mr Trent wouldn't or couldn't confirm in so many words that the offer came from the same bloke that was pestering her to sell. Not a bad guy, though, that Mr Trent; he has agreed to put the feelers out and let me know if he comes up with anything.'

'So why not wait until he gets in touch with you?'

'Because I have this feeling that if he gets Miss Sheldon's flat he'll go for Mrs Hines. He won't play fair, he'll make her life a misery same as he did Miss Sheldon's. He thinks if he's clever enough he'll end up owning the whole caboodle.'

'Don't you ever stop to think, you nuthead? How can he get hold of Dorothy's flat? You own it now and sure as hell he can't make you do anything you've no mind t' do.'

'Dad, I've got a plan hatching in my head, but I'm beginning to think Packard might be a little too dangerous for me to have dealings with.'

'Son, has that couple of nights in a cell turned your grey matter to yellow? Come on through and outline what you're trying to come up with.' He lifted the flap of the counter and led Dennis through into his private office.

It was a bit long-winded, but in the end Dennis managed to outline his idea clearly enough to make his father roar with laughter.

'Nice one, my son, a really nice one, we'll drink to that, 'cos if what we suspect turns out to be the truth, then it will be a case of the biter got bit. If anybody ever deserved to be brought down to earth it's that scumbag. Only the lowest of the low picks on defenceless women, especially when he knows they've got no man behind them.'

'I'm glad you agree, Dad. But what about Mrs Hines? How the hell do we explain to her that we want to sell her place over her head yet also assure her that she can remain living there if that's what she wants t' do?'

'Tough one, my boy, I'll give yer that. Then again, as you've heard me say often enough, never trouble trouble till trouble troubles you. So we'll sort that problem when we come to it. Meanwhile I think you're right. A little reassuring talk with Mrs Hines is in order and there's no better time than right now.'

Dennis was more than pleased. If his father agreed to be involved with his plan then there would be no question of anything going wrong. It might be complicated, but Edward Dryden had a habit of always coming out of a tricky situation smelling of roses.

Edward took his car. The roads were wet but the hard ice had gone, and the overcast sky was slowly lightening.

It was about an hour and a half later when he turned in to the long private drive that led up to Maple House. During the night the wind had dropped somewhat and the two men saw that in places the snow had melted and almost seeped away, revealing patches of rough, tufty grass each side of the driveway. Dennis lowered his side window and there was the fresh smell of moss and damp earth.

Not a bad place to live, he was thinking. If only his Ella had agreed to move out of London when he had first suggested it, who knows where they'd be today. As his father brought the car to a halt and Dennis made to get out he was mumbling, 'Life's full of bloody ifs.'

When Mrs Hines opened her front door in answer to the ringing of her bell, she was fully dressed but walking with two sticks.

'Hello. What have you been doing? You weren't using sticks when you attended Dorothy's funeral.' Edward spoke kindly.

'Hello, Mr Dryden and son I suppose I should say,' Mrs Hines said laughingly. 'Come in, you're more than welcome. I was just about to have coffee. You will join me, say yes, please do, I'm that thrilled to have company.'

She hobbled back into her magnificent lounge and bade them both to sit down. 'I have just put milk in the saucepan but haven't yet put it on to boil. I'll add some more to it and then I'll make the coffee.'

'You'll do no such thing,' Dennis ordered, guiding her safely to the chair with a foot-rest in front of it where she had obviously been sitting.

Having seen her settled and left his father there to talk

to her, Dennis made for the luxurious kitchen. There was a tray neatly laid, one cup and saucer, one teaspoon and a small plate with two biscuits. It was an expensive tray and the delicate bone china hadn't come from Woolworth's; nevertheless, the sight brought a lump to his throat. It spelt lonely.

He found a larger tray, added two extra cups and saucers, took more milk out of the refrigerator and poured some into the saucepan, then put the pan on to the electric plate. The milk came to a boil at the same time as the coffee percolator began to steam. Finding a pretty jug, he poured the hot milk into it and set it down on the tray, unplugged the percolator, added more biscuits from a tin and all was ready.

If Ella had been there, she wouldn't have believed Dennis was capable of such an achievement. Though she would probably be the first to admit that when he lived at home she had encouraged him to be lazy by waiting on him hand, foot and finger.

Entering the lounge, Dennis grinned. 'Since I made it, I suppose the job of pouring it into the cups falls to me,' he said as he tackled the tricky job.

When they each had a lovely milky coffee in front of them, it was Ted who asked what Dennis was dying to know.

'So, why *are* you walking with two sticks, Mrs Hines? Have you had a fall?'

'Not exactly. I was careless, I suppose.'

'Now then, Mrs Hines, you leave us to draw our own conclusions,' Ted said, sounding really serious. 'Just tell us what happened.'

'I had been to our Friday night Bible class and the members of the group always stay on for a hot drink, then usually the vicar drives me home. It takes less than ten minutes in the car. Last week, as the roads were so bad, Mrs Taylor's son came for his mother and he said he had to pass my door almost and it would save the vicar a journey if he brought me home at the same time. He was so kind, he insisted on getting out of his car and seeing me safely inside the house to where the hall light was on. I thanked him and closed the front door, but as I was coming up the few stairs to my front door the light went out and I missed my footing and tripped.'

'Did anyone pick you up?' Dennis was quick to ask.

'No, there wasn't anyone around. I stayed still for a moment or two, then I managed to make it all right. I did have a restless night, quite a bit of pain, so in the morning I telephoned my doctor, who kindly came out to me within half an hour. I've bruised the shin bone on my left leg and sprained my right ankle. A nurse has called each day since, so I am fine. Funny thing, though . . .'

'Go on, finish what you were going to say,' Ted said, leaning forward and taking one of the old lady's hands between his own.

Mrs Hines looked perplexed. 'When the doctor came, he offered to replace the dead lightbulb. A kind thought, for which I was very grateful. However, he switched on the light and it worked, the bulb had not gone. It must have been a power cut.'

'Mrs Hines, think back,' Ted pleaded. 'When you finally managed to get into your apartment, was the electricity on or off?'

'Oh, it was on in here,' she said without hesitation. 'As soon as I got the front door open I remember I felt for the switch without thinking and my hall was flooded with light. Maybe the entrance is on a different circuit.'

And maybe pigs could fly if they had wings, Dennis was thinking.

The look that passed between father and son said they were both having the same thought.

There was unbroken silence while the three of them drank their coffee and nibbled at digestive biscuits. During this time Ted was casting his eyes all over the place. He had to hand it to his son, he might not do much manual work himself, but by God the men he employed were never amateurs or dabblers. Each man had to be an expert in his own trade. Dennis paid top wages and he expected only the best. It was a code he had long stood by and it certainly paid off. This apartment was proof of that. Everything about it was perfection personified.

Ted smiled to himself. Dennis was fond of saying, 'If you pay peanuts, your workmen must be monkeys.' He might cut corners in order to obtain contracts, but whether he got them by fair means or by giving out backhanders when a job was finished, he seldom received complaints. Quite the reverse.

Dennis had finished his coffee and the look his father gave him said it was time to take the bull by the horns.

'Mrs Hines, are you happy living here?' Ted gently asked the first question.

'Well, who wouldn't be, it is such a beautiful place.'

'That was not what I asked you. Please try and tell me and my son exactly how you feel. Can you do that?'

'I'll try.' Mrs Hines sighed softly and took a minute or two to collect her thoughts. 'For years I envied Dorothy and Lady Margaret, they had such a wonderful friendship, but they always had time for me when we met at church. On many an occasion they would bring me back here to have lunch with them. Of course this building was a whole house then, and the interior was rather old-fashioned but graceful. It was Dorothy who suggested I have an apartment here after you,' she nodded her head towards Dennis, 'did the alterations. I thought it was God's will because Lady Margaret decided to go into a care home and Dorothy and I would have each other for company.'

298

Mrs Hines paused and from a small handbag that hung from the arm of her chair she took out a lace-edged handkerchief and wiped the corner of her eye.

Father and son remained silent, letting her take her time.

'Everything was going so well to begin with. Young Mr Marshall was such a gentleman and helped us both in so many ways. We had grown quite fond of him. Slowly she shook her head. 'It wasn't to be. He was only here a matter of weeks when his firm promoted him and he moved away, and Mr Packard bought his apartment. I can't think why a married couple would want two flats.'

Dennis jumped in. 'Mr Packard has a wife?'

'Yes, yes, he does, though I don't think they are exactly amicable, nor even cordial to each other on some days.' Then, in a very childlike voice Mrs Hines added, 'I like her much better than him and so did Dorothy. Now Dorothy has gone and it doesn't seem right for me to be living here.'

Dennis looked at his father, and when he got the nod from him he began.

'Mrs Hines, I am going to tell you some interesting facts and I would like you to listen very carefully. Is that all right with you?'

'Perfectly all right,' she said, and nodded her head just once.

'Once the war was over, there was much rebuilding to be done and repair work was being carried out by men that my father and I would look upon as cowboys. They were causing a lot of unessential reconstruction to listed buildings. Therefore, the powers that be decided that every building, including dwellings, had to be registered at Somerset House. From then on, the Town and Country Planning Act became law. For example, if the title deeds of a property have been lost, new ones have to be applied for. On all such registrations, stamp duty has to be paid.

'As you know, my father and Lady Margaret were friends, mainly because of their mutual interest in horse-racing, and when she decided that this property was far too big for her to manage, she turned to my father for advice.'

Dennis stopped talking, and after a suitable interval during which Mrs Hines assured them she was all right, even saying that she was very interested, Ted took over.

'Over the years, maintenance of this property had not been kept up and matters such as the roof, to name only one item, needed urgent costly repairs. Lady Margaret decided to sell, and she and I between us negotiated a fair price and my son was able to go ahead with the deal. Dennis will tell you what happened from then on.'

'It was a lengthy business.' Dennis smiled at this genteel, white-haired old lady. 'I wanted to come and live here, bring my wife and two children, but it wasn't to be. My wife has her roots in London and no amount of persuasion from me would get her to move. So I decided to go down another road.

'Three times I put in an application and plans to Surrey County Council and each time they were turned down. The council were right, I realize that now. So was my wife,' Dennis quietly confessed. 'If my Ella had come to live in the original house she would have been like a fish out of water.' He paused, looking very thoughtful, before continuing. 'The municipal council were adamant. No outside structural alterations whatsoever to this building would be allowed.

'Then I had a brainwave! This property is detached, double-fronted and on two floors. All it really needed was for a good architect to draw up plans for the inside of the building to be split into four equal parts. Two downstairs and two on the first floor. Costly, mind you, and maybe I was a bit extravagant when it came to the fittings, but in hardly any time at all I had good craftsmen crawling all over the place, and hey presto we had these four luxurious apartments. All registered and all legal. Maybe I did boast a bit,' Dennis admitted, looking shamefaced at his father. 'I told my wife I had built a block of flats but only because I was narked because she wouldn't come to live here.'

'Now,' Ted butted in, 'having told you the basics, I think we need a proper drink before my son sets his plan before you. What do you think, Mrs Hines? A little drop of brandy?' he suggested, pulling his briefcase nearer to his feet and bending down to take out a bottle.

'I am going to put a proposition to you, Mrs Hines, and I want you to think about it very carefully.' Dennis spoke slowly and clearly.

'I will.' Having taken a sip of the brandy that Ted had poured for her, Mrs Hines sounded quite chirpy.

'I want to purchase this apartment from you.'

'You mean buy me out, you don't want me here?'

'Oh, Mrs Hines, please don't sound so horrified. Just hear me out. There is a lot I want to tell you and I did ask you to think about it carefully. That means that you make your own decision and in your own time. It doesn't matter how long you take. Now, shall I continue?'

Mrs Hines let out a deep breath which could have been a sigh of relief. 'Yes, I am listening.'

'Claude Packard wants to buy what was Dorothy's place and he also wants to purchase your apartment. As he already owns the other two apartments, doesn't that say something to you? It does to both my father and myself, something rather fishy, I'm afraid. I know at first you loved it here, and you had Dorothy close at hand, but now she had gone and you are alone again.'

Dennis could not give Mrs Hines a complete picture of his intentions, so what he was about to suggest to her

301

would require as careful an approach as would the other matter of dispensing with Claude Packard. If only he could see that life was made hard for this rotter, get a few London heavies to give him a good beating, get rid of him even, he thought wryly.

But it was far more complicated than that.

'What I am hoping to do is get our own back on Mr Packard for all the torment he put Miss Sheldon through and what we fear he might try to do to you should you refuse to sell your apartment to him.'

'Poor Dorothy,' Mrs Hines murmured. 'She was really afraid of him towards the end. She left her home to you, didn't she, Mr Dryden?'

'Yes she did.'

'Did she really have no other family? No relations?'

'Nobody, it seems.'

'Poor soul, Dorothy was such a sweet person. I think she felt it very badly when Lady Margaret left here. Though she did visit her and I went with her on a couple of occasions, and we both agreed Lady Margaret was so happy it was a good move. We all get so lonely as we get older and our friends and family have mainly passed on. We wonder why we are left.'

'If I did sell this apartment, where would I go? I have means but I wouldn't be mad enough to sink more money into making another expensive move.'

This was just the opening that Dennis was looking for.

'My father and I were thinking that if you sold this place back to us, you might like to go into the same care home in Chelsea as Lady Margaret.'

Dennis saw the doubt in her eyes and said quickly, 'I won't go into detail as to why I need to buy your property – the circumstances are too complicated – but both myself and my father will give you our solemn word that you would not lose out, not by one penny. If I buy your

302

place, I would ask you to move out for the time that it would take us to sort out Mr Packard, and when we have done that you shall have two choices. One, we return the deeds back over to you for a very reasonable sum and you would once again become the owner of this apartment. The alternative you must consider long and hard: you could stay in the care home as a permanent resident. You say you have visited Lady Margaret, so you have seen the conditions, and we could have a word with Anne Riley, the matron. I'm sure she could find you a very comfortable large room where you could stay, kind of test-drive the place, give everything the once-over and see if you think you would be happier there. And if not, there will be nothing to stop you coming back to Epsom once we have sorted this nasty matter out.'

Ted felt he had to give this kind lady a bit of confidence, so it was he that added, 'And we promise there will be no Mr Packard on the scene by then.'

'I don't have any idea how much it costs to stay in that beautiful place where Lady Margaret is. I only know it would be a lot.'

'To begin with, all that would be taken care of by my father.' Dennis also sought to reassure her.

Mrs Hines, quite firmly for an old lady, said, 'No. I can't say that I haven't given the same idea a great deal of thought since Dorothy died, but I cannot understand why you should want to go to such lengths to sort my affairs out.'

'Because we feel responsible for you. We should have checked Mr Packard's credentials before selling him an apartment. With hindsight, we should have sought buyers of the same age group and qualities. It is an old saying but a very true one, you have to live with someone to really know them. What we have learnt from Lady Margaret has led us to believe that Mr Packard is not a true gentleman.'

Dennis would have liked to have used words that were much stronger when referring to Claude Packard, but this was a frail old lady they were talking to.

'You are not to make a rash decision, you are to take your time. The wheels of justice grind slowly but we'll get there, never fear we shall get there.'

'If I decide to go along with your plans, Mr Dryden, I wouldn't own any bricks and mortar, would I?'

'You would if you decided that your stay in Chelsea was only going to be a temporary one. If that was the case, we would sell you back your own apartment and it would be like the move that Mr Marshall made, all expenses paid.'

Dennis felt he couldn't say any more because he didn't want to be accused of badgering Mrs Hines. Ted, however, couldn't leave things so up in the air. He stood up, moved his chair much closer to where Mrs Hines was sitting and gave her a very straightforward look.

'I endorse every word my son has said to you, and whatever you decide, that will be all right by us. Should you decide to stay here, that also will be OK. If you want to go with one of the options my son has offered you, we shall insist that everything is done legally and above board. Naturally you will use your own solicitor at every stage of the proceedings.

'Now,' he stood up, looked down at her and said, smiling, 'Dennis will wash our coffee cups and then we'll be off, because I think we have given you more than enough to think about for one day.'

With Dennis out in the kitchen doing what for him was a very unusual chore, Mrs Hines spoke softly to Ted.

'Lady Margaret often talked about you to me. I know she was quite content to leave her affairs in your hands when it came to selling this house. Therefore I do know that I may trust you, but if you don't mind I shall consult

304

my own solicitor and take a little while before making any big decision.'

'Very wise, my dear. You are a very competent lady, of that I have no doubt. I have put one of my business cards on your coffee table. Should you at any time feel the need to talk to me, or ask any questions, please ring my number. Should I be out of the office, just say who it is ringing and I will get back to you quite quickly.'

'Thank you, Mr Dryden,' she said, attempting to rise.

Ted gently pressed her back down into her chair. 'It has been a pleasure talking to you, we will see you again soon.'

'I hope so,' she said sadly, 'I hope so.'

It was a very thoughtful father and son who drove back to London.

Chapter Thirty-two

'COME AWAY WITH ME for the weekend,' Sam said to Ella one morning halfway through February.

Ella was busy changing an optic behind the bar and was certain she must have misheard what Sam had just said.

'Sorry, what did you say?'

'You heard me right the first time,' he said, smiling broadly. 'I think a few days away on our own would do us both good.'

Ella was still unwilling to believe that she was hearing right. Out of the blue, just like that, he wanted them to spend a whole weekend together.

'How can I, Sam?'

'Just ask Mike for some time off. The club isn't that busy at this time of year.'

He was incredible! 'What about my children?'

'Get your mother to move into your house to look after Babs and Teddy, she won't mind.'

The cheek of the man. He obviously had it all planned out in his mind.

Ella was worried. Not about what Dennis might think

if she went off for the weekend with another man. She hadn't set eyes on her husband since he had taken her out to dinner, and that was way before Christmas. He wasn't in a position to criticize how she led her life. But what about her mother? What would her reaction be?

She was tempted, that much she had to admit. Life at the moment was all work and no play, not that she was complaining. She counted herself lucky to have found herself such a good job and she really liked the people she worked with.

Sam was a nice man, and so far he hadn't taken any liberties, though that little spat he had had with her father-in-law on Christmas Day still rankled.

Ella took a deep breath before asking, 'Where would you be taking me?'

'To Brighton, well Hove, actually, it adjoins Brighton though it is a lot quieter and considered more upmarket. It will be really quiet at this time of the year.'

'So, have you taken a lady there before?'

Sam's face flushed bright red.

'No, I haven't.' His denial came out in a hoarse whisper. 'It's a detached bungalow, out in the wilds a bit. I first discovered it when my firm used a hotel on Hove seafront two years ago for our annual conference. One evening I went for a walk and it had a "For Rent" sign in the front garden. I told my sister and her husband about it and they rented it for two weeks. I went down and stayed three days with them and their two children, and we had a great time.'

'I'll think about it,' said Ella cautiously. To herself she was saying, he hasn't suggested that we take *my* two children with us.

Sam walked away without saying another word and Ella decided he could be very aggravating at times.

There was still the question of Dennis niggling away

in her head. Did he have the right to object? No, he had no right whatsoever, she thought bitterly.

So it was more or less to spite Dennis that three days later she said dubiously to Sam, 'A weekend by the sea sounds just what I need. But Sam, could we make it in a couple of weeks' time, because this Sunday is Babs's birthday.'

Sam didn't delay in making a decision. 'That's fine. It will give me time to contact the estate agent and to book a car.'

'What's wrong with your own car?'

'Nothing, it's just due for a thorough overall and I thought this would be an ideal time.'

Ella was pleased that Sam had agreed so readily to delay their little holiday.

She and her mother were planning a party, though Babs didn't want any boys to be there. That suited Teddy, who declared with a huge grin on his face that he would go and spend Saturday and Sunday with his grandad. Who wanted to hang around with a load of silly little girls when more than likely Grandad would take him to watch a football match?

To Babs a birthday meant presents. This year she had taken great pains to explain to her gran and her mother that she was no longer interested in dolls!

After breakfast, she sat on the rug in front of the front-room fire and opened her parcels, watched with some amusement by her mother and adoringly by her gran. She was not disappointed. Winnie had given her a cream-coloured coat which Babs had tried on in the shop a week ago and declared that she really, really liked. At the time Winnie had insisted it was far too expensive. The very next day, unbeknown to her granddaughter, she had gone back and bought it.

There was a huge jigsaw puzzle from Mike Murray and his wife, a real fountain pen and propelling pencil set together with a diary that had a lock on it from her mother, and a pretty card with a ten-shilling book token inside from Sam Richardson. But Babs's best present came from her father, in a large box that had been delivered by hand yesterday and which Ella had hastily hidden under the stairs.

Babs tore frantically at the brown paper. Then the lid of the box was lifted, showing layers of tissue paper which were quickly torn away, and finally Babs gasped with delight. A party dress. Baby-blue sateen, the skirt of the dress had a top layer of white organdie, the neckline was trimmed with lace, and pearly buttons were sewn down from the neck to the waist. The short puff sleeves had organdie cuffs.

Nothing could have given Babs more delight.

'I want to put it on now, please, Mum, can I?'

'No, sweetheart, it is a party dress. You can wear it this afternoon and show it off to all your friends. What you can do is clear up all this paper and take your presents up to your room. We've got to have the party in here, and we'll need the space to play games.'

Ella was deep in thought, thanking God that Ted had come and collected her son yesterday morning. What would Teddy think about his father sending such a wonderful present to his sister? It was Christmas all over again! Spend money on his children but too much of a coward to put in an appearance. A birthday hug and a few kisses from her dad would have had Babs dancing on the tabletop.

Babs's school friends arrived at four o'clock, and for an exhausting couple of hours Ella and her mother were in charge. At least they tried to be. Each child had brought a small present for Babs, which had to be opened. One child wept when a bigger girl tugged at her ringlets. Another girl asked if there was going to be a magician who would pull rabbits out of his top hat. Ella quickly told her there wasn't.

Games were played, with Pass the Parcel seeming to be the favourite, though every time Winnie lifted the needle from the gramophone record to stop the music there was an argument as to who was rightly holding the parcel.

Mother and daughter looked at the clock and couldn't believe that it was only a quarter to five.

'Tea time,' Ella shouted above the din. The games were thankfully abandoned and they all trooped out into the kitchen.

The scrubbed table was covered by a chenille cloth and then a really pretty cloth had been laid diagonally over that. The curtains were drawn, and the fire was burning brightly.

Winnie and Ella had gone to great lengths to please: there were dainty sandwiches, ham, egg and cheese, all with the crusts cut off. Lemonade, orange squash and cream soda were supplied with straws. There was a huge fruit trifle with a jug of pouring cream, jam tarts that Winnie had made, and, of course, the cake.

The girls took their places at the table, and for a little while all was silent. Of course there were accidents and squabbles, drinks spilt, the last egg sandwich two girls both wanted, a jam tart dropped on the floor, all speedily dealt with.

Winnie came in from the scullery bearing an enormous glass plate on which stood the cake. Ella, having cleared a space, said to her mother, 'Put it down here, all we need is for you to drop it.'

Winnie did as she was bid, then reached over and turned off the centre light.

Finally Ella lit the nine candles. The old kitchen became a magic place, the dancing flames reflected in the wide eyes of the little girls who sat around the table while Babs stood beside her mother and helped her to cut the cake.

The guests had all gone home, and suddenly the whole place was quiet.

'Cup of tea, Ella?'

'Oh Mum, you are a mind-reader,' Ella said as she looked around at all the mess. 'By the way, when it's Teddy's birthday, and in fact all future birthdays, remind me to give the children sixpence each and send them all to the pictures!'

'Get on! You loved every minute of it,' her mother said as she pushed the kettle to the centre of the hob.

While Winnie set about making that most welcome cup of tea, Ella hesitated for a moment, needing time to collect her flying thoughts. This time next week, *if* all went according to plan, she should be in Hove with Sam. She shook her head. A lot could happen in a week. Finally she found a tray, and started on the tedious business of clearing up the remains of Babs's party.

She was in the kitchen washing up when her mother joined her.

'Leave all that and come and have this tea that I've made. I couldn't get Babs to take her new dress off, she'll probably want to go to bed in it tonight.' Winnie sighed and added, 'I'm bushed, I thought that party was never going to end. You'd have thought that Dennis might have shown his face, wouldn't you?'

Ella flicked a towel from the rail, and dried her hands. 'Just pour the tea out, Mother, and stop wishing for miracles.'

Each settled comfortably, the hot tea working wonders.

'Thought Sam might have popped in,' Winnie remarked casually.

'There's no reason why he should, but since you've brought the subject up, I may as well tell you he has asked me to go away with him for the weekend.'

'Well, don't sound so miserable about it. Nothing to be ashamed of, having a fling with a good-looking chap like Sam Richardson, good luck to you.'

'Don't know what you're talking about. I am not having a fling. I like him a lot but I'm certainly not in love with him.'

'Well, a weekend away together might help you to make up your mind.'

Ella turned her head and stared at her mother. Their eyes met, and it occurred to her, at that moment, that they had a remarkable relationship. What she would have done without Winnie over all these years she had no idea. Shared responsibilities, sorrows, frustrations, heartaches and laughter. Oh yes, they had had many a good laugh together and shed many tears. When Dennis had first walked out on her and she hadn't had a penny to bless herself with, her father-in-law had been a great help but it was always her mother to whom she and the children knew they could turn.

Hasn't she really and truly turned my life around? Ella asked herself. It was me who decided to find a job, but who was it who had encouraged me to slim down, wear different clothes, wash and set my hair more often? Just the fact that her mum had introduced her to Sadie and Isaac Cohan had gone a long way to giving her more confidence in herself. There was no way she could have afforded the kind of clothes she wore now if it weren't for them. In fact, as much as any person could be, her mum was practical, worldly and infinitely kind. She would share her last penny with anyone that needed it.

'So you are going to go, aren't you?' Winnie broke into her thoughts.

'I don't know. Dennis would go mad if he found out.'

'Bugger Dennis,' said Winnie. 'Did he ask your opinion when he went off the rails?'

'Two wrongs don't make a right.'

'Oh for Christ's sake, don't go all sanctimonious on me. Go, have a good time, Lord above knows you deserve it.'

'I'm married.'

'Yes, you're married, worse luck.'

'Mum, did you ever like Dennis?'

'Yes, I did, when you first started to go out with him, but like your father kept on about at the time, Dennis was twelve years older than you and you could have had the pick of so many young men. I have to say, though, that you both seemed to be so happy for the first six years before Teddy and Babs came along, and while they were still babies Dennis worked hard, even if he was always pulling dodgy deals. You didn't want for much, he was a good provider and he loved his children.'

'And now?'

'Well, a straight question deserves a straight answer. As the years passed he changed, got too big for his boots. He became a rotten husband and a rotten father.'

Having said that, Winnie felt she was between a rock and a hard place. When Dennis had called in to see her the other Saturday when Ella and the children were out with Sam Richardson, she had found it in her heart to feel very sorry for her son-in-law. He had done some diabolical things, but my God she knew he was paying for them now. Not financially, no, not by any means, but emotionally he was drained. And the thought crossed her mind that he was lonely.

That he deeply regretted his affair with Connie Baldwin and the tragic final outcome went without saying.

None of this could she speak about to Ella because she had given her word that she wouldn't say he had visited.

Ella smiled weakly. 'I never thought you would encourage me to go off with another man.'

'What do you think I am? Some sort of saint? I wouldn't expect you to spend the rest of your life in a state of chastity.'

'Then you won't disapprove if I go?'

'No, I won't. Sam Richardson is a nice fellow, been on his own for years, so why shouldn't the pair of you have a good time? God knows, life's been a big strain for you this last year, just one thing after another, but you've coped.'

Despite everything, Ella started to laugh. 'Mum, you are an absolute wonder. You're urging me to go away with Sam and I haven't even asked you yet if you will move in here and look after Teddy and Babs.'

'Because you know full well you have no need to ask me. It will be my pleasure. Now, we'll have another cup of tea, then we'd better finish clearing up and get all the dirty dishes out of the way before Ted brings young Teddy back and it's time to start cooking the supper.'

It was Wednesday before Ella saw Sam.

'Everything is fixed up,' he said, smiling at her. 'How about you? Was your mother OK about having the children?'

'Yes, she was. Actually she was all for it, said we both deserved a break. Though there is one question I would like to ask you, Sam. Why rent a bungalow for only two or three days? Surely the owners will charge you for a full week. Why not book into a hotel?'

Sam laughed. 'I've never know such a woman as you for raising difficulties. Besides, if we stayed in a hotel, we would either have to book ourselves in as Mr and Mrs or have two single rooms and make sure that at all times we were really discreet. In a bungalow those sort of problems will not arise.'

Ella scowled. 'I'm not raising difficulties. I'm being practical.'

Ella's mind was in a whirl. Now she knew exactly what he had in mind and her imagination flew ahead. Seconds later she was rebuking herself. Wake up, Ella, you're no spring chicken and neither is Sam. He's too much of a gentleman to come right out with it, and you wouldn't let yourself face the truth, but now you've heard it. Face to face, head on. Call it a little holiday, or anything else you like, but if you go to Hove with Sam you are going on a dirty weekend.

'If your mother is all right about having the children, there's nothing to stop us. Get your skates on and go and ask Mike for the weekend off. Go on,' Sam urged.

Mike was a man of few words but swift action. She'd told him the true reason why she would like the time off. He put his arms around her and kissed her. 'Good on yer, me darling, you certainly deserve a break, and come t' that so does Sam. Strait-laced and sober-sides is our Sam; let's hope you bring him back with a smile on his face.'

'Oh Mike, don't let on to the staff, will yer?'

He promised he wouldn't. But all morning he was smiling to himself. When those two come back, if all goes as it should, we'll all be able to tell!

They didn't want to set the neighbours' tongues wagging, so come Saturday morning Sam picked Ella up outside the British Legion. Ever the gentleman, he took her small suitcase and, having stowed it away in the boot, came round to the passenger side of his rented black Humber to make sure that Ella was comfortably settled before they set off.

Ella felt like pinching herself as London was left behind and Sam was soon driving down the fairly new Kingston bypass, where all the signs indicated that they were en route to Brighton in Sussex.

The main approach to Brighton was so fresh and green, with great parks, greenery and healthy shrubs and trees. Sam began to give her a running commentary, which led her to believe that he was no stranger to this journey. The Pavilion was like no other building that Ella had ever seen. Standing majestically in beautiful grounds, every corner of its roof was adorned by an onion-shaped dome. 'It was built by George IV when he was Prince Regent,' Sam informed her knowledgeably.

Suddenly they could see the sea, and almost immediately Sam was driving along the sea front. It was a cold, blustery day, but still a great many people were walking along the promenade. Ella knew what a pier was, she had been to Southend quite a few times. Brighton had two of them!

Hove seemed to be an extension of Brighton, but even at first glance it was vastly different. Sam told her that while Brighton had a railway station, large shops and theatres, Hove had other attractions nearby such as a racecourse and several golf-links.

Even though Sam had stayed at this bungalow before, it took him a while to find it. From the road it was invisible, protected from all eyes by trees and a rutted driveway, bordered by high banks of shrubs.

Not much to look at from the outside, the bungalow was squat and square. They got out of the car together, and while Sam was fetching the two small cases that they had brought with them, Ella had a walk around. In front the small garden was neatly cultivated and she thought that when the spring finally arrived and the flowers came into bloom it would probably look very pretty. Walking around the back, she got a surprise. There were a great number of outbuildings. Old stables which hadn't housed a horse for years was her guess. The whole large area was paved with cobbles and flagstones all protected by high flint walls. Maybe a century or more ago a rich gentleman had had this place built, but it had to have been someone who cherished their privacy.

'Are you going to stand there staring for much longer? Or are you coming inside?' Sam's voice calling brought Ella back to the present.

Her eyes widened when she saw provisions stacked on the table which stood in the middle of the big kitchen. 'Did you bring all that with you?' she asked in disbelief.

'Of course not,' Sam laughed. 'When you rent a furnished cottage, either the estate agent or the owner always provide the essentials. Some folk might have travelled a long way, and the last thing they want to do is find a shop and go out to buy groceries. There is even a small refrigerator over in that corner,' he pointed, 'that's bound to have milk and maybe eggs.'

Sure enough he was right. Ella opened the door; inside there were six eggs, a half-pound pack of butter and two pints of milk.

'Shall we make a pot of tea and rustle up something to eat now, or investigate the rest of the rooms first?'

Ella hadn't stayed to hear the rest of his question; she had gone to explore the bungalow.

The front room cum dining room was very cosy-looking, a fawn tweed three-piece suite grouped around an open fireplace in which a fire was laid, and there and then Ella decided that Sam's first job was to put a match to the kindling wood and get that fire going. It was like an ice-well in here. Beneath the window was an oak dining table and six chairs, four high-backed and two carvers, one each end.

On the opposite side of the hall was a very large bedroom, with big windows that looked out on to a beautiful view, but it wasn't that which had Ella sending up a silent thank you. Someone had been thoughtful enough to lay out on top of the eiderdown which covered the double bed two very large rubber hot-water bottles. She'd fill them straight away, she decided, 'cos it was odds on the bed would be damp. Next door was a neat but slightly smaller bedroom. At the end of the hall she found a bathroom and a lavatory.

Sam made her jump as she turned around quickly and almost knocked into him.

'Everything all right?' he asked.

'Spotlessly clean,' she said. 'Nothing wrong, other than the whole place is absolutely freezing cold.'

Sam put his arms around her and held her close. 'I've already lit the fire in the sitting room and I've also turned the gas oven full on and left the door wide open so that the kitchen will get warm.' He released his firm hold on her but kept his arm around her waist. 'Why don't we go straight out? There is a nice high street down in Hove which has a car park near by. We can either find a decent restaurant or even have a pub lunch. What do you say?'

'Oh, yes please, Sam, but first I must boil a kettle, probably twice. I need enough hot water to fill two bottles. Can't risk that bed being damp. And another thing, before we go out will you please make sure that there's logs or coal somewhere here so that we can keep the fire going.'

'I have done that already. There is a bunker on the left-hand side of the bungalow which is well stocked with coal, and also a small shed housing a pile of logs. I've brought in a basketful of the logs. By the time we get back, the whole place should be feeling a whole lot warmer. I am sorry you're so cold, I should have asked the agent to come in and light the fire before we arrived. If that's all, let's go then and get some warm food inside you.'

Rather than unlock the front door again, they decided to go out through the back door and at the same time give Sam a chance to look at the outbuildings.

'At one time this must have been a vegetable garden,' was Sam's first comment. 'I don't remember it being as bad as this when my sister and her family were here, but then again the weather was hot and we spent most of the time on the beach.'

What they were staring at now was a sagging greenhouse and a cucumber frame. Every pane of glass of both was broken. However, there was a gorgeous smell, and for just one moment Ella couldn't work out where it was coming from. She sniffed a couple of times, then laughed and looked down at their feet. They were standing on an overgrown carpet of mint, the scent of which filled the sharp cold air.

Ella thought it was sad to see so much neglect. 'Shame,' she said to Sam, 'they've let the outside of this bungalow go to rack and ruin. Once it must have been a lovely home.'

She tugged the belt of her camel coat tighter around her waist, turned up the collar and began to run towards the car. The ground was uneven, and she tripped and would have fallen had not Sam been right behind her. His arms stretched out and caught her safely, and holding on to her he guided her to the car. Once inside, she watched as he tucked a car rug around her lap, tucking the ends about her legs. Then he walked around the car and got into the driver's seat.

Once he was seated, Ella said, 'You're taking great care of me today, aren't you?'

'Any reason why I shouldn't?'

Ella just shrugged her shoulders.

Sam had already turned the key in the ignition, but now he turned it off again and twisted round so that he was half facing her.

'Sometimes I get the impression that you ended your life the day Dennis walked out on you. You work hard, you pay your way and you take such good care of your two children, but you have no life of your own. I was like that when Charlotte died but I soon came to realize that life has to go on.'

'Oh, and now you lead such an exciting life?'

'I wouldn't altogether agree that my own life is exciting, but I was quite content until I met up with you again.'

Ella needed reassurance. 'Do you still think it was a good idea to bring me here?'

'Yes, yes, I do.' He leant towards her and laid his hand over hers. His touch was warm on her cold flesh, and she closed her fingers around his wrist, needing his heat.

Suddenly he said, 'I love you.'

She looked up into his eyes. 'At this moment you may mean what you've just said, Sam, but in reality you don't know me.'

'I love you,' he repeated. 'I think I began to love you the first time I met up with you again in the Legion. You were standing behind the bar, beside Mike, being taught how to pull a decent pint. You looked terrified.'

'I *was* terrified. I needed that job so badly, not only for the money but to prove to myself that I wasn't entirely useless.'

Sam sounded dead serious as he said, 'And although I knew you were married and Dennis and I had known each other for years, it made no difference at all. I couldn't get you out of my mind and that's when I started to make excuses to come to the Legion more than was necessary.'

'Sam, have you thought that the attraction was, maybe still is, that through me you still have a link to Charlotte?'

'I didn't try to analyse my feelings. I only know that I felt so much better when you were around.'

'That's understandable, because in all these years you haven't bothered much with female company, have you?'

Sam didn't make any reply and Ella felt bound to add, 'I was someone from the past; you knew I had gone to school with Charlotte and that we were the best of friends. And later, when you met and married her, Dennis and I and you two paired up and we had some good times together. Then Mike gave me a job and you met me again, but a lot of water had gone under the bridge. I was someone from the past.'

'Are you saying you're sorry you have come away with me?' he asked, his face a picture of sadness.

'No, not at all. But I do think it's a bit early for you to start saying that you love me.'

'Don't you have any feelings for me at all?'

'Now that is not what I'm saying. I like you a lot, Sam. It has been great to meet up with you again, and the attention you have paid me has done me the world of good.'

'I haven't paid you attention out of pity,' Sam was quick to reassure her.

He put his arms around her, pulling her close to him, and emboldened by the fact that she didn't pull away, he kissed the top of her head.

They stayed there, arms wrapped around each other, for a long time, both silent and thoughtful, until Sam asked quietly, 'Shall we go back inside? We can go out to eat tonight.'

'Oh, Sam . . .' It was a whisper; she felt like a young girl unable to say more.

'Come on, the fire should be burning well by now.'

She looked up into his face and knew what he was saying, and at that moment what he wanted was what she wanted too.

It had been a very long time since she had experienced

sexual instincts, and even longer since a man had found her sexually attractive.

She smiled, and his lips came down to cover hers and words became all at once totally unnecessary.

The fire was burning really well; even so, Sam added two large nobs of coal and placed a thick log on top of the coal.

Ella sat down on the worn carpet and stared into the dancing flames. Sam, meanwhile, was removing the large cushions from the settee. Having placed them edge to edge on the floor, he lifted her on to them, saying, 'We might as well be comfortable as well as warm.'

Afterwards, in the tranquil peace of passion spent, they lay quiet, entwined in each other's arms.

That evening they did make it into Hove and had a wonderful intimate dinner for two in an elegant hotel.

Come bedtime, Ella wore a beautiful nightdress that she hadn't been aware was in her case. In fact she had never before set eyes on this flimsy peach-coloured article of clothing that was little more than gossamer and lace sewn together with the finest thread. Her mother was more than a matchmaker!

Ella grinned to herself as she slipped this sexy nightdress over her head. Winnie might be old, but she certainly hadn't forgotten her memories!

Ella glanced at herself in the cheval-glass mirror which stood in the corner of the room and slowly slid her hands down over her hips. The feel of that thin material against her skin was fabulous; it was certainly something she wasn't used to. Slowly, before Sam came out of the bathroom, she climbed into bed and was sitting propped up with pillows when he entered the bedroom.

By the look on his face and the way his eyes lit up, he

approved of her night attire. Not that it was long before he was helping her to take it off again.

It was the early hours of the morning before they slept, but when they did they slept well and it was half past nine on Sunday morning when Ella opened one eye to see Sam standing beside the bed holding a tray.

Tea in bed! Now that was a luxury!

Having had a nice hot bath, Ella emerged to find that not only was the table laid for breakfast, but Sam was in the process of making toast and gave her a promise that scrambled eggs would be ready in five minutes.

He was well accomplished in taking care of himself and immediately the thought came to her that Dennis would be useless at scrambling eggs.

Straight off she rebuked herself. Why the hell was she comparing Sam with Dennis?

Later, with the dirty dishes piled in the sink, which was filled with hot soapy water, they donned their heavy coats, hats, scarves and gloves and set off to walk along the beach.

It was a glorious morning, still very cold, but sharp and crisp with the winter sunshine doing its best to light up the sky. The sea was calm and shimmering as the gentle waves lapped regularly against the sand.

Lots of people were out with the same idea of exercise before partaking of Sunday lunch. Quite a few had their dogs with them, and it gave Sam a good laugh when a big German Shepherd dog came bounding up to them and dropped a long thick stick at his feet. Ella was terrified, but not Sam. He stroked the dog's head and told him what a good boy he was. Then he walked to the water's edge, the dog still bounding beside him. Jerking his arm back as far as he could, Sam flung the stick far out to sea. He and Ella watched the strong way that the big dog could swim, and then they started to walk on.

Within minutes the dog had caught up with them and again dropped the stick at Sam's feet, but this time he repeatedly shook himself, jerking his head towards Sam all the time.

Ella thought it was hilarious and got out of the way. Sam, unable to avoid a fast showering of salt water and wet sand, was not so happy.

They came up off the beach, and outside the nearest pub Ella stood back and watched with much amusement as Sam scraped his shoes on the outside iron grid and brushed vigorously at his overcoat. Once inside, however, the atmosphere was so congenial that they stayed for more than one drink.

When they parted from their new-found friends, a table for eight persons had been booked for dinner that evening in the pub's dining room. Ella had never before made friends with strangers so quickly or so easily.

But that Sunday afternoon was perhaps the best of all. With the curtains drawn and the fire blazing, they took their clothes off and lay on a pile of cushions which Sam had again set out on the floor. The sexual activities that Sam indulged in Ella found attractive if not exciting, and no sooner had he rolled away from her than he was sound asleep.

Ella was the first to rise. Wearing only her dressing gown, she drew up a low table and set about laying it with knives, plates and cups and saucers. In the kitchen she made a pot of tea and cut thin slices of bread and butter, and together they ate in front of the fire.

Outside, they could hear the roar of the sea, which meant two things: the tide was coming in and the wind had become more fierce, causing the old windows of the bungalow to rattle noisily. The weather did not worry either of them; if anything, it served to emphasize their own seclusion, their snugness and their undisturbed solitude.

Much later, Sam stirred and suggested they have a nice hot bath and get ready to go out for their prearranged dinner.

Because of the wind, Sam insisted that they drive to the pub. From the moment they walked into the bar, Ella started to enjoy herself, and she even began to see a slightly different side to Sam, proving that he did not act like a dull sober-sides all the time. The meal was great, but it was the good fellowship and the intimacy of comradeship which Ella was enjoying. She felt glad that they had made the effort to dress up, come out and meet up again with these nice people. Somehow, though, that made her feel guilty. Why? Because part of her mind was saying that she and Sam had just spent from lunchtime until seven o'clock alone in the bungalow and there hadn't been a lot of conversation. If they had stayed in for the rest of the evening, would they have been bored?

It was eleven thirty when they said their final goodbyes.

'Our last evening together,' Sam remarked as they made ready for bed, and he sighed. 'So little time, I don't want it to end. How about you, Ella, are you glad that I persuaded you to come?'

'Oh yes, Sam. Really I am.'

'Well, it's not over yet, my lovely Ella.' He smiled. 'We've still got all night.'

Chapter Thirty-three

'WOULD YOU SAY THE weekend was a success?' Winnie asked her daughter as she watched her get ready to do the evening shift.

'Yes, Mum, of course it was.'

'But?'

'I missed the kids, that's all.'

'Ella, don't give me all that old rubbish. You were only away for two nights.'

'I know, but look how they rushed to hug me the minute I came through the door.'

'Course they did, because you're their mum, but they had a great time. Ted took us all to the pictures on Saturday night, *and* we 'ad fish an' chips on the way home. Sam never even came in to see us when you got back, did he?'

'No. He was in a hurry, said he was booked to play in a chess match.'

'Oh my Gawd! That says it all. A weekend quickie and he dashes back to play chess.'

'Mum, it wasn't like that at all. We had a really good time. Now will you please leave it at that?'

And mind my own bloody business is what's she's really

telling me, Winnie said sadly to herself, because Ella was hardly full of the joys of spring. And it was me that encouraged her to go. Ah well, can't win them all!

Once back behind the bar on Monday evening, Ella was glad to hear that there was to be a darts match. She felt really unsettled, not sure if she was glad she had spent the weekend with Sam or not. Such was the restless mood she was in, she got stuck into doing needless jobs, just waiting for trade to pick up, because for once she was hoping that the bar would be packed and they would be really busy.

Molly Riley watched as Ella swept everything off a glass shelf that was fixed to the wall over a mirror, then, with a lot more vigour than was needed, cleaned the shelf, swiping a damp cloth back and forth several times.

She was about to tell Ella that she herself had cleaned all this side of the bar that morning, but instead she bit her lip and waited a moment before saying, 'Ella, shall we have a drink while it's quiet? Have one on me. I missed you over the weekend.'

'I missed you too, yes please, good idea, I'll have a Southern Comfort.' Ella smiled, steering Molly away from the subject of where she had been, and why.

Side by side, the two barmaids sipped at their drinks, probably the only bit of free time they would have during the evening.

Ella knew she had been short with her mother before she came to work and she wasn't being her usual happy-go-lucky self right now. She couldn't help it. Her mind was in a whirl.

Sam had been a considerate, gentle lover, but apart from that very first attempt, which had been done in such haste on both sides, she would not have considered his actions to be passionate. He had just quietly taken her, almost as if he were grateful. It had been such a long time since she had experienced sex. Perhaps it was the same for him. She had loved being held, being kissed, snuggling up to a man's warm body in bed, so in a way you could say that it was she who was grateful.

Being made love to by Dennis, well, there was no comparison.

With Dennis, it had always been because he wanted her, not just needed her. He was her husband. He took her knowing it was his right, and by God he had always known how to arouse her. He only had to run his hands over her body, lingering in places, holding her close, and she would be longing for him to take her.

Now she was getting annoyed with herself. She had left all these thoughts behind a long time ago. Why, after all the bad things that had happened between her and Dennis, was she holding on to these kind of memories?

The next two weeks Ella would have described as humdrum. She went to work, saw the children were well fed, did the washing and the ironing and made sure she took the children out on her day off. Sam Richardson came in only once a week, to collect the till rolls and to talk business to Mike Murray. He did make a point of finding Ella, saying hello and asking after her health. All very civilized and polite. Their weekend together was never mentioned. It was as if it had never happened.

Then came the morning when the postman brought two letters.

One was a very official-looking brown envelope addressed to Mr Dennis Edward Dryden the back of which was endorsed with the signification LCC which told her it was from the London County Council. Ella turned the letter over in her hands several times, pondering on whether or not she should open it. Curiosity got the better of her and taking a blunt knife she slit the top of the envelope.

She was only halfway through reading the typed page when she found she was trembling, and she had to grope for a chair and sit herself down. She didn't have to get to the end of the page nor yet begin to read the second page; she had already grasped the fact that the sole purpose of the letter was to inform all residents in this area that their homes were due to be demolished.

Could the council do that? Ella asked herself, knowing full well it was a silly question. People in authority could do whatever suited them, never mind who got hurt in the process.

It was only after she had drunk a very strong cup of tea that she remembered the second letter.

It was addressed in handwriting to Mrs Ella Dryden, and was short and to the point. As she slowly read it, she was aware that it was not totally unexpected. Despite that, by the time she had read the few short lines, her blood was boiling and her temper was enough to choke her.

The writer was Sam Richardson.

It was not an unkind letter; in fact for just one minute it had her feeling sorry for Sam, though for a bag of gold she could not have said why.

Sam thanked her for her friendship (was that what the weekend had been about, friendship!) and said that he would always remember her fondly, but that he did not think they were compatible. In future his firm, Hirst and Richardson, would appoint another member of staff to be responsible for the accounts of the British Legion. He had already advised Mike Murray of this decision. He wished her well for the future.

Ella got to her feet and without a second thought picked up the poker and used it to lift the top of the hob and threw the letter right into the middle of the fire.

'Pompous git,' she muttered angrily.

As she was replacing the top of the hob, she heard her front door open and her mother calling, 'It's only me.'

Ella took the deepest breath she could manage and told herself to calm down.

Winnie came in slowly, looking thoroughly dejected. Ella was by her side in a flash and had her arms around her.

'I take it you've had a letter from the LCC, but you mustn't worry about it, Mum.'

'Mustn't I? Just 'ad a word with the milkman, and he said we'll all be rehoused in those great hideous blocks of flats that the council have built near the Elephant and Castle. Then the coalman called out that the rehousing programme had already started. I bet the landlords are none too pleased; all their properties will have had a compulsory purchase order slapped on them.'

'Take yer coat off, Mum, sit down and we'll 'ave a bit of breakfast. I'm just as upset as you are but, whatever happens it's not going to take place for some time, so we'll just 'ave t' put our heads together and see what we can come up with.'

They ate bacon, eggs and toast in silence, mother and daughter each deep in thought. With a fresh cup of tea in front of them, it was Winnie that started the ball rolling.

'Can you see me living twenty floors up? That's supposing the landlord even speaks up on my behalf, otherwise I don't suppose the council will be willing to give one of their flats to an old woman like me living on her own. More than likely they'll shove me and a good many more like me into some gloomy, dreary old folk's home. I dread the thought.'

'Oh Mum! Mum, don't keep on.'

'I'm not keeping on, Ella, I'm merely telling it as it is.'

'Yeah, I know. I'm thinking now what a fool I was to

tell Dennis that I wouldn't move out of London, and when he offered for you to move with us, I said you'd never, ever leave your house. If I'd known then as much as I know now, maybe I'd 'ave given his offer a lot more thought.'

'Easy with hindsight, ain't it, gal? If we all 'ad crystal balls we'd lead our lives differently.'

Ella didn't know what to do or say to cheer her mother up. The plain truth was there wasn't much that anyone could do. More than half of London needed to be rebuilt because of the damage caused by German bombs and land mines exploding over all parts of the city. It was inevitable that in the process folk were going to be made homeless. But then when you came to think about it, thousands of homes were bombed during the war and the tenants hadn't had to worry about being rehoused because they had been killed. At least we are alive, Ella thought, and somehow the problems will be solved.

One thing was for sure: she wasn't going to mention the letter that she had had from Sam Richardson. That was an episode in her life that was best forgotten.

Instead she said, 'I've tidied up and made the beds and I've not got to be at work until six tonight, so where would you like to go? We could look round the shops first, then shall we go to that place just off the market and treat ourselves to brown bread and mussels or eels and a nice milk stout?'

'Oh yes, Ella, yes, I'd like that.'

'Then come on, Mum, put yer coat back on and let's get going.'

Bad news travels fast.

It was just half past eight the next morning and Ella was standing on her front doorstep seeing her two children off to school. 'Have yer both got yer dinner money

331

and yer apple an' a clean handkerchief?' she asked as she did every morning.

Teddy looked at his sister and in unison they both grinned and said, 'Yes, Mum.'

They had hardly taken a couple of steps along the pavement when Teddy let out a whoop of joy and fled down the street as if he were being chased by the devil himself.

Ella walked down the short front path and stared up the road. Dennis was standing beside a shiny black car, his arms held wide. As she watched, a lump which felt as big as a walnut got stuck in her throat.

Dennis had swept his young son up into a great bear hug and was turning round and round, never loosening his grip on his boy.

Now Babs was running. She dropped her school bag and left it where it had fallen on the pavement. 'Daddy, Daddy,' she was screaming, and Ella could tell from the tone of her voice that she was crying.

Dennis kept hold of his son with one arm but scooped up his little daughter with the other, and to Ella it was as if time stood still as he held them both close, his head bent down to rest on top of his children's heads.

Ella walked forward and picked up Babs's school bag, then a few more steps and she was silently holding it out to Dennis.

'I'll take the kids to school and then I'll be back, I won't be long,' was all he said.

Jesus wept and well he might! What was she supposed to make of this?

Dennis was helping Teddy and Babs into the back of his car, and then suddenly the car was moving slowly and the two smiling children waved to her as they went past.

Was she dreaming? She certainly had a feeling of relief. It was so good for the children to see their father.

Now that she had had a minute or two to think about

it, she thought she could guess the reason for him being here.

He had heard about the letters from the council, and say what you like about him, there was no way that he would stand by and see his family or his mother-in-law turfed out into the streets or housed in a high-rise block of flats. No way at all. Dennis wouldn't stand for that.

But it was the way he'd turned up! Out of the blue, as if nothing had happened. He might just have got up from the breakfast table and offered to take the children to school. In actual fact, as far as she knew, he hadn't set eyes on either of them for months. Certainly it was the very first time this year that the kids had seen their dad.

She stood still in the street for a moment because suddenly she felt tired, drained, and she wanted to cry buckets, but she checked herself, muttering aloud, 'None of that, come on, pull yerself together. You've coped so far and you'll go on coping.'

Although at one time Ella had vowed she would never forgive Dennis for what had happened to Connie Baldwin, nor for the way he had neglected his two children, she was prepared to be civil to him this morning, because if she were honest she was really pleased to see him. He was the one person who would be able to sort this housing problem out.

He looked completely at home sitting at the kitchen table, almost as if he had never left.

'Would you like some breakfast?' she felt compelled to ask.

'A bacon sarnie would go down well,' he grinned. But he had seen the worried frown on his wife's face, and at that moment he was wishing with all his heart that he could turn back the clock. Just taking his kids to school had tugged at his heart strings. Twice Babs had run back to ask if he were going to be there when she came out this afternoon, and while young Ted had not come straight out with an accusation, he had hinted that his father should look after their mother a bit more. The final rub had been when Teddy had told him he could only go to see a football match when his grandad took him.

'You used to take me every week,' had been his parting shot.

Ella put a plate in front of him and the sandwich smelt good. He'd missed her cooking and a darn sight more things besides. He'd been so stretched out by Connie's death that his whole attitude to life had altered. He would never be a saint, that went without saying, but if any lesson had been learnt it was that family was the one and only thing that mattered in this life. Looking at Ella, and realizing the hurt he had caused, he knew full well that he had left it a bit late in life to appreciate that fact.

Ella couldn't understand her own feelings. She only knew that she needed someone to lean on, to tell her what to do and to sort out where she, the children and her mother were going to live. She no longer wanted to have to cope on her own with all these everyday problems.

As if reading her thoughts, Dennis asked, 'Ella, would you sit down and listen to me for a while?'

'Not if you're going to tell me a pack of lies or make me a load of promises which you have no intention of keeping.' She spoke quite spitefully.

'I deserve that and more,' he said sheepishly, 'but please, let me try. Do you remember the house at Epsom where our problems first began, mainly because I was so bigheaded.'

'And I was so obstinate,' she admitted. 'All past history now, though.'

'Not quite,' Dennis told her with a flicker of a smile.

'Beautiful house, which my builders turned into four fantastic apartments, yet the tenants haven't been happy there. I sold one place to a greedy man who thought he could manipulate lonely old women into doing what he wanted them to do. In other words, he was after their money. I'd be the first to admit that I've pulled a few fast deals in my time, but I've never stooped that low. My father and I only heard about this through Lady Margaret, the original owner from whom I purchased the property. Since then we've worked closely with a solicitor, all legal and above board I promise you . . .'

Dennis paused, and Ella found herself smiling at the fact that he was assuring her that his dealings were all legitimate.

Well, there had to be a first time for everything.

She got up and went to stand at the window, her arms folded tightly under her breasts. In one way it felt so comfortable to have Dennis sitting here in the kitchen, but on the other hand a lot of horrible thoughts were going round and round in her head. Even last November, or was it December, when he had taken her out for a meal, hadn't he said he had a few building contracts to see through but then he would be free, and they would meet and talk things through. Yet here they were in March, and it was the first time since that meal that she had set eyes on him. Recently she had tried to play his game, get her own back if she were truthful, and had gone off with Sam Richardson for that weekend. With that thought she hated herself and she hated him.

Dennis glanced at Ella and asked, 'Have I said something to upset you?'

'No, but I can't see why this ruddy house at Epsom is still occupying your life. When you took me out to eat somewhere near Crystal Palace you pointed out what a great contract you had going on there. Yet me, my mother

335

and all our neighbours have notices stating that every house in these streets is to be demolished. If you're so big in property, why don't you see about finding accommodation for your own family?'

He came to stand beside her and, his voice low, said, 'That is exactly why I came here this morning. You shall have the pick of where you live, and so shall your mother. I swear to you that never, while I can prevent it, will you and my kids live in those concrete blocks of flats that are being thrown up. Please, Ella, believe me, I will look after you, just try and trust me. And before you mock me, I know only too well that you have no reason to believe a word I say, never mind trust me.'

Ella remained silent. What could she say?

Dennis sighed heavily. 'I have to go. My father and I have another meeting with the solicitor, but I promised Babs I would be here when she comes home this afternoon, and I will be if that is all right with you.'

Softly but sharply Ella said, 'If you promised your daughter then you *had* better be here. Letting me down is one thing, but our kids have taken enough knocks.'

Dennis had the grace to look and sound sheepish as he said, 'Bye for now, see you about four.'

Chapter Thirty-four

THAT MORNING, AT TEN thirty, Dennis found himself once more in the offices of Gurney and Trent, but now his father was sitting beside him. Suddenly Dennis was filled with apprehension. What they were about to do was a very tricky business, and to be honest, he was worried sick.

He cleared his throat and looked at his father, and when Ted nodded his head, Dennis began.

'Thank you for the letters you have sent me, Mr Trent, you have kept me well informed. You certainly seemed to have gathered quite a lot of information about this Claude Packard.'

'Yes, though he is a very difficult man to deal with; he doesn't want his left hand to know what his right hand is doing. I have met with Mr Packard twice, and against all my advice he is still determined to do his best to purchase what was Miss Sheldon's flat, and he is also hoping that the remaining tenant is going to decide that she will be better off in a care home rather than living on her own. Should that turn out to be the case, he is aiming to purchase that remaining apartment.'

'Mr Trent, can you see that happening?' Ted asked a direct question and he expected a straight answer.

'Hmm . . .' Mr Trent hesitated. He was in a position to charge a hefty fee for the work he was doing for this pair, but all the same he had to tread very carefully.

'To my knowledge Mr Packard has approached two banks and a mortgage broker for a loan, and on all three attempts he has been unsuccessful.'

Ted had a deep thought that he was keeping to himself at least for the moment. It hadn't been hard for him to discover that Claude Packard was a gambling man, and not a very successful one at that. But he himself liked to cover his back, and when his son had told him of this scheme to beat Packard at his own game, he had made it his business to buy up Packard's gambling debts. Should one idea fail, it always paid to have another up one's sleeve.

This hedging wasn't getting them anywhere. 'Have you made any progress on offering the man a loan?' Dennis asked impatiently.

'Yes, I made an appointment with him to come to this office and I put your proposal to him.'

Dennis cut in far too quickly. 'You didn't name names, did you?'

Poor Mr Trent looked totally shocked. 'There was nothing illegal in the proposition that I put forward. As per your instructions, Mr Dryden, I informed Claude Packard that I was in touch with two wealthy businessmen who had money to invest and were willing to take a risk.'

'And he has no idea who might be putting up the money?'

'No, definitely not, those were your instructions. I set the facts out very straight,' Mr Trent continued. 'I informed Mr Packard that should Mrs Hines decide to give up her residence in Maple House, my two clients would be willing to loan enough to cover the purchase price of both apartments. He was extremely happy with that agreement until I disclosed the fact that my clients would want Maple House as a whole to be put up as security against the loan. Needless to say, he was very dubious about that clause being part of the contract.'

Now it was Ted who almost blew his top.

'If that devious bloke wants to borrow our money t' buy both of those flats, the terms are non-negotiable. Other than that he can go to hell.'

Mr Trent stood up and held out his hand. 'I think we have gone as far as we can at the moment, but I would point out one thing. I think Mr Packard's interest in the flats is only marginal. I'm pretty sure he is more interested in the grounds that Maple House stands in.'

Neither father nor son made any reply. They both shook the hand of their solicitor, and it wasn't until they were in the safety of Ted's car that they allowed themselves to have a good laugh.

'Packard doesn't know us, does he, son?' Ted said. 'We can see him dreaming about how many dwellings he can get a builder to stack up in those grounds if he greases enough palms and gets planning permission, can't we?'

'What he doesn't know, Dad, is that you taught me well. He'd have to get up early in the morning to put one over on us. Anyway, he has got t' be soft in the bloody head not to even give a thought to the fact that owning the whole building doesn't mean that he will ever own the freehold.'

'Nice one, son.' Ted laughed loudly. Then he became serious and said quietly, 'I'm pretty sure that Mr Trent has an inkling of what we are about, but at this point in time it pays him to turn a deaf ear. He can't prove anything and I don't somehow think he would want to. Whatever happens to Claude Packard is nothing more than his just deserts. Picking on lonely women, and for what? Nothing more than sheer greed.'

'He hasn't taken the bait yet,' Dennis reminded his father.

'Well, we'll wait an' see, but greed will get the better of him, that's a dead cert.'

It was the second Saturday morning in March. The sun was shining and in the few pots that Ella had planted in the back yard the daffodils and primulas had opened up, their lovely colours brightening the yard up no end. It had been a strange time, with Ella just plodding along from day to day with not much to look forward to as far as she could see. Wherever she went and whoever she spoke to, the whole conversation revolved around the fact that within the very near future their houses were going to be razed to the ground. Oh, there had been tenants' meetings, council meetings and even a meeting chaired by the local vicar. A lot of questions had been asked, yet not one satisfactory answer from those in charge had been forthcoming. Men, and women also, lost their tempers, but as always shouting and hollering never got anyone anywhere.

Whole families were at a loss as to where to turn. Some folk had been born in these streets of terraced houses and had not even been driven away during the horrific years of the war. They had stood together, sweeping up broken glass as their windows were smashed during the air raids, visiting the badly injured in hospital, and attending so many funerals of long-standing friends and neighbours whose bodies had had to be dug out from beneath ruined buildings and great piles of rough masonry. Now those who had survived all that were worried as to where they were all going to live.

Ella was afraid to pin her hopes on Dennis.

He had said that she and her mother would have a choice as to where their future home would be.

Was that too good to be true? So many promises Dennis had made had never been kept.

Now, having seen Dennis's car draw up outside the house, Ella opened the back door and called to Babs and Teddy, who were bouncing a ball up against the back wall, 'Don't look now, but your father is here again.'

They both came racing in, and Teddy's mouth fell open with surprise as his father walked into the kitchen waving three tickets for West Ham's match that afternoon.

'We'll take Grandad with us,' he said, grinning.

'I haven't forgotten you, sweetheart,' Dennis told Babs, sweeping her up into his arms. 'I've brought you a real grown-up present.' Setting her safely down on her feet, he drew from his pocket a dark red velvet box. Inside was a silver chain from which hung a tiny heart, shaped in silver.

Babs was thrilled, and when her mother had fastened it around her neck, both her brother and her father said how pretty it looked on her.

'Go get yerself ready, son, we'll pick Grandad up and have something to eat before the match.' Then, turning to Ella, he said, 'I want a word with you.'

As Teddy flew upstairs to get himself ready, Ella said to her daughter, 'Walk down t' yer Gran's, will you, pet? Ask her if she's coming out with us this afternoon.'

'Oh Mum, you know she is, she always does.'

'Yes, I do know, but it will give you a chance to show off the lovely necklace yer dad has bought for you.'

Babs's face brightened at the thought and she was out of the door before Ella could tell her to put a coat on.

With both children out of the way, she turned to Dennis, raised her eyebrows and said, 'Well?'

His lightness of mood changed and his voice was quite

341

firm as he said, 'Let me know which day you can have off in a couple of weeks' time and by then I should have two or three houses which you might like to give the once-over. Better if you don't bring yer mother first time around; too much walking. Wait and see which district you think you might like and what the school situation is for the kids. A lot to sort out, but then you know that, don't you?'

Before she had time to form a reply of any sort, Teddy was back in the room, tugging at his father's arm, eager to be gone.

'Boy, oh boy!' Dennis Dryden muttered aloud as he replaced the telephone receiver in his father's office.

'Is that a cry of triumph?' Ted asked.

'To be honest, Dad, I'm not sure. I just cannot believe what lengths some folk will go to to get what they want. Packard must know the risks he is taking and yet he has jumped in with both feet and grabbed the offer of our enormous loan. I bet he hasn't given a thought as to how he is going to keep up the repayments, given that he already has one if not two mortgages to repay.'

'You almost sound as if you feel sorry for him, son. Are you having feelings of regret?'

'Oh no, Dad. He walked into this with his eyes wide open. True, we laid the bait, but nobody forced him to take it. I've only to remind myself how he made Dorothy Sheldon's life a misery and was well set to do the same to old Mrs Hines. I'm glad we were able to step in and help her. Whatever mess Packard sinks into is of his own making.'

'Mrs Hines is well set for the moment,' Ted remarked thoughtfully. 'We saw to it that her furniture was packed well and safely stored, and if she should decide to make her stay with Lady Margaret a permanent one, we can always make sure that she gets the best price possible for her goods.'

'Yes, you did well by her, Dad, and I wouldn't be at all surprised if she does stay put. Best thing, probably. Company when she wants it, good food, and all her needs attended to.'

'Well, if everything is done and dusted, we'd better get over to Trent's office and add our signatures to the documents.'

Within half an hour, they were once again sitting across from Mr Trent's desk.

'You will be pleased to know that we tied it all up this morning,' was Mr Trent's opening statement.

'What?' Dennis sounded really surprised. 'Mr Packard has signed already, has he?'

'Oh yes, he's signed, and I would say at this moment he is eagerly awaiting the arrival of a large cheque.'

Mr Trent watched the look that passed between father and son, and his own thought was that Mr Packard had at the very least acted recklessly. He banished the thought quickly from his mind and merely said, 'I have the papers here.' He just couldn't leave the matter there, however. Slowly and deliberately he added, 'I wouldn't say you own the man body and soul, but he certainly owes you both a considerable amount of money. However, as you stipulated, the loan is secured against the whole building. So let's hope for Mr Packard's sake that his proposed business deals go ahead.'

Dennis took the file of documents that Mr Trent had handed across the desk and passed them to his father, and Ted handed a cheque over to Mr Trent.

Edward Dryden would this very morning lock these papers away in his safety deposit box at the bank, with the knowledge that the good wishes that Mr Trent had hoped for Mr Packard was never going to happen.

Men, real men, didn't treat old ladies the way Packard

343

had treated Dorothy Sheldon. Ted and Dennis could bide their time in the full knowledge that payback time would come when they were ready.

As the old saying went, give a scoundrel enough rope and he'll hang himself!

Chapter Thirty-five

ELLA FELT HEARTSORE AND weary as she tried to turn the mattress on her double bed. Nothing was going right for her at the moment and she felt really washed out, aching from head to foot before she'd halfway finished her shift at the Legion.

Most of her neighbours had already been to inspect the flats which were on offer from the council, but both she and her mother were holding out, hoping against hope that Dennis was going to come up with an alternative. This time she wouldn't be so fussy, nor so dogmatic in her determination to stay in this part of London. No matter how hard she tried, she just could not see herself cooped up with her two children in a high-rise flat.

What about during the summer holidays? Their back yard might not be much to write home about, but at least she could put a table and chairs out there and they could eat their meal in the fresh air. Teddy had gone through a phase when he wanted to keep rabbits, and Dennis had built him a double hutch. What fun he'd had letting them out and chasing them around the yard, and he'd been pretty good about feeding them and keeping the hutch clean. In a flat, who knows how she would keep the pair of them amused. Or what trouble they would get up to. One nightmare thought she'd had lately was what if they were allocated a flat several floors up and one day Teddy decided to climb out of the window and fell?

It didn't bear thinking about.

Dennis was quite a frequent visitor these days: once a week, and sometimes twice. Was she glad about that?

She didn't let herself dwell on that question. Certainly the kids were a darn sight happier when their dad was around, which didn't seem quite fair to her. Both Teddy and Babs were so excited each time his car pulled to a stop outside the house, rushing to greet him excitedly because they knew darn well he never came empty-handed. It was like he was buying their love. If his visits should suddenly cease, what would they do then? Ella knew what she would do. She'd sort out where he'd got to this time and she would kill him. 'I would,' she muttered aloud. No way was he going to get away with messing up his children's lives again.

It had been ages since he had mentioned finding them a decent house, and she had felt so under the weather that she couldn't face another hostile argument.

Having struggled to put two clean pillowcases on, she plumped up the pillows and propped them against the brass head-rail at the top of the bed. Thank God she was finished in here. She had changed Teddy's bed first thing this morning, and now her own, so she would leave Babs's room until tomorrow. Time she put her feet up and had a cup of tea.

She had barely sat down when her mother was to be heard calling, 'Cooee!'

'I swear you smell the pot.' Ella grinned at Winnie as she came through the kitchen door. 'Be a love and get yerself a cup. There's plenty of tea in the pot and I did put the cosy over it.'

They were seated opposite each other, sipping their tea, and Ella felt a bit guilty. Getting to her feet, she collected two plates, knives, butter and jam, all of which she set out on the table. Then from the dresser she brought a huge round tin, and lifting the lid said, 'I made these scones yesterday. D'you fancy one?'

Ella didn't have to ask twice. Already her mother had a scone on her plate, had cut it through the middle and was busy spreading both butter and jam on it.

'Mum, at what age would you say a woman starts the menopause?'

Ella had asked the question quietly, but Winnie was startled. She could tell that her daughter was more than a little worried.

'Normally somewhere around forty, but it can differ. Some start much earlier and some much later. Why? Are you having hot flushes? To be honest, I have noticed that you've been under the weather lately but I put it down to all this bother about us being compelled to move out of our homes.'

'No, not hot flushes, but I don't feel right. Any strong smell seems to make me feel sick. Molly and I were making cheese sandwiches yesterday and suddenly I just had to get out into the open air. I couldn't breathe.'

As Ella was speaking, her mother's eyes did not leave her face, and she was clenching her hands together in her lap to stop them trembling. There was a moment of silence that hung heavily between them until Winnie knew she had to ask that one vital question.

'You haven't missed any periods, 'ave you?' she said.

Ella's face had gone pale and she was twitching. At last she managed to murmur, 'Haven't seen anything for two months. I thought I was going through the change.'

'Oh my God!' her mother cried. 'I thought you 'ad more sense than that. Menopause in a pig's ear! Sounds

347

to me that more than likely you're pregnant.'

Ella was astounded. Of course she had suspected it, but so far she had been able to convince herself it couldn't be true.

She bit her lip, eyeing her mother, trying to assess if she was being serious. Then Winnie's lips began to tremble and with utter disbelief Ella realized that it wasn't just a possibility; her mother was serious and it was ten to one she was carrying a baby.

'Jesus Christ!' she cried, anxiety showing plainly in her eyes. Everything in the room was moving; she couldn't breathe. She was weak with horror, anger and guilt.

Winnie was beside her in a flash, pushing her head down between her knees. The sickening feeling passed and her mother insisted that she lean back in the chair and stay still while she fetched her a glass of cold water. Eventually the dizziness passed and she stared at Winnie, her eyes wide with apprehension. She was very scared. Yes, I'm a grown woman, she chastised herself, yet I'm scared stiff.

'What will Dennis say, he'll kill me,' she gasped

'Sod Dennis.' Winnie gave Ella a swift but knowing glance. 'He's hardly in a position to 'ave a go at you, and if he so much as tries he'll 'ave me to answer to,' she informed her daughter bluntly, her voice harsh with anger.

'What in God's name am I going to do?' Ella asked.

'Well, yer could tell the father, for a start.'

'Never, not in a million years! According to him we are not compatible. Besides, he doesn't come near the club now. I got the impression that I didn't come up to his expectations.'

Winnie loved her daughter dearly, and at this moment in time she could cheerfully have killed Sam Richardson. Instead she just sat there staring into space, not knowing whether to laugh or to cry. The fact was that it was she who had encouraged Ella to go off for the weekend, thinking that her daughter richly deserved a break, someone to make a fuss of her, let her know that she had changed from being an overweight slob into an elegant-looking woman who combined a full-time job with being a really good mother.

'I'm too old to have another baby, I'll be thirty-nine this year, but I can't be that far gone. I suppose one of our neighbours would know what I could do to bring on a miscarriage.' It had taken all of Ella's self-control to speak normally, for she was shaking with anger.

'For Christ's sake, gal! Give yerself time to think.' Winnie was in danger of losing her temper. 'You don't mean a word of what you've just said. We'll 'ave no more talk about going to a neighbour nor to some quack.'

Her mother did her best to ease the tension by laughing lightly, but it was a cynical laugh because her thoughts were well and truly dwelling on Sam Richardson. If she didn't have a go at him, given half a chance Dennis would.

Ella broke into her thoughts. 'Please, Mum, tell me what to do. I suppose at the back of my mind I've known for a couple of weeks that I was pregnant. I just wouldn't let myself admit the fact. I've been dying t' tell you. I couldn't tell anybody else. It's been awful for me, it really has, especially when Dennis has been here. I 'aven't been able to look him in the face.'

Winnie was racking her brains. Eventually she cleared her throat and her voice was firm as she put forward her point of view.

'The first thing we've got to get settled is this housing business. When Dennis next appears, send one of the kids to fetch me and I'll tell him straight that it's about time he kept his promise and took you to see a couple of places. God knows he's bragged loud enough that no way was his family going to live in those council flats.'

'But, Mum, he might not even want to know me when he finds out about the baby, never mind helping to get me a house.'

'All the more reason why you don't tell him yet. Are you sure, really sure, that you don't want to contact Sam Richardson?'

Ella straightened her back and her head flew up sharply. She was shaking with anger, feeling really hurt as she thought of that curt, unkind letter that he had written to her, and it took all of her self-control to speak normally.

'Mum, I don't care what I have to go through, nothing on this earth would make me go to Sam for help. We didn't have a bad weekend, and OK, he decided that I wasn't what he wanted in his life. That's fair enough, but there are ways of saying things without hurting folk. It wasn't as if I expected him to marry me. No, I think me having two children put him off. Children would be a hindrance in the kind of life that he leads.'

She paused for a moment and actually smiled. 'I think he'd run a mile at the thought of having to cope with a newborn baby. It would disturb the pattern of his safe, dull life.'

Winnie sniffed. 'He knew about Teddy and Babs from the beginning, but what about taking precautions?' Sighing heavily, she added, 'I suppose it's a bit late now to pursue that subject. Just remember, not a word to Dennis until he sorts something out about where you're going to live.'

'Where *we're* going to live, Mum? What about you?'

'Don't start worrying about me, you've more than enough on your plate. The council wouldn't dare put me in a high-rise flat. I'd be straight on to the papers. Can't you just see the headlines, "Old age pensioner with bad legs and a heart problem has twelve flights of stairs to climb".'

'Mum! Since when did you have bad legs? Or a heart problem, come to that?'

Winnie adopted a hurt look. 'Since the council put a compulsory purchase order on my house just so that they can bulldoze the whole street.'

'Mum, you're dead wicked,' Ella managed to say as they both fell about laughing.

Two days after Ella had talked to her mother, Dennis appeared. The front door was wide open because the weather was pushing towards spring and it was so nice to see the sunshine. In he walked, like he'd never left home, picked up a magazine and last night's evening paper from the seat of what had always been his armchair, tidily placed them on the dresser and sat himself down, his long legs stretched out right across the hearth rug which lay in front of the kitchen range.

'Kids at school?' he asked.

Ella looked at him and raised her eyebrows. 'No, they've both got jobs down on the docks.' She let her sarcasm come out with a sneer.

'Oh, you're on good form this morning, aren't you, my luv.'

'Wrong on both points,' she shot back at him. 'How the hell can I be in good form? Day and night all I can think about is that me and the kids will probably be thrown out into the street if we don't accept the council's offer to rehouse us soon. And as for being your luv, I thought you dispensed with me a long time ago.'

'Touchy, eh? Can't say as I blame yer. Got a bit of news for you, though. Couple of houses I can take yer t' see. Mind, the mood you're in today, I'll be lucky if you decide that you like either of them.'

'Thanks. Like I've got a choice now.'

In spite of all her cares and woes, Ella found that she was smiling. Like it or not, Dennis was a sight for sore eyes. Lazily stretched out, he did look great. He'd probably come here straight from the barber's shop: his thick mop of dark hair was neat and tidy, his face freshly shaved. He had nice teeth, even and straight, and although he wore an expensive suit he still had that boyish look and his intense bright blue eyes twinkled as he exchanged gibes with her.

No wonder the women fall for him, Ella said mournfully to herself.

She stood at the door to the scullery and said seriously, 'Do you want me to make you a pot of tea? Or are you taking me to see these houses right now?'

'No thanks to the tea. Yes to your second question, just as soon as you're ready to go. I might even treat you to a slap-up lunch if you're not too stroppy.'

God, this fellow could drive a person to drink. He comes here looking like a million dollars with no warning whatsoever and expects me to get myself ready within minutes.

Her beautiful glossy hair had been rolled into a secure French pleat with enough strands left loose to pile into curls around her forehead. She had selected a sage-green suit that Sadie Cohan had sold to her about a month ago; this would be the first time that she had worn it, and with it she had teamed a dark green high-necked blouse. Time taken over her make-up had been well worth while. Black high-heeled court shoes, handbag and gloves and she was ready.

When she had a final look in the mirror she checked that the seams of her stockings were straight and she was pleased with herself.

In all it had taken her twenty minutes.

As she came down the stairs her husband let out a low whistle of approval.

Ella couldn't have said why, but she was feeling extremely nervous as she sat beside her husband as he drove them to view the first of the two houses. When they had started out he had kept up a running commentary on the first place he was taking her to view. Ella felt that she had to give him a great deal of credit. He had left nothing to chance, really toured the areas and had the facts ready on the tip of his tongue.

It wasn't too long before Dennis was saying, 'This is Sydenham, and we're looking for Langham Avenue. I've already done a recce so I'm pretty sure if I take a left down here the first on the right will be the road we are looking for.'

It was.

He pulled the car in to the kerb and asked Ella to look up at the number of the house which they were parked outside.

Lowering the window, she poked her head out, looked up and said, 'This house is number twenty-two. What number are we looking for?'

'Forty-seven,' he replied. 'Must be on the other side of the road. The property is empty, but the agent let me have the keys. We'll get out and walk, shall we?'

He came round to the passenger side and helped his wife to get out of the car. It was little things like this that made her realize how much she had missed him. Not that he had often taken her out in his car, or even in the old van he drove in those early days when they were first married. Stop comparing how things used to be, she chided herself. After all, when the kiddies had been small she'd be the first to admit that she'd always put them first. More than likely Dennis had felt that he hadn't been getting enough attention at home. That could be part of why he had looked elsewhere, that and the fact that she knew now that she had lost interest in how she looked.

Dennis took her hand and linked it through the crook of his arm as they walked. It felt good.

'God Almighty! What a long road,' he remarked, adding, 'It's never-ending.'

'I thought you said you had looked the place over,' Ella reminded him.

'I did, late at night, an' I was more interested as to where it was than how it looked.'

'To me it looks a long, cold road. Not much different to where we live now. The houses are still terraced; the only difference is they are much bigger and there are more of them.' Ella was watching the numbers: 43, 45. 'Here's forty-seven.'

Dennis went ahead up the short flight of stone steps, but before he put the key in the front door lock he leant over the metal hand-rail and looked down. Then he straightened himself up, took a sheaf of papers from his inside pocket and quickly scanned the details. 'I thought not,' he muttered angrily. 'There's no mention of basement rooms on these estate agent's details.' He half turned to go, but Ella put out a restraining hand.

'We're here now, Dennis, we might as well go inside. At least it will give us something to compare other properties with.'

'All right, if you say so,' he agreed somewhat reluctantly, standing back to allow her to enter first.

Ella didn't like the house and that fact showed on her face. The place smelt musty, as if it hadn't been occupied for years.

Front room, back room, kitchen and scullery downstairs, rooms bigger than she was used to, higher ceilings and much larger windows. First floor, three bedrooms, one double, two singles, both looking out over a long, untidy, overgrown garden.

Up a flight of just five stairs and there was one huge

354

room which had a sloping ceiling. On this floor there was a bathroom and a separate lavatory. Ella wrinkled her nose. Both could do with a damn good cleaning.

'Almost a dormitory,' she said.

'Could fill it up with lodgers,' Dennis chuckled.

'On yer bike, mate, I'm not thinking of catering for the masses. By the way, you told me you would enquire about schools for the children and about a place for me mum.'

'I did both. The nearest school is a huge place, mixed scholars, about half a mile away, and there are no flats or small houses near that would be suitable for Winnie. Course, we could always shoot my mother-in-law, take the kids and move abroad.'

Ella turned her head so fast she stumbled, then she saw the laughter in Dennis's eyes and she laughed with him.

'You don't really dislike my mum at all, do you?'

'Course I don't, and I really did enquire about accommodation for the elderly but the agent was a hundred per cent sure there wasn't anything suitable in the area.'

'Why the hell did we come here then?'

Dennis thought it best if he counted to ten before he answered.

'The air raids reduced the number of houses in London and in fact all major cities by a very great deal; plus the fact that when the solders, sailors and airmen were demobbed they wanted to set up home with their wives. Many had had war-time weddings and had never had the joy of actually living with their wives and children. Hence the shortage of houses to rent. We are lucky we can afford to buy a house . . .' Under his breath he added, That's if we ever find one that is to your taste, then quickly went on. 'At the moment the only choice for most people is the high-rise flats that have been thrown up or the corrugated-iron huts known as Nissen huts which the

Government are placing on every available open space and charging ten shillings and sixpence every week for the privilege of living in them.'

The fact that Dennis had said '*we* can afford to buy a house' affected Ella in different ways. It was kind of him not to rub it in that she had asked for his help in finding them somewhere to live, and she had to feel grateful that apparently he could afford it. But there again, Teddy and Babs were his children as much as hers and it was a long time since he had recognized his responsibility.

In the hallway Dennis opened what he thought was a door to a cupboard; instead he found himself looking at a rickety flight of dusty steps. 'I think we'll skip the basement,' he said.

Ella took a quick look and agreed.

She hadn't meant to ask, but it came out without her thinking. 'How much is this large house?'

'Four thousand six hundred pounds. Freehold, but there's no garage.'

Ella looked at him in amazement. 'And you can afford that much?'

Straight-faced, Dennis replied, 'Money begets money and it talks all languages.'

Then suddenly they were both laughing fit to bust and he had her in his arms.

When their laughter had subsided he said quietly, 'Remember the times when I sold almost everything in the house that was movable just to give you enough to pay the rent?'

Ella wasn't having that! She still had both feet firmly on the ground where Dennis was concerned, and her voice was harsh as she gave him her answer.

'I well remember! Also I can recall the times you pawned or sold everything we owned that was worth anything just so you had the money to back a horse.'

'True,' he admitted sheepishly, 'but we're both older and a darn sight wiser now, aren't we?'

'Are we?'

At that moment Ella almost blurted out that she had made the biggest mistake of her life and was carrying Sam Richardson's baby.

Coming quickly to her senses, she broke free from Dennis's arms and told herself that now was certainly not the time for confessions.

Back in the car, Dennis turned to face her and said, 'The second house is in West Dulwich, which is actually quite near Camberwell. A gentleman is still living there but we have an appointment to view the property at two o'clock. We've plenty of time to eat first, so what shall it be? Posh restaurant or pub lunch?'

Without hesitation Ella said, 'I'd like a ploughman's, only ham not cheese, if that's all right by you.' She was hungry, but she remembered that the smell of strong cheese made her feel sick and there was no way she wanted to show herself up.

Matters between herself and her husband were going so well today, not one argument. She didn't want to spoil the situation at this stage.

It was a public house frequented by businessmen at lunchtime and the food was good. Dennis ordered rump steak for himself, asking that it be thick and rare. The ham that came with Ella's ploughman's was really tasty home-cooked gammon, and Dennis made no comment when she said she would prefer just a tonic water to drink. He ordered Scotch for himself.

It wanted just ten minutes to two o'clock when Dennis pulled into the drive of Zenith House.

No idea what Zenith is supposed to mean, Ella was

thinking, yet already she had decided that this was a nice residential area, and she certainly liked the look of this detached property which was situated in Court Lane, West Dulwich SE21.

For a start the road was tree-lined, and most of the trees were just about to burst with pink blossom.

From the moment the elderly gentleman opened the door in answer to Dennis's knock, shook hands with each of them and introduced himself as Mr Hamilton, Ella knew that she liked him. He had been tall in his younger days, but now his shoulders stooped and his brown hair was thin on top. He wore trousers with a Prince of Wales check, a fawn shirt, a tie embossed with a regimental badge and a beige woolly cardigan.

'Come in, come in, I had my cleaning lady come in an extra morning today just to make sure everything was neat and tidy, but would you mind showing yourselves around the house? I find the stairs a bit trying these days.' As he turned to go back into the front sitting room, Ella noticed that he walked with a stick.

Dennis and Ella went straight up the stairs to the bedrooms. Almost unable to believe her eyes, she asked, 'Do you have the agent's particulars on this property?'

He smiled to himself; he could tell Ella was smitten. 'Yes,' he said, giving her two printed pages but keeping hold of the third.

The landing was big and wide with two bedrooms on each side. Large double rooms to the front; the other two only slightly smaller looking out over a large, well-kept garden which had a wooded area at the far end.

'Does that piece of ground come with the house?' Ella queried.

'According to the agent's survey, yes, it does.'

'Marvellous. Imagine Teddy climbing trees in his own back garden.' Ella stopped short. 'Just a minute. There

358

are four bedrooms and they are all wonderful. We haven't even seen the rest of the house, not even the bathroom, but would you mind telling me how much the asking price for this house is, 'cos I can't for one moment believe that we can afford to buy it.'

'Ella, let's just continue, and when we have seen the whole house I will give you this third page of the details to read.'

With that she had to be satisfied, because Dennis had already opened two doors which were set back at the top of the stairs. One was a walk-in airing cupboard and housed what Dennis told her was a boiler which gave constant hot water.

The second door led to a bathroom. Ella was dreaming. A huge white bath set on iron claw legs dominated the room. Oh, to fill that bath even half full with scented hot water and just lie there! A toilet *and* a wash basin.

On the landing Ella stood staring through a small window which gave her a great view of the tree-lined road in which this house stood. Daydreaming wasn't in it. Fancy even thinking that she and her family could ever come to live in a place like this. Dennis was cruel to have brought her here. It was like looking into a palace and being told that normal people didn't get to live in such places.

Dennis broke into her thoughts. 'Ella,' he touched her arm, 'come on, we haven't seen the downstairs yet.'

She shook herself, not at all sure that she wanted to do as he was suggesting. It would only make her feel even more envious than she did now.

Mr Hamilton was standing at the foot of the stairs, smiling up at them. 'I have laid a tray and made a pot of tea but am unable to safely carry it through into the lounge. Would you mind having it in the kitchen? Or perhaps you, Mr Dryden, would be kind enough to take the tray through.'

It was Ella who quickly said, 'The kitchen will be fine,

it is very kind of you to have gone to so much trouble.'

'No trouble at all, Mrs Dryden,' he answered, leading the way.

Oh, bless the man! Ella was saying to herself. The tray even had a lace cloth and the cups and saucers were so delicate that she thought Dennis's big fingers would never manage the handles of the cups.

'Shall I be mother?' she asked, as the three of them seated themselves around the large table.

Conversation was a bit difficult until Mr Hamilton started to speak and then there was no stopping him.

'This has always been a family home. My wife and I were blessed with four boys. One served in the Royal Navy and we lost him early on in the war. He was serving on HMS *Hood* which was sunk by the *Bismarck* off Greenland in 1941. Another son was in the RAF and he was shot down during a bomber raid over Cologne in 1942.'

He paused and smiled at Ella. 'I think living alone makes me talk too much when I have visitors.'

'How long since you lost your wife?' Ella asked, showing great concern.

'Only two years. We had a great life. My other two boys see that I want for nothing, and I have three grand-children. They all visit as often as they can, but they have their own lives to lead.'

'So are you going to live with one of your sons? Is that why you have put your house up for sale?' Dennis asked.

'Oh, no, no, actually things could not have turned out better. On the corner of the road behind this one there is a very beautiful large old house which the elderly owners left in their will to some charity organization. It has taken some years to sort things out but I think their wishes have finally come to fruition. The building is to remain but some restoration has been carried out, a warden has been installed and it has become sheltered accommodation under the umbrella of the British Legion. Their aim is to assist ex-service men and women. Some tenants will pay rent, some will buy a lease, but those who are not financially well placed will receive help. The funds for this and many more such good causes are derived largely from the sale of poppies on Armistice Day.

'I am lucky to have secured a lease on a one-bedroom apartment there; or at least I have put down a deposit. Now I have to find a buyer for this house.'

Ella almost blurted out that she was employed as a barmaid in a British Legion working men's club; instead she asked, 'Will you mind very much moving?'

'Not at all, Mrs Dryden. I shall still be in the same vicinity, able to visit friends and neighbours. But look, I should stop my ramblings and allow you to finish your tour of the house, that is if what you have seen already drives you to continue.'

'It certainly does.' Ella got to her feet quickly. She had already noticed all the main features of the kitchen: white tiled to halfway up each wall, though some of the tiles were cracked and needed replacing; loads of cupboards; deep white sink; huge wooden draining board with a large wooden plate-rack above. No wiping up of plates and dishes here, just leave them to drain. But it was the spaciousness of the room that she liked so much. The whole family could eat in here.

Stop it, she scolded herself. What family?

That was a question she couldn't bring herself to think about.

'Stop daydreaming, Ella, and come and see the lounge and the dining room,' Dennis was calling her from the hallway.

Lounge? Dining room? What would she do with rooms like that?

Goodness gracious me! This front room looks more like a hotel. No it doesn't, Ella chided herself, it is far more cosy and comfortable than that. And what about the dining room? Even if, and it was a great big if, Dennis did buy this property for her, when on earth would she ever use this room? The table was enormous, with six chairs arranged around it, and Dennis was down on his knees looking beneath it. 'Thought so,' he said, looking up at her and grinning. 'There's a leaf here that pulls out so that more people can get round it.'

More people? What was he imagining? That she was going to feed the five thousand?

From the dining room French doors led into the garden. Dennis undid the bolts and flung them open wide. This was a different world. Ella had never known anything other than a small back yard. Having lived in the East End of London all her life, a place like this seemed impossible, and it was wicked of Dennis to tantalize her so.

Thank God the children weren't with them. To see all of this and then be told it would cost far more than they could afford would be a cruel joke.

But just supposing Dennis did have the money and was willing to buy this lovely house. What then?

From the moment they had left the house this morning, she had shoved the thought that she was pregnant by another man right out of her mind. Be realistic, she told herself now. You have to tell him sometime and then sit back and watch him explode!

Dennis had gone back inside the house and she could see the two men sitting in the dining room talking to each other.

Ella walked towards the wooded area at the bottom of the garden, her eyes brimming with tears as she told herself what a fool she had been to think that an educated man such as Sam Richardson would really have been interested in her. They came from two different worlds. Perhaps he had just wanted to find out if he was still able to perform the sex act.

Now she was being really nasty!

She hoped with all her heart that he would never find out that he had made her pregnant. Bit one-sided to put all the blame on him, she rebuked herself. She had been up for it; she had had the sweets and now by golly she was having to put up with the sours.

'Ella, Ella, where are you? Time for us to go.'

Hearing Dennis calling her brought her back sharply to the present. For the moment she had to try not to think about the predicament she was in. Hastily she rubbed at her eyes with her handkerchief, buttoned up her jacket and came out from between the trees with a smile on her lips.

At the front door she shook hands with Mr Hamilton and thanked him for allowing them to see his lovely home.

'My pleasure, Mrs Dryden, my pleasure,' he assured her.

'Thanks, Mr Hamilton.' Dennis held the old gentleman's hand longer than was necessary. 'We've a lot to discuss but I will be in touch with you in a day or two.'

On hearing this, a faint hope flickered deep inside Ella. Maybe, just maybe, Dennis would end up buying this lovely house.

It was a silent drive home, but not strained, Dennis looked very thoughtful, while Ella remained hopeful.

'Are you coming in?' she asked as he brought the car to a halt.

'No, I've a lot to do, but I'll leave the last page of the estate agent's details with you. Yer might like to show them t' yer mother.'

Ella was flabbergasted as she stood on the narrow pavement and watched him drive away.

Why did he have to have a dig at her mother?

Another thing, why was he grinning from ear to ear when she closed the car door?

363

Chapter Thirty-six

BY THE TIME ELLA had seen her two children off to school, her heart was pounding and her head ached.

Having spent the previous evening going over and over the estate agent's details that Dennis had left for her to read, she had had a restless night. She didn't know what she was going to do.

It wasn't so much the particulars of the property that had inspired her to want to move heaven and earth to make things right. It was the few lines that Dennis had written in pencil on the bottom of the last page.

She wished her mother would hurry up and arrive; she could usually come up with a sensible solution to any of her daughter's problems. Though not this time, Ella sighed. If only she could 'disappear' this troublesome pregnancy.

She had never looked at another man since the day that she married Dennis, though the Lord above knew that he had given her enough cause to. Then along came Sam Richardson, and to be honest she had felt flattered. But now it was as if a whole new life was being offered to her on a plate. A proper family life, not one where she had to make all the decisions and some weeks do her best to make ten shillings do the work of a pound. She had blown all her chances. When she did get around to telling Dennis that she was pregnant, it would be goodbye to all the dreams that had only yesterday started to form.

'Something tells me that all is not right in your world.' Her mother had not received any answer to her usual 'Cooee!' and had been standing in the doorway to the kitchen, but now she walked over to the black-leaded range, reaching for the big black kettle. After checking that there was enough water in it, she pushed it to the centre of the hot plate, then, before even taking her coat off, delved into her shopping bag and produced a half bottle of Bell's whisky.

'Nothing like a drop of the hard stuff in a nice cup of tea when you don't know if you're coming or going,' she said cheerfully. 'Two questions an' then I might know what is causing you to look as though you've lost half a crown an' found a tanner.

'First, how did the house hunting go? And second, did you tell Dennis about the baby?'

'Oh Mum, one of the houses we saw was a place to die for. As for telling Dennis that I'm pregnant, I just couldn't bring meself to do it.'

'But during the day, how were things between the pair of you?'

'That's just it, Mum, they couldn't have been better. He was Dennis as he was years ago. Kind and considerate. Didn't try to play the big hard man, not even once.'

'And did you both like this house, or was it just your choice?'

'Mum, I'll make the tea; you read these details that Dennis got from the estate agent, and when you come to the last page, prepare yourself for a shock.'

Ella passed over the three typewritten pages, got to her

feet and busied herself laying out cups. As the steam started to spurt from the kettle, she poured the boiling water on to the tea leaves which she had ladled into the pot. Waiting for the tea to draw, she watched her mother's reaction. So far it was delightful to see such a happy smile on that well-worn face.

Thank you, God, for my mum, Ella prayed silently. If anyone had the knack of putting everything on a level footing again, it would be dear old Winnie.

She poured out two cups of tea and placed one near to her mum's elbow.

Winnie looked up. 'Where's the whisky? I didn't bring it to sit on your dresser, and by all accounts we are both going to need more than one tipple.'

'So you've reached the last page! What are your thoughts?'

Winnie didn't hesitate. 'I expect I've made the same assumption that you have.'

'Pass me that last sheet, Mum, I'll read out loud what Dennis has scribbled and see if we are both of the same mind.

'"Ella, you obviously like this house a lot. It has four bedrooms, so why not ask your mother to come with us?"'

Ella's voice wavered and it was a moment or two before she could continue.

'Can't be all bad, can he?' Winnie Paige had not felt so emotional in a very long time.

Ella made no reply, but continued to read.

'"Winnie could have her own bedroom, and the dining room, that you said you would never use, we could turn into a private sitting room for her. Naturally she'd have all her meals with us. Ask her to give it a try. If she decides after a while that she can't live with me we'll take our time and find her something nice nearby."'

Winnie was the first to say what was staring them both in the face.

'Dennis is expecting you to take him back. All of you move in together and become one big happy family again. Isn't that the impression you got?'

Ella couldn't stop the tears from rolling down her cheeks. 'Course he is. A blind bat could see that. Oh Mum, please, tell me what to do.'

Winnie reached for the whisky bottle and topped their cups up before saying, 'Ella, luv, you don't need me to tell you. You know full well what you have to do. Tell him. And the quicker the better.'

'But Mum, what if—'

Winnie cut her short. 'No ifs or buts. He has to be told now. No good putting it off. You'll be starting to show before you know where you are.'

'Supposing he goes mad and walks away?'

'Are you saying that you want Dennis back in your life, or is it just this house you want?'

'Christ, Mum, that's a bit below the belt.'

'No it's not. You have to decide. Course, there's always the chance that he will buy the house, let us have it and walk away,' she laughed, and added, 'But I can't see Dennis Dryden doing that. He may well 'ave changed quite a bit, but seeing him as a saint doesn't work for me. By the way, I got another letter from the council this morning.'

Ella looked up sharply. 'Does it give a date for when the demolition is going to start?'

'No, but it does say they can offer me a flat in Hackney, a first-floor flat apparently.'

'You're going to turn it down, aren't you? You don't want to live in Hackney of all places, do you?'

'Of course not. I'd much rather come with all of you to Dulwich.'

The look Ella gave her mother was cynical. 'And you

think any of us stand a chance of living in that big house?'

Her mother didn't have an answer to that!

The next hour was spent at the kitchen table with more cups of tea and a huge dish of well-buttered toasted teacakes.

There were several times during the course of this hour that Ella wanted to throw her arms around her mum and hug her hard. She knew that Winnie was blaming herself for having encouraged her to go off with Sam Richardson for that weekend, and that wasn't fair. Ella was a grown-up woman, albeit a neglected one, and she should have thought harder about what she was doing.

'Let's go over those estate agent's details together and you can describe the house as we go so that I'll be able to see it in my mind's eye,' Winnie suggested, doing her best to lift Ella's spirits.

Slowly Ella began to read. '"Double-fronted detached house. First floor: four bedrooms, bathroom and lavatory, linen cupboard which houses boiler. Ground floor: large half-tiled kitchen, spacious dining room with French doors leading to the garden and a woodland area at the far end which is also owned by the owner of the property, sitting room with tiled fire surround and bow-fronted window. The hallway is ten feet wide and to the left of the front door there is a second lavatory and a small wash-hand basin. A garage stands to the right of the property but is not adjoining.

'"Dulwich College, which also has a prep school for younger children, is within close proximity. The oldest part of Dulwich is known as Dulwich Village and boasts a beautiful public park.

'"The asking price for this freehold property is £5,995."'

When Ella stopped reading you could have heard a pin drop. Then Winnie rose from her seat, walked round to her daughter and put her arm across her shoulders.

'Look, luv, Dennis Dryden almost destroyed you, and for a while he didn't give a toss for his children. Even today I can't bear to look Mrs Baldwin in the eye. He hurt that family more than you or I can imagine. Worse than that, he destroyed that family.' She spoke quietly, her voice shaking with the depth of her feeling.

Ella nodded.

Her mother began again. 'It might be asking too much of him to accept another man's child; on the other hand, if he's suggesting that you try to make a fresh start, then there has got to be give and take on both sides. I understand more than you think, but you must do what seems best to you. First things first, though. He has to be told that you are having a baby. There is no other way I can think of.'

'What about Teddy and Babs?' said Ella sullenly. 'Their reaction won't be pleasant, I bet.'

'And who's going to tell them that their baby sister or brother has a different father than they do? I'll lay odds that Dennis never will.'

'Mum! What you're suggesting is that we all live a lie.'

'Oh for God's sake. Dennis won't be the first husband to pass another man's baby off as his own. Have yer never heard the saying, it's a wise man that knows his own father?'

Ella shrugged off-handedly as though she hadn't also been considering the fact that Dennis might decide to accept the baby as his own. Whether he agreed or not, she was going to stick to her guns over this. One way or another she was going to make sure that he provided a decent place for them to live.

She and the kids at least deserved that much.

Later that same evening, after having seen the children into bed, Ella was sitting darning Teddy's socks when she

369

thought she heard the front door open. Glancing at the clock on the mantelpiece, she saw that it was twenty minutes past nine. Who the hell was coming in at this time of night?

She dropped her work on to the floor and got to her feet. Hardly had she got the kitchen door opened when Dennis came striding down the passage calling, 'It's only me.'

Once inside and seated opposite her, Dennis apologized.

'Sorry, luv, for coming so late, but I've had a helluva day. Still, this evening has made up for it. I've been on the phone to Mr Hamilton, and guess what, I told him we were interested in buying his house. He asked how much my offer was going to be, and I told him that I was willing to pay him the full asking price. Apparently the estate agent had said that he would have to accept a slightly lower price. Anyway, he was that pleased that he went on an' on about what furniture he was going to take with him, reminding me that he was only having a one-bedroom apartment, ended up by telling me that anything he did not require he would leave in the house at no extra cost, including all the carpets and curtains, though not the rugs he said, those he would make good use of.'

Ella's eyes lit up. He'd be leaving most of the bedrooms fully furnished! Unbelievable.

Then, like a bolt out of the blue, it struck her. No longer could she keep this pretence going.

'Dennis, will you listen to me for a minute? You haven't once attempted to make your position clear to me. Are you intending to move into this new house, or is it just for me, the kids and my mother? By the way, Mum was over the moon that you had given a thought to her. Only this morning the council had offered her a place. In Hackney, would you believe!'

All the time Ella had been speaking, her eyes had not left his face and now she saw his cheeks flush up.

For a moment he hesitated. 'I . . . I,' he stammered at last, 'took it for granted that we'd make a new life for the kids. You and me together. It was what I wanted right from the moment that I bought the place out at Epsom, but you would have none of it. You wanted to live an' die in the East End. Now you and I are getting on so well, aren't we?' He leant forward and touched her shoulder gently.

Impatiently she shook his arm away and in the moment of silence which followed Ella was not able to control her temper.

'You take too much for granted,' she cried loudly. 'And don't you dare try to lay the blame on me for all the bad things that have happened.'

'You've every right to be angry,' Dennis agreed.

'Humph! Too true I have. Besides, Dennis, I'm going to have a baby!'

She had blurted the last sentence out really harshly, not knowing how to tell him more gently. She was past caring now she couldn't keep this awful secret to herself any longer.

She clenched her hands together so tightly the knuckles showed white. She had given him a shock, but at least it was out in the open now.

She watched as Dennis moved so that he was sitting up ramrod straight in the chair. The colour of his cheeks heightened and his look of disbelief was incredible. That piece of news had quickly wiped the smile off his face. His hands clutched at his stomach. It was almost as if somebody had dealt him a violent and crippling blow. He looked utterly devastated.

At last he managed to speak. 'Ella, why? Who with?'

She wasn't sorry for him; in fact she almost spat her

371

answer at him. 'Dennis, ask yourself how many times I have wanted to ask you those very same questions.'

'Oh my God!' he cried. 'I knew that bloody Sam Richardson was sniffing around you. He was here in my house over Christmas. Just like him to go for another man's wife.'

'At least he chose a woman and not a girl barely out of school.' Ella was shaking, and her anger, hurt and disgust were choking her.

She hadn't meant to retaliate so fiercely. This was getting out of hand. She bit her lip and moved her chair further away from his. Any moment he might let fly with his fists.

'Jesus bloody Christ! I thought better of you,' Dennis muttered, before clenching his teeth.

'Yes, and I've wished better of you so many times that I've lost count. I made one mistake. I let Sam take me away for two days, but what you need to remember is that you left me a long time ago. I was on my own, not knowing how to cope, while you did exactly what you wanted to do and with every girl that happened to take your fancy.'

Then she added spitefully, 'But two wrongs don't make a right, do they?'

Dennis had the sense to realize that what his wife was saying was the truth, and so he swallowed hard and said sadly, 'I didn't do right by Connie. I stood by and let her mother send her away, and then that rotten sod of an uncle raped her. If it wasn't for him, I keep telling myself, she would never have been on that train. I hadn't even got the guts to go to her funeral. I should never have left you. I should have stayed but still stood by Connie. I didn't do either. I cleared off when I should have damn well stayed. You know it, I know it, and everybody knows it. But I didn't . . . and it's too late now for me to put things right. I made a bloody mess of so many lives and I'll spend the rest of my life paying for it.'

It was then that Ella began to calm down, and as she watched the emotions pass across his face she realized she could find it in her heart to feel sorry for him.

Anger on both sides had subsided, and now there was this ominous silence. Dennis had played by his own rules, but never in his life had he thought that his wife might be tempted to do the same.

He thought of her as his. She belonged to him, joined at the hip almost. Since the sad death of Connie Baldwin he had always intended to come back home and make a good life. He'd really missed his wife and seeing his kids grow up.

Now he'd left it too long and he needed no telling that he only had himself to blame for what had happened between Ella and Sam Richardson.

Sam had been there for her. He hadn't.

'Do you want this baby?' Dennis asked, his voice little more than a whisper.

'I didn't,' Ella answered truthfully, 'but then at first I wouldn't let myself believe that it was true. Then I dallied with the idea of having an abortion, but that I could not bring myself to do.'

'Does Sam know that you're pregnant?' he asked awkwardly, not meeting her eyes.

'No, he does not. And he is never going to find out, if I have my way. Since we spent our weekend together I 'aven't seen hair nor hide of him. I don't want to neither.'

Ella felt she had every right to keep secret the matter of the letter that Sam had written to her. If she were to tell Dennis that Sam had practically said she wasn't good enough for him, it would be like giving him a big stick with which to beat her.

Dennis stood up and went to the dresser. 'Since when 'ave you taken to drinking whisky?' he asked.

Ella gave him a tight smile. 'Mum brought it in.'

'There's still some left. Shall we have a drink? I think we could both do with one.'

Ella stayed silent as she watched him pour the same amount into each glass before handing one to her.

He remained standing, watching as she took the first sip.

Ella raised her head. 'I wish things hadn't gone so wrong,' she said, her beautiful eyes brimming with tears.

He tossed half of his measure of whisky back in one gulp. Then he said, 'You're right, Ella. With my record I'm 'ardly in a position to condemn you, am I? Are you sure you don't want an abortion?'

'Definitely not.'

'Why not?'

'Partly because I'm too scared, and partly because it would be taking a life.'

Dennis took a deep breath, walked across the floor and stood with his back against the door, putting the widest possible space between them. 'Ella, would you consider letting me take care of you?'

By now Ella was spent, unable to lift her head, let alone give him an answer. She was sitting hunched up in her chair, softly crying.

The very sight of her was tugging at Dennis's heart-strings. How could I have been such a fool? he was asking himself. I threw so much away, and for what? In so many ways I couldn't have been more lucky; every deal I've pulled off has made me a small fortune, but with no one to share it with it's worthless. This room, this house might not be much, but it was our home, my children upstairs in bed, and I jeopardized everything. He was almost praying, and that, he knew, would be a first for him.

'Ella, will you hear me out?'

She nodded her head slightly.

374

'Long ago I started to look back and I began to realize exactly what a selfish man I had become. When I left you and the children in the lurch it was a cruel thing to do. I'm not proud of my past, I only wish that I could turn the clock back, but no one gets that chance. I will buy this house in Dulwich, but whether you decide that I can become part of your life, of this family, will be up to you. If you decide that I am not to put a foot inside the door, you have my word that the house will still be yours and all necessary payments will be made by me. You will have no worries and you will not be getting another job. You will have three children to look after and I will do my utmost to treat the baby you are carrying as if it were my own.'

He hadn't moved, he'd still kept his distance, but all the time he was speaking Ella listened carefully, and she had the feeling that for once in his life her husband was speaking from the heart. Yet somehow she felt she had lost control. It seemed that both of them were experiencing a sense of terrible guilt.

'Ella?' His voice was softer now. 'Please, look at me.'

Ella didn't want to look up. God knows, every fibre of her being wanted to trust him. To have her whole family, even her old mum, all safely under one roof, with Dennis coming home every night to sit and share their evening meal round one table. Teddy and Babs would be over the moon. But there would be another child to consider. Would Dennis really accept this one as his own? He had painted a picture that said it would happen. Could she really trust him?

'Ella?' It was unbelievable but it was true: there were tears in the voice, and such sadness. 'Please . . . look at me.'

Ella raised her eyes, and what she saw tore at her heart. Her husband was crying. 'I'm sorry,' she murmured.

Most of this was not her fault, but at that moment it felt as if it was.

'I do still love you, Ella. And you know my feeling for our kids. Is there even a slight chance that we might put the past behind us?'

Ella blinked away her own tears and said quietly, 'We both know that what's done is done and can't be undone, more's the pity, so it's no use us laying the blame on each other.'

She forced herself to look up, and somehow Dennis was standing directly in front of her. Without warning he bent his head and gently kissed her. When she made no attempt to push him away, he pulled her to her feet, and this time his kiss was a long, slow, lingering one. When finally they broke apart, he had the look on his face of a schoolboy who had been caught out doing something that he shouldn't.

Ella grinned. Suddenly it was as if a great weight had been lifted from her shoulders.

Dennis remained holding her close within his arms and whispered against her hair, 'God above knows how long I've been longing to do that.'

'Really?' Ella asked.

'Yes, it's true, I've been longing to kiss my own wife.'

Epilogue
1958

ELLA AND DENNIS SAT in the well-padded swinging hammock out in the garden of Zenith House, Court Lane, West Dulwich.

They both looked sun-tanned, fit and well, and their friends and relations only had to look at them to see how settled and happy they were. They both loved these summer Sunday afternoons. Having had family and friends to midday dinner, they could relax in the hot August sunshine.

'Who would ever have thought things could have changed so much for the better since we moved from the East End of London,' Ella reflected aloud to her husband, as they watched the antics of their children and their friends.

'I know.' Dennis reached along and took hold of his wife's hand. 'It's almost unbelievable, isn't it?'

Their thoughts were running along similar lines.

Young Ted was down in the overgrown wooded area with his two German Shepherd dogs and three of his mates. All four were privileged young men, attending Dulwich College, and it was so hard to believe that their son would be eighteen years old this autumn.

Ella's eyes moved and settled on her two daughters. Babs was fourteen and into the stage where fashion and make-up was beginning to be a big item in her life, though she did take her studies seriously.

As Ella lazily let her mind wander back over the last five years she knew she had a great deal to be thankful for.

Their children were being given so many advantages that she herself and Dennis could never have dreamt of. But then again, five years ago would they have imagined that their own lives would have changed so drastically?

Suddenly Claire let out a scream. One of the other girls had pushed the swing too high and just for a moment Claire had been afraid. Dennis was on his feet in a second, running down the garden, making sure that their youngest child wasn't hurt.

Ella allowed herself a happy, grateful smile. In three months' time Claire would be five years old.

There wasn't a more loved child anywhere in the country, on that she would stake her life. Also, never a day went by that Ella did not thank the Lord for all his blessings. It had always been a known fact that Teddy was the image of his father and Babs favoured Ella's side of the family. If you saw the two girls together, you would have to assume they were sisters. Claire had the same long chestnut-coloured hair, the big brown eyes and the angelical look that came from the Paige side of the family. If the truth be known, it was a fact that both Dennis and Ella were extremely grateful for.

If she had been born with different colouring, however, it was doubtful that it would have made the slightest difference. From the day she had been born she had brought love with her. And to the whole family it was a lasting love.

*   *   *

'Tea's coming!' the cry rang out, and children and adults came from all directions.

Winnie Paige and Ellen Hines each came carrying a tray loaded with fruit scones, jam and cream plus at least four very large home-made cakes.

Bringing up the rear were Edward Dryden and Mr Hamilton, now lovingly known as the Major. All four adults were, as usual on these occasions, in charge of the china and the two huge teapots.

Mrs Hines had enjoyed her stay in Chelsea in the company of Lady Margaret, but after a year she had decided that she would prefer to return to her own apartment.

No problem. Dennis and his father had asked the bank to send out the official documents calling in the loan on the apartment that had previously belonged to Ellen Hines. To his own detriment, Claude Packard had ignored the warning from the bank. This had resulted in a visit from the Drydens. Very reluctantly Mr Packard had allowed them to enter his flat.

Dennis had made the initial move by saying, 'Mr Packard, you should not take out loans that you are unable to pay back.'

Then Ted had quickly chipped in, 'Another lesson you need to learn is that you shouldn't gamble if you cannot pay up when your horse doesn't win the race.'

Ted had almost found it in his heart to feel sorry for the man as he spluttered, 'What the hell have my gambling debts got to do with you?'

'Everything, Mr Packard. It is to me that you owe the money! I own three bookmakers and I bought your debts.'

It had been a joy to both father and son to watch the man squirm.

They had reminded Packard of his dirty tricks when Miss Sheldon had been alive, and warned him it was payback time, though actually they let him off lightly, reclaiming only the apartment for Mrs Hines. However, they did remind him that should he fall short in just one mortgage payment in the future, they would send the bailiffs in and he would be homeless.

'The same applies if you pester Mrs Hines in any way whatsoever. Have we made ourselves clear?' Ted asked loudly.

Mr Packard had nodded his head.

'I would like a verbal answer if you don't mind, just so that I know we have made ourselves clear,' Ted had insisted.

Quickly enough Claude Packard had said, 'Yes.'

'He's got the picture,' Dennis said, loud enough for Claude to hear as they left.

So Mrs Hines's furniture had come out of store, she was back home in Epsom and the family had remained friends. Once a fortnight Winnie Paige went to spend the day with her. Then the next fortnight Ted would drive to Epsom and fetch Ellen to spend the day in Dulwich with the Drydens.

Another turn-up for the books was the fact that Mr Hamilton had revealed that he was a great lover of horse-racing, and so Ted had befriended him and made a point of inviting him to attend all the main races of the season.

'The Major' was a frequent visitor and a great favourite with all the family.

As Ella took the hot cup of tea that her mother was holding out for her, they exchanged happy smiles.

The fact that Mr and Mrs Dryden and their children had moved to West Dulwich had been of great benefit to a lot of people.